Atonement

by Richard J Greene

Sequel to God's Coffin

by Richard Greene

1

ISBN: 978-1-4349-3166-5 eISBN: 978-1-4349-7233-0

For my parents, Edward Lee Greene and Bertha Viola Patterson Greene.

I think of you often

About the Author

Richard and his Lhasa Apso Jackson

Richard Greene was born in Denver, Colorado, in 1939, and grew up in a small two-bedroom house in Englewood, a suburb of Denver attending Hawthorne Elementary School and Flood Jr. High. In 1954, his parents divorced, and his father moved to Houston, Texas. Soon after that, he dropped out of ninth grade, worked at various jobs, including sacking groceries at a local Miller Supermarket and as an electrician's apprentice for a neighbor. He spent his summers with his dad, who owned 'The Texan' bar on the outskirts of Houston, Texas, where he got an education in life unlike his friends back in Englewood, Colorado.

In August 1956, at seventeen, Richard enlisted in the United States Navy. After boot camp and Yeoman School in March 1957, he was transferred to the USS Belle Grove LSD-2 (Landing Ship

Dock), serving in the South Pacific and taking part in the atomic testing at Eniwetok and Bikini Atolls in 1958.

Honorably discharged in 1960, he worked at Samsonite Luggage for a short spell and then went to work for Burlington Truck Lines as a billing clerk. The trucking industry fascinated Richard, so he attended Denver Traffic School to learn the trucking industry's ins and outs. He worked as a dock supervisor for United Buckingham in Denver, a sales representative for Californian Motor Express in Fresno, California, and Los Angeles. Moving back to Denver, he went to work as Claims Prevention Manager for Consolidated Freightways, which included investigating road accidents of CF trucks within 100 miles of Denver. After a year with Consolidated, he was transferred from Denver to the General Claims Department in Portland, Oregon. In 1973, Richard left the Claims Department to become a supervisor in the Collection Department for Consolidated, where he remained until his retirement in December 1995 as Manager of Collections.

Still residing in Portland, Oregon, Richard and his wife Cathy spend much of their time with their children and grandchildren. Richard's other interests are golf, long walks, reading, and oil painting.

Please visit my web page, www.richardjgreene.net, or visit me on Facebook at https://www.facebook.com/richardgreene.7393 or on Twitter at https://twitter.com/@dickiejoe All of my books are available on Amazon as ebook or paperback.

Atonement

Pup the coyote

Preface

Wade Garrison took his vengeance against the men who took his unborn daughter's life and tried to kill his wife and son to settle a score. When the last man was dead from Wade's Sharps Rifle, he rode out of Harper, Colorado, a wanted man, and disappeared into the Montana Territory.

Morgan Hunter was a forty-eight-year-old gunman from west Texas wanted for killing a sheriff and his deputy. Fleeing from those killings and riding away from the sorrow that caused them, he rode into the Montana Territory. Unaware of the other, both men rode toward the same destiny.

Sarah looked toward the top of the hill every day, waiting for Wade and his red sorrel mare to come home. The days turned into weeks, and then into months, and still no word of him or from him.

Chapter 1

Harper, Colorado

August

Wade Garrison turned his sorrel mare south and rode away from Levi Wagner's Livery and into an arroyo to a sparse, scraggly, Pinyon tree and climbed down. Tying the mare to the Pinyon, he took the long glass out of his saddlebag and walked up the bank of the arroyo of rocks and sagebrush, stopping well below the top.

Careful not to hurt his wounds, Wade sat on his hip and peered over the top of the hill at the rear of the Hoskins Hotel. Putting the long glass to his eye, he found the windows of the top floor and searched for George Hoskins.

Not seeing Hoskins, he lowered the long glass and looked at the distance between him and the top floor windows, estimating the range to be around four hundred yards. The blades of prairie grass between him and the back of the hotel barely moved, and the sleeves of two shirts hanging on a clothesline behind the house next to the hotel were motionless.

Pushing the glass together, he slowly stood feeling the stitches Levi had replaced pull and walked back to the mare and put the long glass away. He untied his bedroll, took one .50 caliber cartridge out of the bandolier hanging from his saddle horn, pulled the Sharps out of its scabbard, and headed back up the embankment. Wade found a spot behind a small, rugged, almost square rock and carefully laid down on his stomach. Placing his bedroll on the rock in front of him, he placed the Sharps on it and then put his eye to the rifle's scope. Finding the third story windows of the Hoskins Hotel, he moved the scope from one window to the next, knowing he needed but one clear shot.

He shoved the lever of the Sharps rifle forward, opening its breech, shoved the cartridge in, and pulled the lever back, closing it. With the Sharps resting on the bedroll, he put the scope to his right eye and searched the windows for George Hoskins with the scope's crosshairs. The moments passed, the sun was climbing higher, and it was getting warmer. Wade knew that with the warmer air, a slight breeze would come that could affect his shot. The minutes passed, and then he saw movement inside one of the windows. He pulled the first trigger of his Sharps Rifle, softly placed his finger on the second trigger, looked through the scope, and waited.

George Hoskins, dressed in suit pants and white, long sleeve underwear, with suspenders hanging loosely down his legs, suddenly appeared at the window. He raised the lower half of the window and poked his head out as he leaned on the sill with his hands looking at the Rocky Mountains. Wearing a smile, he took a deep breath of the fresh morning air and never heard the explosion of the Sharps Rifle.

Chapter 2

Wyoming Territory

It was early evening when Wade approached Charlie Peters' place. The sun was well below the western horizon, and darkness was close at hand. Sitting in his saddle, he stared at the warm, inviting lights in the windows of the Peters house and thought about riding on, but it had been a long ride from the gully behind the Hoskins Hotel. He was tired and hungry, and so was the mare that shook her head, rattling the reins and bit. She turned her head and looked back at him with an irritable snort breaking the stillness of dusk as if complaining.

Wade stroked her neck. "Tired, girl?"

The door of the cabin opened, and Charlie Peters stepped out with the light of the doorway surrounding him like a halo. He closed the door engulfed by the darkness, and as he stepped off the porch, he saw the dark image of the lone rider. Fearful, he backed toward the porch thinking of his Winchester just inside the closed door.

Wade quickly spoke. "It's Wade Garrison, Mr. Peters."

Charlie leaned into the darkness straining his eyes in the dim light. "Marshal Garrison?"

Wade nudged the mare forward. "Sorry if I startled you."

Peters scoffed with humor, "You scared the shit out of me is what you did, Marshal. What the hell are you doing sitting out here in the dark?"

Pulling his mare up a few feet from the porch, Wade chuckled. "Trying to decide whether to climb down or ride on. Mind if I step down?"

"Of course not," grinned Charlie, then he gestured at Wade with one hand. "How's them wounds?"

"Shoulder is doing better than the side, but both are a mite sore."

"You were lucky the bullet that went into your shoulder was a small caliber. Want me to take a look?"

Wade thought back on the night Levi re-stitched the wounds. "Won't be necessary, Charlie."

Having the look of a hard day, Peters took the mare's reins to steady her while Wade eased down from the saddle. "We'll put your horse in the barn with some fresh hay and water."

Wade held out an open hand. "How's the missus?"

Charlie grinned as he shook Wade's hand firmly. "Sassy."

Wade chuckled. "Think she'd mind if I stayed for supper?"

As they started toward the barn, Peters grinned again. "You know she wouldn't. Fact is, we'd both be disappointed had you rode past our place without stopping."

The door opened, and Nora stepped out of the house then walked across the porch, wrapping herself in her shawl. "Who you talking to, Charlie?" she asked as her green eyes searched the dark face of the man next to her husband.

"It's Marshal Garrison, Nora," said Charlie.

She watched the figure walk into the light from the window, wearing the blue shirt and pants that once belonged to her dead brother, and smiled. "Why, hello, Marshal Garrison."

12

Wade took off his hat, looked at her green eyes, freckled face, and smiled. "How are you, Mrs. Peters?"

"I'm fine, Marshal." Then, looking concerned, she asked, "How are your wounds?"

"Healing slowly, I'm afraid, Mrs. Peters."

"They might heal a lot faster if you stayed off that horse for a while." She held out her frail hand, thinking of the men that tried to kill his wife and son. "And that family of yours?"

Wade took her hand and gently shook it. "They're fine, ma'am, thank you for asking."

"You hungry, Mr. Garrison?" she asked.

"I'm always hungry."

She smiled at that. "You look a mite tired, too," she said in a soft voice. "Start calling me Nora, Marshal." She wrapped her arms around her thin body as if feeling a chill and rubbed her arms with her hands. "Gets a mite chilly at night these days." She gestured toward the barn. "You go help Charlie while I finish supper."

The smell of dinner and hot coffee greeted Wade and Charlie when they stepped into the house. Hungry and anxious to eat a hot meal, Wade hung his black hat on a wooden peg next to the door, slipped out of his black duster, hung it on another peg, and followed Charlie to the long table.

Charlie Peters combed his sandy hair with one hand and gestured to the chair at the head of the table with the other. "You sit here, Marshal." He pulled his dark blue pants up and waited for Wade to sit down

Wade sat at the head of the table and with Charlie on his right. Wade glanced around the large familiar room then at Nora busy over a black, cast-iron cooking stove.

Nora turned from the stove, placed two platters of food on the table, and then sat down across from Charlie, on Wade's left. After a quick, thankful prayer, they filled their plates to the music of silverware on china. As they ate, she smiled at how Wade attacked the food on his plate with some degree of enthusiasm. "What brings you back this way, Marshal?"

Wade shoved a fork of food into his mouth. "Making my way up north into Montana Territory."

Charlie lifted his fork to his mouth, paused, and looked at Wade while recalling his last visit. "Hope you don't mind me asking Marshal, but who are you trailing this time?"

"Ain't after no one this time, Charlie," said Wade thinking of his badge tucked away in his saddlebags. "And I not a marshal anymore."

Looking surprised, Charlie glanced at his wife and then looked down at his plate, filling his fork. They were both curious but figured if he wanted them to know more, he'd tell them. So Charlie went about the task of eating and making small talk about some things he'd like to do with the ranch when he had the time.

Charlie set the fork on his empty plate, picked up his coffee cup, and asked Wade how long he was planning on staying.

Wade pushed his empty plate away. "I'd like to spend the night if that'd be alright with you folks and be on my way in the morning."

"You can stay as long as you like," offered a smiling Nora.

"That's a fact," agreed Charlie with a quick nod, thinking he could use some help around the place.

Nora filled Wade's cup with coffee thinking about the last time he was here. "Don't mean to be nosey, but are your wife and child safe?"

He looked up and smiled. "Yes, ma'am." Remembering George Hoskins falling back from the window of his hotel. "That business is taken care of."

"Glad to hear that," she said. "The spare room's all made up and wait'n."

Wade glanced toward the door of the bedroom, recalling how he lay in the darkness of the room filled with fever for several

14

days, afraid he would die without finishing what he had to do. He smiled at her. "It's been a while since I've slept in a soft bed."

Charlie gulped the last of his coffee and stood. "I'm going out on the porch for a pipe. Bring your coffee Wade, and we can talk."

Wade stood with his cup of coffee, thanked Mrs. Peters for a fine dinner, then followed Charlie outside, where he stood at the edge of the porch. The sounds of crickets in the yard and frogs down by the small stream that wound its way through the Peters's place filled the quiet night air. He leaned against the roof post and looked up at the black moonless sky of a thousand stars listening to a coyote's call from somewhere far off in the darkness. Taking a drink of coffee, the sounds of a match exploding into flames told him that Charlie was lighting his pipe

Peters blew out the flame, tossed the dead match into the darkness, sat back in his chair, and puffed his pipe while billows of smoke surrounded his head disappearing into the darkness.

Wade took a drink of coffee as he stared into the black night toward the south with his mind full of Sarah and their son. Then he thought of Friendly's, the shootout, and the fire. "Any more said over what happened out at Friendly's?"

Charlie puffed his pipe, blew a cloud of smoke, which caught the light from the window before disappearing into the darkness. He shook his head, "No. That business has died."

The door opened, Nora Peters stepped onto the porch and took a seat in the chair next to her husband. "You plan on bringing your family up to Montana after you get settled?"

Wade stared south toward Colorado, knowing he would never see them again. "Don't know if I'll stay yet. Have to see what it looks like first."

She smiled. "Well, if you do, you be sure and stop by so's I can meet that wife and child of yours."

He turned, and for some reason, thought of the woman he killed at the Hoskins ranch. "I'll be sure and do that, Nora."

Charlie sat in front of the small window. The light from inside shone on the back of his head, lighting up the billows of smoke that softly rose as he puffed on his pipe. "Montana's pretty country, I hear."

Wade looked at Charlie's face in the light of the window, thinking it didn't much matter, then returned his stares to the south and Harper.

"What time you plan on leaving?" asked Nora.

Without turning, Wade replied, "First light, I reckon."

She stood and wrapped herself in her shawl. "I'll go turn your bed down." Then she reached out, took Wade's empty cup, and turned to her husband. "Don't stay up too late." Then she stepped inside the house.

Charlie stood and walked to the edge of the porch next to Wade and tapped his pipe against the porch post to empty it. After he blew air through the empty bowl, he put it in his shirt pocket and glanced around into the darkness. "Guess we best get to bed."

After the Peters said goodnight and went into their room, Wade walked into his room, undressed, and quickly checked his bandages finding a small spot of blood on his side. Easing himself between the cool sheets, he rested his head on the cool, soft pillow and stared up at the dark ceiling listening to the noises of Charlie and Nora preparing for bed. His mind filled with thoughts of Sarah in the evening when they undressed, climbed into bed and made love. He turned from the ceiling to the wall, closed his eyes, and waited for the sleep that came quickly.

Banging pots and pans made their way from the kitchen, waking Wade from a sound, restful sleep. The morning sky above the cliffs outside, the high narrow window of the bedroom was turning from black to blue. Starring at the cliffs outside the narrow window, he watched as the light from the rising sun slowly make its way down toward the base of the cliffs painting them a soft morning orange. A rooster crowing, a cow answered in protest, followed by the pigs and horses, filled the morning calm. Holding his side, he slowly sat up and put his bare feet against the cold floor. The bandage on his left shoulder showed a small spot of blood that was not there last night. He checked the one on his side, finding it had bled a little more during the night. He slowly stood to the pain of pulling stitches and managed to put on his pants, shirt, and boots. Leaving his gun hanging on the peg near the bedroom door, he walked to the kitchen, greeted by the smell of bacon and Mrs. Peters busy at breakfast.

She looked up with a towel in one hand and a large fork in the other as her freckled face filled with a smile. "Did you sleep well, Mr. Garrison?"

"Yes, ma'am."

Looking pleased with that, she gestured to a chair at the head of the table. "Sit yourself down, and I'll pour you a cup of coffee."

He did as told while asking where Charlie was.

Nora poured the coffee into one of her nice china cups she used for special occasions while saying that her husband was visiting the chicken coop, stealing eggs from the hens. His cup filled, she smiled and then turned back to the stove.

Wade picked up his cup, smelled the strong aroma of the hot, black coffee, and took a quick sip. Sitting back, he watched Nora while she worked over the stove and thought of Sarah as she cooked breakfast back in Santa Fe. Looking down at the black coffee in his cup, he found himself wishing they were still in Santa Fe and had never made the trip to Sisters to help Seth.

The front door opened, and Charlie stepped inside, carrying a small bowl of eggs, looking angry. "That damn hen of yours pecked me again, Nora." He held up one hand, showing her a small amount of blood, and then he looked at Wade. "Morning, Wade."

Without turning from the stove, Nora asked, "Why is that one mine, and the rest yours?"

17

He set the bowl on the counter next to the stove, picked up a rag, and wiped his hand. "Cuz that's the only one that won't give up her eggs."

Nora paused from what she was doing and looked at her husband. "Ever think that maybe she just doesn't like anyone taking her eggs?"

Charlie tossed the rag down on the kitchen counter, picked up the pot of coffee, and headed for the table and his cup. "The others don't seem to mind."

"Well," began Nora thoughtfully. "Maybe the others ain't as smart as she is." She turned with a triumphant smile. "But maybe that's why she's mine."

Wade grinned at that while Charlie ignored the comment, poured himself a cup of coffee, returned the pot to the kitchen then sat down at the table. After taking a drink, he looked at Wade. "Is that blood on your shirt?"

Wade looked down at a small spot on the side of his shirt. "Bandages need changing."

"We can take a look after breakfast," offered Charlie.

After a breakfast of eggs, bacon, and biscuits, followed by another slice of Nora's rhubarb pie, Wade took off his shirt so Nora could clean both wounds, saying the wound in the shoulder looked good. She applied some of her Indian ointment and bandaged both wounds. After she finished, she told him to get another of her brother's shirts out of the bedroom.

Wade did as told, picked up his shirt, and headed for the bedroom.

Nora stared after him. "Leave the dirty one on the bed."

Wade paused at the door and turned. "Yes, ma'am." Then he disappeared into the bedroom, returning a few minutes later wearing a clean, yellow shirt tucked into his blue pants with his red bandana tied loosely around his neck.

Nora turned from what she was doing and glanced at her brother's shirt, and then the gun belt Wade was buckling. "You leaving?"

Wade adjusted his holster. "I have a long way to go before sundown." He looked at her with an appreciative smile. "Thanks again, Mrs. Peters."

"You're welcome, Mr. Garrison." She smiled. "Seems funny, not calling you Marshal."

Wade smiled with embarrassment. "Wade sounds better, Nora. Well, ma'am, I best be on my way."

A slight look of disappointment filled her face. "I suppose you do." She looked at the shirt that fit Wade perfectly and thought of her dead brother as she turned and picked up a small burlap sack. "I fixed you some food in case you get hungry."

Grateful, Wade looked down at the burlap bag and thanked her as he took it, then glancing around for her husband, asked, "Where's Charlie?"

Nora gestured toward the door. "Getting your horse, I imagine." She moved closer, stood on her toes, and kissed his cheek. "You take care of yourself, Wade Garrison. Be sure and have someone look at them stitches."

"Yes, ma'am."

She turned, went back to what she was doing while humming a song that sounded like an old hymn.

Wade carefully shrugged into his black duster, picked up his hat, and headed for the door, where he turned and glanced back at her going about her chores while humming. He picked up his Sharps, leaning against the wall next to the door, stepped outside, and closed the door. Stepping off the porch, he walked toward the barn just as Charlie Peters walked out of the barn leading the mare, all saddled and ready. Wade thanked him, shoved the Sharps into the sheath hanging in front of the saddle, careful not to disturb the scope. Then he opened the flap to his saddlebags, shoved the

19

burlap bag inside, turned, and extended his hand to Charlie. "Thanks for everything, Charlie."

Peters shook Wade's hand and then held the reins while Wade carefully climbed up into the saddle without using his left hand and arm, feeling the stitches pull. "I put some of Nora's salve and clean bandages in your saddlebags."

Wade settled into the saddle to the sound of leather, resting his left hand on his thigh, adjusted his duster and gun belt, then looked down at Charlie. "Thanks."

Peters looked curious. "Where ya headed?"

Wade looked north and frowned. "Ain't exactly sure. North is all I know at the moment."

Charlie looked envious. "Wish I could go off exploring."

Wade thought of Santa Fe, Sarah, and their son, Emmett. "You have a nice place here, Charlie. I bet there's a lot of men who'd love to be wearing your shoes about now."

Charlie grinned, thinking Wade was probably right, stepped back, and let go of the mare's reins. "Well, I hear there's still a few Crow and Cheyenne poking around up there, so be careful."

Wade tipped the edge of his hat with two fingers. "I'll do that." Then he nudged the mare and looked north while talking over his shoulder. "Take care of yourself and the missus, Charlie."

Considering the Indians in Montana, Peters called out, "Mind what's around you!"

Wade heard but never responded as he rode away.

Charlie stared after him, pondering the heavy burden that held Wade Garrison in its grasp. He couldn't know that as a lawman, Wade had betrayed everything he had ever believed in. He couldn't have known that Wade was riding away from a wife he loved and a child he adored, neither of whom he would ever see again. Charlie could only wonder what devils were deep inside the man who rode north.

Chapter 3

Montana Territory

September

A solitary rider guided his Appaloosa and big brown packhorse through a grove of cottonwoods to the grassy banks of a wide, shallow stream. A soft breeze rustled the fall leaves of the trees while the horses drank from the cool stream that had taken on the color of the gray sky. The rider wrapped his right knee around the horn of his saddle, taking in the golden grass, sagebrush, plateaus of steep rocky cliffs, and rolling hills. Far off in the distance, tall, rugged peaks that disappeared into the gray stormy clouds showed signs of the approaching winter.

A soft rumble of thunder filled the quiet afternoon as it rolled across the Montana plains toward the blue haze of mountains in the West, drowning out the trickle of the stream. The horses raised their heads from drinking, and as their wide eyes glanced toward the rumble, each snorted softly through flared nostrils.

The rider spoke softly to the Appaloosa and patted her neck while he raised his head to sniff the air that smelled like rain. Turning in the saddle, he looked eastward at the silent flashes of lightning above the prairie, rolling hills and cliffs that had become dark gray and thought of cover from the storm. Turning as he took his leg from around the saddle horn, he stood in the stirrups and glanced around. Rolling hills of fir trees and a low plateau of rock cliffs loomed in the near distance beyond the cottonwoods on the other side of the stream. Hopeful of finding cover from the approaching storm, he held the reins to the packhorse tightly in one hand and nudged the Appaloosa into the shallow gray water.

Chased by thunder as they trotted across the stream, a sudden light breeze picked up, blowing limbs of the trees back and forth. Reaching the other side, he rode up a low embankment and galloped through the cottonwoods toward the bluff. Pausing but a moment, he looked up, seeing a bowl-shaped cave in the rocky cliff. Partially hidden by boulders, scrub brush, and Pinyon trees, it looked big enough for both horses, so he nudged the Appaloosa up the hill while tugging at the packhorse. Reaching the cave, he climbed down, backed the horses into it, and quickly hobbled their front legs. As he stood and held onto their reins tightly in both hands, he turned to watch the storm that was upon them.

The breeze that had been gentle by the stream now howled, whipping about the heavy limbs of the fir trees, sagebrush, and Pinyon trees near the entrance to the bowl-shaped cave. Outside the shallow cave, a thick metallic curtain of heavy rain covered the landscape. A sudden flash of lightning lit up the walls of the hollow with loud, crackling thunder bouncing off the walls of the cave, causing the horses to squeal and pull at the reins the rider held firmly in both hands.

Minutes passed filled with strong wind, white lightning, and the loud bang of thunder. It was all the rider could do to keep the horses inside the shallow cave. Within minutes, the wind began to soften, and the heavy rain let up, becoming a quiet, soft, friendly shower while the thunder and lightning moved north with the front of the storm. With the end of the soft rain came the fresh smell that always follows a rainstorm, and suddenly the late afternoon sun broke through the clouds with a gift of a rainbow in the distance above the shiny, wet, golden grass of the Montana plains.

The rider was Morgan Hunter, who, as a young, brown-eyed boy of seventeen, rode bareback out of Oklahoma into the Texas Panhandle with an old pistol tucked under his belt. Now at thirty-five, the dark brown hair was mixed with little gray, and the old gun replaced by an eight-inch .45 Caliber Colt Navy pistol, the same favored by Bill Hickock. Morgan was right-handed but preferred the cross draw wearing his Colt high on his left hip, lying more across his belly than at his side. This made the wooden grips of the pistol butt within an easy reach of his right hand, whether standing, in a chair, or sitting his horse. He was a quiet, soft-spoken man of five feet nine inches, narrow of hip and broad-shouldered. Not having seen the inside of a barbershop in weeks, his hair bulged from under his wide-brimmed, Texas flat hat. The dark red bandana he wore was faded, as were his black shirt and black pants.

Morgan stepped from the concave hollow, taking in the rainbow above the wet, grassy plains, smelling the fresh air left by the storm. As the storm headed north with its flashes of lightning, he decided this was a good place to make camp and unsaddled the Appaloosa. After unloading his supplies from the packhorse, Morgan gathered what dry wood he could find for a fire. After building a fire near the entrance of the shallow cave, and while the day fought with the night, he ate a dinner of beans, jerky, and boiled black coffee.

After dinner, Morgan Hunter let the horses dine on the grass below his camp before putting them back inside the shallow cave, making sure their front legs were secure in their tethers. Deciding to stretch his legs, he took a walk filled with thoughts of Texas. As the mountains in the West are wallowed up by the darkness of night, the weight of the day soon found him. He walked back to the warm fire and the small lighted room it created outside the shallow cave and sat down. He poured another cup of coffee from the dented coffee pot, picked up his cup, and leaned back against his saddle. Taking a drink, he gazed into the dancing flames of the crackling, warm fire as images of Texas raced through his mind. The cry of a coyote somewhere in the dark distance broke the quiet night, taking away the images of men he had killed and places of his past. Hearing a nervous snort from the horses, he glanced into the bowl-shaped cave at the dark images whose big dark eyes reflected the colors of the fire.

Relaxing against his saddle, he drank his coffee and watched the flames as they danced above the wood they consumed while scenes of the past walked through his memory. The bottom of the burning wood gave way to its own weight and collapsed into the red, glowing embers beneath it, reminding him of another fire and the collapsing of a house. Setting the empty cup down, he reached into his shirt pocket and pulled out a locket with a strand of black ribbon through its eyelet. He opened the locket, held it close to the fire, and looked at the picture of a beautiful Mexican woman with dark hair, a shawl draped around her shoulders, and a young boy sitting on her lap. He closed the locket, returned it to his shirt pocket, and returned his stare to the dancing flames.

Becoming tired and sleepy from the miles he had traveled, he placed some wood on the fire, then checked once more at the horses in the shallow cave. Seeing they were content and relaxed for the moment, he lay down with his head on his saddle, pulled his single blanket up over his shoulders, closed his eyes, and waited for sleep.

The morning sun broke over the eastern horizon and slowly crawled down the side of the bluff above the cave and campsite. The dead fire was the first thing Morgan saw when he opened his eyes, feeling the September morning chill. He sat up, tossed his blanket back, and stood feeling sore and stiff from the hard ground. Morgan stretched, built a fire, and heated what was left of the beans and coffee from the night. He was about to fill his plate when he heard the neigh of a horse.

Setting the plate on the ground next to the fire, he turned to his holster lying next to his saddle, drew his pistol, and looked toward the sound that came from the shallow stream and cottonwoods he rode through the day before. Standing, he stepped away from the fire to a large boulder several feet away, crouched behind it, and searched the tree line and stream beyond for the horse. Moments passed before he spotted a lone rider wearing a black hat and black duster and walking his horse toward the stream from the east. He watched as the rider approached the stream, pulled his horse up, and slowly dismounted. While the sorrel drank from the stream, the rider knelt, dipped his hand into the cold water, and took a drink. Shaking the water from his hand as he stood, the rider glanced around, then swung up onto his saddle. When the horse finished drinking, he nudged it into the stream and up the opposite bank, disappearing into the cottonwoods. Several moments passed before the rider emerged from the cottonwoods.

Morgan watched as the rider pulled up, dismounted, and tied the horse to a small bush, then opened his saddlebag, taking out a small bag, opened and shoved something into his mouth. Glancing around, the man eased himself down against the trunk of a cottonwood tree and took off his hat. Setting it next to him, he leaned his head back against the trunk and closed his eyes, feeling the warm September sun on his face.

Morgan watched for several minutes deciding whether or not to call out to the man, then, making up his mind, yelled, "Hello, there."

Startled, the rider rolled behind the tree, drew his pistol, and looked up the hill.

"I mean you no harm!" yelled Morgan.

25

Wade Garrison lay flat on the ground while his tired eyes searched the trees and boulders for the owner of the voice. Wishing he had his long glass that was in his saddlebags on the mare, he continued to search the trees and boulders on the hillside.

Morgan stood so Wade could see him and gestured toward his camp. "I have a pot of strong, hot coffee and a warm fire." Lowering his gun, he yelled, "Name's Morgan Hunter!"

Wade stood, stepped out from behind the tree, and holstered his Colt. "Emmett Spears," he said, not wanting to give his true name, adding, "I could use a cup of coffee."

Morgan waved him up, "Come on up!" Then he returned to his campsite while Wade picked up his hat and got his horse.

Morgan was kneeling next to the fire pouring a cup of coffee into a dented tin cup when Wade reached the campsite. Tying his horse to the branch of a Pinyon tree shaded by a large fir tree, he noticed the two horses inside the bowl-shaped cave.

Morgan turned from the fire with a cup of coffee in his left hand. "It may be bitter."

Wade grinned as he took the cup. "I'm not all that choosey." He shook Morgan's outstretched hand, and when Morgan turned and sat down next to his saddle, Wade found a nice size rock to sit on. Sitting the cup down, he took off his hat, setting it down on another rock, took off his leather gloves, and gently tossed them on his hat. Glancing at the man who offered his camp, he took a drink of coffee, thinking it was a little on the strong side but hot and good just the same.

"Can I offer you some breakfast?" asked Morgan. "It's only beans and jerky, but it's hot."

Wade hadn't had a hot meal in two days since the small town where he stopped to let a doctor look at his stitches. He was hungry, and the pot of beans looked mighty tempting.

"There's enough," grinned Morgan thinking the man probably hadn't eaten in a while since he had no packhorse and lied. "I already ate." Picking up the empty tin plate, he filled it with beans and jerky, then handed it and an old fork to Wade. Then he got a spoon, picked up the pot, and started eating what was left of the beans.

Wade watched him for a moment. "You sure you already ate?"

Morgan smiled. "Just cleaning up.

Wade wondered if that was true then attacked the plate of food like a hungry child. Wade shoved a fork of food into his mouth and looked into the shallow cave at the two horses. "Nice looking, Appaloosa."

Hunter glanced at the animal, shoved a spoon of food into his mouth, and considered the man sharing his camp, who traveled with no packhorse and supplies. "Where you headed?"

Wade shoved another fork of food into his mouth, thinking it tasted good, and shrugged as he took a drink of coffee. "Not quite sure." He looked down at his fork as it moved through the beans. "Looking for work." He looked up. "You?"

"Same." Morgan picked up his coffee, took a drink then set it back down on the rock. "Ride far?"

Wade thought on that a quick moment. "Santa Fe. I worked on a ranch near there." He moved the fork around the tin plate, filling it with what little juice remained on his plate, then licked the fork clean. He set his empty plate on the ground next to the fire, picked up his cup of coffee, and grinned at Morgan. "Guess I was a little hungry after all, thanks."

"Happy for the company." Morgan looked out at the vast prairie. "Gets a bit lonely at times."

Wade glanced at the land and nodded in agreement. "Where you from?"

"A little town in northwest Texas." Hunter thought Santa Fe was a long way to travel without supplies, but some drifters traveled light and eat when they could.

Wade had been taking stock of the man who shared his campsite and quickly decided that he liked the stranger. "Never been there, but I heard it's pretty country."

Morgan sipped his coffee and gestured around at the landscape. "So's this."

Wade drank his coffee and glanced around at the hills, prairie, and mountains in the distance. "It is that." In the moment that followed, Wade thought Morgan was no ordinary drifter, and he certainly was no ranch hand. He looked back down the hill to the cottonwoods and stream. "That was some storm we had yesterday."

Morgan gestured to the bowl-shaped cave and his two horses. "Barely made it into that cave." He looked at Wade. "You find cover?"

Wade looked down the hill past the cottonwoods and stream into the distant plains. "Found a small canyon with a slight overhang a few miles to the southeast of here. Most of the storm passed to the north, but me and the mare got wet all the same. We just spent the night where we were."

Morgan poured the last of the coffee into their cups, set the empty pot down, leaned back against his saddle, and started to take a sip of coffee when the neigh of horses broke the morning stillness. Both he and Wade sat up and looked down the hill past the bushes at a half dozen Indians three hundred yards to the north, leisurely riding toward the cottonwoods and the shallow stream.

"Crow," whispered Wade.

"Good thing you're not still sitting by that tree down there," whispered Morgan.

Thinking on that while fearing the horses would give away their hiding place to the Crow, Wade glanced at his mare and then at the horses in the shallow cave. "Horses," he whispered, and then he hurried to the mare, wrapped one arm around the mare's nose to hold it still, and then put his left hand over the mare's mouth.

Morgan rushed into the cave, put one arm around the nose of each of his two horses, and then they watched the Indians ride into the cottonwoods, where they paused at the stream to let their ponies drink. After their ponies had drunk their fill, the Indians rode into the shallow stream toward the far bank.

"Best break camp," said Morgan, stepping out of the bowl-shaped cave. "I suggest we ride north together for a spell."

Wade let go of the mare's nose. "Might be a good idea." Watching the Indians ride out of the stream, heading east, he helped Morgan pack up.

They had traveled less than a mile when Wade turned and looked back over his shoulder. Pulling up, he turned the mare and stood in the saddle. "We got company."

Morgan pulled up, turned his horse toward a small cloud of dust in the distance, and knew it was the Crow.

Wade took his long glass out of his saddlebag, pulled it apart, and looked back at those who followed.

"Indians?" asked Morgan, hoping it wasn't but knowing it was.

Wade lowered the long glass and handed it to Morgan. "Must be another group." He glanced around. "Place must be crawling with them."

Putting the glass up to his eye, Morgan Hunter said, "They're coming pretty fast." Then he gave the long glass back.

Wade took it and pushed it together. "They'll be on us soon." Wade turned in his saddle, looked at the landscape around them, and seeing a rise about four hundred yards to the north, he pointed to it. "There."

Morgan turned and looked. "Not much cover."

"No," said Wade. "But it's high ground."

Morgan turned to look up at the rise, unsure of his new friend's choice, and repeated, "Not much cover."

"Don't need much cover," replied Wade. "Just elevation. When we get to the rise, you and that slow packhorse head north."

Morgan glanced back at the approaching Indians and then looked at Wade. "And where will you be heading?"

"I'm gonna slow 'em up a bit." Then he turned the mare toward the rise and spurred her into a gallop.

Morgan took another quick look at the Indians, spurred his Appaloosa, and followed Wade up the hill tugging at the reluctant packhorse while considering letting go of the reins.

Reaching the top of the rise, Wade pulled his mare up and looked back at the pursuing Indians.

Morgan pulled up. "I ain't gonna let you stay behind while I run for it."

Wade looked at Morgan with a determined look as he climbed down. "We can't outrun them with that packhorse in tow. He'll slow us up. Besides, there's only eight of them." He nodded north. "You go on ahead." He smiled. "I'll be along."

Morgan quickly considered that as he glanced back at the cloud of dust closing in on them. Able to hear the hooves of their ponies against the hard Montana soil mix with the faint war cries, he turned his horse and rode after Wade. He watched as Wade tied his mare to a small scrub brush, pulled his Sharps from its scabbard, and took the bandoleer of cartridges off his saddle horn.

Wade looked up at Hunter. " Go on. I'll catch up."

Morgan's face held an expression of uncertainty as he glanced back at the dust cloud and the Indians riding in front of it. He turned back to Wade, who had just pulled a metal shooting rod from its slot in the Sharps scabbard. "How long you plan on staying behind?"

"Not long," replied Wade. "Now get that packhorse out of here." Then he turned and ran to the edge of the rise, falling to his knees.

Morgan watched Wade shove the steel shooting rod into the ground and then twist it as if screwing it into the soil. Figuring he knew what he was doing, Hunter gripped the reins to the packhorse tightly in one hand, looked back at the Indians, and then at Wade. "Don't dally!" Then he spurred his Appaloosa and rode up a slight draw onto flat ground and rode away from the ridge and into the Montana plains, leading the slower packhorse.

Wade turned in time to see Morgan disappear over the ridge, picked up his rifle, shoved a cartridge into the breech, and rested the long barrel of the Sharps on the u-shaped on top of the rod. He glanced at the Indians, estimating their distance, which grew shorter with each moment, and thought of the day he, Seth, and Frank Wells rescued the Indian, Dark Cloud, from a band of renegade Apache. Wade estimated them to be about three hundred yards out and closing fast. The wind was calm, the air crisp and clear as he looked through the scope and, after adjusting it, put the crosshairs on the lead rider and squeezed the first trigger. Resting his finger on the second trigger, he steadied the crosshairs on the Indian's chest and gently squeezed the trigger.

Hearing the sound that resembled cannon, Morgan pulled up and looked back, knowing it was the Sharps. Hearing a second shot, he considered going back but instead turned and rode north, tugging at the slower packhorse, deciding he would stop in a few minutes and wait for Wade while wishing he hadn't left him alone.

Back at the knoll, Wade reloaded and fired, knocking another Indian from his pony. The band of Crow turned their ponies and scattered in different directions while Wade pulled a cartridge from the bandoleer, shoved it into the breech, and found another target. The gun recoiled against his shoulder, followed by the explosion that imitated cannons in the vastness of the landscape. His target jerked and rolled backward off the rear of the pony. He watched as the Indians pulled up, turned their ponies, and rode back toward the stream while one of the Crow he shot slowly get up and staggered after his pony that was trotting after the other ponies.

Wade thought about putting another cartridge into the Sharps but instead watched as another Crow galloped toward the wounded Indian, stop and helped the wounded Crow climb up onto the rear of the pony. Watching as they rode away, Wade figured they'd had enough of his Sharps, pulled the rod out of the ground, and headed for his mare. Shoving the Sharps into its scabbard, followed by the rod into its tiny slot on the side of the scabbard, he untied the mare and swung up. He stood in the stirrups, looking at the dust in the distance left by the Crow before he turned the mare and followed the trail left by Morgan Hunter up the ridge.

He rode for about a quarter-mile before he pulled up, looked down at Morgan's trail letting his eyes follow it for a short distance, then looked toward the northeast. He turned, looked behind him to make sure he wasn't followed, and then studied the landscape around him. His eyes followed the tracks left by Morgan's horses until they disappeared into the distance. He smiled, tipped his hat, wishing him a safe journey, turned the mare, and rode northeast.

Chapter 4

Morgan Hunter

Morgan rode due north for about a half-hour before stopping in a deep arroyo, taking advantage of what little shade the walls of the arroyo offered. After climbing down, he took a drink from his canteen, poured some water into his cupped hand, and gave both horses a drink before tying them to a nearby scrub brush. Pulling his Winchester from its scabbard, he climbed up the sloping bank taking position behind a large rock that gave him a clear view of the prairie, and waited for his new friend.

The minutes quickly passed into an hour and that into two, and there was no sign of the man, Emmett, and his Sharps rifle. Visions of him being killed and scalped by the Crow filled Morgan's mind, and he became angry with himself for not staying with him. He liked what little he knew of the man and would have enjoyed getting to know him a little better. Another few minutes passed, and he considered riding back but decided that it would serve no purpose. What was done was done, and he felt terrible for leaving him. He climbed out of the arroyo and looked back into the distance for several minutes, hoping to see some sign of

Emmett. Seeing none, he turned and walked back into the arroyo, sheathed his Winchester, climbed into the saddle, and rode out of the Arroyo heading northeast.

It had been two days since the incident on the knoll when Morgan pulled the Appaloosa to a stop atop a sloping hill. The sun was almost gone, and feeling the fall chill of the approaching night, he turned and untied the straps that held his duster securely to his saddle, slipped it on, and buttoned it. He looked at the scene covered in that faint light that stubbornly hangs on before giving way to darkness. A wide, winding river stretched out before him, both sides populated with stands of willow, cottonwood, and oak trees as far as the eye could see. The land was a mixture of dry grasslands and sagebrush with tall mountains to the north and west. Cattle country, he thought to himself, recalling the cattle wars in west Texas.

He rode down the hill tugging at the packhorse and followed the river north until he saw a ranch house, barn, and corral nestled among the trees on this side of the river near its bend. His mind thought of a soft bed and hoped the people were friendly. In the dim rose-colored light of dusk, smoke drifted lazily from the chimney. Soft yellow-orange lights, warm and inviting, filled the windows. Feeling tired and hopeful for a night's comfort and maybe a home-cooked meal, he looked back over his shoulder. He thought briefly of Emmett, then nudged the Appaloosa and tugged at the packhorse.

The colors of sunset were almost gone when he reached the house, and darkness close at hand as he pulled up several yards from the front porch and called out, "In the house!"

Moments later, the door opened, spreading light from within across the porch as the dark figure of a man silhouetted against the light stepped from the house. Holding a rifle across his belly, the figure stepped to the edge of the covered porch. "You lost?" the man asked, sounding puzzled.

34

Morgan chuckled. "Guess some would believe so. I ain't all that sure myself."

The lean figure cautiously stepped off the porch. "Come closer, so's I can have a look while you tell me who you are." The man looked past Morgan and asked, "You alone?"

Morgan thought of Emmett as he nudged his horse into a slow walk. "I am."

"That's far enough," said the figure as he turned the barrel of the rifle toward Morgan.

"Name's Morgan Hunter. I ride alone, and I mean you no harm, sir."

Still suspicious, the man took another step closer, keeping an eye on the stranger's hands while glancing at the tired-looking packhorse and the unusual markings of the horse of the rider. "Come far?"

"Texas."

The man thought about that. "That's a long ride, all right." He studied the man who called himself Morgan Hunter and decided he was an honorable man, so he lowered the rifle. "Might as well, step down." He motioned toward the house with the barrel of the rifle. "Me and the missus were just about to sit down for supper. It ain't much, and if you ain't particular, you're welcome to join us."

Morgan smiled as he climbed down. "I let go of particular a long time ago. The last good hot meal I had was in Laramie, Wyoming. Since then, it's been beans, dry beef jerky, an occasional rabbit, and a few quail eggs." He wiped the palm of his right hand on the front of his black duster and offered it in friendship. "So, I'm sure what your missus is putting on the table is fit for kings."

The man chuckled as he shook Morgan's hand and introduced himself. Jessup Thornton was a lean man of sixty-plus years with a full head of ruffled white hair, dark brown eyes that had a friendly but questioning gaze, and his lined tan face had a day's growth of gray whiskers. He was without a shirt dressed in faded red long johns and dirty gray pants held up by suspenders.

Morgan was surprised at the strength of the hand he shook.

Jessup Thornton turned to the door. "Louise!" he yelled. "We got company for dinner!"

A small, plump woman stepped out of the house onto the porch holding a lantern, wearing a faded yellow dress with a high collar and long sleeves. Her gray hair was cut short, like most of the women on the frontier. She paused for a moment wearing a faint, uncertain smile as she looked at Morgan through tired brown eyes.

Jessup gestured to his wife. "Mr. Hunter, this here's Louise, my wife of forty-odd years."

Mrs. Thornton walked to the edge of the porch, nervously fidgeting with her hair and obviously unprepared for company. She wiped her empty, small hand on her stained apron and then held it out. "We ain't got much, Mr. Hunter, but you're welcome to what we do have."

Jessup looked at his wife. "Mr. Hunter's rode all the way from Texas."

"My, that is a long way," smiled Louise.

Morgan took her hand and shook it gently while thanking her.

"You're welcome to spend the night," offered Jessup, gesturing toward a small bunkhouse near the barn. "There's plenty of room in the bunkhouse."

Morgan glanced at the bunkhouse, thinking of a soft mattress instead of the cold, hard ground. "I'd appreciate that." He looked at Thornton. "How many men do you have?"

Thornton looked annoyed. "Had four, but they up and left about a week ago."

Looking curious, Morgan asked why.

"We can talk about that later," replied Jessup. "Right now, we best get these horses inside." He handed his Winchester to his

36

wife as he looked at Morgan. "While you take care of your horses, I'll get my stock out of the corral and inside the barn."

Pickering, Montana

Wade Garrison

Soft orange and yellow light from windows and open doorways spilled across the boardwalks and into the dark streets of Pickering, Montana, as Wade rode into town under a black starry sky. He proceeded up the dark, lonely street, riding in and out of the lighted images of doorways and windows to the sound of the mare's hoofs on the hard, rutted street. Wade was thinking of Morgan and wondered if they'd ever meet again. As the mare walked past the saloon, soft piano music and faint laughter made its way out of the closed door, reminding him of the Blue Sky Saloon, back in Harper. Several horses tied up at the hitching rail, looking like statues waiting for their riders. An empty wagon and its team of horses waited alongside the boardwalk across the street in front of the general store. The sound of a woman's soft laughter coming from the boardwalk as a man and a woman walked arm in arm, seemingly having a good time.

The smell of cooked food suddenly found him as the door to the café opened, and a man and woman stepped onto the boardwalk. The man closed the door while giving Wade a glance before escorting the woman to their waiting buggy, helping her into the seat. The man hurried to the other side, climbed up, and slapped the horse with the reins disappearing into the darkness.

Finding the livery on the north edge of town, he pulled up, climbed down, and looked at the name above the livery doors painted in white that was barely visible in the dim light. "Bennett's Livery, Albert P. Bennett, Prop." As he walked the mare to the big doors, he thought of Levi Wagner, recalling how Levi had stitched up his wounds and gave him breakfast the morning he killed George Hoskins. Knocking on one of the big doors, he waited, and when no one answered, he led his horse to the side of the livery. Seeing the lighted windows of a small house several yards beyond the livery, he led the mare to the house, tied her to the porch roof post then knocked on the door.

"Who's there?" said a deep voice from inside.

"Name's Emmett Spears. I'm looking for Mr. Bennett?"

The door opened, and a bearded man of six feet, with broad shoulders filling most of the doorway, holding a pistol in one hand. He was wearing black pants and a shirt with sleeves rolled up to his mid-forearms, exposing white long johns. His dark, deep-set eyes looked at Wade. "I be Bennett," he said with a curious stare. "What can I do for you, Mr. Spares?"

"It's Spears," corrected Wade as he gestured back toward the livery. "Like to put my horse up if you've room."

Albert gave him a quick, thoughtful glance up and down and then turned his head, talking over his shoulder. "Shelly, I'm going down to the livery to put this man's horse up."

"All right," answered a woman's voice from somewhere inside. "I'll put your dinner in the oven to keep it warm."

"Be back soon," Bennett said, and then as if in a hurry, he tucked the pistol under his belt, reached back inside, taking a ring of keys off a nail, then a lantern from a small table, and stepped outside. "Come far?" he asked while closing the door.

"Seems far," replied Wade dryly as he followed Bennett off the porch.

Albert waited while Wade untied the mare, and then they walked toward the livery immersed in the light from the lantern. "Got friends in Pickering or just passing through?"

Wade frowned, not liking the questions. "No, I don't know anyone here."

Bennett waited for the rest of the answer to his question, and when none came, he decided, the stranger was passing through. Bennett shoved a key into an old lock holding a chain together that ran through the door's handle and a steel ring on the door jamb. He turned the key, the rusty lock opened, and then pulled the chain free, opened the door, and turned to Wade. "I'll meet you around front." Then he disappeared inside and closed the door.

Wade led the mare around the corner of the livery, and when they got to the big doors, he heard the board across the doors being removed, and then one opened to a creaking, moaning sound.

Holding the lantern in one hand, the other hand on the door, Albert stepped aside. "Bring her in; you can put her in the third stall."

Wade led the mare into the stall, where he took the Sharps from the scabbard, leaned it against the stall, and started with the cinch of the saddle. "That two-story hotel across the street expensive?"

Bennett gave the rifle and its scope a curious look. "The Grande? To some, I guess it would be." Then he gestured back toward the middle of town. "There's one across from the saloon that's a mite cheaper called the Howard Hotel. It ain't the Grande, but it's nice and clean."

Wade recalled seeing the Howard Hotel as he rode up the street as he gently pulled the saddle off the mare.

Seeing he was in some distress, Albert Bennett quickly stepped into the stall. "Let me give you a hand with that."

Wade stepped back while Albert tossed the saddle on the railing of the stall and thanked him. "How much for a bag of oats? It's been a while since she's had the pleasure of a good meal."

Bennett glanced at the mare and thought of his supper sitting in the oven, getting dry. "Oats, clean hay, and water are included in the price," He set the lantern down, turned, and walked toward the other end of the barn while talking over his shoulder. "I'll get a bucket of oats while you take that bucket by your feet."

39

He stopped and turned. "There's a pump just outside the big doors."

Wade finished with the harness, picked up the bucket, and went outside for water, and when he returned, Bennett was stepping out of the stall with a grin. "She's a hungry one."

"Don't doubt that." Wade walked past Bennett and placed the bucket of water next to the bucket of oats, patted the mare on the neck, and tossed his saddlebags across one shoulder. He picked up his Sharps, tossed the bandoleer of cartridges over the other shoulder, and looked at Albert. "Want me to pay you now?"

Albert Bennett smiled friendly-like while thinking of his dinner getting dry. "Tomorrow will do." He gestured toward the door and started walking while talking over his shoulder. "Now, if you don't mind, I'd like to get back to my supper."

The two men walked to the open doorway, where Bennett waited for Wade. "See you in the morning, Mr. Spears."

Wade put one hand against the door that Albert was closing. "Is there a doctor in town?"

Bennett thought of helping him with the saddle. "You all right?"

"I'm fine. Just want to ask him a thing or two."

Albert Bennett wasn't sure about the reason but figured it was none of his business as he motioned toward the street. "Doc Reid's place is just down the street, around the corner from the hotel." Bennett nodded. "I'll say goodnight now. My dinner's getting dry." The door closed, followed by the sounds of Bennett putting the wood brace across them.

Wade turned, walked along the dirt, rutted street in and out of lighted images of windows on the dirt street, and wondered what sort of place this Pickering is. As he approached the corner, where he was to turn, he looked across the street at the saloon and decided Doc Reid could wait until morning and crossed the street thinking of a beer. Stepping up onto the boardwalk in front of the saloon, he paused at the window with white lettering spelling

40

"Saloon" encircled by white fancy, curly designs, and looked inside. Hunched over the bar, talking to the heavyset bartender, were two men looking like farmers, each nursing a beer. Laughter came from four men he figured to be drovers sitting at a table near the stairs leading up to the second-floor balcony. The two at the bar turned their heads, looking over their shoulders at the four men. The bartender looked past them at the four men with an annoyed look and said something as he wiped the bar with a white bar towel.

In the far corner, next to the bar under the second-floor balcony, a short, heavyset man on a stool played the piano. He moves from side to side as his chubby fingers glide across the keys playing a soft melody. At a table not far from the piano, two men in their late fifties or early sixties talked with three whores. Thinking it must be a slow night, Wade stepped away from the window to the closed door, turned the knob, and pushed the door open, stepping inside. As he walked toward the bar, the four men at the table near the stairs gave him a quick unimportant glance then went about their business. The bartender and the two men he talked with turned, gave him a glance, and then continued their conversation.

Noticing a large buffalo head hanging on the wall above the bar, he set the Sharps on the floor, leaned the barrel against the bar, and then set the saddlebag and bandoleer of cartridges down. Feeling tired, Wade rested on his elbows, folded his hands, and glanced at the images in the mirror behind the bar.

Laughter from the four drovers interrupted the stillness and soft music of the otherwise quiet saloon.

The bartender approached wearing an unhappy expression. "What'll it be?" Dressed in a white shirt with gartered sleeves, a stained apron over dark pants, he looked around fifty. He stood around six feet and a little on the heavy side with black hair, blue eyes, and a pleasant face even though he wore a frown.

"Quiet night?" asked Wade.

The bartender raised his brow with a disappointed look, pulled the towel from his shoulder, and wiped down the bar. "What'll it be?"

"Beer."

The bartender flipped the towel over his left shoulder, turned, got a mug from the counter behind him, and placed it under the spigot.

Wade watched the beer flow from the tap into the mug, anticipating the taste when the sharp yelp of a pup caused the piano player to stop playing, turn his head and look toward the four men.

Wade turned toward the sound and the four men, seeing what appeared to be a frightened coyote pup tied to the leg of one of the men's chairs with a thin rope.

The bartender glanced at the four men as he set the mug of beer in front of Wade. "That'll be a nickel."

Wade took a coin out of his pocket and tossed it on the bar. "What's that all about?"

The bartender looked irritated. "They're teasing the pup before they take it outside and shoot it."

"Seems a little cruel," said Wade. He picked up his beer and took a drink, wondering about the pup's mother. Wade wasn't fond of coyotes but couldn't help feeling sorry for the pup. He set the mug down and wiped the foam from his mouth, remembering how frightened Dog was that day he found him.

The bartender watched the four men as he wiped the bar with his towel. "Yeah, I ain't fond of coyotes any more than the next man, but they should just shoot the poor thing and get it over with."

"Why not stop it?"

The bartender looked at him. "You're new in town, mister. No one messes with Brodie."

Wade looked over his right shoulder. "Which one's Brodie?"

"Has his back to us."

Wade looked at the bartender and thought he was no Sam Carney, took another drink of beer, and watched the four men in the mirror while they laughed and teased the pup. "Who are the other three?"

Dave wiped the bar with his wet towel. "The one teasing the pup is Harry Anderson, the one with sandy hair is Jimmy Wilson, and the other is Todd Young. None of them are worth a shit."

Wade took a drink of beer, then turned his head and looked over his right shoulder at the four men.

Harry yanked the rope and kicked at the pup that yelped and snapped at his boot. Harry turned to the others with a surprised look and laughed. "Mean little shit."

Brodie turned in his chair to the barkeep. "Need four beers over here, Dave." Then he gave Wade and the Sharps rifle leaning against the bar a quick, curious look, and then turned back to his friends.

Deciding to mind his own business, Wade leaned on the bar with his elbows, took a drink of beer, and stared at his image in the mirror, thinking he could use a bath, shave, and haircut. He took off his leather gloves, tucked them under his gun belt, and picked up the beer just as the pup yelped. Turning, he saw it was trembling and afraid, and then he looked down the bar at the angry bartender.

The pup yelped again, and then the one named Jimmy Wilson took out the makings for a cigarette. "Let's see how sensitive her nose is."

Harry laughed, knowing what Jimmy had in mind. "She won't be needing it much longer anyways."

Wilson was making a cigarette, spilling more tobacco than he was putting on the thin paper. He looked at Harry. "I'm gonna burn her little nose." Then he laughed.

Wade picked up his beer and took a big drink, thinking they were just a bunch of assholes picking on a helpless pup. He set the

43

mug down and wiped his mouth while his eyes quickly roamed around the room of empty tables, small dance floor, and an upright piano with its fat player watching the four men. Wade thought of the player in Paso Del Rio he shot the night the Indian and Frank Wells died, and then his eyes climbed the stairs to the second floor with five closed doors. He thought of the bar in Whisper Creek, Colorado, and the tearing eyes of young Josh Martin as he lay dying on the saloon floor. His eyes found Wilson lighting his cigarette while the others looked on in joyful anticipation. Wade looked at the trapped, scared coyote pup feeling sorry for the animal.

Harry Anderson pulled the coyote closer, took the cigarette from Jimmy Wilson, and leaned down at the pup.

"I wouldn't do that," said Wade stepping away from the bar.

Anderson paused and looked up at Wade with curious eyes.

"You want something?" asked Brodie. He was a big man, unshaven, his clothes dirty, and his long black hair bulged under his old tan hat. The others who looked no better gave Wade a curious look.

"I want to buy the pup," offered Wade.

Harry paused and sat back in his chair, letting go of the rope.

"Why?" asked Jimmy Wilson, who had unruly sandy hair and a long handlebar mustache. He pushed his hat back, letting it drop to his back held by the string around his neck.

Noticing his missing front tooth, Wade wondered if someone had knocked it out. "When I was a kid, I had a pet coyote."

"So?" frowned Brodie.

"So," said Wade. "I'd like to buy him."

Harry puffed on his cigarette. "It's a bitch."

The others chuckled as Wade glanced around the table before looking back at Harry. "Bitch," he corrected. "I'd like to buy the bitch."

"She ain't for sale," said Harry.

Brodie gestured to Harry. "Just a minute." Then he looked at Wade. "How much?"

Wade looked at the she pup, who couldn't be more than three months old. She stood against the wall, trembling in a puddle of her own piss. "Two dollars and a round of beer."

Brodie looked up at Wade for a moment. "Four dollars and two rounds of beer."

Wade thought for a minute, knowing what lay in store for the pup, agreed on the amount, then reached into his pocket for the money.

Brodie turned away, looking irritated as he gestured Wade away. "Get lost, asshole."

A stillness fell on the table as the four men watched to see what Wade would do. He stood there, feeling the fool for the moment, and that angered him.

The fourth man, whose name was Todd Young, looked up at Wade. "The man said to get lost." He was an angry-looking young man wearing the scars of acne. He had black, greasy hair and dark eyes that stared up at Wade with foolish pride.

Harry Anderson stood, giving Wade a mean look. He stood six feet, a little on the heavy side, with dark hair. "The man said to get lost."

Wade was about to bust him in the face and then draw his gun, but Brodie yelled for him to sit down.

Harry took a drag from his cigarette, blew smoke toward Wade's face, and then sat down.

Wade wanted to shoot the bastard, but he wanted to get the pup without a fight if he could. He looked at Brodie. "Four dollars and two rounds of beer."

Brodie simply gestured Wade away with one hand and repeated, "Get lost, asshole." Then Brodie looked at Harry. "You gonna burn her damn nose or not?"

One of the whores sitting at a nearby table stood. "Don't burn her, Harry."

Brodie turned to her with an ugly look. "Stay out of this, Estelle, damn it."

Wade wanted to kick the shit out of all four but knew he couldn't win a fistfight, and he'd pull all of the stitches in him anyway, so he looked at Harry. "You ain't gonna burn that pup."

Harry looked up at Wade with a questioning face. "Who says?"

Wade's hand moved to the butt of his gun. "I do."

"There's four of us," chuckled Brodie.

"I can count," said Wade

Todd laughed. "You better count again, stranger."

"No need," replied Wade. Knowing Brodie was the leader, he looked straight into his eyes. "Are the lives of two or three of you worth that bitch pup?"

Brodie sat back in his chair, considering the question and the man standing at their table. "I'll ask you the same question, stranger. Is your life worth that bitch pup?"

Wade looked at the pup standing next to the wall, trembling with fear, and spoke in a soft, calm voice. "I don't plan on dying." Then he looked at the others. "Any of you boys ever draw from a sitting position?"

The table was quiet while they thought that over, noticing that Wade's hand was already at the butt of his Colt, and they knew he had the advantage even if there were four of them.

Brodie stared up at Wade, wondering if he was crazy, but didn't want to back down. "Do you think you can take all of us?"

"Maybe not," said Wade without hesitation. "But I know who I'll shoot first." Then he looked at the others. "And I sure as

46

hell could get two more, and I'll take my chances with the last man."

A deafening silence fell on the big room as everyone watched to see what Brodie and the others would do, including a worried Dave Goody, the bartender. Fearful of what might happen, he slowly pulled a shotgun from under his bar but didn't cock it, afraid the sound would resonate across the quiet room and cause someone to draw.

Feeling restless, Brodie moved his chair slightly.

Hearing the noise, Wade looked from Harry to Brodie and drew his gun, "You anxious to die?"

Brodie raised his hands. "Hold on, mister, I ain't drawing." Not used to backing down, his dark eyes held a mixture of fear and hate, knowing he was in the worst of positions to call a man's hand. Especially the hand of a man who appeared crazy enough to die over a coyote pup. Brodie relaxed in his chair and placed both hands on the table, telling Harry to untie the pup. "Looks like you just bought yourself a coyote pup, mister."

"It's my pup," complained Harry.

Brodie gave him a dirty look while talking through clenched teeth. "Give him the damn pup."

Harry gave Wade a mean look then did as told.

Wade gestured at the bar. "I'll leave your money with the bartender."

Harry handed the rope to Wade, who carefully took it with his left hand while keeping his Colt pointed at the table. He backed away from the table with the reluctant, growling pup fighting the rope that was dragging her across the wooden floor.

Goody raised the shotgun over the bar, pointing it at the table. "You boys just stay seated while the man leaves with the damn coyote."

When Wade and the pup reached the bar, he holstered his gun and turned to put the money down.

Seeing his chance, Brodie quietly pushed his chair back and started to stand, thinking he could gun down Wade.

Dave cocked both hammers of the shotgun. "Not tonight, Brodie!" He pushed the barrel of the shotgun toward him. "No one's getting shot in the back in my place tonight."

Brodie looked at Dave and raised his hands as he turned to Wade. "Another time."

Realizing he had made a mistake in holstering his gun, he looked at Brodie. "You're a sneaky bastard, but lucky."

"Maybe," said Brodie. "And maybe you're the one who runs with luck this night."

Dave Goody looked at Wade. "You and that pup leave right now, stranger."

Wade laid money on the bar for the pup and beer, picked the bandoleer of cartridges, his saddlebags, and then grabbed his Sharps. Dragging the growling pup along the hardwood floor, he backed toward the door, turned the knob, opened it, and stepped outside. Pulling the angry pup along the boardwalk, Wade stepped off into the shadows, and while watching the door, put on his gloves. He bent down and tried to pick the pup up, but she was uncooperative, growling and snapping at his gloved hands.

"Yeah, you're tough all right," he told her, and then he dragged her across the street to the Howard Hotel, regretting his getting involved. Stepping up onto the boardwalk in front of the hotel, he knelt and spoke in a soft voice. "I ain't gonna hurt you none."

The pup backed away with a low growl, bearing her sharp puppy teeth.

He stared at her for a moment and then asked, "What the hell am I going to do with you?" Deciding he would pick her up, he put one gloved hand over her face, the other under her belly, and picked her up. She twisted and growled, trying to get free, but he held her tight and tucked her under his arm but kept her mouth and those sharp little teeth covered. "There," he said softly, looking into her dark eyes. "Now, this ain't so bad, is it?"

She trembled and struggled as she whined.

"Hey, I'm not going to hurt you. I'm the guy that saved you." Deciding to take a chance, he let go of her mouth, and she immediately snapped at his gloved hand. Chuckling, he gripped her nose and covered her mouth once again. "You ain't about to let this be easy, are you?" He glanced across the street, fearing Brodie and the others would come after him, so he picked up his Sharps, turned, and walked toward the door of the Howard Hotel.

The hotel lobby was empty and quiet as the tiny bell above the door announced their arrival. He looked at the empty counter just as a thin woman pushed a black curtain apart and stepped out of the backroom to the counter. She was wearing a dark blue dress, her black hair worn in a braid atop her head, giving her a matronly look. "No dogs allowed."

Looking disappointed, Wade turned away and walked outside, where he stood on the boardwalk next to the window of the hotel, wondering where he could spend the night. Without realizing it, he had taken his hand away from the pup's mouth and was gently petting her shoulder. He looked down at her dark eyes. "Fine mess you've gotten us into."

The door of the saloon opening caught Wade's eye, and seeing Brodie and the others step out of the saloon, Wade stepped back into the shadows. He watched while they climbed up on their horses and rode out of town in the other direction. Relieved, Wade walked to the edge of the boardwalk, looked in the direction they had ridden, then looked at the clock in the hotel lobby. Seeing it was nine-thirty and feeling tired, he looked at the pup that had settled comfortably into his left arm and stepped off the boardwalk. Not knowing where else to go, he hoped Mr. Bennett had enjoyed his dinner and was in a good mood.

Chapter 5

The Thornton Ranch

It seemed to Morgan that whenever he took a bite of food, Mrs. Thornton filled his plate. Pausing once as she did so, Morgan glanced around the big room of a brown leather sofa, two wooden rocking chairs, and a bear rug on the floor in front of a stone fireplace that took up most of the east wall.

Morgan learned during dinner conversation that their only son had died after falling from the roof of the barn eight years earlier. Mrs. Thornton talked about her son in a soft voice while she moved her fork through her food. He could sense the sadness she still carried as she asked, "He never married?"

She looked sad and disappointed. "No, my son never did."

"Got engaged once," offered Jessup.

Mrs. Thornton smiled. "She passed away before they could get married."

Jessup's voice broke the stillness changing the subject. "That's a mighty fine looking animal you're riding," he said, referring to the Appaloosa that was black with a spattering of white spots, a white rump covered in black spots, and a solid black tail. "Never saw a horse with such unusual markings."

Morgan Hunter smiled proudly. "He's one of a kind, all right."

"Mind asking how you come by such a piece of horseflesh?"

Hunter glanced up at Mrs. Thornton as she picked up his empty plate, then he turned to Jessup. "About two years ago, I ran across an old man sitting against a rock down in Texas. He'd been gutshot, and I could tell he was dying."

Thornton looked curious. "Did he tell you who shot him?"

Morgan shook his head no as he leaned on the table with his elbows. "Never had the chance." He paused, looking sad. "I climbed down from my horse with my canteen to give him a drink of water, but as I knelt, he slipped away." He sat back with a shrug of his hands. "So, I buried him and kept the horse."

Jessup thought about the old man and felt downhearted while Louise placed a plate of fresh apple pie and a clean fork in front of Hunter.

Morgan stared at it a moment, smelling just a hint of the warm crust, cinnamon, and apples thinking it looked good. He smiled as he looked up with anticipation. "Been a long time since I've had apple pie."

She smiled in memory. "My son Johnny loved apple pie. Used to make it for him when the trees filled with apples." She walked behind his chair, carrying a second plate of pie and a fork for her husband. "Our two trees were good to us this year." She placed the plate in front of her husband. "What brings you to Montana, Mr. Hunter?" She smiled. "Or am I getting nosey?"

Images Morgan wanted to forget ran through his mind as he cut through the crust of pie and thin slice of apple with his fork. "Needed a change."

Disappointed at the answer, She smiled, figuring there was more to it than that said, "Reason enough, I suppose."

51

Morgan shoved a fork of warm apple pie into his mouth and looked at Jessup. "Maybe it's none of my business, Mr. Thornton, but why'd your hands up and leave?"

Jessup considered the question while he shoved a fork filled with pie into his mouth and watched Louise walk behind Morgan and sit down at the table across from him. "I think they were scared off."

Morgan looked puzzled. "By what?"

Louise's face had a bitter look as she picked up her coffee cup. "That rabble who works for Ben Croucher." She looked at her husband with a quick, determined nod of the head, "That damn Brodie, that's who."

Jessup looked unhappy as he stabbed his pie with the fork and made a clean cut across the tip of it. "Afraid Lou's right." He looked at Morgan and smiled. "Brodie's first name is Francis." Thornton raised his brow, looking serious. "He don't like being called Francis, though. Answers only to Brodie. Anyone that calls him Francis gets a boot in the groin."

Morgan grinned. "Sounds a bit sensitive."

Mrs. Thornton enjoyed her husband's and Morgan's humor and softly laughed as she stood. "More coffee, Mr. Hunter?"

"Thank you, ma'am."

She made a hot pad from her apron, picked up the large gray coffee pot from the stove, and filled his cup.

Jessup put his hand over his cup, indicating he didn't want any more as he looked at Morgan. "You ain't by chance looking for work?"

Morgan sat back and smiled at Mr. Thornton. "No, sir, I ain't."

"Too bad," answered Jessup, showing his regret. "Just where is it you're headed if I ain't being too nosey?"

Morgan took the last bite of his pie and considered the old man's question. "Well," he began as he placed his fork on the empty plate and pushed it toward the center of the table. "It's been

52

a while since I visited a town, and if there's one nearby, I'll probably head there." He paused. "Don't know what I'll do after that."

The old man wondered why anyone would want to visit a town. There wasn't anything in a town but nosey people looking for you to spend money in their stores. "The only town close by is Pickering, a few miles north of here." He paused in thought. "There ain't nothing else around but a fort on the Tongue River and another farther north, where the Tongue meets the Yellowstone River." He paused. "Guess you could call them towns." He glanced at the clock standing in the corner. "Get'n late, and sunrise comes early. As soon as you're done with that coffee, I'll show you out to the bunkhouse."

A full moon sat motionless above them in a black sky filled with stars from horizon to horizon as they stepped off the porch into the night. The moon's faint white light cast ghostly shadows as the two men surrounded by the orange glow of the lantern the old man carried walked across the yard. Singing crickets mixed with the call of bullfrogs that lived along the banks of the Powder River, and something shuffled across the ground giving both men reason to pause.

"Wonder what that was?" asked Morgan.

"Maybe you don't want to know," chuckled Jessup.

Neither spoke again until they reached the porch of the bunkhouse where Jessup Thornton opened the door. As they walked inside, light from Jessup's lantern filled the room with a soft glow, leaving dark shadows here and there.

Morgan stood by the door glancing around the small room while Thornton set the lantern on a table and lit another. Bunk beds occupied the east and west walls, separated by a long table where the two lanterns spread their light. There was another lamp waiting life at the far end of the table, and two benches on either side looking like someone just stood and walked away. Two crudely built wooden chests sat under a small window in the center of the north wall, and two more at the foot of the two bunk beds.

Thornton pointed to the bunk beds. "Take whichever you want." Then, gesturing at the chests and closet, he thoughtfully added, "You can put your belongings anywhere since you're the only one here." A small stack of wood and a potbellied stove occupied one corner of the wall away from the door, and a narrow nook or open closet was next to the door. Jessup gestured to the small potbellied stove. "Still gets a mite chilly in the morning."

Morgan made a note of that and walked to the nearest chest and set his saddlebags, bedroll, and duster on top. "It'll be good to sleep in a bed and not have to worry about snakes." Then he set the Winchester in the corner near one of the bunks.

Jessup picked up the lantern. "Morning comes early, so I'll say goodnight."

"Goodnight, sir, and tell the missus I enjoyed dinner."

Thornton paused at the door. "I'll come out and roust you when breakfast is on the table." Then he opened the door and stepped outside.

The sound of Jessup Thornton walk faded across the small porch while Morgan took off his hat and hung it on a peg next to the door. He paused at the small window to watch the old man walk toward the house bathed in light from the kerosene lamp. Morgan turned from the window, took off his gun belt, laid it on the table next to the lamp, and started working on a fire in the small potbellied stove to take the chill out of the air.

Once the fire was going, he sat down on the bench, took off his spurs and boots, and got undressed down to his long johns. After he neatly folded his pants and hung his shirt from the post of the bunk bed, he took the locket out of his shirt pocket and wrapped the black velvet string around his fingers. Holding it securely in his right hand, he blew out the lantern on the wall next to the door, and after he shoved the lock into place on the door, he blew out the lantern on the table, leaving the room in darkness, but for the dim light escaping through the cracks of the stove.

Climbing into one of the lower bunks, he adjusted the pillow, then snuggled down under the blankets and got comfortable, being thankful he wasn't spending another night on the cold ground. Waiting for sleep to take him, he thought of Emmett lying dead and scalped under the black night sky, now food for coyotes and vultures and an Indian owning his Sharps and horse. He felt guilty about leaving him and wished he hadn't done so, but he had, and nothing could change it. Pushing Emmett from his thoughts, he gripped the locket he held in his right hand and thought of the girl and small child whose picture was inside. As his eyes found the flickering light of the fire coming through the tiny slits of the potbellied stove door, sleep visited.

Pickering, Montana

The early morning sun broke over the eastern hills filling the livery with long lines of light that shone through the cracks between the boards of the east wall. The bitch pup sat up, ears alert, eyes staring toward the back of the livery while giving a soft growl deep within her throat. Wade raised his head and looked toward the rear of the livery through the narrow lines of sunlight. He touched the pup to quiet her with his left hand, while his right found the butt of his Colt still holstered and lying next to him. The sound of the key in the lock and chain removed from the door broke seemed loud in the quiet morning. Knowing it was Albert Bennett, Wade took his hand away from the Colt and looked at the pup who owned the top of the blanket they shared. "He owns the place."

The pup turned from the noise and looked at Wade with dark questioning eyes, and he wondered what he was going to do with a coyote pup in cattle country. Hearing the door open, he looked through the side of the stall at Albert Bennett's big frame walking through the doorway. The pup's eyes fixed on the big figure, her ears alert as she softly growled.

Wade picked her up, pushed the cover off, and set the pup back on the blanket.

Bennett was at the entrance to the stall. "Sleep well?"

"I did," responded Wade as he grabbed his boots.

Bennett looked into the dark eyes of the pup as she growled at him. "Mean little shit."

Wade smiled at her. "Gives her character." He put his boots on and stood with the help of the railing of the stall.

Remembering helping him with the saddle the night before, Bennett asked, "You sure you're all right, Mr. Spears?"

Wade nodded that he was.

Bennett doubted that as he looked back down at the pup while he talked to Wade. "My missus told me to send you down to the house for breakfast."

Wade was hungry, and the thought of a hot, home-cooked breakfast appealed to him, but just the same, he didn't feel right about Mrs. Bennett fixing his breakfast. "Imposing on you is one thing, Mr. Bennett, but I surely don't mean to impose any on your wife. I'm sure she has other things to tend to besides my breakfast. I can eat at the café."

Albert frowned. "Nonsense. You do like I say and take the pup with you. I'm sure my misses can find some scraps for her as well."

Wade smiled as he looked down at the coyote pup staring up at Albert with intense eyes. "I'm sure she'd like that." Then he looked at Bennett. "I appreciate the use of this stall for the night."

Albert Bennett was wearing a leather apron over a dirty blue shirt with his sleeves rolled up, exposing his long underwear covering powerful arms. He combed back his black hair with the fingers of his left hand. "You ain't the first that's spent the night in one of my stalls instead of a horse, and you won't be the last." Then he turned his head, looking toward the rear of the livery in

56

the direction of his house. "Now, you take that pup and go have some breakfast."

Wade reached down, picked up the rope, and gently tugged at the pup, that followed with tail wagging. They had walked but a few steps when Wade stopped and turned. "What can you tell me about that Brodie fella I was telling you about last night?"

Bennett leaned on the stall's railing with his big arms. "Brodie's one of Big Ben Croucher's men." He quickly added, "He's a no-account as far as I'm concerned."

Wade thought of George Hoskins. "Who's this Big Ben Croucher?"

"Ben Croucher owns the Big C, a cattle ranch northwest of here. Every time his men come into town, they get drunk and raise hell. Most times, it's harmless." He looked at Wade. "I ain't saying all the Croucher gang is like Brodie and his three friends. The rest seem like hard workers who let loose a little steam now and again."

"Can't fault a man for that," said Wade. "Is Brodie the Big C foreman?"

"Ted Giles is the foreman, and a good one. I've never heard of him getting drunk or causing trouble. Stays out at the ranch most of the time."

"If Brodie and his friends are that much trouble, why doesn't this Ted Giles fire 'em?"

"Well," began Albert, "there's the rub for Ted Giles. A couple of years back, Brodie, Harry Anderson, Jimmy Wilson, and Todd Young rescued Ben's only son from a band of Crow Indians."

That interested Wade. "How'd the Crow get him?"

Albert looked puzzled. "Don't rightly recall how all that happened." He paused a moment. "Seems to me, the boy rode out alone and was taken captive." He paused again. "Not sure. But to make a long story short, Brodie and them trailed the Crow and traded the boy for two of their horses. When they returned, Big

57

Ben and his wife were more than grateful, and ever since them, boys can do no wrong."

"What about the sheriff?"

"Sheriff Jim Styles was near seventy and no match for the likes of Brodie and a few others, so he quit and headed west last spring." He paused, looking thoughtful. "California, I think it was." Then he looked at Wade with a sad face. "A nice young man by the name of Carl Cole took the job and clamped down on the Big C hands, especially Brodie and his friends. Then one night, someone beat the shit out of him, so he rode out of town and never came back."

"Was Brodie responsible for that?"

Albert shrugged. "Can't say for sure. Most of the hands of the Big C are good boys. But a few like Brodie are trash." He gestured toward the back door. "You best go eat."

Wade turned to leave but paused again. "How long ago was it this Cole fellah got beat up?"

Albert thought a moment. "Two, three weeks ago, maybe."

Wade quickly considered that. "Pickering is without a sheriff?"

Albert frowned with a troubling look. "That's right." Then he grinned with a small chuckle as he joked, "If you've the hankering, you can walk into Smith's General Store and ask Mayor Robert Smith for the job."

Wade smiled, letting that suggestion run around in his head as he turned to walk away. "C'mon, girl, let's get something to eat." Wade tied the pup to the post of the porch roof, knocked on Bennett's door, turned, and smiled at the pup, scratching herself behind the ear. The door opened, and when Wade turned, he looked into the face of a pretty woman in her late twenties or early thirties. She had long brown hair and big brown eyes. She was thin but not skinny, and she was wearing a gray and white polka dot housedress with long sleeves and a spotted apron.

She smiled as she spoke with a southern drawl. "Why, you must be that Mr. Spears, my husband told me about?"

Wade took off his hat. "Yes, ma'am," he said while combing back his long, messy brown hair with his right hand.

She stepped back. "I'm Shelly Bennett, Mr. Spears. Do come in." After he had stepped into the house, she started to close the door when she noticed the coyote pup sitting on the porch tied to the post and smiled. "What a cute little thing."

Wade turned and looked at the pup wondering why women always find things cute.

"Albert told me about you and that cute coyote pup this morning over breakfast and how y'all rescued her."

Wade looked down at the pup staring up at him with questioning eyes as Mrs. Bennett closed the door. He never considered the pup cute, but in a way, he had to admit that she was just that. "Well, I only hope she's worth the trouble," he said thoughtfully.

Shelly gestured toward the kitchen. "Right this way, Mr. Spears." She walked toward the kitchen while talking over her shoulder. "What are y'all gonna name her?"

Wade followed her thinking of the conversation with Sheriff Seth Bowlen's wife, Molly Bowlen, about naming Dog and his horse. "Don't know yet."

"I'll fix some scraps for that coyote pup of yours if you'd like."

"I'm sure she'll appreciate that, Mrs. Bennett." Wade looked around for somewhere to set his hat.

She noticed his dilemma. "Just set it down anywhere, Mr. Spears.

He set it on a nearby chair that occupied a wall by the doorway to the kitchen.

Mrs. Bennett filled a small plate with meat and potatoes. When she finished, she handed it to him and smiled. "Feed your pup, Mr. Spears, while I fix your breakfast."

He thanked her, took the plate, thinking it was awful good food for a coyote, and headed for the door.

As he walked away, she asked, "How do you like your eggs, Mr. Spears?"

Wade thought it was going to take a while to get used to being called Emmett Spears. "Whatever's easiest, Mrs. Bennett. I ain't particular," he said over his shoulder. When he opened the door, the pup anxiously greeted him, having already smelled the food on the plate he carried. Wade knelt, placed the dish in front of her, and before he could take his hand away, she was eagerly devouring the food. He watched her eat for a moment, then stepped back inside, asking Mrs. Bennett for a bowl so he could give the pup water. She gave him a big pan and gestured to the inside pump on the corner of the counter. Wade filled the pan, and as he carried it outside, he thought of the pump he had put in his home in Santa Fe for Sarah. Finding the pup licking the empty dish, he no sooner put the water down when she went after it much the same as she had the food.

"Breakfast is ready, Mr. Spears," called Mrs. Bennett

The Thornton Ranch

Jessup Thornton stepped out of the house, looking up at the sun hiding behind the treetops along the Powder River. Although a slight September chill filled the air, he knew it was going to be one of those warm September days. Stepping from the porch, he walked toward the bunkhouse to the song of the big red rooster sitting on top of the hen house with his outstretched neck and flapping wings. One of three cats the Thornton's kept for mice, a black-and-white female, walked out of a slit between loose boards in the barn wall and quickly disappeared into the bushes. Jessup walked across the small porch of the bunkhouse, knocked on the door, and waited. When his guest never responded, he opened the door, stuck his head inside, and looked around. Seeing Morgan's things were still on the chest, his Winchester leaning against the wall, Jessup figured Mr. Hunter couldn't have gone far. He turned and looked first at the outhouse seeing the door partly open, then he looked toward the barn, thinking Morgan may be saddling his horse to leave. He hurried to the barn, and when he walked inside, he was surprised at finding Morgan Hunter cleaning out one of the stalls. "No need for that, Mr. Hunter."

Morgan paused and looked over the railing of the stall with a smile. "Least I can do for the dinner and soft bed." Then he turned and continued working.

Jessup walked up to the stall, rested his arms on the top rail, and watched the man for a moment, noticing he wasn't wearing his sidearm. He recalled Louise's question the night before and Morgan's answer. "Hope you don't take offense, Mr. Hunter, but you don't look like a man who shovels shit for a living."

Without pausing, Morgan chuckled while recalling the days as a young man working in liveries for scraps of food and a place to sleep. "No offense taken, but I've shoveled my share of horse shit." He paused while resting the shovel on the dirt floor, wiped his forehead with his shirt sleeve, and smiled. "But I have to admit; it has been a while."

Looking hopeful, Thornton grinned. "I could use a good hand."

"I ain't exactly looking for work," replied Morgan as he continued his task.

"Hope you don't mind me asking, but what exactly are you looking for?"

Morgan never looked up. "I don't mind you asking, Mr. Thornton. Guess I'll know when I see it." Then he set the shovel down, picked up a pitchfork, and started in on the dirty hay that covered the floor.

Feeling a bit disappointed, Thornton walked to the center of the barn where the Appaloosa and Morgan's big brown packhorse stood. He rubbed the Appaloosa gently on its neck and looked up into her big black eyes. "Mighty fine horse. Yes, sir, a mighty fine horse, Mr. Hunter."

Morgan paused and looked at Jessup. "How about I call you Jessup, and you call me Morgan, and we both do away with this 'mister' stuff?"

Jessup turned with a grin looking pleased. "I guess we can do away with that sort of formality all right."

Hunter smiled with a quick nod of the head, indicating his approval, and went back to work in the next stall. "What do I look like I do, Jessup?"

Taken aback by the question, Thornton thought about Morgan's big Navy Colt pistol and the way he wore it high on his hip. Thornton wasn't a gunman, but he still knew a few things, such as a man with a conventional belt and holster sitting down in a chair or saddle doesn't have much of a chance if he has to draw.

"Well," he said cautiously, "I don't rightly know for sure what you look like, but you don't have the look of a farmer. And, I see you prefer the Navy Colt pistol, the same weapon of choice as Bill Hickok."

Morgan tossed a pitchfork of dirty hay out of the stall, stopped, and looked at Jessup. "He had two, but I can't say they did him much good at the time of his death." He looked into Jessup's curious eyes. "Let's just say I wasn't a farmer or ranch hand back in Texas and let it go at that."

Feeling uncomfortable, Thornton gestured toward the house. "Breakfast is ready."

After eating breakfast, Morgan pushed his empty plate away and stood. "Thanks for supper last night and breakfast this morning, Mrs. Thornton. Hope I didn't cause you any bother."

Louise stood as Morgan shoved his empty chair back under the table. "Weren't no bother, Mr. Hunter. You're always more than welcome to drop by for a meal."

He looked into her kindly face and thought of his mother. "You never know, I just may ride in here again one day."

She smiled, looking pleased. "I'll look forward to that." Then she hugged him and held his broad shoulders in her small hands. "You go on your way now, Mr. Hunter, and try and be careful."

"Yes, ma'am," replied Morgan softly. "And thanks again."

"You're more than welcome." Then she gestured toward the door. "Now, go on and be on your way."

Morgan turned and followed Jessup out the door to the bunkhouse for his belongings and then on to the barn, greeted by the smell of straw, urine, horse manure, and other barn smells.

"Where ya headed?" asked Jessup as he followed, carrying Morgan's saddlebags.

Hunter leaned his Winchester against the stall and laid his duster over the top railing. "Not sure." He took the gun belt and pistol draped over his shoulder, laid them on his duster, and picked up his saddle blanket. "What's the name of that town you mentioned last night?"

Jessup placed Morgan's saddlebags on the railing. "Pickering."

Morgan laid the saddle blanket on his horse, pulled the saddle off the railing, and tossed it onto the Appaloosa. Then he bent down and tightened the saddle cinch. "What sort of place is this Pickering?"

Jessup shrugged thoughtfully, not fully understanding the question. "Town like most towns, I reckon."

Morgan took the stirrup off the saddle horn and started with the bit and bridle, thinking that was good enough for him. Finished, he tied, tossed the saddlebags onto the saddle, slid the Winchester into its sheath located in the front of the saddle, and led the Appaloosa out of the barn.

Jessup followed, still filled with the hope of hiring Morgan. "Should you change your mind about a job, I could sure use the help." Then, hoping he needed money, he added, "I can afford thirty a month."

Morgan tied his horse to the top rail of the corral and patted it on the shoulder as he glanced around. After a moment, he turned to Jessup with a thoughtful look. "Nice place you have here, Jessup." Then he looked off into the distance, thinking of Emmett and the Crow Indians. "Have any trouble with Indians?"

"I find what's left of a steer now and again, or I see a small band of Indians off in the distance. But we've had no trouble from them."

Hunter turned. "Well, Jessup, as I said, you have a fine place, and if I were looking for work, it'd be a place like this."

That brought a smile to Jessup's disappointed face. "Can I help you with the packhorse?"

Morgan patted the Appaloosa on the rump and smiled at Jessup as they walked toward the barn. "Sure thing."

After Morgan led the packhorse out of the barn, tied him to the corral next to the Appaloosa, he returned to the barn for the rest of his gear. He strapped on his gun belt then adjusted the stiff holster that rested across his left hip. He smiled at the old man while holding out an open hand. "Thanks for everything, Jessup."

He shook Morgan's hand firmly. "If you're heading for Pickering, just follow the Powder River north about ten miles. You can see the town in the distance."

Morgan took the reins to both horses and climbed up, settling in his saddle. He glanced around once more, wrapped the reins of the packhorse around the horn of his saddle, and thought of the small place he had in Texas. "Yes, sir, mighty nice place you have here." Then he looked down at the old man, tipped his hat with two fingers, and turned the Appaloosa toward the river.

"Good luck to ya," called Jessup as he watched Morgan ride around the far side of the corral toward the river.

Pickering, Montana

It was nearing eight o'clock in the morning when Wade and the pup reached Smith's General Store. The walk from the livery had been quiet amid the curious onlookers sharing the story they heard that morning about the stranger and the coyote. He tied the pup to the porch post and glanced around as he stepped onto the boardwalk. As he started to open the door, he paused to look back at the pup, "Don't go anywhere."

The coyote pup looked up with black eyes, tilted her head, and whined softly as if in protest at being left alone.

Wade walked into the store to the tune of a tiny bell above the door that announced his arrival, and as he closed the door, it rang again. He looked through the glass of the window on the door at the coyote sitting on the boardwalk, watching a wagon pulled by a team of horses pass. He turned and started walking toward a

65

stocky man with oily brown hair wearing a slightly dirty apron over a white, long-sleeved gartered shirt and black vest.

The man looked up, letting his gray eyes examine the stranger and his lack of a sidearm. Setting his pencil down on the paper, he smiled. "Something I can help you with?"

"You, Mayor Smith?"

He gave Wade a curious look. "That I am."

"I'd like a minute of your time," said Wade as he approached the counter.

"A minute you have, Mr. ...?"

"Emmett Spears," Wade told him, and then he turned and looked through the glass of the door at the coyote pup to see if she was alright.

Mayor Smith leaned to one side to see what he was looking at. "That a coyote?"

Wade turned to the mayor with a friendly smile. "Yes, it is. I understand you're looking for a new sheriff?"

Smith stared at the small coyote remembering the story he heard earlier that morning, then looked at Wade. "You must be the fella that has everyone talking. You going to keep him as your pet?"

Wade glanced back at the pup. "It's a she, and yes, I guess she is a pet of sorts."

The mayor's gray eyes went from the coyote pup to Wade's blue eyes while considering his question. "The town is currently without a sheriff." He paused. "Mr. Spears, was it?

"That's correct."

"Have you had any experience?"

"I've been a deputy in a place or two."

Mayor Smith looked interested. "Mind telling me where?"

Wade had taken notice of the lack of telegraph lines leading into town, so he figured the man couldn't be too fussy. "Here and there."

The mayor stared at Wade. "Can you be more specific?"

"Texas and New Mexico territory."

Smith looked thoughtful. "The last man we hired is someplace west of here, licking his wounds."

"So I heard."

Mayor Smith stared at the stranger. "May I inquire as to what brought you to Pickering, Mr. Spears?"

Tired of the questions, Wade looked at him. "I robbed a bank and killed the mayor of a little town in Arizona."

Smith stared into Wade's blue eyes for a moment and then began to laugh. "Very funny. It's always good to have a sense of humor."

Wade grinned. "Let's say I needed a change and leave it at that."

Smith gestured at Wade's empty hip. "I see you're not wearing a gun."

Wade glanced down at his side and smiled. "Came looking for a job, not to shoot anyone."

Finding humor in the answer, Smith grinned. "You do have a gun?"

"If you heard about last night in the saloon, you should know that I do. I have a Colt that I'm not afraid to use and a Sharps rifle with a long reach for those who've tried to get away." He paused. I'm not bragging, but not many have."

The mayor thought about that for a moment believing this may be the sort of man the town of Pickering needs.

Wade glanced back at the small coyote to make sure she was all right, and then he looked at the mayor. "Mr. Smith, you need a sheriff, and I need a job."

"That's true enough," replied the mayor. "But you'll have to excuse my concern after our last sheriff. We can't afford to have another law enforcement officer run out of town." He smiled. "Makes the town council look bad."

"So does not having a sheriff." Then he looked at the mayor. "All I can tell you is that I'm an honest man. I like to think that I'm fair-minded, but at the same time, I won't take a lot of shit off drunken cowboys, trail hands, and drifters." Wade glanced back at the pup then looked at the mayor. "I ain't never been run out of a town, and I ain't never backed down. Now, if that interests you, I'm your man, and if not, then you can hire someone else, and I'll keep heading north."

Mayor Smith liked this man's frankness and believed that he was probably an honest man as he said he was. Further, no one else wanted the job, and there was last night with Brodie and the coyote, so he decided to take a chance. "Fair enough, Mr. Spears." Then he turned and glanced up at the clock on the wall behind him. "Give me an hour to get the town council together, and we'll meet over at the jailhouse."

"Where is the jail?"

Smith gestured with one hand. "It's just up the street between the Bank and the Gunsmith shop."

Wade thought that was an interesting place for a jail.

"I'll get the others and meet you there in an hour?"

Wade glanced at the clock on the wall and then looked at Smith. "Can you tell me where Doc Reid's office is?"

Smith looked concerned. "You feeling okay?"

Wade looked at him with a reassuring smile. "I'm fine."

Looking relieved, Smith told Wade where Doc Reid's office was.

Wade thanked him, walked outside, untied the pup, and headed for Doc Reid's.

Chapter 6

Wade and the coyote pup stood in front of a small white house with dark blue trim that had a sign hanging on a post next to the porch; "William Reid, Doctor of Medicine." Wade tied the coyote pup to one of the porch posts, walked up the steps, and knocked on the door. While waiting, he turned and looked at the pup lying on the bottom step eyeing a man on a horse riding past.

The door opened, and a plump elderly woman with soft brown eyes in a green dress and clean white apron smiled pleasantly, "May I help you?"

Wade took off his hat. "Is the doctor in?"

"Yes, he is." She stepped back and motioned him inside, noticing the coyote pup. "Is that a coyote you have tied to our porch?"

Wade was getting tired of everyone asking the same question. "Yes, ma'am, afraid it is."

She took another long look and quietly said, "How strange."

He looked back at the pup. "Yes, ma'am, I suppose it is."

"What?" she said while closing the door.

"I was just agreeing with you."

She stared at him for a long moment. "Agreeing over what?"

Confused, Wade said, "About the coyote pup being strange."

She glanced again at the door. "Yes, it is strange." Then she smiled as she pointed to a closed door. "This way."

Wade followed her across a room of fine furniture, shelves of knick-knacks, and floral wallpaper, beginning to feel a little unsure about the doctor's age.

She knocked softly on the door, opened it, and stuck her head inside the room. "Man to see you, William."

After a voice inside told her to show him in, she stepped aside. "The doctor will see you now."

Wade thanked her and stepped past her into the room. As the door closed behind him, he was surprised at seeing a man much younger than the woman, by twenty or more years, sitting behind a desk in front of a wall of medical certificates.

The man looked up, smiled as he stood, and walked around the desk. "Good morning." Then he gestured at an empty chair in front of his desk. "I'm Doc Reid, but most people call me Doc. Please sit down, Mister..."

"Emmett Spears," replied Wade as he sat down next to the desk filled with papers and an open book. "I hope I didn't interrupt your reading."

Doc Reid returned to his chair and closed the book. "I recently received an updated medical book and was reading up on some new procedures." He looked at Wade. "Now, what can I do for you, Mr. Spears?" Dr. William Reid was a good-looking man of forty, with thinning brown hair gray at the temples. His face was tanned, and the spectacles he wore sat low on his broad nose, helping his brown eyes that are not as good as they once were.

Wade shifted nervously in his chair. "I was shot a while back, and a friend dug the bullets out, leaving some pretty good cuts that had to be stitched."

"I see," he said thoughtfully. "You want me to take a look?"

"If you wouldn't mind."

The doctor stood. "Of course, I don't mind, Mr. Spears." He smiled. "That's what I do." He motioned to another chair next to a small table containing several towels and assorted instruments. "Have a seat over here, and I'll have a look."

Wade stood and placed his hat on the chair just as a knock came at the door.

Doc Reid looked toward the door. "Yes, Mother, what is it?"

"I'd like to ask the young man if I can take the coyote around back and give it some water. She's sitting in the sun and looks thirsty."

Reid looked at Wade. "So, you're the man with the coyote?"

"Afraid so," replied Wade as he looked at the closed door. "That'd be fine, ma'am." Wade took off his shirt, exposing the bandage with several small smears of dark, dried blood, and then sat down. "I had the stitches in my shoulder removed in a small town south of here a few days ago.

Doc Reid sat in another chair and carefully took off the bandage.

Worried about the coyote pup and Mrs. Reid, hoping the pup didn't run away, Wade watched as Doc Reid took off the bandage.

Tossing the old bandages on the floor after he smelled them, Doc Reid started to examine the wound. "That was dried blood on the bandages. It doesn't look like there's any new seepage."

Mrs. Reid spoke from the other side of the door. "I fed your coyote just a little and gave her some water."

Doc Reid's face held an irritated expression as he looked toward the door.

Wade's eyes went from the doc to the closed door. "Thank you, ma'am."

"You're welcome!" yelled Mrs. Reid, adding, "She's tied up out back! Thought it might be safer."

Doc Reid returned to the wounds. "You'll have to excuse my mother, Mr. Spears."

Wade smiled, imagining Mrs. Reid with the pup. "That's all right, Doc. I don't mind."

Reid gently touched the skin around the stitches. "Nasty looking wounds. That hurt?"

"No."

"Good." Reid sat back. "Your skin is a little red, but that's to be expected. I'd say you're healing quite nicely." He paused. "The bullet must have gone in a ways. I'm surprised more damage wasn't done."

Wade felt relieved and lucky.

Doc Reid turned to the table behind him. "I smelled something on them bandages. What have you been putting on the wounds?"

"Some stuff a lady in Wyoming gave me." He suddenly looked worried. "Was that all right?"

The doc turned with a pair of tweezers and thin scissors. "Thought it smelled funny is all. What is it?"

Wade shrugged. "Something she got from the Indians."

"I see," replied the doc thoughtfully. "Whatever it was, it didn't do any harm, and it looks to me like it's time to take out the stitches.

"The man that took the stitches out of my shoulder took some out but said the wound hadn't fully healed, and it'd be best if he left them in and have someone else take them out."

"I can see that," said Reid. "Some have already torn loose, but that happens when you over do things. The skin has healed, but you need to take it easy for a few more days."

Feeling relieved, Wade gazed at the certificates and diplomas hanging from the wall behind the desk while Doc Reid cut and pulled out the stitches.

Curious, the doc asked, "Was it the woman that gave you the Indian medicine who did the handy work?"

"Her husband."

Reid kept working. "Well, whoever dug the slugs out did a lot of cutting." He stopped what he was doing and looked a little closer at the stitches. "Got a second set here."

Wade told him about the stitches tearing and Levi stitching him up, minus Levi's name.

Doc worked in silence and asked no more questions. He had learned a long time ago that men didn't want to explain every gunshot and always felt that he was better off not knowing anyway. When he finished, he looked at Wade's shoulder. "The looks good." He looked at Wade. "None of my business, but it looks like a smaller bullet hit your shoulder." He looked at Wade. "I'd say you had an issue with two different men.?"

Wade looked at the Doc and then at his shoulder and said nothing.

Doc finished bandaging the side then warned him to leave the bandages on for another few days. Reid stood and handed Wade his shirt. "Might be a good idea if you came back to see me in two or three days."

Wade took the shirt. "All right, Doc."

"What kind of work do you do, Mr. Spears? The reason I'm asking is I don't want you tearing the wounds open. They could become infected."

Wade stood, put on his shirt, buttoned it, and as he carefully stuffed the shirt into his pants, he thought about the town council. "I'm meeting the town council about the sheriff's job."

Reid's face held concern while recalling what happened to the last sheriff. "That can be a dangerous profession in Pickering, Mr. Spears."

"So I've heard."

Reid looked concerned. "So, you've heard the story of our last sheriff?"

"I have." Wade finished tucking in his shirt and then buckled his belt. "What do I owe you, Doc?" After Doc gave him a figure, Wade reached into his pocket, took out some money thinking his funds were getting low, placed it on the doc's desk, and thanked him.

"Don't forget what I said about taking it easy, Mr. Spears," warned the doctor as he picked up the money.

Wade picked up his hat, opened the door, and turned. "Should I continue with the medicine I have?"

Doc shook his head. "No, I don't believe that'll be necessary." Reid looked at him. "I'm serious about you taking it easy. You could still do some damage."

Wade nodded his understanding. "I'll do that, Doc." Then he walked out of the room, closing the door behind him. Hearing the sound of pots and pans from the next room, he walked toward the noise finding Mrs. Reid busy over the stove.

She turned with a smile and wiped her hands on her apron. "Well, I see my son has finished with you." She gestured toward the back door. "Your coyote is out back. I tied her to the back porch."

Wade returned the smile. "Thank you."

"Sure is a cute little thing."

"So, I've been told."

"What's her name?"

Wade furrowed his brow. "Haven't decided yet." Then he said goodbye and walked out the back door, thinking he had some time before the meeting with the town council. Concerned over the mare after the long ride, he decided to pay Bennett a quick visit and check on her.

Albert Bennett was busy over the anvil working on a horseshoe, and at seeing Wade and the pup walk around the corner, he paused from his task and looked up. Steam and hissing sounds escaped from the bucket of cold water as he dipped the hot shoe into it.

Glancing first at the pup and then at Wade, he placed the nippers and horseshoe on the table next to the anvil then wiped his hands on a dirty rag. "Enjoy your walk?"

"We did," replied Wade as he grinned. "I think I've found a job."

Bennett looked curious. "A job, you say?"

Wade grinned. "Sheriff of Pickering."

"Sheriff?" said Albert, with a surprised look. "I didn't think you'd take me seriously."

Wade grinned again as he fussed with the rope holding the pup. "You said the town needed a sheriff, and I need a job. I have to meet with the town council at 10:30." He shrugged. "They may not want me."

"I don't think they can be all that choosy." Albert looked at Wade curiously. "You ever do that line of work before?"

Wade nodded. "A time or two."

Albert Bennett wiped his big hands with the dirty rag once again. "Well," he said with a concerned look. "I sure as hell hope you know what you're get'n yourself into, Mr. Spears." He tossed the rag onto the table. "Have you forgotten what I told you about the last sheriff getting beat so bad he could hardly see the day he left town?"

Wade shook his head and spoke in a soft voice. "No, I ain't forgot."

Bennett scratched his beard, then his thick head of black hair, thinking of Brodie. He smiled and softly chuckled. "Brodie and his bunch are gonna be surprised."

Wade thought of Seth and Billy French, wishing they were here, but he knew he'd never see either again, knowing the same was true for Sarah and little Emmett. "I'm sure they will be," he said softly, having already realized that he would have to deal with Brodie and the others when the time came. He pulled his watch from his pocket, looked at the time then looked at Bennett. "Well, no sense in keeping the town council waiting."

"Good luck to ya."

"Thanks."

Bennett watched Wade and the pup walk away, thinking that he would need all the luck he could get.

Opening the door to the sheriff's office, Wade found Mayor Robert Smith sitting behind an old desk talking to three men sitting on a tattered black leather sofa next to the window. All four men had on their Sunday suits, white shirts, string ties, all looking official and important.

Smith stood with a pleased look. "Come in. I want to introduce you to the town council."

Wade closed the door, eyeing each of the men as they stood, looking quite serious and business-like.

"Emmett," began the mayor as he walked from behind the desk, pointing to a thin, balding man in his fifties. He had brown eyes set deep under bushy eyebrows and a nose that looked like it had been broken at one time. "This is the Pickering Bank President, Jonathan Moore." They shook hands, and then Smith gestured to a plump, short man of five feet three with slightly bulging eyes, a pug nose, a small mouth, and a double chin. "Meet Tom Purdy, owner of the Pickering Saloon."

Wade shook the man's hand. "I was in your place last night."

Tom stared at Wade a long moment before he shook his hand. "So I heard from Dave Goody, my bartender. He told me all about you and the coyote."

"Yes," said the mayor. "We've all heard the story of the run-in, Purdy."

Wade grinned. "Not exactly a run-in, more of a small difference over the price of a coyote pup." He looked at Tom Purdy. "I like your man Goody."

Tom wasn't just looking at Wade; he was staring at him. "It appears the feeling is mutual, Mr. Spears."

Purdy's stare made Wade a little uncomfortable.

Mayor Smith put one hand on Wade's shoulder and introduced him to the last man. "This is Earl Noonan." Smith laughed and looked at the others. "Earl here doubles as the town mortician and barber."

Earl smiled as he shook Wade's hand. "Nice to meet you, Mr. Spears." Noonan was a tall, slender man with dark red hair and a handlebar mustache, a rough-looking face, and friendly green eyes. He winked as he said, "I always make sure my customers look nice before they're put in the ground." Then he chuckled as he glanced at the others.

Wade only managed a small grin, finding little humor in the joke.

Mayor Smith told the others to sit down, and then he gestured to two wooden chairs sitting in front of the desk, each missing a couple of spindles in the back. "Have a seat, Mr. Spears."

Wade took off his hat, sat down in one of the chairs that moaned from his weight, and waited.

Mr. Noonan sat forward on the sofa. "So tell me, Mr. Spears, where is that coyote pup I've heard so much about?"

Wade gestured toward the front door. "Outside, tied to the porch."

"Are you planning on keeping the pup?" asked Purdy.

Wade looked at Tom Purdy. "Any problem with that?"

Tom glanced at the others as he leaned back on the sofa. "I don't mind, but there are some around who might not like our sheriff to have a coyote as a pet. This is cattle country."

Wade smiled wryly at the man. "Well, I guess that'd be their problem."

Purdy took a hanky out of his inside coat pocket, wiped his forehead and cheeks, and then stuffed it back into the pocket.

Wade watched the little man wondering how he ever became the owner of a saloon and whorehouse in a small town like Pickering.

"That's not why we're here, Tom," said Mayor Smith sternly.

Jonathan Moore spoke up. "That's right. What Mr. Spears does with that coyote isn't any of our concern." Then he looked at the others. "Our concern— or our purpose, if you will— is to see if Mr. Spears is the sort of man we can count on while dealing with the rovers and other riffraff that come into our town causing trouble."

"It's a fine line you'll have to walk," offered Purdy while looking at Wade and then quickly turning to Moore. "Our businesses rely on that riffraff as you called them, Jonathan."

Moore leaned forward and looked at him. "I realize that, Tom, but it's about time the town takes a stand. We have to decide what kind of town we want for our families."

Purdy's eyes narrowed. "All I'm saying—"

Mayor Smith interrupted. "Gentlemen, gentlemen, please." He looked at the council. "I say we give Mr. Spears a chance. He is willing after all and has full knowledge of what happened to the last sheriff." He looked at Wade. "Appears to me, Mr. Spears here has what it takes to do the job after that little ruckus in the saloon last night."

Earl Noonan cleared his throat and glanced at the others. "If Mr. Spears' actions in any way bring unwanted results, we can always terminate his contract."

Mayor Smith looked embarrassed. "Now's not the time to discuss such matters, Earl."

Tom Purdy stood in anger. "We can't bite the hands that feed us, gentlemen."

"Feeds your hand, you mean," said Moore angrily. "There is more to this town than your damn saloon and whores."

Wade looked down at his boots and listened to the arguing for several moments, and then he shook his head and stood. "Sorry, gentlemen, you'll have to find yourselves someone else."

Mayor Smith stood then hurried around the desk. "Please, Mr. Spears, sit back down."

Wade looked at him, ignoring the others. "I don't think I'm interested any longer."

Smith glanced at the others as if soliciting their help, letting his eyes settle on Tom Purdy. "The drovers have had their way in this town long enough. They're good for your business of whiskey and whores." Then he looked at the others. "But they're keeping the honest folks off the streets, and that's bad for our business." He turned to Wade. "Please sit down, Mr. Spears."

Noonan and Moore joined in. "Please have a seat, Mr. Spears."

As Wade sat down, he couldn't help but notice that Purdy remained silent but continued to stare at him. Wade wanted to ask what his problem was but decided to ignore the little man.

Mayor Smith returned to his chair and looked at Wade with a nervous smile. "Please reconsider, Mr. Spears." He looked at the others. "There is no one else, gentlemen."

Moore spoke up, asking Wade to reconsider, as did Noonan, while Tom sat on the sofa in smugness with arms folded across his chest.

Smith turned to Wade and repeated himself. "Please reconsider, Mr. Spears. We need you."

Wade thought about that for several moments. "I want a special contract."

Mayor Smith looked puzzled. "What sort of special contract?"

"I want a one-year contract signed by a majority of the town council stating that if I am fired for any reason, I get paid for the rest of the year. If I stay, the contract has to be renewed each year if the council wants me to stay."

"Preposterous," replied Purdy, looking irritated.

Jonathan Moore, the banker, pursed his lips in thought. "A year is not that long, gentlemen." Then he looked at the mayor. "We need a sheriff, Bob."

Smith looked at Jonathan. "So you agree?"

Moore nodded. "If we want a sheriff, I do. If not, then we take the chance of anarchy taking over Pickering."

Noonan leaned forward with a worried look. "What will keep Mr. Spears from being roughed up and run out of town, the same as our last sheriff?"

Wade leaned forward in his chair and looked at him. "The only way I'll leave this town is in a pine box." Then he grinned. "And if that happens, you won't be bound by the contract."

Earl Noonan thought for a moment and then chuckled. "I'm in."

Purdy looked down at the floor and shook his head. "I disagree." Then he looked at the others. "A contract of this sort is preposterous. Simply preposterous."

The room fell silent again as the mayor looked at Jonathan Moore and then Earl Noonan. "Let's take a vote. All in agreement, raise your right hand." Three hands raised while Purdy's arms remained defiantly folded across his chest. Smith turned to Wade, looking relieved. "You have your contract, Mr. Spears."

Tom Purdy stood and looked at the others. "I'll have no part in this." Then he walked to the door, opened it, and turned, giving Wade a long, silent look before stepping outside.

"He'll come around," said Smith as Purdy's footsteps faded across the boardwalk. The mayor stood. "The job pays sixty a month and cartridges." Pointing to a closed-door, he said, "There's a room and bed in the back, you get two meals a day at Laurie's Café, and your stock can stay at the livery for free."

Wade looked uncertain. "Does Mr. Bennett know that?"

Smith chuckled. "That is Mr. Bennett's contribution to the town." Then he looked at the others. "We all have to make them." He looked at Earl Noonan. "Earl cuts your hair and shaves your face for free."

Wade unconsciously rubbed his stubble covered chin.

Mayor Smith stood as if in a hurry, picked up a Bible he brought with him that was sitting on the desk, and walked around it.

Wade stood.

"Place your right hand on the Bible and hold up the other."

Wade did as asked.

"Do you solemnly swear," began the mayor, "to uphold the laws of Pickering, Montana, to protect and serve the town and its inhabitants to the best of your ability? So help you, God?"

"Yes, sir," replied Wade with a quick nod.

The mayor smiled, looking pleased. "You're the new sheriff, Mr. Spears." He turned back to the desk, picked up a badge, and pinned it onto Wade's yellow shirt. Finished, he shook Wade's hand eagerly. "Congratulations, Sheriff."

Jonathan Moore and Earl Noonan shook Wade's hand, congratulating him, while the mayor took a folded piece of paper out of his coat pocket and laid it on the table. He took a pen from the inkwell sitting on the desk and handed it to Wade. "Make your mark on the line if you can't write."

"What about the contract?" asked Wade.

"I'll have it ready in a day or two."

Wade stared into Robert Smith's gray eyes as he took the pen, then signed the paper, 'Emmett Spears' and then wrote: Not binding without the agreed-upon contract.

Mayor Smith picked up the paper, looked at what Wade had written, and held it up for the others to see. "I see you're a cautious man." The mayor folded the paper and stuffed it into his coat pocket. "Don't concern yourself, Mr. Spears. You'll have your contract, signed by the three of us and ready for your signature soon."

Wade grinned, "I'm not worried, Mayor. I know you're all gentlemen of your word."

Mayor Smith looked at Wade for a moment considering that. "Any questions?"

Wade quickly considered the question. "Just how far is my jurisdiction?"

Smith frowned. "As far as the crime takes you. Montana is still a territory, Mr. Spears. There are no county lines, no fences, and Indians still roam about, killing our cattle, or a fool panning for gold, and now and then a settler."

Wade nodded, thinking of the Crow Indians he and Morgan had encountered.

Mayor Smith smiled. "If we run into trouble, there's an Army Post on the Tongue River, some forty or fifty miles to the west, and Fort Keogh twenty-five or so miles north, where the Tongue flows into the Yellowstone River. There's also a small town called Miles City north of us. Anything else?"

Wade thought a moment. "Do we have a judge?"

"I'm the judge," replied Mayor Smith, who then proudly added, "I have a law degree."

Wade chuckled. "Well, that takes care of my concerns for the moment."

"Good," replied the mayor. "I have things to take care of." He looked at the others and gestured at the front door. "Gentlemen."

Moore and Noonan both smiled, wished Wade good luck, and then followed Mayor Smith out the door.

Wade stared at the closed door a moment, wondering if he was making the right decision, and then he looked around the tiny jail, thinking of the US Marshal's office in Santa Fe. Looking down at the badge pinned to his yellow shirt pocket, it felt good to be wearing one again. Walking around the old desk to the chair the

Mayor had been sitting in, he sat down, hearing the chair creak, reminding him of Seth's chair. He turned in the chair to the long, narrow table sitting against the wall under the gun rack that contained a single, double-barrel twelve-gauge shotgun. Three tin cups, turned upside down, next to a large beat-up coffee pot. A small potbellied stove occupied the corner between the cells and a door. A hat rack occupied the opposite corner next to the door, and an old sofa under the big window, where Purdy and the others had been sitting. A large window bearing the word "Sheriff" in fancy white lettering above the sofa gave him an unobstructed view of the street and buildings across the street.

After his eyes completed their trip around the room, he was startled at seeing an old man sitting on the cot in the second cell watching at him. "What's your story?"

The old man stood and walked to the bars, gripping them lightly with both hands. "What do ya mean?"

"What are you in jail for?"

The old man grinned. "Oh, I ain't in jail."

"Then what the hell you doing in that cell?"

The old man glanced around the cell and shrugged. "I sleep here."

"You sleep here?"

The old man's grin quickly disappeared. "Yes, sir, I have for a long time."

Wade thought of Levi back in Harper. "Come out here, so's we can talk."

The old man walked out of the cell, closed the door, and sat down in one of the two chairs in front of Wade's desk.

"What's your name?"

"Jed Canon." Jed was near sixty. He was skinny, his clothes were dirty, and his shoes looked old and too big for his feet. His hair was gray and thinning, he needed a shave, and he had a crooked smile of yellow teeth.

"How long have you been sleeping in that cell?"

Jed considered the question and shrugged. "Few years, I spect." Then he went on to tell that when Jack Styles was sheriff, he'd keep the coffee pot filled, make sure there was plenty of firewood, sweep the place out, and anything else the sheriff asked him to do.

"I see," Wade said thoughtfully.

"Did the same for Sheriff Cole until they...." Jed let the sentence die.

Wade finished the sentence for him. "Beat him up and ran him out of town?"

Jed shook his head. "Yes, sir. And that's too bad cause he was a likable sort."

Wade leaned forward, placed his elbows on the desk, and gestured to the cell. "You hear what was said earlier?"

Jed glanced back at the cell. "Yes, sir, I did."

Wade rubbed his chin with his right hand while considering everything that went on between him and the others.

Sensing his concerns, Canon shrugged. "You don't have to worry about me, Sheriff. Nobody in this town talks to me all that much, and I wouldn't say anything about what was said here today no-how."

Wade turned from Jed, deciding he'd have to trust in what he said, and then looked at the door next to the pot-bellied stove leading to his bedroom and then another door by the sofa. "What's behind that door?"

"A closet of sorts. That's where the broom and mop are kept. There's a couple of shelves for things like food and coffee when we have some." He looked at Wade. "We're out of coffee, by the way, but there may be a couple of jars of fruit left if you're hungry. There's also some plates, cups, small frying pan, and a pot or two." He shrugged. "Stuff like that."

Remembering the coyote was still outside, Wade got up and hurried out to get her.

84

Jed Canon slid to the edge of his chair and looked at the coyote pup as Wade walked past. "That the coyote pup, everyone's talking about?"

"I guess it is."

"What's its name?"

Walking past Jed toward one of the cells, Wade caught a whiff of Jed and quickly decided he needed a bath, and wondered why everything had to have a name. "Ain't got one."

Jed reached out to pet the pup, but she snapped at him. He quickly pulled his hand back and grinned as he looked down at her curled, snarly upper lip showing her sharp puppy teeth. "Mean little shit."

Wade thought of Harry Anderson. "She's been mistreated by some assholes."

Jed bent at the waist to have a closer look. "Ain't never heard of anyone having a coyote for a pet before." Wearing a grin, he knelt to one knee, making sure he was a safe distance from those sharp teeth. "You and I will be friends before you know it. We're gonna have to find a nice name for you." He bent down, trying to see whether it was a male or female. "You a boy or girl?"

"It's a bitch," replied Wade, then he took her into the first cell, picked up a folded blanket from off the foot of the cot, and dropped it on the floor. He knelt, took the rope from around the pup's neck, and looked at Jed. "Is there a bowl or pot around? I think she could use some water?"

Jed headed for the closet. "I think there's an old pot we can use in here." Moments later, he returned with an old dented pot. "The pump's out the back door. Do you want me to fill it?"

"If you wouldn't mind."

Jed hurried past the cells and down a short hall to the rear door, disappeared outside, and returned a couple of minutes later carrying a pot of cold water.

Jed ignored Wade, walked past him, and set it down on the floor in front of the coyote. "There ya go, little gal." Standing over the pup, he smiled, watching her lap up the water. "Yes, sir," he said, grinning. "You and I are gonna get along just fine."

Wade felt a little jealous as he walked out of the cell with a grinning Jed Canon close behind. He closed the door leaving it unlocked, and walked to the door that led to his new bedroom. He opened the door and stood in the open doorway staring at his new home. A small single bed containing a soiled and stained mattress with two folded blankets sat against the far wall near the window. The dirty, torn curtain hung over the small dirty window. On top of the mattress was a coverless gray-and-white-striped pillow that didn't look much better than the mattress. A single straight-back chair occupied the opposite corner next to an old six drawer dresser with a cracked mirror hanging on the wall above it. A small potbellied stove sat in one corner, and a wardrobe closet the corner next to the door.

Jed was behind him, peering into the room. "Clean sheets and pillow covers are in the bottom drawer of the dresser."

"Well, that's something," said Wade.

"I take 'em to the laundry twice a month."

Glancing around the room, Wade thought of the bedroom in their house in Santa Fe and the Double J, where he and Sarah shared their mornings over a cup of coffee. He backed out of the room and closed the door, thinking it was not much of a place to end up. He turned and looked around the office while Jed took a seat on the tattered black leather sofa. Wade again thought of old Levi. "You interested in working for me, Jed?"

Canon looked puzzled. "Sure, I guess so."

Wade extended his open hand across the top of the desk. "Name's Emmett Spears."

"Yes, sir," said Jed as he stood. "I heard the mayor when he introduced you to them, others." Then he shook Wade's hand firmly. "Glad to know you, Sheriff."

Wade thought he needed to clean this place and Jed up a bit. He turned and looked at the old beat-up coffee pot and three tin cups on the table against the wall behind his desk. "I'll get us some coffee a little later." He turned to Jed. "What were your arrangements with the other sheriffs?"

Jed looked puzzled. "Arrangement?"

Wade nodded. "Yeah, what did they pay you?"

Jed's face lit up as he laughed. "No one ever paid me, Sheriff." He grinned and gestured to the cell he previously occupied. "I got to use that bed." Then he pointed to the coffee pot. "And all the coffee I could drink."

Wade was suddenly concerned for the old man. "What do you do for food and clothing?"

Jed's brow furrowed in thought. "Well, I chop wood for Laurie's Café across the street, haul their garbage out back and feed it to the pigs for one meal a day. That's usually in the evening when they're about to close up."

Wade figured that was why Jed was so skinny.

"Dave," continued Jed, "up at the saloon is always good for a drink when he wants the spittoons emptied and cleaned, and sometimes I chop firewood for the saloon as well." He shrugged. "I do a few odd jobs around town to earn a little change."

Wade considered that as he stood. "If you're gonna work for me, Jed, you'll have to take a bath and get some clean clothes."

Jed looked down at his clothes then at Wade, looking worried. "I ain't got money for new clothes, Sheriff, and I ain't sure about a bath."

Wade felt sorry for the old man, thinking he'd been taken advantage of by the whole town. "The job pays four dollars a month."

Jed's eyes lit up. "Four dollars a month?"

Wade headed for the front door. "Plus, all the coffee you can drink, a bed, food, and a place to stay out of the cold." He opened the door and looked back at Jed. "Think on it. I'll be back in a while. Don't let the coyote out."

87

Chapter 7

Wade walked into Smith's General Store, finding the mayor busy helping a lady asking questions about one of the bolts of cloth that interested her. The mayor looked up but then continued helping the lady. Thinking the mayor would be a while, Wade walked around looking at this and that until the lady bought the bolt of cloth and left.

As the front door closed, ringing the tiny bell above it, Mayor Smith looked at Wade. "I don't have your contract ready yet, Sheriff. But I will tomorrow."

Wade gestured him off. "Not here about that, Mayor. I need some supplies."

Smith looked relieved. "What sort of supplies?"

Wade walked to the counter and looked at the shelves behind it filled with glass jars of fruit and cans of various types of food. "Six jars of peaches and two pounds of coffee to start with."

The mayor set six jars of peaches on the counter. "Anything else?"

Wade glanced around the store, thinking of the pup. "Need a couple of small bowls."

Smith pointed to a shelf against the wall. "I think you'll find what you need on the bottom of those shelves." He turned, picked up a large scoop, filled it with coffee beans from a barrel, dumped the beans into a grinder, and began turning the handle.

Wade found two bowls he thought would do and placed them on the counter next to the six jars of peaches.

Smith placed the white cloth sack containing two pounds of coffee next to the bowls. "Anything else?"

Wade made a thoughtful face as he looked around the store. "You have any shirts?"

Smith stepped from behind the counter. "Right over here."

Wade followed him to a table piled with shirts of various colors and sizes. The sound of the tiny bell above the front door softly rang as two women, one young and one a little older, entered the store. Wade looked at Smith. "Go ahead."

The mayor turned away and walked toward the two ladies, smiling while asking if he could help them.

Wade sorted through the piles of shirts until he found a dark blue shirt and a tan one and set them aside while turning to another table with an assortment of pants. After sorting through the stack, he found a dark blue pair and a tan pair and set them on top of the shirts. Turning from the mayor and the two ladies, he picked up the shirts and pants and returned to the counter, where he watched the mayor's pleasantries with the two women.

After the two ladies bought what they came for and left the store, Mayor Robert Smith returned to the counter where Wade waited. He looked at the stack of clothes. "This everything?"

Wade considered the old coffee pot. "That coffee pot in the sheriff's office looks like it made a trip from New York. The town needs to replace it."

Mayor Smith looked at Wade for a moment, then walked to a shelf, picked up a large coffee pot, and set it on the counter. "No charge, Sheriff."

Wade leaned on the counter. "What can you tell me about Jed Canon?"

Smith shrugged, looking puzzled. "Not much to tell. He's been around for years doing odd jobs. I know Sheriff Styles, and

Sheriff Cole let him sleep in one of the cells. He seems harmless enough. Why do you ask?"

"I hired him."

Smith looked surprised. "As your deputy?"

"No," chuckled Wade, finding humor in the mayor's reaction. "A handyman of sorts to keep the place clean. He'll be sleeping in one of the cells just as he always has."

The mayor gave Wade a stern look. "Any arrangements you make with Jed concerning money is strictly between the two of you."

"I understand."

Smith smiled with relief.

"I'm paying him four dollars a month out of my salary."

The mayor thought on that a moment. "Sounds very generous."

"Glad that you agree, Mayor," replied Wade. "Since he's been taking care of the place for the past month while you were without a sheriff, it's only fitting that the town pays him four dollars."

Smith looked stunned. "You can't be serious."

"Dead serious," replied Wade. "I'll pay him for what he does for me, but I think you and the council owe the man for keeping the place clean while you looked for a new sheriff." He paused. "I'm sure none of you ventured down there to clean the place and scare away the rats."

Smith thought on that for a quick moment looking guilty. "No, I'm sure we didn't."

"Well," grinned Wade. "I'm sure the town can afford a few dollars."

Smith looked embarrassed. "I suppose we do owe him something, but he also got to sleep there and drink coffee for free."

"There is no coffee, Mayor; that's why I'm buying some now."

Seeing it was useless to argue, Smith nodded. "All right, I agree that the town owes Jed Canon something. But not four dollars. I'll agree to two."

Wade grinned. "Make it three."

Smith's eye narrowed as he stared at Wade. "Two and a half."

Wade considered the offer. "Done."

The mayor reached into the till, took out two and half-dollars, and handed it to Wade. "But he works for you now."

"Wouldn't have it any other way." Wade shoved the money into his pocket. "I have one more thing."

Not sure he wanted to hear this, Smith leaned on the counter and waited.

"I aim to clean Jed up a bit as well."

"What do you mean, clean him up?"

Wade looked around to see if anyone was listening and then leaned on the counter. "I'm sending Jed in here later today on his way to the bathhouse. I'd like you to help him get some new clothes. You can take it out of my first month's wages."

Smith stared at Wade a long moment, and then he grinned with a chuckle. "I doubt that Jed's had a bath in five years."

Wade grinned. "You're probably right. Now how much do I owe you?"

The mayor glanced through the articles, picked up a pencil, and began writing figures on a piece of paper. When he finished, he turned the paper so Wade could read it and smiled at Wade's expression. "Shipping into the territory is expensive."

Wade reached into his pants pocket and pulled out a small roll of bills. "Seems to me, the sheriff should get a discount."

The mayor grinned. "Discount's already included in the price, Sheriff."

Wade gave Smith a look, not sure he believed the man, then counted out the money and laid it on the counter.

Smith turned and tore two lengths of brown wrapping paper from a big roll attached to a spindle on the edge of the counter. After picking up the money, he wrapped the supplies into two packages and tied them with string.

Wade watched the mayor tie the last package. "Speaking of cleaning things up a bit. That bedroom I will be sleeping in needs new curtains and some new towels."

Smith walked from behind the counter to a table, picked out two new towels and two washcloths, then walked to another table and picked out a white lace curtain for the window. Returning to the counter, he wrapped them in brown paper, tied it with string, and looked at Wade with a proud grin. "No charge."

Wade picked up the packages. "Thanks. Nice doing business with you, Mayor." He turned and walked toward the door, stopped and turned with a grin. "By the way, you could have won at two dollars."

Smith grinned. "And you at three."

Walking into the sheriff's office, Wade found the cell door where he had put the coyote pup open, the cell empty, and no sign of Jed. Hearing the sound of someone chopping wood out back, he walked to his desk, set the packages down, and walked down the short hallway to the back door. Stepping outside, he found Jed busy chopping firewood and the pup tied to the water pump. Seeing Wade, she got up, pulled against the rope, and whined.

Jed stopped what he was doing and wiped the sweat from his face with his dirty shirt sleeve. "Figured she could use some fresh air."

Wade walked toward the pup. "I'm surprised she let you put the rope around her."

Jed chuckled. "Took a bit of doing." He held out his left hand, bearing scratches. "Got these from those damn little teeth. She's a fast one."

"Warned you," chuckled Wade. He untied the rope and started for the back door. "Come on, Pup." Reaching the door, he turned. "Come inside, Jed. We need to talk."

Jed looked at Wade, being curious about the talk, put down the ax, and wiped his hands on his pants as he followed.

After Wade put Pup back in her cell, he pointed to one of the chairs and told Jed to have a seat.

Jed looked past Wade at the coyote. "Pup her name now?"

Wade looked at the coyote. "Seems to fit the little shit."

Jed chuckled. "It does at that." It was then that Jed noticed the packages on the desk. "What's in the packages?"

"Two pounds of coffee, six jars of peaches, and four tins of beans, and a brand new coffee pot." Wade picked up the packages containing his clothes, towels, face cloths, and curtain placing them on his bed in the other room. When he returned, Jed was standing over the other package. "Go ahead and open it up." While Jed did that, Wade sat down at his desk.

Jed opened the package, and at finding coffee, he grinned. "Want me to fix some coffee in our brand new coffee pot?"

"Fix yourself some if you want. I need to get the rest of my gear from the livery." Then he reached into his shirt pocket, pulled out the money he got from the mayor, and handed it to Jed. "Mayor Smith sent this for taking care of the place."

Looking surprised, Jed hesitated but then took the money and stared down at it as if he had never seen money before.

"Have you thought about our agreement?"

Looking a little befuddled, Jed looked up from the money he was holding. "Guess I'll stay. But I ain't too happy about that bath."

Wade chuckled. "You'll like it. On your way for your bath, stop by the store. The mayor will help you with a new outfit."

Jed looked worried. "New outfit?" Then he looked at the money. "I ain't gonna spend this on new clothes."

"Ain't asking you to."

Jed looked puzzled. "Then who's paying for the new clothes?"

"The city is since you're working for me."

Jed rubbed his chin, looking baffled. "Sure is a lot going on all of a sudden?"

Wade grinned. "You'll get used to it."

"I'll put on them clean clothes, Sheriff," said Jed, looking defiant. "I'll even take that bath, but I ain't gonna let that barber shave me."

"Bath is good enough," agreed Wade as he looked at Jed's dirty clothes. "You can either get them washed or burn 'em." Then he walked out the front door and headed for the livery.

Jed stared at the door for a moment, then looked down at his clothes, wondering why he would burn perfectly good clothes.

Albert Bennett was busy inside the livery cleaning out a stall when Wade walked in to get his gear. Bennett stopped what he was doing, turned to Wade, and leaned on the shovel. Noticing the sheriff's badge, he smiled. "I see you survived the Town Council scrutiny."

Wade smiled, thinking of the scrutiny he went through with Sarah's pa, Jasper Talbert. "Faced worse."

Bennett laughed softly. "They're all cowards when it comes to getting involved in anything risky. Something you'll find out soon enough."

"Men like that usually are." Wade turned and looked back through the big open doorway toward town and thought about Purdy. "What's the story on Tom Purdy?"

Bennett thought a minute. "Tom owns the saloon and runs the whores who work there. Stays to himself mostly, which is why I find it difficult to understand why he's on the town council." He looked at Wade. "Why you asking?"

94

Wade sighed. "Seems a little strange. He kept staring at me."

Albert considered that. "Can't say why he'd stare."

Wade shrugged it off. "Ain't important. Came to get my stuff and check on the mare."

Albert gestured toward the back of the livery. "Your horse is doing fine. She ate a hearty breakfast, and I let her out into the corral for a while. Your belongings are still where you left them." Then he returned to the arduous task of shoveling horseshit.

Wade gathered up his gear, said thanks to Bennett, and headed back to the Sheriff's Office, finding Jed gone and smiled, imagining him taking a bath. He dumped his gear in his room, put the towels away, and hung the new curtain after cleaning the window and made the bed. Wanting to thank the bartender for last night, Wade walked across the street to the saloon. It was still early, and the place was near empty when he walked in and bellied up to the bar.

Goody was drying a whiskey glass as he glanced up, seeing Wade's image in the mirror. He put the glass with the others, put the towel down, and turned with a friendly smile noticing the badge on Wade's shirt. "I heard you were the new sheriff." He held out an open hand. "I guess congratulations are in order."

"Not quite sure about that yet." Wade glanced around. "Tom Purdy, tell you about me being sheriff?"

Dave chuckled softly and shrugged. "He wasn't too happy about it."

"I figured as much."

With a wide grin, Goody picked up a clean mug. "First beer's on the house."

"Later, maybe. I just came in to buy a bottle of whiskey, and thank you for last night."

Goody grinned cleverly. "I wasn't much in the mood to clean up after a killing."

"Well, whatever the reason, I'm obliged."

Dave bent down behind the bar, came up with a bottle of whiskey, placed it on top of the bar, and quickly glanced around at the other customers. "The first one's on me. I enjoyed watching Brodie get it for a change." He leaned toward Wade. "I'd be careful of him. He's a hard case and mean as they come."

Wade picked up the bottle. "I'll keep that in mind." He held the bottle up as he turned toward the door. "Thanks."

Wade was greeted by the smell of freshly brewed coffee when he walked into the jailhouse, finding Jed sitting in the sheriff's swivel chair, enjoying a cup of coffee, hair still damp from the bath, and all dressed up in his new clothes.

Canon stood and gestured to the big gray coffee pot on the stove. "Cup of coffee?"

"I believe I will," said Wade.

Jed jumped up and began pouring Wade a cup of coffee.

Wade put the whiskey bottle in the bottom drawer of the desk, thinking that Jed looked a little younger, all cleaned up, and wondered what he would look like without the beard.

Jed set Wade's coffee on the desk and then sat down on the sofa, holding his coffee in his hands. "It's been a while since I had any coffee to make." Then he smiled. "Sure, missed my coffee."

Wade walked into his bedroom, brought out the Sharps, and set it in the gun rack next to the twelve-gauge shotgun along with the bandolier of cartridges. He hung his wide-brimmed, black hat on one of the four pegs between the gun rack and the supply room thinking he'd empty his saddlebags later. Sitting down, Wade picked up his cup of hot coffee and took a drink, surprised at how good it tasted, and suddenly realized he was hungry. He looked up at the clock thinking the morning had passed all too quickly, and then he looked at Jed. "You hungry?"

"Guess I could eat."

Wade stood. "Come on. I'll buy you lunch."

When they returned from Laurie's Café, Wade put the plate of scraps he had brought back on the cell floor, and while Pup devoured her supper, he picked up the coffee pot, opened the lid, and looked inside. Seeing it was about half full, he placed the pot on the stove and then opened the door in the front of the stove, stoked the fire with some wood, sat down, and waited for it to heat up.

Jed was at the gun rack, eyeing the Sharps. "Knew a man who owned a Hawkins once."

Wade thought of his old Hawkins. "I owned a Hawkins once myself." He then thought of the day Mr. Grimes gave him the Sharps before he rode out after the four men that killed his friend Emmett Spears. "But a Sharps, in my opinion, is a better weapon."

"I wouldn't know," replied Canon. Jed leaned closer and looked at the scope. "How far will this shoot?"

"Accurate at eight, nine hundred yards, lucky at a thousand."

Jed thought on that while he stared at the rifle. "That's fair shooting."

Wade turned to him. "Hope I ain't getting personal, Jed, but how'd you end up in a place like Pickering?"

Jed sat down on the leather sofa under the window and stared into his cup of black coffee in memory. "Me and my wife of just a few years, Lisa was her name, decided to leave Boston and head west about fifteen years ago." He paused in thought to correct himself. "Seventeen years it were. When we reached St. Louis, we joined a group of wagons heading into the Oregon territory. I'd heard there was plenty of rich soil, lots of trees for lumber, and land for the taking." He looked into his coffee. "Everyone with the train was anxious to get west, but it was late in the season, and the wagon master refused to leave, saying we had to wait until next spring. Well, most of us were itching to get going, so we hired another man who claimed he'd made the trip several times, so we packed up and started out. Everything was going okay until we hit Wyoming. The snow started falling, and we got snowed in by a big blizzard." Jed frowned, looking sad. "My Lisa got sick with the fever and died."

In the stillness that filled the room, Wade opened the bottom drawer of his desk and pulled out the bottle of whiskey he had bought earlier that day. He uncorked it, stood, and poured some into Jed's coffee.

Jed looked up appreciatively, smiled, and took a drink.

Wade returned to his chair, poured some whiskey into his coffee, stuck the cork back into the bottle, and set it on top of his desk. He sat back in his creaky chair, put his feet on the edge of the desk, and stared into the cell where Pup lay sleeping and waited for Jed to continue his story.

"The ground was frozen hard," continued Jed. "And I couldn't bury her, so I wrapped her in a blanket and kept her under the wagon." He took a drink of coffee. "A week or so passed, the weather finally broke, so I gave all my stock but one horse to another family who had befriended Lisa and me. They all left, but I stayed to wait for the thaw, so's I could bury her proper." He paused in memory.

"Why not go with them and bury her along the way to Oregon?"

"No longer felt like going on. One night a band of hostiles happened upon us, so I got under the wagon to hide, but they found my Lisa and me and pulled me from under the wagon and then my precious Lisa. I was screaming at 'em to leave her alone, and when they pulled the blanket off, they jumped back." He grinned. "I never saw an Indian looking so afraid. They began yelling at one another and pointing to me as I crawled to Lisa, like the end of the world was coming. Well, they just hopped on their ponies, rode away, and never bothered us no more."

"Probably thought you were crazy," offered Wade thoughtfully. "Indians won't mess with crazy people."

"That's what I supposed." Jed paused in thought. "Well, come spring, I buried my Lisa at the base of the cliff where we had wintered and covered her grave with rocks so the coyotes and wolves wouldn't get her."

"That when you headed north into Montana?"

Jed shook his head. "No, I wandered into Colorado for a few years, got tired of that, and headed back into Wyoming. I happened upon a trading post by the name of Friendlies."

The name hit Wade's memory like a bullet. He gave Jed a look and then looked into his cup, remembering that night in the store.

Jed continued. "Ed Reese took pity on me and gave me a job. I stayed a year, but then one day, I just saddled my horse and rode out."

Wade often wondered about Ed Reese. "What sort of fella was this, Ed Reese?"

"He was a nice enough fellah. Looked mean as hell, but he had a kindness to him. Felt bad about leaving 'cuz his brother rode out the week before."

Wade recalled the look on Ed Reese's face when he saw his badge and the surprise in his eyes when he had to shoot him.

Jed continued. "I bounced from place to place for a while and ended up in the great town of Pickering some years back."

Wade considered all that Jed had told him as he drank the last of his coffee, then stood and took the coyote outside to do her business.

Chapter 8

Morgan Hunter

The August afternoon sun threw long shadows of the buildings across the dusty street of Pickering, Montana, as Morgan Hunter, his Appaloosa, and packhorse made their way in and out of the shadows of the wagon-rutted street. Late shoppers hurried along the boardwalks, and two elderly men sat in front of the Howard Hotel with a small table between their chairs, playing a game of checkers. One of the men looked up and gave Morgan a friendly wave, which he acknowledged with a nod as he proceeded up the busy street. He rode at a walk through the maze of horses, wagons, and people with only a few of the curious turning to take a quick look at another drifter.

Soft piano music spilled from the open doorway of the saloon, and he imagined the player hunched over the keys, maybe smoking a cigarette. Perhaps he was like Samuel Brumwell down in Texas, who always thought of some far-off place or a woman while playing to the noise of loud drunks, fistfights, and the occasional shooting.

The pleasant smell of food rushed at him from Laurie's Café, reminding him that his last meal was breakfast at the Thornton Ranch. His empty stomach growled as he rode past the windows with their red curtains pulled to the sides, allowing him to see inside and the people enjoying their quiet meals. He turned from the café, and seeing the livery and a two-story hotel at the far end of town, he gently nudged his horse and tugged at the reins of the packhorse.

Pulling the Appaloosa up in front of the livery, he read the words, 'Bennett Livery, Albert Bennett Prop.' in faded white paint above the open doorway. The building with its two big open doors looked weathered, while the roof had a newer look. The sound of a hammer on steel broke the stillness as Morgan turned the horse toward the corral of two horses and a mule.

A big man with black hair and beard, wearing a leather apron over a light gray shirt with sleeves rolled up, wielded a five-pound hammer. In his left hand was a pair of leverage nippers he used to hold the hot steel on the anvil while the other swung the hammer, hitting what would soon have its shape. He stopped what he was doing and studied Morgan for a moment, then set the hammer on a table behind him and stuck the steel back into the hot coals of the furnace. After he set the nippers on the table next to the hammer, he picked up an already dirty rag, wiped the sweat from his bearded face and hands while eyeing the stranger. Stepping from behind the big anvil, he noticed the broad-billed black hat he recognized as a Texas flat hat, the handcrafted leather holster, and the handle of a fine-looking Colt pistol that lay across his stomach. "Can I help you?"

Morgan gestured to the Appaloosa and packhorse. "I'd like to put these two up for the night if you've room."

The big man tossed the rag onto the table behind him and walked toward the gate of the weathered fence. A friendly smile quickly filled his face. "Got plenty of room."

Morgan climbed down and turned to the man with an outstretched hand. "Morgan Hunter."

The big man's hand dwarfed Morgan's. "Albert Bennett." He looked at the Texas saddle and then stepped back to admire the horse. "Fine-looking animal."

"So I've been told," replied Morgan proudly.

Bennett walked toward the open doorway of the livery. "Bring them inside. Come far?"

"Texas."

"Thought as much. Don't see many Texas saddles this far north." Albert Bennett gestured at two empty stalls. "These'll do."

Morgan led the Appaloosa into the first stall. "You been to Texas, Mr. Bennett?"

He shook his head no. "I was born in a little town called Conchos, down in New Mexico. We used to see a lot of Texas saddles." He pointed to Morgan's boots. "And Mexican boots."

"I know the place," replied Morgan as he led the packhorse into the other stall.

Albert Bennett looked pleased but not surprised. He remembered a few gunmen from Texas crossed into New Mexico Territory back then on the run from Texas Rangers. He looked at Morgan. "You a Texas Ranger?"

Morgan chuckled. "No, sir, I'm not. Do I look like a Ranger?"

Bennett smiled, wishing he hadn't asked, and stepped away. "Not really. I'll get some oats for your stock."

Morgan watched the big man walk toward the rear of the livery, then returned to the stall with the Appaloosa.

Bennett returned with two buckets of oats. "Didn't mean anything by my question. It's just that you being from Texas, and the way you wear that fine-looking Navy Colt made me curious."

Morgan lifted the stirrup, placed it over the saddle horn, and started with the saddle's cinch. "I'm sure you didn't, Mr. Bennett. I passed through Conchos on my way out of Texas." After loosening the cinch, he pulled the saddle off and set it on the stall's rail. Wanting to change the course of the conversation, he asked, "How'd you end up this far north?"

"My older brother was killed by some hired guns one day, so my folks came north when I was thirteen, and we ended up here."

Morgan started on the bit and bridle. "Your brother, a gunman?"

Bennett shook his head no. "Jim just happened to be in the wrong place."

Morgan frowned. "Sorry to hear that."

Albert Bennett shrugged with a sad look. "Happened a long time ago."

Morgan pulled the harness over the Appaloosa's ears and then took out the bit. "Was your pa a blacksmith?"

"Yes, sir, he was. He passed away several years ago, leaving me this place. Ma followed a year later."

Morgan hung the harness on the wall and started working on the packhorse in the next stall, noticing that he was almost finished with the oats.

The big man stepped into the stall to give Morgan a hand with his supplies. "We can put your stuff in the back room. My place is just out back, and I lock this place up at night tighter than hell."

"Appreciate that, Mr. Bennett. Don't rightly believe I could carry all this to that hotel across the street."

Not sure if Morgan could afford the Grande, Albert said, "The Grande is a fine hotel all right, but the Howard just down the street's a mite cheaper. It's also close to Laurie's Café and the saloon."

Morgan gave that some thought while they unloaded the packhorse.

When they finished, Albert said, "I still have some work to do, so I'll let you take care of your stock. When they're done with them oats, you can fill them buckets with water." He motioned to the open doors. "The pump's just outside them doors."

103

Morgan watched him walk away and then turned and watched the horses finish their dinner of oats as the sound of hammer on steel filled the air. He picked up the buckets, filled them with water at the pump, and returned to the livery smelling of stale, heavy air, of straw and horse urine. The smells reminded him of Texas when he was a young boy working in old man Johnson's livery. He set the buckets down, and while the horses drank, he flung his saddlebags over one shoulder, picked up his carpetbag of clothes, his Winchester, and walked toward the big doors. Noticing a familiar horse as he walked by a stall, he stopped. "I'll be damned," he said, then he walked outside. Albert Bennett was taking off his leather apron when Morgan approached. "Can you tell me who that sorrel mare inside belongs to?"

Bennett slipped the apron over his head, folded it, and laid it on the anvil. "Belongs to a man named Emmett Spears."

Morgan chuckled. "I'll be damned."

"You know the man?"

"We met a few days back. Had a run-in with some Crow and got separated." He glanced back toward the street of Pickering. "I was afraid the Crow got him." Then he turned back to Bennett. "Any idea where I might find him?"

"You might try the Sheriff's Office."

Hunter grinned. "He get tossed in jail already?"

"No," said Albert with a serious face. "He's our new sheriff."

Morgan's eyes lit up. "What?"

Albert nodded. "Has been for two days."

"Well, if that don't beat all," replied Morgan in a quiet voice. "I thought for sure he was a dead man."

"Well, if he is, he sure don't act like it," said Albert. "Since he's been in town, he's pissed off four hands of the big C ranch over a coyote pup. He spent one night in my livery with that mean little shit of a coyote and got himself hired as sheriff."

104

Morgan grinned. "Sounds like he's been busy." Then he looked at Bennett. "Did you say coyote?"

Al nodded. "That was the cause of him pissing off them four men. They was gonna torture the poor thing and then kill it." He paused. "The way I heard it, he drew on them four to convince them to sell him the pup."

Morgan smiled at the story, thanked Bennett, and headed for the Sheriff's Office.

The sun had set, bringing with it the faint light of dusk when Morgan walked down the street looking for the Sheriff's Office. Lantern light-filled many of the windows and doorways of the town as people prepared for another night. With the thought of seeing Emmett again at the forefront of his mind, he hurried along the boardwalk toward the sheriff's office, thinking of the story Bennett told him.

Finding the Sheriff's Office tucked between two larger buildings, Hank's Gun Smith and Saddle Shop on one side, the other the Pickering Bank, he opened the door and stepped inside. The top of an old desk was covered with a mess of papers and a one-sheet newspaper. The swivel chair behind it was empty. He turned from the chair toward the growling sound coming from one of the two cells along the west wall. Taking a step closer, he saw it was the coyote pup the man at the livery had mentioned, baring her teeth and growling deep inside her throat. He hadn't seen the man lying down on the cot in the next cell, watching him.

"She won't bite," Jed said in a scratchy voice.

Morgan turned in surprise, his hand on the butt of his gun.

Jed got up from the cot, thinking the man was a little edgy. "You looking for the sheriff?"

"That's right," replied Morgan while wondering why the old timer was in jail.

"Well," grinned Jed, "he ain't here."

Finding no humor in that, he asked, "Know where I can find him?"

"Can't say for sure." Jed opened the cell door and stepped out, wondering who the stranger was and what he wanted with the sheriff.

"Thought you were a prisoner?" asked Morgan.

Jed combed what was left of his gray hair with his right hand. "Nope." He walked past Morgan to the window and looked outside at the street as a rider passed the window. "Name's Jed Canon." He looked at Morgan. "I work for the sheriff."

"You, the deputy?"

Jed chuckled, holding his arms out to his side. "Do I look like a deputy?" Before Morgan could answer, he said, "You might find the sheriff across the street at Laurie's Café, eating his supper."

Morgan thanked him, walked outside, and as he closed the door, he saw the café across the street. Filled with anticipation at seeing Emmett again, he stepped off the boardwalk, hurried across the busy street, dodging wagons and horses. Reaching the café, he opened the door, stepped inside, and quickly glanced around the room. It took but a moment to find Wade sitting alone at a table in the back corner. Grinning like a child, Morgan made his way through the small maze of crowded tables.

A surprised Wade looked up as his hand and fork stopped at his mouth. He smiled, put the fork of food back onto his plate, and stood holding out an open hand. "Never thought I'd see you again."

Hunter grinned and shook the hand vigorously. "I thought the Crow got you."

Wade motioned to an empty chair. "Have a seat."

Morgan set his belongings on the floor, rested his Winchester against the back of the empty chair, and sat down. "I waited a long time and started to go back, but I thought if the Indians got you," he said, grinning. "They weren't gonna get me."

Wade grinned. "Smart thinking for a Texan." He picked up his fork of food and shoved it into his mouth.

Morgan failed to see the humor.

A slender woman in her mid-thirties with long brown hair, a turned-up nose, and big blue eyes, looking like she'd had a tough day, approached the table with a white apron stained with today's supper. She smiled at Wade. "How is everything, Sheriff?"

"Food's great, Laurie."

Looking pleased by that, she turned to Morgan. "Would you care for something?"

Without looking up, Morgan pointed at Wade's plate. "I'll have what he's having and a cup of coffee."

As Laurie turned and walked away, Wade began his story of the Indians turning back to the river and leaving the knoll. "I followed your trail a ways but decided to head in another direction."

"Why?" asked Morgan.

Wade thought on that a moment and shrugged. "I wasn't sure where you were heading." Then he cut a piece of ham in two. "Can't really say. It just occurred to me."

Morgan smiled. "Well, no matter. I'm damn glad the Crows didn't get you."

The waitress brought Morgan's dinner, and as the two men ate, Wade told Morgan all that had happened to him since he hit the town, including how he came by the coyote pup.

Morgan pushed his empty plate away. "That Brodie fellah sounds like trouble. What's the story with the old man over in the jail?"

"Jed?" Wade took a drink of coffee, set the cup down, and told him briefly about Jed. When he finished, he listened while Morgan told him about the Thornton's, riding into town and seeing his horse at the livery.

Wade turned to Laurie and motioned to her. "Can I get a plate to go for Jed and some scraps for my coyote?"

She grinned. "Everyone's talking about that little coyote of yours." Then Laurie frowned. "Some say it's cruel to keep a wild thing."

Wade smiled. "Some say the same about a woman keeping a man."

She smiled. "You men like being corralled, and you know it."

Wade glanced at Morgan and laughed, then looked up at Laurie. "And what about you, Laurie? What do you think about me keeping the coyote?"

She considered the question. "It ain't any of my business, but I'm glad you took her away from that, Mr. Anderson. He's a terrible man." She smiled. "I'll get your food and a special plate for that coyote pup."

The street was nearly empty, and the town quiet when the two stepped out of the café into the dark, chilly night. "Today's the last day of August," said Wade. "Winter ain't far off."

Morgan glanced up and down the street of riders and wagons as soft piano music from the saloon spilled into the street. "Only saw snow once in my life."

Wade looked at him amusingly. "I believe you'll wish you were back in Texas soon." Then he stepped off the boardwalk. "I'd walk you to the hotel, but I best get this food to Jed before it gets cold. Want to come over for a drink?"

"No," replied Morgan. "I'm a bit tired." He adjusted the saddlebags on his shoulder. "I think I'll head up to the hotel. See you tomorrow." Then Morgan stepped off the boardwalk and walked toward the Howard Hotel.

Wade watched him for a moment, glad he had come to town, then walked toward the jail.

Jed met Wade at the door. "Some fella was here looking for you."

Wade handed him the plate of food. "He found me."

Getting nothing further to ease his curiosity, Jed took the plate and headed for the desk. He set the plate down, poured a cup of coffee, then sat down and started on his dinner.

Wade put the plate of scraps on the floor, and while the coyote pup gulped it down, he sat at the desk and looked at the wanted posters that had arrived on the afternoon stage from Miles City. Relieved at not seeing one with his name on it, the sound of the plate sliding across the floor told him that Pup had finished. He stood, picked up the plate, and set it on the edge of the desk. Seeing that Jed was done, Wade told him he would take the plates to Laurie's and make his rounds.

Wade stopped by the saloon after he dropped the plates off at Laurie's Café and took a quick look through the window seeing it was a slow night. Somewhat relieved that Brodie and the others weren't inside, he turned and walked down the boardwalk of the quiet town, occasionally twisting a locked doorknob.

Jed Canon was sitting at the desk, reading the single page of the Pickering Newspaper, when Wade walked in. He looked up as he pushed it away. "Everything okay?"

Wade nodded. "Nice and quiet. Let's hope it stays that way." He gestured to the coyote pup. "Guess I better take her out so she can do her business."

"Want me to take her?"

Wade shook his head. "I'll take her." Then he and Pup stepped outside, where she immediately squatted while he looked up and down the deserted street. A scattering of lights shone across the boardwalks and spilled into the street, leaving perfect images of the windows. Several horses stood at the hitching rail, showered by the light from the saloon window. A solitary coyote somewhere in the darkness cried out, and Pup stiffened and stared into the black night. Wade looked in the direction of the sound, then turned and tugged at the rope and pulled her inside. He locked the door, pulled the shade down over the door's window, and then the shade on the big window above the old leather sofa.

Jed was lying on his cot, lifted his head, and looked at Wade. "You turning in?"

"Been a long day," Wade said, sounding tired. Then he took the lantern from his desk, said goodnight, and instead of putting Pup in her cell, he picked up her blanket and took her into his room, closed the door, and set the lantern on the dresser. After placing the folded blanket on the floor, Wade took the rope off Pup, set it on the dresser as she lay down on the blanket. He blew out the lantern and climbed between the cool sheets, looking forward to a good night's sleep.

The minutes passed, and his thoughts quickly turned to Morgan, being glad he showed up in town and hoped he would stay a while. Then he thought of Brodie, the town council, and the story Jed had told him over coffee and whiskey, about his wife. He closed his eyes, wanting to shut off his mind so sleep would come, when he heard the coyote pup trying to jump up on the foot of the bed. He sat up, looked at her dark image, reached down, grabbed her by the nape of the neck, and lifted her onto the bed. She curled up into a ball by his feet and closed her eyes. Resting his head on the pillow, he lay in the darkness staring at the broken mirror on the wall waiting for sleep, but Sarah crept back into his mind, and he wished he could see her and Emmett for just five minutes.

For the first time in his life, he felt lonely and all alone. Feeling Pup move, he looked down at her, and he was glad he had saved her from those assholes. Wanting to think of something else, images of the Hoskins' rushed at him. Men screaming as they climbed out the windows of the bunkhouse, and the old lady he killed, filled his mind. Pushing those images from his mind, the look on Booth Fox's face as he fell back along the bar in the Blue Sky Saloon replaced them. He knew he was going to kill Booth before he and Seth ever walked into the saloon. Seth had been right; he stepped over the line.

He turned over, bringing a soft, protesting growl from the coyote. She got up, walked the short distance from the foot of the bed to a spot next to his stomach, laid down, and curled up against him. After she settled in with a few soft groans, Wade reached down and gently stroked her fur, finding comfort in her small body, thinking the life of the solitary coyote wasn't much different from his now.

Chapter 9

Morgan's room in the hotel was on the second floor overlooking the street. It was a small room with a double bed that proved to be lumpy and the springs noisy. A dresser and framed mirror hanging on the wall occupied one wall, and an uncomfortable wooden chair sat next to a small table by the window. The room was, as Albert Bennett had said, reasonable. He got undressed, climbed into the bed with noisy springs, the locket, and picture in his right hand. As Morgan waited for sleep, his thoughts turned to the Thornton's, their hired hands up and quitting, and of Emmett's story about Brodie and the coyote pup. He looked out the window into the black night, filled with concern over his new friend. Morgan wasn't sure Emmett was up to handling the likes of such men. Soon his eyes felt heavy, and as he thought of the woman and child in the locket he held in his hand, sleep found him.

September

The morning sun rose above the eastern horizon shining through the window of Morgan's room, then slowly crawled down the wall until it found his face. Opening his sleepy eyes to the bright morning sunshine, he raised his hand to shield his eyes. He sat up and tossed the covers back, feeling the chill of the morning as he swung both legs over the edge of the bed, letting his warm feet meet the cold wooden floor. He sat there a moment with his head in his hands, fighting the sleep his mind still wanted, and then he looked up at the sunshine coming through the window. Suddenly realizing that he no longer held the locket, he searched the bed, lifting the one pillow, and then he knelt to the floor, finding it under the bed. With clumsy fingers, he picked it up, sat on the edge of the squeaking bed, opened it, and looked at the picture.

Grabbed by the morning chill, he placed the locket on the table next to the bed, then stood dressed in his faded long underwear and hurried across the room to the small potbellied stove while briskly rubbing his upper arms. He built a fire, hurried back to the warm covers of the lumpy bed and noisy springs, where he waited for the fire to warm the room. The minutes passed while he held the locket in his hand, and when the room no longer carried the morning chill, he returned the locket to the small table and tossed the covers back. Thinking of breakfast, he walked across the room to the dresser and mirror, poured some cold water from the pitcher on the dresser into a white basin, and shaved.

Dressed in clean clothes, he sat on the edge of his bed, opened one side of his saddlebags, and took out a small bundle wrapped in an old yellow bandana tied with a big knot. Unbuttoning his shirt, he stuck the bundle inside next to his stomach. After buttoning his shirt, he put the saddlebag back on the chair next to the window. He strapped on his gun belt, and after adjusting the pistol across the front of his stomach, he picked up the locket and put it into his shirt pocket. After taking a glance around the room, he picked up his carpetbag of clothes, stepped into the empty hall, locked his room, and walked downstairs.

The same thin woman he met the night before, who introduced herself as Beatrice, was sitting behind the desk reading a book and wearing the same dark blue dress she wore the night before. "You ever sleep?" he asked, wearing a smile.

She looked up and smiled, showing her uneven, yellow teeth, closed the book, and pushed it to one side. "I don't require much sleep. Did you sleep well, Mr. Hunter?"

Morgan thought of the lumpy mattress as he placed the key to his room on the counter. "Until the sun hit my face."

Beatrice quickly apologized. "You might try and remember to pull the shade before going to bed."

Morgan filed the suggestion away and set the carpetbag of clothes on the floor. "Is there a laundry somewhere's in town?"

She gestured toward the front door. "Go out that door and around the corner of the building. You can't miss it."

Morgan thanked her, picked up the carpetbag, and headed across the small lobby decorated with two red chairs and one brown leather sofa surrounding a small oval table. Stepping into the warm September morning filled with the scent of fall, he paused on the boardwalk and glanced up and down the street. A single wagon and its driver were coming down the street at a slow pace while two riders slowly rode by, heading in the opposite direction. A boy, not more than ten or twelve wearing an apron that was too big, was busy sweeping the boardwalk in front of Smith's General Store. Otherwise, the town was quiet and peaceful as he continued along his journey to the laundry.

Mrs. Ida Walker, an unsmiling, slightly plump, middle-aged woman of forty, looked up from whatever it was that she was doing and smiled at the handsome man as he placed his carpetbag on the counter.

"I need these washed," he said, and then he smiled. "Have to warn you; they're pretty dirty."

She smiled. "We're used to that sort of thing, Mr...."

Morgan took off his hat. "Morgan Hunter, ma'am."

"Are you staying at the Howard Hotel?"

"I am."

"I'll have your clothes delivered to the desk in the lobby when they're clean."

"Thank you."

Noticing his full head of brown and gray hair needed a trim, she asked, "Could I interest you in a haircut and bath, Mr. Hunter? The water is hot and fresh. No one else has used it yet today."

He thought about that for a moment. "I believe I will have that bath, ma'am, but not the haircut."

She gestured toward a closed door. "Just step through there, Mr. Hunter. You can take off your clothes and get into one of the tubs. After you're in, give me a holler." She glanced at his clothes. "I'll collect your clothes and give them a good brushing even though they don't appear to be dirty."

He thanked her and walked through the door for his bath, remembering other baths he and the lady in the locket would take together.

Laurie's Café was busy, but Morgan managed to find the same small table in the back corner that he and Wade had occupied the night before. He pulled one chair out, placed his hat on it, then sat down in another with his back against the wall giving him the view of the room, the windows, and the front door.

Laurie approached the table wearing a yellow dress and a clean white apron. "Coffee?"

He looked up and smiled. "Please."

She disappeared through an open doorway into the kitchen and returned with a mug of steaming coffee. "Eggs and ham is this morning's special."

Morgan smiled. "That sounds good." He watched her walk away, picked up the coffee cup, and took a small sip. Setting the cup down, he glanced at the other faces while quiet laughter and inaudible conversations spilled from one table to another. He thought about the early mornings in Texas when Ana would have his breakfast ready and always marveled at how she could manage to set hot food on the table just as he walked out of the bedroom, shaved and dressed. He smiled in memory of the way she would sit at the table with her coffee and watch him eat, always looking beautiful with her raven black hair and big dark eyes that he swore could look deep into his soul.

Wade walked in and took off his hat as he made his way through the maze of tables to Morgan's table and pulled out a chair. "How did you sleep?"

Morgan grinned. "Besides the lumpy bed and noisy springs, not too bad."

Wade chuckled as he placed his hat over Morgan's and sat down.

Laurie placed a plate of food in front of Morgan and looked at Wade. "Good morning, Sheriff. Would you like some breakfast?"

"Good morning, Laurie. I'll have what he's having and a cup of coffee."

She smiled. "Be right back."

The warm morning greeted Wade and Morgan Hunter as they stepped out of the café.

Wade paused at the edge of the boardwalk while Morgan stepped into the street covered in sunshine. "What are your plans?"

Hunter considered a moment. "Well, I need to visit the bank."

Wade glanced at the bank down the street next to the sheriff's office. "You ain't planning a robbery in my town, are you, Morgan?"

Hunter chuckled and shook his head. "You have too long of a reach with that Sharps."

Wade stepped off the boardwalk holding the plate of leftovers. "I've gotta take this food to Pup and then do some walking around town to get better acquainted with some of the folks."

"Ain't it about time you gave that coyote a proper name?"

Wade started across the street toward the jailhouse. "She has a proper name."

Morgan walked into the Pickering, Montana, bank and paused just inside the door to have a quick look around. An elderly lady wearing a dark red dress and matching bonnet was standing in front of the only open teller window. The plump bald man behind the window of thin wooden bars was listening intently while the lady talked. Morgan's eyes roamed the inside of the bank then settled on a pretty woman beyond the railing that separated the lobby from the rest of the bank. She was sitting at a large oak desk looking at something on her desk wearing a perplexed look.

She wore a light green dress with a white collar and sleeves. Her complexion was fair and soft, something few women in this hard country had. She wore her hair atop her head, and Morgan imagined how it would look when she let it fall around her shoulders. She looked up with big brown eyes, gave him a quick smile of even white teeth, and quickly looked down at the papers on her desk.

Guessing her age to be about thirty, his eyes went from that woman back to the older woman at the window in front of him that suddenly raised her voice, scolding the teller sounding quite unhappy. Morgan could not make out what it was that had her so upset, but the woman at the desk quickly stood and hurried behind the teller's cage. He couldn't hear what she said to the teller, but whatever it was, it seemed to please the elderly lady. The younger woman smiled at the elderly woman while reaching through the bars of the window, gently touching her hand. The teller looked relieved as the younger lady walked back toward her desk.

Pausing next to the gate of the railing, she smiled as she looked at Morgan. "May I help you, sir?"

He took off his hat and stepped toward the railing. "Yes, ma'am." Noticing some ink on the side of her narrow straight nose, he said, "I'd like to open an account and make a deposit."

Smiling, she pulled the small gate toward her. "I can help with that. This way, please."

Morgan stepped through the gate she held open, catching a slight scent of her perfume, then followed to her desk. He estimated her height to be around five feet three and slender with a small waist.

Reaching her desk, she turned and gestured at the chair next to it. "Have a chair, please." Then she sat down.

He waited for her to sit, then he sat down, holding his wide-brimmed black hat on his lap. As she shuffled the papers on her desk, his eyes made a quick trip around the bank.

After she gathered the papers she had been studying and set them on the side of her desk in a neat pile, she folded her delicate hands and smiled. "I don't remember seeing you before, so I'm assuming you're new in Pickering, Mr...."

"Morgan, ma'am. Morgan Hunter and I rode in late yesterday."

She held out her right hand. "Welcome to Pickering, Mr. Hunter. I'm Mrs. Katharine Jordan."

He shook her soft, delicate hand, disappointed in her marital status. "Thank you." Then he grinned and gestured with one hand. "You've some ink on your nose."

Looking embarrassed, she took a handkerchief from her dress pocket and wiped the side of her nose.

He smiled. "The other side."

Her face blushed as she quickly wiped the ink off. "Where are you from, Mr. Hunter?"

"Texas."

Still feeling flush from her embarrassment, she opened the center drawer of her desk and took out a small, thin book. "That's quite a ways."

"Yes, ma'am, it is at that."

She placed the small book on the top of her desk. "I hope you don't mind me asking, but what brings you to Pickering?"

He thought of the woman and child in the locket. "There was nothing to keep me in Texas any longer."

Believing there was more to his reasons, she accepted what he said, opened the small, thin book, and picked up an ink pen from the inkwell on her desk. She wrote his name on the top line, blotted the ink, and then asked where he was staying. He told her, and she wrote that on the second line while telling him if he moved, he needed to come in and tell her. With pen poised above the book, she asked how much he was depositing.

He sat back in his chair, unbuttoned his shirt and pulled out the faded, yellow bandana tied in a big knot, and set it on her desk. She watched with curiosity as he untied the bandana revealing a small stack of money. He sat back in his chair. "Five thousand two hundred seventy-five dollars, to be exact."

She stared at it for a moment, looking a little surprised, and then she looked at him. "A deposit this size will require our bank president's approval."

"And who is that?"

"Jonathan Moore is the bank president." Looking apologetic, she stood. "Excuse me while I see if Mr. Moore can see you. I'll return shortly."

He watched her walk to a door on the far wall, open it then disappear inside. While he waited, his eyes found a round, white-faced clock on the wall behind the teller cages. Pulling out his pocket watch, he compared the time then replaced the watch into his pocket. A large oil painting depicting a scene of a cattle drive that reminded him of Texas was on the far wall, above a dark brown leather sofa, sitting smugly near the door she disappeared in. The bank's front door behind him opened, and as he turned, he saw Wade standing just inside the door, grinning. Morgan picked up the bandana with the money and put it on his lap.

Wade took off his hat and approached Morgan just as Mrs. Jordan stepped out of Mr. Moore's office.

She looked first at Morgan and then at Wade and smiled warmly. "Good morning Sheriff Spears."

Wade returned her smile. "Good morning, Mrs. Jordan."

"Is there something you need?" she asked.

Wade shook his head no as he gestured to Morgan with the hand that held his hat. "I just saw this one walk in and thought he looked a little suspicious."

Morgan turned to Wade. "Funny, Emmett, real funny!"

Wade grinned.

Mrs. Jordan looked curious. "You two know one another?"

"We do," said Wade as he grinned at Morgan, looked at Mrs. Jordan, and nodded as he turned to walk away, saying, "Mrs. Jordan."

"Good day, Sheriff," she said in a pleasant voice.

"I'll see you later, Morgan," Wade said over his shoulder.

Mrs. Jordan looked at Morgan. "Mr. Moore will see you now, Mr. Hunter."

He stood, holding his money, and followed her to the closed door.

She opened the door and then stepped aside.

As he walked past her, he caught another whiff of her perfume.

A thin, balding man dressed in a black suit in his fifties stood from a large mahogany desk. Having friendly, brown eyes under bushy eyebrows and a nose that looked like it had been broken, he looked at Mrs. Jordan. "That'll be all for now, Katherine."

"Yes, sir."

Morgan turned and thanked her as she backed out of the room, closing the door. Turning, he walked toward the man who had stepped from behind the desk.

"Jonathan Moore," the man said with a smile and an outstretched hand.

Hunter shook the man's hand. "Morgan Hunter."

Jonathan gestured to one of three comfortable red velvet chairs. "Mrs. Jordan tells me you want to make a rather sizable deposit."

Morgan sat down in the nearest chair, adjusted his pistol, placed his hat on the chair next to him, and folded his hands, holding the yellow bandana of money on his lap. "That's correct." He paused and leaned forward, laying the yellow bandana of money on the desk. "Six thousand two hundred seventy-five dollars, to be exact."

Moore looked down at the money and then at Morgan. "That is a substantial amount. Are you planning on staying in Pickering, Mr. Hunter?"

"Haven't quite made up my mind yet. But until I do," Morgan said, gesturing at the money, "I don't want to walk around carrying that with me or leave it in the hotel room."

Jonathan grinned. "Well, I can't say that I blame you."

"But so far, I like what I see. The town is small and seems friendly enough, and the country looks like good grazing land."

Moore appeared thoughtful. "Now that the Army is getting the Indian situation in hand, the town is growing." He paused. "Perhaps too fast." He leaned forward, placing his forearms on the top of his desk. "And as you just said, this country is good for grazing." His face filled with an inquiring look. "Are you interested in a piece of land, Mr. Hunter?"

Morgan quickly considered that. "I might be if there was any land along the Powder River."

Jonathan Moore sat back in his chair. "Most of the land along the river has been sold." He smiled. "However, you're in luck."

Morgan didn't believe in luck.

"Kyle Chandler's place," said Jonathan, "is about ten or eleven miles southwest of here."

Morgan thought of Jessup Thornton. "That'd be close to the Thornton place."

Jonathan appeared curious. "You know Jessup Thornton?"

"Not very well. I stopped at their place on my way here. They were kind enough to ask me to stay for dinner, and I spent the night in their empty bunkhouse."

Moore gave an understanding shake of the head. "Nice people." His face turned sad. "They're having a hard time of it, I'm afraid."

Morgan was curious but said nothing, figuring it wasn't any of his business.

Jonathan had the look of someone caught at something he shouldn't be doing. "Now about this place I was telling you about. It's on the other side of Thornton's place, so you'd be neighbors."

"How many acres?"

"Close to five hundred, I believe," replied Moore. He opened the top right drawer of his desk, pulled out a stack of papers, and set them on his desk. He began thumbing through them, and after passing several pages, his eyes lit up. "Ah, here it is." He paused to read the words on the document. "Six hundred forty acres," he said, then he looked at Morgan. "One section, to be exact. The Powder River cuts a line right between the Chandler Ranch and the Thornton Ranch, and I believe there's a small tributary that feeds a lake not far from the house, so you won't have any water issues."

Interested, Morgan sat back. "What borders the other side of the property?"

"The Big C, owned by Ben Croucher."

Morgan filed that away. "How much is this, Mr. Chandler asking?"

Jonathan Moore looked down at the papers in front of him and quoted the price.

Morgan raised his brow, thinking that would take over half his money, but he knew it was a good deal figuring another may not come along.

Seeing the concern on Morgan's face, Mr. Moore said, "I suppose you could negotiate the price." Then he leaned forward. "It's a good piece of land, Mr. Hunter. I know for a fact that Mr. Croucher would love to have this piece of land because the north boundary borders the Big C Ranch."

"How big is the Big C?"

He frowned in thought. "Close to twenty sections, I believe."

Morgan recalled the Thornton's mentioning Ben Croucher. "Why doesn't Mr. Chandler just sell to Ben Croucher?"

Jonathan sat back, looking amused. "Bad blood." Then he frowned. "The two men hated one another from the first time they met. Before he left for Cheyenne, Mr. Chandler left strict orders not to sell to Croucher under any circumstances."

Morgan sat back and wondered what he was getting himself into. The acreage was perfect for a small operation, and he may need to hire a couple of men, maybe three. It was just what he was looking for. "Why is this Chandler fella selling?"

Jonathan looked sad. "Old Man Chandler couldn't keep up with it any longer. He lost his wife, Maybelle, several years ago, and then his only son got lost in a blizzard a couple of years back and froze to death."

Morgan thought of the Thornton's son.

"After that," said Jonathan sadly, "he just lost interest in the place. A few months ago, his hired help up and quit, so he decided to sell."

"Seems odd."

Jonathan looked concerned as he turned to the window and looked out at the street. "Old Man Chandler blamed Croucher for

123

his men up and quitting." He turned to Morgan. "Mr. Chandler complained to Sheriff Jack Styles and the mayor a couple of times." He shrugged and gestured with both hands. "Neither could do anything without proof, and of course, old Sheriff Styles said he talked to Croucher, but naturally, Ben denied everything."

Morgan had known men like Ben Croucher in Texas. Hell, he even worked for one. Suddenly he was curious about the Thornton's. "You said something about the Thornton's having a bad time of it."

Moore looked embarrassed. "Well, I shouldn't have said anything, Mr. Hunter, and I'd appreciate it if you'd forget I mentioned that. It was wrong of me."

Morgan thought on that for a short moment and decided to let the matter drop. "I'd like to ride out and take a look at the Chandler place later today."

"Of course," replied Moore. "Ride south past the Thornton place and stay close to the river. It winds a bit, but you'll run into the Chandler place. You can see the house and barn from the river." Moore stood opened his desk drawer, pulled out a key, and walked around the desk as Morgan stood. They shook hands, and then he gave him Morgan the key. "Enjoy your ride, Mr. Hunter. The bank will be closed tomorrow, being it's Saturday. Hopefully, I'll hear from you on Monday." He put one hand on Morgan's back and guided him toward the door. "We'll use your deposit as a retainer, so to speak, and I'll make sure the place does not sell until you've had a chance to see it."

"I appreciate that." At the door, Morgan glanced back at his money, sitting on the desk.

Jonathan Moore smiled. "Your money is safe with me, Mr. Hunter." He opened the door, stepped into the other room, and quietly called out to Mrs. Jordan.

She turned in her chair, and seeing Mr. Moore motioning for her, she stood and walked toward them. "Yes, Mr. Moore?"

"Give Mr. Hunter a receipt for six thousand two hundred seventy-five dollars, Mrs. Jordan, and one of our passbooks." He looked at Morgan. "Mrs. Jordan will take care of you. It's been nice doing business with you, Mr. Hunter." Then he turned and walked back into his office and closed the door.

Morgan followed Mrs. Jordan to her desk and sat down in the same chair he was sitting in before. Deciding to make small talk, he asked, "What does your husband do, Mrs. Jordan?"

She paused for a moment without looking up. "My husband of eight years was killed two years ago this past August, Mr. Hunter."

Being regretful for asking, he said, "My apologies for asking, ma'am."

She finished what she was doing and smiled softly at him. "No need to apologize, Mr. Hunter. You couldn't have known." She opened a ledger, wrote his name on an empty line, and then the amount of six thousand two hundred seventy-five dollars opposite his name along with the date of the transaction. After sliding a piece of paper in front of him, she took a pen out of the inkwell on her desk and offered it to him. "Can you write your name?"

The question was not out of the ordinary, and he took no offense. Many men knew only how to write their name, nothing else, and many others who only made their mark. He smiled. "Yes, ma'am," and signed the paper.

She looked at the signature, gave him a receipt, and the small book containing his name and the balance of his account. "That should do it." Then she stood. "I'll show you out, Mr. Morgan." They walked to the gate in the railing, where she pulled it toward her so he could pass into the outer lobby. As he walked by, she smiled and offered her hand. "It was a pleasure meeting you, Mr. Hunter. If there is anything else we can do for you, please don't hesitate to ask."

He shook her hand gently. "I'll do that."

Smiling, she turned and walked back to her desk, sat down, picked up a piece of paper, and began reading.

Morgan walked to the glass door with the bank's name in white lettering and paused to look back at her. Disappointed that she did not look up, he opened the door and stepped outside.

Mrs. Katherine Jordan glanced up as he closed the door, smiled to herself, and then looked back down at the paper, thinking he was an interesting man.

Chapter 10

The Thornton Ranch

Approaching the Thornton ranch, Morgan saw the barn door was open and, thinking he would find Jessup Thornton inside, guided the Appaloosa toward the door, pulled up, and called out. "Hello, Jessup!"

Curious as to who was calling his name, Jessup laid the pitchfork he was using against the stall he was cleaning and cautiously stepped outside. Looking pleased at seeing Morgan, Jessup extended his hand. "Good day to you, Mr. Hunter."

Morgan smiled while shaking the old man's hand. "I thought we decided to do away with the formalities?"

Jessup grinned. "I guess we did at that. What brings you back this way so soon?"

"What can you tell me about the Chandler place?"

"Not much to tell," responded Jessup with a curious look. "Why you asking?"

Morgan took off his gloves. "I'm thinking about buying the place."

Surprise and delight filled Jessup's face. "Buying it?"

"I'm on my way now to take a look but thought I'd stop by and see what you had to say about the place."

"It's a good piece of land and butts up against mine," offered Jessup. "The Powder River is what separates both places from the Bic C. There's a wide but shallow part of the river that's easy crossing. A small tributary feeds a small lake not far from the house." He grinned in memory. "Me and old Kyle used to pull some pretty good Cutthroat Trout out of it." He suddenly looked sad. "Big C takes up a lot of land."

"So I've been told, but that doesn't worry me none."

Jessup's expression was tense. "Sure as hell would prefer you a neighbor than that damn Ben Croucher."

"Well, if you ain't too busy, how'd you like to ride over there with me while I take a look?"

Jessup glanced back at the barn, deciding it could wait. "I'll tell the missus and then saddle my horse."

Hunter grinned. "You go tell the missus, and I'll saddle your horse."

After telling Morgan which horse to saddle, he turned and hurried toward the house.

Sitting in their saddles in front of what looked like a well constructed single-story house with a covered porch that ran from one end of the front of the house to the other, Jessup said, "Sturdy place. Helped build it myself."

Morgan turned from the house and looked at a nice sized barn, large corral, empty pig sty, empty chicken coop, and a bunkhouse. Climbing down, he tied his horse to the railing next to the porch, took off his gloves, and stuck them under his gun belt.

"Sure, do miss old Kyle," said Jessup as he climbed down from his gray horse.

Morgan pulled the key to the house out of his coat pocket. "Let's see what's inside."

Jessup tied his horse next to the Appaloosa then stepped onto the porch glancing around the place in memory.

Morgan turned the key, pushed on the door, which had swollen from dampness and lack of use, pushed a little harder, and the door opened with a creak. Entering the dim room, greeted by that stuffy smell that lingers when a house has been closed up for a long time, he paused to look around.

Jessup stepped in behind him and closed the door.

Morgan walked to the nearest window and opened the shutters flooding the room with dusty sunshine. Turning from the window, he walked across the hardwood floor, chased by the sound of his heavy footsteps, and lifted a covering from off a deep brown leather sofa. After examining the sofa, which appeared in good shape, he dropped the cloth and walked around the room, lifting covers to inspect the rest of the furniture. A large stone fireplace took up the center of the wall with a set of young elk horns on either side. The walls were empty of pictures except a large painting of snowcapped mountains and a winding river left by Mr. Chandler.

Jessup was on a journey of his own, looking at this and that, remembering his and Louise's visits before Mrs. Maybelle Chandler passed away.

Morgan turned from the fireplace to the adjacent dining room, with its long oak table and eight chairs covered by several white cloths. A long window with a view of the land to the tree-lined river filled the wall behind the table. Seeing a closed door, he walked past the covered table and another low cabinet and opened the door. Stepping into a dim kitchen, he opened the shutters giving light to a wood cooking stove, cabinets, counters, and an inside pump.

Jessup was standing behind him. "Maybelle sure loved her kitchen," he said sadly.

As if he hadn't heard Jessup, Morgan turned and walked back through the dining room to a hallway of two doors and opened the first. A big room greeted him with a large bed, sitting between two shuttered windows, end tables, and two covered chairs in front of a fireplace the room shared with the living room. Curious, he bent down and looked through the fire pit into the living room full of covered furniture.

Jessup was at the door. "Another bedroom is across the hall. It's quite a bit smaller than this one."

"I've seen enough," said Morgan. Then he walked past Jessup, closed the shutters in the kitchen then walked into the living room with Thornton following. Morgan closed the shutter that he had earlier opened. "Let's step outside."

Jessup followed him to the edge of the porch, and while he waited for Morgan to speak, he looked out across the ranch remembering his old friend Kyle Chandler. "Nice place," said Jessup. "You'd have to buy cattle, chickens, and such."

Morgan's memory pictured a little piece of land in the Texas Panhandle as his gaze went to the willow and cottonwood trees along the small lake fed by the Powder River. Pushing the memory of Texas from his mind, he thought about herding cattle across his own land. He turned from the scene to Jessup with a worried look. "I don't know much about ranching."

"What do you know?" asked Jessup.

With a smile, Morgan stepped off the porch, bent down, and picked up a handful of soil with his hand, then watched it drift between his fingers to be carried away by a slight breeze. "Not much."

"If you don't mind me asking, what did you do in Texas?"

Morgan stood and put on his gloves as he stared at the scattering of white clouds against a blue sky in the distance. "Something I ain't going to do here."

Jessup considered that with a fair idea of what the man did do for a living in Texas. "Mind me asking a personal question?"

Morgan turned to the old man and grinned. "Depends on the question, Jessup."

Thornton smiled. "Why'd you leave Texas?"

Morgan stared into the distance, thinking about the woman and child in the locket. "That's a story I ain't ready to tell just yet." Then he looked at the barn, thinking of it full of hay, the corral full of horses, and the empty chicken coop with a red rooster on top of the roof and fat hens inside laying eggs, and a couple of pigs snorting in the empty sty.

Jessup stepped off the porch next to him. "I can teach you a few things."

Morgan turned, appearing interested. "I'm a quick learner."

"You ain't exactly dumb when it comes to working, Son. I saw that in you the morning you were cleaning out the stalls."

Hunter chuckled. "Anyone can shovel horseshit."

Thornton grinned. "That's true, I suppose, but not with the enthusiasm you showed." Jessup grinned as he patted Morgan on the shoulder. "Tell you what, if you have the money to buy this place, do so. Then you and I will partner up."

Morgan considered that quickly. "What's on your mind?"

Jessup Thornton turned, looked down at the two chairs on the front porch, and sat down in one that moaned softly from the unaccustomed weight.

Morgan turned and leaned against the porch post with his left shoulder and waited.

"The way I see it," began Thornton, "I need a hand, and you need an education on cattle ranching."

Hunter shook his head and looked at the barn. "Can't deny that."

Jessup looked up. "I'll sell you a hundred head at a reasonable price, and we work both places as one." He pointed to the house over his shoulder with his right thumb. "You can live here if you like and come over each day or stay in the bunkhouse at our place. Whichever you prefer."

Morgan quietly considered both options.

Jessup shrugged. "Hell, you're only a short ride to my place." He sat forward in the chair, looking determined. "If you decide to take me up on my offer, I have to tell you; it's damn hard work. Ten, twelve hours a day of nothing but hard work. The winters are cold and hard up here, not like they are where you come from." He looked at the barn in memory. "There are days you snow is so deep you won't be able to get out of the house to the barn. Sometimes you lose cattle to the cold and lack of grazing from the drifts." He stood and walked to the edge of the porch. "Yet the spring always comes, and somehow with it, you find new calves, green grass, and cool, clear water from the melting snow." He turned to Morgan. "It's then you know that you've been blessed by God Almighty."

Morgan thought on all that for a moment. "I'm willing to give it a try if you're willing to put up with me."

Jessup chuckled. "Need to warn you, son; I can be a hard man at times."

Morgan recalled the days with his father before both parents and his younger brother was murdered and how he secretly called his pa "Old Ways" because his pa always talked about the old ways. He held out an open hand, which Jessup gladly took. They shook firmly and congratulated one another on their new adventure, climbed in their saddles, and headed back for the Thornton place.

Pickering, Montana

It was dark when Wade and Jed stepped out of Laurie's Café, carrying a plate of scraps for the coyote pup. Pausing at the edge of the boardwalk, Wade glanced up and down the dark street of images of lighted windows and doorways. "I ain't much in the mood for checkers tonight, Jed." Wade was feeling a little down with Sarah and Emmett on his mind.

Jed glanced at the jailhouse up the street and lied. "I'm a bit tired myself."

"Do me a favor," said Wade. "Take the plate and see that Pup eats? I think I'll take a walk."

Figuring something had a hold of Wade, Canon took the plate. "Sure thing."

"See you after my rounds," said Wade, and then he turned and walked along the boardwalk toward the saloon.

Jed watched him a moment, wondering what it was that had a hold of him, then stepped off the boardwalk and headed toward the jailhouse.

Wade turned the knob of the door to the saloon, opened it, and stepped inside, greeted by piano music and laughter. He walked to the bar, leaned on it with his forearms, looked at Dave Goody standing several feet away, and signaled for a beer. Instead of the chubby piano player, Tim Martin, one of Sam's whores, named Mary Lee, was at the piano, and Wade wondered where the man everyone called Chubby was.

Dave nodded and started toward him to warn him that Brodie and the others were sitting at a table near the stairs. Before he could warn him, Wade saw their images in the mirror behind the bar, walking toward him.

As Goody approached, Wade softly said, "I see them. Give me a beer."

Dave picked up a clean mug and began pouring beer into it while watching Brodie and the others, who had stopped a few feet behind Wade. He set the beer on the bar, took the money Wade had tossed down, and walked toward the register and hidden shotgun he kept under the bar.

Wade lifted his beer with his left hand, looked into Brodie's eyes, took a long drink, and then set the mug down. As he wiped his mouth with the sleeve of his left hand, he turned, letting his right hand rest on the butt of his Colt. "Gentlemen."

Brodie stood a couple of feet from Wade with his feet spread apart, thumbs hooked in the belt of his holster, looking arrogant. He glanced at the badge pinned to Wade's shirt. "We heard you were the new sheriff, but we had to come and see for ourselves."

Harry stepped forward, looking angry. "Where's my damn coyote?"

"She ain't your coyote any longer. I paid you, boys, for her."

Dave quietly picked up the shotgun he had hidden under the bar and held it with both hands just below the top of the bar out of sight.

The whore, Mary Lee, had stopped playing the piano, and the place was suddenly quiet with everyone watching Wade and Harry.

Harry spoke through clenched teeth. "I'll buy the bitch back."

Wade picked up his beer with his left hand and took a long drink, wiped his mouth, and set the mug back on the bar but held onto the handle. "Sorry, but she ain't for sale. Besides, you'd only shoot her, so why not save your money?"

Harry lowered his voice. "That's right, and that's just what I intend on doing."

Wade suddenly slapped Harry up beside his face with the mug, hard enough to break it and turn Harry sideways, knocking off his hat. The move was so sudden and unexpected that Brodie and the others just stood there while Wade drew his pistol and cocked it.

About the same instant, Dave raised the shotgun over the bar pulling back both hammers.

Harry was holding the side of his wet face as he turned back to Wade. Tiny lines of blood trickled down his neck onto his shirt collar and his beer-soaked coat. He took his hand away and looked at the blood mixed with beer on his hand, and then at the gun pointed at his stomach. "You bastard!"

"No, Harry, my folks were married." Wade looked at the cut along Harry's jawbone and then into Harry's dark, hateful eyes. "It's a little different when you're the one getting picked on, isn't it, Harry?"

"I don't want any trouble tonight," Dave said.

Brodie glanced at the shotgun and then at Dave. "You're gonna pull that thing on me once too often, Goody."

"I doubt that, Brodie," said Dave. "And if you're wondering, damn right, I'll use it."

Brody looked at Wade while talking to the bartender. "There won't be any trouble tonight, Dave. You can rest easy." He turned, putting one hand on Harry's shoulder. "Let's get that cut fixed."

Harry bent down and picked up his hat, gave Wade a hateful look, then followed Brodie and the others out the door.

Dave leaned across the bar, looking at Wade. "You carrying a death wish, Sheriff?"

Wade stared at the closed door, considering the question, and then he looked down at the floor covered in beer and broken glass and then at his trembling hands. "Appears I need another beer."

"You're gonna have to arrest them or kill 'em," said Dave as he turned to put the shotgun away.

"How many of those shotguns do you have back there?" asked Wade.

Dave grinned. "Three."

Wade's face held a small grin. "Give me another beer." While Dave got the beer, Wade glanced back at the door, knowing that Dave Goody was right about Brodie and the others. At some point, he would have to either arrest them or kill them.

Dave set a mug of beer on the bar. "On the house," he said and then walked away.

The whore went back to playing a soft tune while the hushed sound of conversation and laughter filled the room. Dave yelled at one of the whores to clean up the mess Wade had made.

Wade picked up his beer, took a drink, and stared into the foamy beer thinking of Booth Fox falling back along the bar in Harper. He could still see the surprised and afraid look on Booth's face, knowing he was going to die. A hand on his shoulder startled him, and as he spun away from the bar, his Colt was halfway out.

Morgan stepped back with hands waist high, looking surprised. "Hold on, Emmett."

Wade slid the pistol back into its holster. "Brodie and his pals were in here earlier wanting the coyote back."

The bartender walked up. "What'll it be, Morgan?"

"Beer." Morgan watched Dave walk away, and then he leaned on the bar with his elbows. "Sooner or later, those four are gonna be a problem."

Wade took a drink of beer and softly chuckled. "Gonna be?"

Morgan grinned, and as Dave set his beer on the bar, he tossed some coins down, picked up his beer, and took a drink. After Dave picked up the money and walked away, Morgan turned to Wade. "I'm available if you need me."

Wade was grateful for the offer and smiled. "Where the hell you been all day?"

Hunter picked up his beer and gestured to a table in the corner. "Let's sit down, and I'll tell you about my new occupation."

Curious, Wade picked up his beer and followed Morgan to a table in the corner away from the windows and piano music. While they drank their beer, he told Wade about the Chandler Ranch and the deal that he and Jessup Thornton had made. While Hunter talked excitedly about the day, Wade stared into his beer and thought of Sarah wishing he could go home.

The minutes passed, and soon Morgan stopped talking. "What do you think?"

Wade looked up from his mug. "Sounds like a plan, Morgan. A hell of a lot of work, but a plan just the same." He paused, "A man has to have a plan." Then he leaned on the table with his forearms. "You ever punch cattle before?"

Hunter thought of the little place in Texas and the few cows he owned. "Can't say I have. Leastways not for a living."

Wade sat back in the chair, thinking he knew what he did for a living. "It's damn hard work." He lifted his mug and drank the last of his beer, feeling happy for Morgan. "This Jessup fella seems like an all-right sort. I hope it works out." He looked at the clock above the bar near the buffalo's head. "It's getting late." He stood. "Old Jed's probably wondering about me, and Pup needs her exercise."

Morgan pushed his mug, which still contained a small amount of beer, toward the center of the table and stood. "I'll walk out with you."

The chilly night air greeted the two when they walked out the door of the saloon. While Wade closed the saloon door behind them, Morgan moved from the light coming through the window into the shadows. Wade figured it was out of habit and glanced around into the shadows of the streets, thinking of Brodie and the others. "Gotta make my rounds before I head back."

"Want company?" asked Morgan.

Appreciating the offer but wanting to be alone, Wade said, "No thanks, I'm just gonna check a few doors and head for the jailhouse."

Morgan stepped closer. "You sure that little coyote is worth all this trouble?"

Wade thought on that, realizing the pup was the closest he had to family now. "Yeah, she is, Morgan. Don't expect you or anyone else to understand, but she is. At least she is to me." He patted Morgan on the shoulder. "Don't concern yourself. It's my problem. See you at breakfast, and you can tell me how you and Mrs. Jordan are getting along."

Wondering what Emmett meant by that, Morgan watched him walk away, thinking maybe he should tag along but instead stepped off the boardwalk and headed toward the Howard Hotel.

The town was dark and quiet, and the only noise Wade heard once away from the saloon was his own footsteps on the boardwalk and the occasional twisting of the doorknobs he turned to make sure the doors were locked. His mind was full of Sarah and little Emmett as he walked, and after checking the last door of a small dress shop at the edge of town, he stood at the boardwalk's edge and looked south toward Colorado. The dark sky was full of stars from horizon to horizon, and a big orange full moon slowly made its way over the treetops to the east. A coyote broke the stillness, causing a dog to respond somewhere behind the buildings on the other side of the street. Thinking of Pup, he took one last look in the direction of Harper, then stepped off the boardwalk and walked across the street toward the sound of the barking dog.

Stepping from the dark street onto the dark boardwalk, he checked a couple of locked doors then continued on his silent journey toward the jailhouse. A dog barked from somewhere in the night, and he paused to listen, but it stopped as suddenly as it had begun. Checking another door, he looked down the street as the light from the jailhouse windows. Anxious to see the coyote, he walked a little faster. He was thinking about a cup of hot coffee and never saw the pistol that delivered the blow to his head. His legs buckled as he collapsed, sprawling across the boardwalk. Barely conscious, he felt someone grabbing his arms and then dragging him along the boardwalk and across the dirt into the alley.

Dazed by the blow, Wade opened his eyes to a blurry figure kneeling over him while voices spoke soft words in a whisper he could barely hear. His hand found the warm, moist cut on his head as he tried to get up, but the blurry figure took his hand away and held it against the ground. "Stay put, Sheriff."

Wade thought he recognized the voice, and though still dazed, he watched the man standing next to the other three, and as his mind began to clear, he knew who they were. He rolled onto his side and reached for his Colt but found an empty holster.

One of the figures bent down and laughed softly. "Lose something, Sheriff?"

Another pushed him over onto his back with his boot. "I told you to stay put." That was followed by a kick in his ribs.

Wade turned onto his side, curled into a ball, and wrapped his arms and hands around his head, trying to protect himself from the kicks that kept coming to his back and head. After the kicking stopped, he was lifted to his feet and held up by two men while another punched him in the stomach, then grabbed his neck. "Look at me," the voice said.

He opened his swollen eyes, but blood from a cut above his left eye blurred his vision.

"Hey, Sheriff," said a voice with laughter.

Wade looked at the figure standing in front of him and then felt a blow to his jaw that brought unconsciousness for a moment.

When he opened his eyes, the figure grabbed his hair in one hand and held it so tightly he thought he was going to pull it out.

"Look at my face, Sheriff. See what that beer mug did to me?"

Wade could only see a dark blurred head but knew it was Harry Anderson.

"See this knife?

Wade's eyes went to the blade of the big knife, thinking he was going to cut his throat.

"When we're done, you get on that horse of yours and ride out of Pickering and don't ever come back."

Wade could smell the bad breath that accompanied the words, and knowing it was Harry Anderson, Wade spit in his face.

"You son of a bitch yelled Harry, and then he punched Wade in the stomach. He felt a gloved hand cover his mouth and struggled to get free while his muffled words filled the otherwise quiet alley. Feeling something cold touch his skin just under the ear, he felt the blade cutting him along the bottom of his jaw from his left ear to his chin, turning his muffled words into muffled screams.

"Now, we both got scars, asshole!"

Wade screamed into the glove, fighting to get free, feeling the warm blood run down his neck onto his shirt while someone punched him in the stomach just before he passed out. Moments later, he opened his eyes, lying face down on the alley's hard, cold dirt. Wade tried to push himself up to his knees, but a boot pushed him back to the ground. Slowly rolling over, he opened his eyes and looked up at the four men, certain this dark, lonely alley would be the last thing he would see before they killed him. At that moment, Wade thought of Sarah and Emmett and then of Pup waiting for him, knowing these men would kill her next. Filled with resolve, he sat up, swung aimlessly at one of the figures, missed, and fell over. He tried to get up amidst their laughter but fell back to the hard ground, followed by several kicks to the ribs and back with one final kick to the head.

Wade opened his eyes to a large black dog licking the blood from his face. He turned his head and pushed the dog away with one hand. "Go away," Wade managed in a hoarse voice, then slowly sat up. Feeling unsteady, he looked around into the darkness through his one good eye for Harry and the others, but all he saw was the dog disappear around the corner of a building. His mind was groggy, and it seemed as if his whole body hurt. Remembering the knife, he touched his wet, sticky jaw with his left hand, feeling the long gash and worried he would bleed to death. Slowly, he made it to his knees, fighting the pain in his back and ribs. Knowing he was badly hurt, Wade had to get out of the alley for help but collapsed onto his stomach. Then, trying to get up again, a single gunshot echoed through the dark night. "No," he said softly. Picturing Pup dead in its cell, he passed out.

Chapter 11

Jed Canon leaned back in Wade's chair, put his feet on the desk, and drank his coffee while looking out at the lighted windows across the dark street. He took a sip of hot coffee and then looked at the clock on the far wall, thinking the sheriff had been gone a long time. The old chair moaned as he took his feet down from the desk and stood. While setting his cup on the desk, he looked out the window, having a strange feeling he couldn't explain. He turned to the gun rack, took the twelve-gauge shotgun, and opened its breech seeing both barrels were loaded. Opening the center drawer, he picked up the keyring containing several keys and walked to the cell where Pup was lying. "I'll be back soon, girl," he said.

The door opened, and Brodie, Harry, Jimmy Wilson, and Todd Young walked in. Todd closed the door and pulled the blind down over the door's window while Jimmy rushed to the big window above the sofa and lowered the blinds.

Fear gripped Jed as he stepped inside the cell with Pup and closed the door wishing he could lock it, but he was on the wrong side of the door.

Brodie chuckled. "Where you going, old-timer?" They were all grinning as they walked toward the cell.

Jed dropped the keys, jingling as they bounced on the floor, raised the shotgun, and cocked both hammers. Noticing the bandage on Harry's face, he wished the sheriff would get back. He shoved the shotgun through the bars while tiny beads of sweat filled his palms and forehead. "What do you boys want?"

Brodie pointed at the pup sitting on the cot. "There's your bitch coyote pup, Harry."

Harry's lopsided grin looked evil as he started toward the cell.

Recognizing him, Pup jumped off the bed, ran under the cot and into the corner. She turned and growled, showing her baby teeth.

"Don't come any closer," warned Jed.

"I came for my pup," said Harry.

Jed glanced at the small coyote then looked at Anderson. "It ain't your pup no more, Harry." His hands were sweating, and his mouth felt like cotton. "She belongs to the sheriff now."

Pup began to whine, pushing herself back against the corner where two walls meet.

Harry stared at the coyote pup. "Go on and cry, you little bitch. You and I have some unfinished business."

Sweat covered Jed's face. "You boys go on and get out of here before the sheriff comes back."

Harry gave Jed a look. "You crazy old folks, you ain't gonna shoot no one." Then he looked at the coyote and stepped toward the cell. "But, I'm gonna shoot myself a little bitch coyote."

Jed saw Harry's hand reach the butt of his pistol. His heart pounded, his head throbbed, and he couldn't suck in enough air.

Harry drew his pistol, cocking the hammer as it cleared the holster.

Jed knew Harry was going to shoot Pup.

Harry was so close to the barrels of the shotgun that he never heard the blast that knocked him five feet past the desk and onto the floor ending up against the leather sofa. The room was deathly quiet as the smoke slowly rose out of the barrel of the shotgun. Jed's mouth was open, and he had a surprised look on his face while sweat ran down his forehead and neck, soaking the collar of his new shirt.

The other three turned from Harry and looked at him. "You crazy old bastard!" yelled Brodie.

Jed pointed the shotgun at him. "I'll kill you, Brodie, if you draw down on me. I swear I'll kill the first one who draws." Jed Canon wanted to run away, but there was nowhere to run, and figured he and Pup were both dead.

The door opened, and Morgan walked in with his gun drawn.

Jed started to point the gun in Morgan's direction, but the cell bars prevented it.

Morgan's gun went to Brodie. "What's going on, Jed?"

"Harry was gonna kill the sheriff's coyote pup."

Brodie pointed at Jed and yelled, "That crazy old man killed Harry!"

Morgan looked at Harry's bloody body, having forgotten how much damage a shotgun at close range could do, and then he looked at Jed. "What happened?"

Jed looked scared. "He was gonna kill Pup."

Morgan motioned to the body with his pistol. "Get your friend out of here."

Brodie looked at Jed. "You crazy bastard, you killed a man over a damn coyote." He had a mean look on his face. "This ain't over."

Morgan shoved the barrel of his big Navy Colt into Brodie's face. "Unless you want another mouth, it is for tonight."

Brodie looked at the barrel of the pistol that right now seemed awfully big, gave a last angry look at Jed, and then he and the other two men picked Harry up and carried him outside. Morgan followed them out the door and onto the boardwalk, where he watched them load Harry's lifeless body over the saddle of his horse. After tying it down, they swung up onto their horses and rode out of town with Harry in tow.

Morgan watched them until they disappeared into the darkness, then waited until the sound of their horses' hooves faded before he stepped back inside.

Jed stepped out of the cell, looking afraid. "He was gonna shoot the sheriff's coyote." He looked back at Pup, cowering in a puddle under the cot next to the wall, and then at Morgan. "I didn't know what else to do." Looking afraid and regretful, he leaned the shotgun against the cell. "They're gonna hang me, ain't they?"

Morgan felt sorry for the old man but had no words of comfort for him. He looked down at the bloody floor, contemplating the question, and then at Jed. "Where's Emmett?"

"I was just about to go find the sheriff when they came in."

Morgan looked worried. "They wouldn't come for the coyote unless they knew Emmett wasn't here." He looked at Jed. "Stay here and lock up after me and put another shell in that shotgun."

"Where you going?"

"To look for Emmett." Afraid something terrible had happened to Emmett, Morgan hurried along the boardwalk, which was coming alive with a few of the curious asking what happened.

"A gun went off accidentally!" yelled Morgan. "No one's hurt, so you can all go back inside!" He rushed along the dark street, running from dark corner to dark corner, looking for some sign of Emmett. As he ran down the center of the street, looking here and there, he saw something lying on the boardwalk. He ran over, knelt, and picked up Wade's hat. Holding it in his hands, he glanced around, fearing the worst, then hurried along the boardwalk and disappeared into the small walkway between two buildings.

Reaching the alleyway, he saw what looked like a dog standing in the middle of the dark alley and drew his pistol, thinking it strange that the dog never ran away or barked. Then hearing what sounded like soft moaning, he realized it was Emmett, rushed to him, and knelt. "It's Morgan," he said as he dropped the hat, holstered his pistol, and put one arm under Wade's shoulders.

"I'm hurt bad, Morgan."

"What happened?"

Wade could barely speak. "Got jumped by Brodie and them others."

Morgan helped him stand, and as Morgan put Wade's right arm around his shoulder, he said, "I'll get you back to the jail, and then send for a doctor."

Wade looked around into the darkness. "Where's my hat?"

Morgan put one hand against his chest to steady him. "I have it." Then he bent down, picked up the hat, and put it on Wade's head.

"My gun," said Wade as he glanced around.

Morgan thought it was like dealing with a drunk as he looked around in the dim moonlight. Seeing it on the ground a few feet away, he said, "I'll get it."

Wade watched on unsteady feet while Morgan picked up his gun and shoved it into his holster.

Not sure how badly he was hurt, Morgan put one arm around Wade's waist, pulled Wade's right arm around his shoulder, and slowly walked up the small passageway toward the street. "I better get you to a doctor."

No," protested Wade, fearing for Jed and the coyote pup. Barely able to speak through bruised and bloody lips, he told Morgan to take him to the jail. "I heard a gunshot."

"Jed killed Harry Anderson."

Wade stopped and looked at Morgan with his one good eye. "What?"

"Let's keep going," said Morgan, and as they walked, he told Wade about the four bursting into the jail. "Harry was gonna

146

shoot that coyote of yours, so Jed unloaded a shotgun on him before he could."

Wade let out a small chuckle. "Good for Jed" Then, looking concerned, asked, "Is he all right?"

"He's fine," said Morgan as he stopped to look at Wade in the light of a window. His left eye was swollen shut, his lips were cut and bleeding, and his face was bruised and cut. Then he saw the gaping cut along his jaw. "What the hell did they do to you?"

"Knife," replied Wade in a tired, raspy voice thinking of Seth's bad eye. "Shit," he said softly. "I was kind of looking forward to killing the son of a bitch myself."

"Well," said Morgan as he helped him along the boardwalk. "There's three more."

Though it hurt like hell, Wade managed a smile. "Looking forward to it."

"I'll get you to your bed, and then I'll get the doc. Now no more talking, Emmett. You need to save your strength."

Wade stopped.

Morgan looked at him, fearing he was going to pass out.

Wade hung on to Morgan's shirt, leaned closer, and looked at him with his good eye. "If I die, kill the bastards."

Morgan chuckled. "Consider it done." He helped Wade along the boardwalk to the jailhouse, where he knocked on the door. "Jed, open up."

When Jed opened the door, "Good Jesus" is all he could say as he looked at Wade's swollen eye, bloody face, and torn shirt. Then he set the shotgun down and put Wade's arm over his shoulder to help Morgan get him to his bed.

Wade looked at Jed with his good eye. "Thanks for saving Pup."

Jed didn't respond as he helped Morgan walk Wade to the bedroom.

As they passed, the coyote whining and scratching at the bars of the cell, Wade looked down, thankful she was still alive.

147

After they gently laid him on his back in his bed, Morgan looked at Jed. "Go get the doc."

Jed nodded and hurried toward the bedroom door.

Pup continued her whining and scratching at the bars, only now her whining was louder and faintly resembled a coyote cry. It was beginning to get on Morgan's nerves, so he turned and yelled after Jed, "Shut that damn coyote up!"

"No," said Wade in his low, raspy voice as he grabbed Morgan's arm and looked past him at Jed. "Let her in."

Morgan looked back at Jed. "Get the doc. I'll take care of the coyote." Morgan walked into the other room, opened the door to the cell, and the coyote pup bolted between his legs straight into Wade's room. When Morgan got to the bedroom door, she was on the bed cuddled next to Wade, licking his face and softly whining. Morgan thought it was unnatural.

Wade pulled Pup away from his face, held her against his body, and as she settled against him, he closed his eyes, drifted off to sleep, and never heard her growl protectively at Morgan.

Morgan and Jed were sitting in the Sheriff's office drinking coffee while the doc tended to Wade, but only after Jed removed the coyote from the bedroom, where she had held Doc Reid at bay by showing her sharp puppy teeth. She protested with mean growls as Jed put her in the cell, but she eventually lay down on the floor next to the bars where she could keep an eye on the bedroom door.

The floor had been cleaned of Harry Anderson's blood, and the shotgun was back in the rack. Jed was sitting on the sofa drinking his coffee, worried about what would happen to him for killing Harry Anderson over the coyote.

Morgan sat in the sheriff's chair, worried about Emmett, and knew Jed was concerned over his fate.

Jed took a drink of coffee. "Doc sure is taking a long time in there."

Morgan turned his head toward the door, causing the chair to moan. "Sure is." Then he looked at the blinds covering the front window seeing the morning sun against it. "Sun's up."

Jed leaned forward, rested his elbows on his knees, and looked into his cup of black coffee. "They gonna arrest me, Mr. Hunter?"

Morgan thought about that. "Can't say for sure, Jed." His chair moaned as he stood, stretched, and walked to the front door, where he raised the blinds and looked out at the deserted street. He turned away from the window, noticing the barrel of a pistol under the desk, walked over, and picked it up.

"What ya got there?" asked Jed.

Morgan smelled the barrel and then opened the cylinder. Finding one spent cartridge, he looked at Jed. "Whose gun is this?"

Jed stood and walked over to Morgan and looked at the gun. "Don't know." Then he looked at him. "Hey, do you suppose that's Harry's gun?"

Morgan looked at the gun. "Where was Harry standing when you fired?"

Jed thought a moment and then pointed to a spot on the floor. "Right about there. Why?"

Morgan looked at the spot and then at the spot in front of the sofa where Harry ended up after Jed shot him. "I don't think you have to worry about getting hung, Jed."

Canon looked at Morgan. "Why not?"

Morgan walked to the spot where Harry had been standing and curiously looked around, then opened the cell door, stepped inside, walked toward the far wall, and began examining it.

Jed walked to the cell and watched him with curiosity. "What ya looking for?"

Hunter was running his fingers across the wall and then stopped, leaned closer, and put his fingers to the wall. After a moment, he stepped away and turned to Jed. "I'd say this gun, and

149

that bullet hole says you killed Harry in self-defense. He got off a shot about the same time you did."

"I never heard him fire his gun."

"Don't doubt that," said Morgan as he stepped out of the cell, allowing the coyote to bolt past him to the bedroom door, where she began scratching at it.

Morgan started for the coyote, but before he could pick her up, the door opened, and she disappeared between Doc Reid's legs.

Startled, the doc looked down at the blur running past him, then watched as she jumped on the bed and lay down next to a sleeping Wade Garrison. Thinking they would be alright, he stepped out of the room with his black bag in his left hand, his coat draped over his forearm, looking tired. He quietly closed the door and set his bag on the desk, his coat on top of it, noticing the gun in Morgan's hand. Instead of asking about the gun, he asked Jed if there was any coffee.

Jed said there was and began to pour a cup while Doc rolled down his sleeves and buttoned them. Anxious to hear about Emmett, Morgan put Harry's pistol in the top drawer of the desk and then sat down. Jed handed the cup of coffee to Doc, who had sat down in one of the two empty chairs in front of the desk, while Jed returned to the sofa. Doc Reid tasted the coffee, thinking it was terrible, but it was hot, and he couldn't be choosy. He looked at Jed and then Morgan. "The Sheriff's hurt bad. The cut on his chin took twenty-three stitches." He looked at Morgan. "Came damn close to his jugular." He took a drink of coffee. "The cut above the left eye, three, the one under the eye, another five. I put seven more above his left ear." He paused, looking worried. "He's lost a lot of blood and is pretty beat up, not to mention some badly bruised ribs and bruises on his back. Both arms are bruised as well. My guess is he was covering his head with them. I put a bandage over his left eye so's to help with the swelling, but I couldn't do much about his cut lips." He looked at his coffee. "He's a mess."

150

"He gonna be all right?" asked Morgan.

Doc looked at Morgan with a worried look. "I'm concerned over his previous wounds that opened up again from the kicking he took. I had to stitch part of them up again, and I'm afraid of infection."

The room fell silent as Morgan looked at Jed and then at Doc. "What other wounds?"

Reid looked surprised. "You didn't know?"

Morgan leaned on the desk with his elbows. "Know what, Doc?"

Reid regretted saying anything but saw no need to keep it a secret now. "Sheriff Spears was shot in the shoulder and left side a while back and was just healing." He sipped the coffee. "I warned him when he came to see me about taking it easy for a while."

Morgan thought back to that first day, recalling Emmett moved a little cautiously but dismissed it at the time, thinking he was naturally slow.

Reid put the cup down, stood, picked up his coat, and slipped his right arm into the sleeve. "I left some laudanum for the pain on the dresser. See that he gets a spoonful every few hours to keep the pain away." He slipped his other arm in and then shrugged into his coat. "Don't overdo it. That stuff is habit-forming and dangerous."

A worried Morgan stood. "All right, Doc."

Jed stood, looking worried.

Reid walked to the door, opened it, looked out at the street filled with the morning dawn, and turned to Morgan. "That young man took a pretty good beating. I'll stop by later today after I have a rest and some breakfast."

After the door closed, Jed turned as Morgan carefully opened the bedroom door to take a quick look inside the dim room. Wade was resting, and Pup was lying next to him. She raised her head, looked at Morgan briefly, and then laid her head back down and closed her eyes. Morgan stared at the coyote,

151

thinking it wasn't natural, closed the door, and walked to the sofa. "I'm gonna stretch out for a couple of hours."

Jed was a bit tired himself, and while Morgan lay down on the sofa, he locked the front door, made sure the back door was locked, and pulled the blinds. He started for his cell and bed but paused to look at Morgan, who had already drifted off. Thinking Morgan may get chilly, Jed got a blanket from the other cell, covered him, and then Jed quietly pulled the loaded shotgun off the rack and walked into his cell. Glancing at Morgan once more thankful he was here, Jed laid down, covered up with a blanket, and closed his eyes.

Chapter 12

Pounding on the door startled Morgan from a sound sleep. Sitting up, he tossed the blanket Jed had covered him with, then stood and reached for his holstered pistol lying on the desk. Drawing the Colt, he heard a voice yell, "Jed, open up!"

Morgan glanced at a sleepy Jed standing in the doorway of his cell, holding the 12 gauge shotgun across his body, looking fearful. "Stay put." Then he yelled, "Who is it?"

"Mayor Smith, Jed! Open up!"

Morgan walked to the door, parted the blind enough to see two unfamiliar faces and the banker, Jonathan Moore. "Just a minute." He lowered his pistol and opened the door.

"Who might you be?" asked the mayor as all three rushed in.

Morgan nodded to Jonathan Moore. "Mr. Moore."

"Mr. Hunter," replied Moore.

Mayor Smith looked from Morgan to Jonathan Moore. "You two know one another?"

Moore looked at Smith. "Mr. Hunter and I met yesterday when he opened an account at the bank. He's considering buying the Chandler place."

Morgan held out an open hand to Smith. "Name's Morgan Hunter."

Smith shook the hand. "Robert Smith, Mayor of Pickering." Then he gestured to the third man. "This is Earl Noonan. He runs the barbershop down the street."

Morgan shook Noonan's hand, turned, and walked to the desk where his empty holster lay and shoved his pistol into it. As he turned, he noticed the clock on the far wall said it was eight-thirty. "What can I do for you, gentlemen?"

"How's the sheriff?" asked Mayor Robert Smith as the three walked toward the desk.

Morgan walked to the potbellied stove. "I see you've heard the news." He picked up the coffee pot and looked inside.

Smith asked again. "How is the sheriff?"

Finding the coffee pot empty, Morgan looked disappointed as he turned and softly said, "The sheriff's resting," He set the pot down and looked at Jonathan Moore. "How'd you learn about the sheriff?"

"The doc stopped by Robert's store," said Moore, then he gestured to the mayor. "Then Robert came to us."

"Do you know how it happened?" asked Noonan.

Morgan nodded. "Four men attacked him while he was making his evening rounds."

"Just the same as Sheriff Cole," said Smith.

Morgan looked puzzled. "Who was Sheriff Cole?"

Mayor Smith looked at Morgan. "Carl Cole was sheriff before Mr. Spears. He was beaten pretty badly and left town soon after."

Morgan looked curious. "Was Emmett aware of that?"

Smith nodded. "He was. I told him myself when we hired him."

Morgan looked from one to the other. "Any idea who beat up Sheriff Cole?"

Moore shook his head. "He wouldn't say."

Smith looked up. "Does Sheriff Spears know who did this to him?"

Knowing that Emmett wanted to handle this when he was well enough, Morgan lied. "He hasn't said." Then he looked at Jed, standing at the cell door holding the shotgun. "Jed, would you make some coffee?"

Jed nodded, put the shotgun down, and headed for the stove and empty coffee pot to fill it with water.

Morgan knelt next to the potbellied stove and filled it with wood and kindling while talking. "The doc says Wade will be all right." He struck a match on the stove side, lit the kindling, closed the door, and stood.

Jed returned from outside with a coffee pot filled with water and placed it on the stove.

Smith looked disappointed. "I suppose he'll be leaving soon as he can ride."

Morgan thought about that while watching Jed pour coffee grounds into the coffee pot, thinking the coffee would be strong. He turned to Smith. "I doubt it."

Smith and the others looked surprised. "You think he'll stay?" asked Smith.

Morgan thought about what Wade had said when he was helping him back to the jailhouse. "He won't run." Then he stood and walked around the desk and sat on its corner, glancing from one to the other. "There's something else you need to know." Morgan went on to tell about Brodie and his men walking into the jail, intent on killing Wade's coyote pup. "Harry drew his gun, and Jed shot him with the shotgun." Then he went on to tell of finding the gun and its spent cartridge and the bullet hole under the window in the cell wall where the coyote was hiding.

Mayor Smith looked at Jed standing by the stove, waiting for the coffee to boil. "Sounds to me like it was self-defense, Jed. Being the Judge of Pickering, as well as the mayor, I'm declaring it as such in front of witnesses."

Jed sighed with relief.

Noonan looked at the mayor. "What about the men who beat up Sheriff Spears?"

Mayor Smith looked uncertain. "Can't do much of anything until the sheriff's well enough to say who they were." He looked at Morgan. "You sure he didn't say who they were?"

Hunter looked thoughtful as he walked back to the swivel chair and sat down. "If he did, I didn't hear it. Emmett was pretty bad off last night."

The room fell silent, and then Smith said, "That's too bad."

"Even if we did know," said Morgan, "who'd arrest them? The three of you?"

"I see your point," said the mayor.

Noonan looked at Smith. "We could deputize Mr. Hunter until the sheriff's well enough."

"That might be a good idea anyway," agreed Moore. Then he looked at Morgan. "If you'll take the job."

"I'm not a lawman, Mr. Moore," replied Morgan. "The only thing I plan on doing right now is making sure nothing else happens to Emmett until he heals, and I don't need a badge for that."

The mayor started to say something when the door opened, and Doc Reid walked in. He paused a moment glancing from one to the other, closed the door, and after saying good morning, he asked how the sheriff was.

"Still resting," said Morgan.

"He gonna be all right, Doc?" asked the mayor.

Doc looked worried. "I'm sure he will, but it will take some time. He's in serious condition." Saying nothing more, he walked into Wade's bedroom and closed the door. Moments later, the sound of the coyote growling brought a smile to Morgan's face as he looked at Jed. "Get the coyote so Doc can take a look at Emmett."

Jed disappeared into the room and returned with a growling, fighting Pup in his hands. "I'll just take her out back to do her business."

The mayor watched Jed and the pup as they walked by then looked at Moore and Noonan. "Well, gentlemen, let's get about our own business and let the doc tend to our sheriff." As they got to the door of the jailhouse, Mayor Smith turned to Morgan. "You sure you won't take the deputy job until the sheriff heals up?"

Hunter smiled. "I'm sure."

Smith nodded, looking disappointed. "We would appreciate it if you would let us know how the sheriff's getting along."

"I'll do that."

As they left, Jed walked in with Pup.

Morgan watched as Jed put Pup in the cell then turned toward the stove. "I need a cup of that coffee."

Morgan was sitting in the swivel chair and Jed on the sofa when Doc Reid stepped out of the room with his suit coat draped over the same arm holding his black bag. He had a solemn expression as he closed the door, and both Morgan and Jed stood with a worried look. "He's resting comfortably," said Reid while he walked to the desk and set his black bag down. "Rest is the best thing for him right now. There's no sign of fever, and that's good." He started to put on his coat but paused. "He got hit pretty hard on the head, so one of you needs to check on him every couple hours. Just shake him gently, so he stirs a bit, and check to see if he's got a fever. If he gets a fever, one of you come and get me at once. I don't care what time of day or night it is."

Hunter nodded his understanding. "All right, Doc."

Reid shrugged into his suit coat and picked up his bag. "The sheriff needs some nourishment. I'll stop by the café and see they fix him something bland, not greasy, and have them bring it over in a couple of hours. I just gave him some laudanum, so he'll sleep a bit." Doc Reid walked to the front door and looked back. "I'll stop back later and see how he is." He opened the door and paused, looking back at them. "That man's body is full of bruises like he'd been in a stampede." Doc Reid turned and shook his head in disgust. "Bastards." Then he stepped outside.

Hunter looked out the window above the sofa, watched the doc walk across the street toward Laurie's Café, and decided to look in on Emmett.

Seeing Morgan open the door to Wade's room, Pup started whining and howling. Feeling sorry for the animal, Morgan opened the cell door, and as he reached down to pick her up, she darted past and headed for the bedroom.

Morgan hurried after her, and upon entering the bedroom, saw that Emmett was sleeping comfortably with the coyote curled up against him. Still thinking it was unnatural, he closed the door and strapped on his gun.

"Where you going?" asked Jed.

"Nowhere." Then he poured himself a cup of coffee and sat down at the desk.

Jed considered that then walked into his cell to get the shotgun he left leaning against the wall to put it away when the front door opened. A big man dressed in an expensive suit stepped inside, having the look of a politician, followed by a younger man.

The big man looked at Morgan. "You, the sheriff?"

Hunter sat back, put his feet on the desk, and adjusted his pistol. Looking up at the man, he picked up his coffee cup, not much caring for the man's attitude, then sipped his coffee. "Nope."

Big Ben Croucher, as they called him, was just that. He was a big man over six feet, with broad shoulders and a robust chest. The suit he wore fit well, as did his hat and boots. His neatly cut dark hair had a hint of gray. He was clean-shaven except for a thin mustache under a broad nose. He glanced around. "Where is the sheriff?"

"He's sleeping," replied Morgan.

"What the hell's he sleeping for?" asked the big man. "Wake the man up and tell him Ben Croucher wants to talk to him."

Morgan recalled the name from his conversation with Mr. Moore at the bank and understood Kyle Chandler's dislike of the man. He'd seen lots of men like Ben Croucher with big egos and large appetites and knew the best thing to do when they were upset was to distract them. "He belong to you?" Morgan was looking at the younger man standing behind Croucher.

Big Ben turned and looked. "My son, Harold."

Harold Croucher was a young man of twenty-three, built big like his father with dark brown hair and eyes. He sported a handlebar mustache, but instead of wearing the fancy clothes like his father, he wore clothes of a working man, which told Morgan that Ben Croucher was not the kind of man to spoil his children.

Morgan lifted his coffee cup to his mouth, noticing the new shiny Colt pistol in a new oiled holster the younger Croucher wore. "There's a bit of resemblance, I guess," offered Hunter.

"Some say there's quite a bit of resemblance," offered Croucher proudly. "And men usually stand when I'm talking to them."

Morgan took a drink of his coffee. "Well, I'm a bit tired, Mr. Croucher. You see, I had a bad night, so I'm sure you'll understand me not getting up."

Croucher's face reddened, and then he noticed Jed standing in his cell. "Well, I see he's been arrested."

Morgan glanced at the cell and Jed. "Who?"

Ben looked confused. "Him, damn it," he said, pointing to Jed Canon. "The man who killed one of my men."

Hunter looked at Jed and then at Ben. "Oh, he's not under arrest. He works here."

Fed up with getting nowhere, Croucher started toward Wade's door. "I'm gonna wake the sheriff and see about this."

Morgan slipped out of the chair with coffee in hand and stepped in front of him. "Sorry, Mr. Croucher, but you're not going in there."

Ben's face turned a dark red, and his chest swelled. "Who's gonna stop me?"

Hunter set his dented, tin coffee cup on top of the stove and looked at Mr. Croucher. "I will." Morgan noticed Harold's hand move toward the butt of his pistol. "If you want to walk out of here, Harold, I suggest you keep your hands from the butt of that shiny new Colt pistol you have."

Ben turned. "Take it easy, son. We didn't come here looking for trouble." He turned his attention to Morgan. "Just who the hell are you?"

"Name's Morgan Hunter, Mr. Croucher." He looked into the big man's dark eyes. "You may run the men that work for you and your son, but you don't run me."

Croucher smiled wryly. "I can see that."

Morgan settled down, took a breath, and let out a soft sigh. "I don't mean to be disrespectful by stopping you from going in to see the sheriff, but he's in a bad way. And I'm a little overprotective at the moment."

"Why didn't you say so in the first place?" asked Ben with a concerned look. "What's wrong with the man?"

Morgan stared into the big man's dark eyes, wondering how much he knew. "Some men jumped the sheriff while he was making his rounds last night and beat the shit out of him." Morgan picked up his cup from the stove and sat down on the edge of the desk. "One of them used a knife and cut his face up."

Ben sat down in the nearest chair, looking upset. "Who'd do such a thing?"

Morgan wondered if it was just an act. "You look surprised."

Croucher looked up with defiance. "I am surprised."

160

Morgan stared into Croucher's dark dyes. "I understand this same thing happened to the previous sheriff."

"Well," said Ben thoughtfully. "I guess it did, but I had nothing to do with either incident. I'm responsible for a lot of things that go on around here, but neither was my doing."

Morgan looked at Harold. "You ever say anything?"

Big Ben looked at his son. "He talks when I tell him to." Then he pointed at Jed. "I'm sorry about the sheriff, but what about him?"

Morgan shrugged. "It was clearly a case of self-defense."

"That's not what my men tell me," Ben said angrily.

"And of course, your men are honorable, truthful men," said Hunter.

Ben stared into Morgan's cold, dark eyes. "Just who are you, anyway?"

"I done told you. Name's Morgan Hunter."

"Just what is it you do around here?" asked Ben, looking curious.

"Right now, it's looking after my friend, the sheriff, and I'll kill any man that tries to cause him harm." He paused. "And I don't care who that individual is."

Croucher glanced at his shirt, seeing the absence of a badge. "Are you the deputy? If not, what do you do?"

"I'm not a drover, Mr. Croucher. Ain't a dirt farmer neither, nor a businessman, and no, I ain't the deputy."

"You ain't answering my pa's question," said Harold.

Morgan glanced at Harold and then looked at Big Ben. "I believe your pa knows what I do, Harold."

Ben Croucher looked at the big Navy Colt Pistol and fancy holster sitting across Morgan's belly. "Where are you from, Mr. Hunter?"

"Texas."

Ben thought about that for a moment. "That's a long ride for someone without an occupation."

"What makes you think I don't have an occupation?"

Ben Croucher looked at Morgan's graying hair. "Aren't you a little old for that line of work?"

Morgan smiled softly. "I'm not past my prime if that concerns you, Mr. Croucher. Some have made that same mistake."

"Maybe," replied Ben in thought, then looking angry, said, "I feel bad about the sheriff, and I'd appreciate you telling him so. But you tell him that I said if Jed Canon ain't arrested soon, I'll have my men arrest him."

Morgan considered that quickly. "That sort of thing usually leads to a lynching."

Ben stood taller. "He shot one of my men in cold blood."

Morgan opened the top center drawer of the desk and pulled out a pistol. "You recognize this, Mr. Croucher?"

"Can't say I do."

Morgan put the gun back. "Four of your men burst in here last night. I don't know if they were all liquored up or just plain crazy. Maybe both, but it was soon after the sheriff was beaten up pretty bad, and your man Harry drew this pistol, and Jed pulled the trigger of his twelve-gauge."

Croucher considered that only a moment. "Why would Harry draw his pistol?"

Morgan glanced at Jed and then looked at Ben. "To kill a coyote pup, the sheriff bought off of him."

"Well, I was told different," said Big Ben.

"I'm sure you were," said Hunter. "But consider this, if Jed shot Harry in cold blood, how did his pistol end up under this desk after he fired a bullet from this gun that's still lodged in the far wall of that cell?"

Ben considered that for several moments.

Harold quickly offered, "Maybe Harry drew as he fell backward."

Surprised that Harold spoke, Hunter looked at him. "That's a good theory, but there's a problem with it. Being hit by a twelve-

162

gauge shotgun at four feet blows the life right out of a man. He doesn't have time to react." Morgan looked at the elder Croucher. "Harry never had time to draw, cock his pistol, and fire after he got shot. He drew first, thinking that old man over there didn't have the sand to pull the trigger. Well, he was mistaken, and now he's dead instead of Jed and the sheriff's pup coyote, which is what those men of yours were trying to do."

"My men tell it differently," said Ben Croucher stubbornly.

Morgan looked angry. "Screw your men, Mr. Croucher. From what I've heard in my short stay in Pickering, your man Brodie and his friends are just a bunch of bullies that you can't control."

Croucher raised his voice. "What my men do on their own time is no concern of mine!"

Morgan looked at Ben Croucher and raised his voice. "It is when they pull this shit, and you should know it! If not, then you're not the man I heard you were."

Croucher was not used to being talked to in this manner, so he turned toward the door. "Come on, Harold; we'll not get any justice here."

Hunter watched them walk out and wondered how much sand Mayor Smith had, and then he turned to Jed. "I'm gonna check on Emmett."

"You sure told him," replied Jed with a big grin. "Want me to go across the street and get us something to eat?"

Morgan thought for a moment and became worried that some of Harry's friends might try and take Jed out of town and hang him. "No, I think it best that you stay inside. I'll go over after I check on Emmett." He gestured toward the windows. "And keep them blinds closed."

Chapter 13

Three days had passed since the night of the incident in the alley and Jed, killing Harry over the coyote. Doc Reid made visits each morning and evening, and he was pleased with how well Wade was getting along. On occasion, the mayor would stop by and ask about the sheriff, and he never mentioned Ben Croucher, and neither did Morgan or Jed Canon.

On the afternoon of the third day, Jed took the coyote out back to do her business, put her back on the bed with Wade, and quietly shut the door. He poured himself the last of the coffee, and in the stillness of the room, he sat down in the creaking swivel chair. Holding the cup in both hands on his lap, he thought about the night he killed Harry Anderson. A soft tap at the window of the front door seemed loud in the stillness of the lonely jailhouse. Jed slowly stood while setting the cup on the desk.

Eyeing the door and drawn shade, he took the twelve-gauge from the rack behind the desk, made sure it was loaded, and walked cautiously to the door. He stood there a moment with his hand on the blind and was about to look out when he heard Morgan tell him to open up. Jed moved the blind enough to see Gin's smiling face from Laurie's Café, so he unlocked the door, opened it, and stepped back.

Gin was carrying a tray of food covered with a towel, and Morgan another. She smiled as she walked by. "Hello, Jed."

"Howdy, Miss Gin," replied Jed while catching a whiff of whatever was under the towel.

Morgan set his tray on the desk next to the other tray. "How's Emmett?"

"Seems okay. I took Pup out for her business not long ago, and when I put her back in the room, he was still sleeping."

Morgan walked to Wade's door, opened it a crack, and peered inside, seeing that he was resting easy with the coyote curled up next to him, so he closed the door.

Gin smiled at Morgan. "If there's nothing else, I best be getting back."

Morgan escorted her to the front door, where she paused, saying she hoped the sheriff would recover soon, and then stepped out onto the boardwalk. Morgan watched as she stepped into the street before he closed the door and returned to the trays on the desk. He took the towel off of the tray containing a large bowl of soup, a spoon, and a dish of scraps for the coyote. "I'm gonna see if I can get Emmett to eat." Then he told Jed to sit down and eat.

"Ain't you eating?" asked Jed.

"I ate at the café." Hunter went into the bedroom with the food, closed the door with one foot, and walked to the chair next to Wade's bed. Having smelled the food, Pup watched with anticipation as Morgan set the bowl and spoon on the chair and then placed the plate of scraps on the floor. She jumped down and began eating while Morgan looked down at the bruised face of his friend. The head bandage was gone, as well as the one covering his left eye, but the eye was still swollen and bruised. He picked up the bowl and spoon, then sat down, leaned toward the bed, and gently put one hand on Wade's shoulder. "Emmett," he said softly.

Wade slowly opened his good eye, clearly confused.

Morgan looked at Wade's deep red injured eye, unable to see any white in the eye. "Hungry?"

Wade's voice was hoarse. "No."

Morgan noticed the blood spotted bandage that covered his jaw and cheek. "You have to eat something, Emmett." Then he set the bowl and spoon on the dresser and helped him sit up enough so he could eat. "Doc's orders."

"What's that sound?" Morgan looked down at the coyote pushing her empty plate across the floor. "She was hungry." He saw a hint of a smile on his friend's face, then he turned and picked up the bowl and spoon then turned to Wade. "You need to eat."

Wade watched Morgan dip the spoon into the bowl and stir the soup. "Tell me that's not chicken soup again."

Pleased he was regaining a little of his sense of humor, Morgan chuckled. "Beef."

"Any beef in it?"

Hunter handed the bowl and spoon to Wade. "I'm sure there's a big piece in there somewhere."

Wade moved the spoon around in the soup. "Don't see it." Then he started eating, being mindful of his swollen cut lips.

Morgan sat back in the chair, watching while Wade slurped the soup from the spoon, leaving some on his chin. He reached over with the napkin and wiped it off.

Wade moved his head away as a child would.

Hunter chuckled and thought of his younger brother. "You've been doing some talking in your sleep."

Wade was curious. "Like what?"

"Oh, several names like somebody names Hoskins, Sarah, and Emmett, mostly." He looked down at the coyote, licking her plate. "You say Sarah more than the others."

Wade continued eating. "I say anything else?"

Morgan picked up Pup's empty dish and looked around for somewhere to set it. "Quite a lot, actually."

That made Wade more curious.

Hunter set the plate on the dresser. "You mentioned a burning building— a house maybe— and you kept saying you were sorry about something."

Suddenly Wade wasn't hungry, put the spoon in the bowl, and handed both to Morgan.

"Finished already?" asked Morgan as he took the bowl and turned to put it on the dresser while talking. "You also mentioned Friendly's once or twice. I heard a story about a place with that name when I passed through Laramie."

Worried that he may have said too much, he listened as he stared at the far wall.

Morgan continued. "Seems the place burned down a while back. You also mentioned Billy French. There aren't a lot of Billy French's, but there is one who happens to be the US Marshal in Santa Fe."

Wade looked surprised. "You know Billy?"

"He rode with a couple of Texas Rangers a couple of years back on the heels of some outlaw he was after. Had a drink with them in a saloon."

Wade remembered Billy's trip into Texas, trailing a man who killed a young girl while attempting to rob the bank in Santa Fe. Wanting to end the conversation, he looked at Morgan. "I'm tired."

Morgan stood and picked up the laudanum and gave Wade some in a spoon, then picked up the dishes. "I'll let you get some sleep." He started to leave but paused and looked at Wade. "I am curious about something."

"What's that?" asked Wade, not really wanting to hear what it was.

"Once you mentioned Emmett being killed. Did you know someone else named Emmett?"

A mixture of fear and anger filled Wade. "You just come in here and listen to me talk in my sleep?"

The outburst caught Morgan by surprise, and he gave Wade a look. "I heard you talking and came in to see what you wanted. You were talking in your sleep. Of course, I was curious. Who wouldn't be? No one's sneaking in here to listen to your jabbering. Don't go making more out of it than what it was." Then he turned and walked toward the door saying in a cold voice, "I'll check on you later."

Wade watched Morgan close the door and felt terrible about getting mad, but at the same time, he was worried and was sure Morgan was curious. Wade reached down, petted the coyote that had jumped back upon the bed next to his stomach, and wondered if Morgan would put two and two together. His mouth hurt, and so did his back and shoulder, but now the laudanum made him tired, so he closed his eyes and slept.

Wade next opened his eyes, needing to visit the outhouse. He called out, and moments later, the bedroom door opened, and Morgan poked in his head.

"I have to go."

Morgan walked across the room and started to bend down for the pan under the bed when Wade protested. Morgan insisted, but Wade said he wanted to go outside. Thinking Wade was stubborn, Morgan helped him with his boots, thinking Wade looked funny in his long underwear and boots. Then with Wade's arm around his shoulder, he helped him stand.

Wade looked down at the coyote, thinking she needed to go outside. "Come on, Pup." With the help of Morgan, he walked into the outer office and asked what time it was.

"Still early," replied Morgan. "Hold up a minute while I get my boots on."

Wade leaned against the desk and looked down at the checkerboard. "Who's winning.

Jed looked up. "Morgan, everything all right?"

"Everything's fine," replied Morgan as he pushed his boots on. "Emmett has to go to the bathroom."

Canon watched as they walked toward the rear door wondering why the sheriff didn't use the mug under the bed.

Pup followed them to the outhouse, and while Wade took care of his business, Morgan watched the coyote sniff the weeds and dirt, looking for a place to go. The sun was just about gone, leaving behind a hue of rose and orange colored buildings among dark shadows. Noises from the street spilled over the roof of the jailhouse, bank, and gunsmith shop. Hearing a noise near the rear of the bank, Morgan's hand quickly found the butt of his Colt. Seeing something tiny moving in the shadows next to the building's wall, he stepped a little closer, seeing it was a small skunk. He reached down and picked up Pup. The coyote growled, wanting down, but he held her firmly until the skunk disappeared under the gunsmith shop next door. He looked at the coyote and her black eyes. "That's all I'd need."

With Wade settled back into bed, Hunter returned to the office, sat down at the desk, took a drink of his cold coffee, and made idle conversation with Jed Canon while they continued their game of checkers. Jed considered his next move at checkers, and Morgan had just swallowed the last of his cold coffee when a knock came at the door. Morgan looked at Jed, motioned toward the door, sat back in the chair, and pulled his gun halfway out of its holster.

Canon went to the door, lifted the blind just a little, peered outside, then turned to Morgan as he opened the door. "It's Doc."

Reid stepped in and asked of no one in particular, "How's the sheriff?"

"He ate most of his soup," said Morgan. "After I gave him some laudanum, he slept until a while ago, when I helped him make a trip to the outhouse. I just got him settled back into bed."

Reid looked puzzled. "Why didn't you use the mug under the bed? After all, that's what it's for."

169

Morgan felt agitated. "He wanted to use the shitter instead. Wouldn't listen."

Reid raised his brow. "That's a good sign. It means he's getting his strength back. I best take a look." He glanced at the checkers as he set his bag down and slipped out of his heavy coat, wondering whose move it was.

Morgan watched the doc. "The bandage along his jaw has some blood soaking through."

Doc Reid made a mental note of that as he placed his coat in one of the chairs, picked up his black bag, walked into Wade's room, and closed the door. Hearing muffled voices, Morgan stood to pour a cup of coffee but found the pot empty.

Jed got up, saying he'd make a fresh pot, but Morgan said he would.

"That's my job," said Jed as he took the pot and headed for the pump out back.

Morgan took a seat in the swivel chair, put his feet on the desk, and turned his thoughts to the ranch he had bought two days earlier. He was anxious to start his new life and looked forward to his partnership with Jessup Thornton. The thing of it was he couldn't leave Wade helpless and Jed in danger of being lynched with Brodie and the others still around.

Jed returned with the water and went about making coffee, sat down, and studied the checkerboard.

Morgan thought about the town council asking if he would take on the duties of deputy until the sheriff was feeling better. He didn't want to be shackled with laws that, most of the time, were inadequate for what he had to do. The sound of boiling coffee running down the side of the pot onto the hot stovetop took Morgan from his thoughts.

Jed stood and hurried to the stove, grabbed an old rag, and moved the pot to the side where there was less heat so the grounds would settle to the bottom of the pot. "Coffee?" he asked.

The door to Wade's room opened, and Doc Reid stepped out, closed the door, placed his black bag on the desk, and shrugged into his coat. "Has a bit of a fever, but I don't think we need to concern ourselves at this point. If it gets worse or he starts getting delirious, come get me." He buttoned his coat and picked up his bag. "I changed the bandages on his jaw, shoulder, and side." Reid slipped on his leather gloves while eyeing Morgan. "The sheriff needs to stay in bed a few more days, but maybe he can take some short walks and get some fresh air in a day or two. A walk to the outhouse is just the thing."

"All right, Doc," said Hunter as he stood to walk Reid to the door.

"Almost forgot," said Reid. "The sheriff wants to see you."

Curious what Emmett wanted, Morgan opened the door and stuck his head inside. "Doc says you wanted to see me?"

Wade was sitting up in bed, resting against the pillow and petting Pup that lay beside him. "I do, Morgan."

Hunter stepped in, closed the door, and walked across the room.

Wade gestured to the chair. "Have a seat."

Wondering what was on Emmett's mind, Morgan moved the chair closer to the bed and sat down, then he reached out and petted the coyote.

"Sorry about earlier."

Morgan sat back and grinned forgivingly. "No need."

The room was quiet as Wade looked at Morgan. "I never worked on a ranch in Santa Fe, Morgan. I was Billy French's deputy."

That was a big surprise for Morgan. "What the hell are you doing in Montana?"

Wade knew it was time for the truth. "Running away as any outlaw would."

Puzzled, Morgan asked, "Running from what?"

Wade spent the next hour telling Morgan who he really was, what happened after he made the trip north to Harper right up until the two met. When he finished, he let Morgan digest the story.

Morgan stood looking bewildered. "I need a drink. Be right back."

Wade waited while Morgan walked into the other room, hearing the desk drawer open and then close.

Morgan walked back into the room, carrying a bottle of whiskey and two tin cups. He pushed the door shut, walked across the room, sat down, uncorked the bottle, and poured a drink. "I was gonna pour you one but remembered you're on laudanum, so you'll just have to watch me drink."

Wade smiled and watched Morgan gulp the whiskey, pour another without looking at him and place the bottle on the floor next to his chair.

Morgan looked at Wade with a frown. "That's one hell of a story."

"I guess it is," replied Wade hoping he hadn't misjudged Morgan.

Hunter looked a little puzzled as he took another drink. "I ain't sure what the hell to call you. Wade doesn't feel right."

Wade grinned. "It took some getting used to at being called Emmett for me as well."

Morgan smiled. "I bet." He took a drink and stared into his cup in thought. He considered all that Wade had told him, then pulled the locket out of his pocket and opened it. "My wife, Ana, and our son, Vance."

Wade looked at the picture. "She's pretty. I was curious about that locket."

Morgan stared at the picture, looking sad. "She's dead now."

Wade looked sorry. "And your son?"

Hunter closed the locket. "He's with someone who will take better care of him than I could." He returned the locket to his shirt pocket and took a sip of whiskey as he sat back in the chair. "I worked for a wealthy rancher in the Texas Panhandle whose name's not important, nor what I did for him. But I can tell you that over the years, I earned a lot of money doing some things I'm not too proud of." He paused in thought then smiled. "A few years back, I met a Mexican girl named Ana Ramos. Her pa owned a little store in the town of El Pamito, and he wasn't too keen on the idea of a gringo courting his daughter." He chuckled. "You should have seen the look in his face when I asked for his daughter's hand." He grinned shyly. "You see, not only was I a gringo, but I was a few years older than Ana. For some reason, her mother liked me, and somehow the two of them worked on Mr. Ramos, and eventually, he consented to the marriage."

Morgan took a small drink of whiskey, looking sad. "Soon after we were married, I quit working and bought a small spread along the Punta de Agua River, south of El Pamito in the Texas Panhandle." He sipped his drink and then continued. "We had a son we named Vance Juan Hunter, after my pa and Ana's father. Mr. Ramos was happy about that because he had three daughters and no sons." His expression turned sullen. "Little over two years ago, we had just finished our dinner when two men rode up and asked if they could bunk in the barn. I had a funny feeling about the two, but they looked harmless enough, so I agreed. Ana, being the kind and thoughtful person she was, offered to fix them something to eat."

Morgan paused to take a drink, and at seeing his cup was empty, poured a little more whiskey into it, put the bottle down, and took a small drink. "After they ate, I walked them out to the barn, and after saying goodnight, I turned to leave when one of them hit me over the head. When I woke up, it was dark, and I was groggy but managed to get up, staggered out of the barn, and made my way to the house. I found Ana lying on the floor." He looked at Wade. "She'd been beaten and raped."

Thinking of Sarah and Emmett, Wade asked, "What about your son?"

Morgan looked down into his cup. "I didn't think of Vance for a few moments; I was so upset and fearful for Ana that I grabbed a cloth and dipped it in some water, and started cleaning the blood from her face. She opened her eyes, said his name, and that's when I got scared and went looking. I found him hiding in his room where he had been crying, and his little body trembled as I picked him up." He paused. "He hugged me with those little arms of his as I held him. I didn't want him to see his mother, so I comforted him a few minutes, put him into his bed, and then covered him."

He sipped his drink and let out a soft sigh. "When I returned to Ana, the Good Lord had taken her." Morgan paused for several minutes. "I sat on the floor and held her in my arms, crying like a child, and I either passed out or went to sleep, but when I opened my eyes, the sun was coming up, and little Vance was crying in the next room. I covered my wife with a blanket, got Vance, saddled my horse, and rode into El Pamito." He looked at his drink. "The news almost killed Mrs. Ramos. She took little Vance in her arms and cried while Mr. Ramos hitched up his wagon, and then he and I returned to my place. When he saw Ana, he sat down next to her, held her hand, and cried. Ana was buried the next day in the graveyard behind an old mission church at the edge of town."

Wade sat back on the pillow feeling sorry for Morgan and wishing he had some words of comfort but knew of none.

Morgan started to refill his cup but changed his mind and set it down next to the bottle. "I told Mr. Ramos that I was going after the two men. He wanted to come along, but I told him that I could travel faster by myself, and I didn't want to worry about him getting killed. Not knowing if I'd ever return, I signed the ranch over to the Ramos family and left Vance with them. I said goodbye, closed my bank account in El Pamito, and headed out with a packhorse. I stopped at every town I found but never saw them. A few months passed, and I was about to quit the hunt when a man at a livery in the town of Good Luck told me he shod a big yellow a couple of months back. I asked if he knew where they were heading, and he said he heard the one riding the brown, saying he'd be glad when they were back in a place called Deer Creek."

Wade was familiar with the place. He and Billy French had trailed three men there a few years back. It ended badly with French getting wounded in a gunfight and the deaths of two of the men they were after, but the third got away and rode out of town. Wade had followed as far as the Rio Grande but never followed into Mexico. He always hoped the bastard would find a little Mexican justice someday.

Morgan continued. "It was early morning when I rode into Deer Creek. I was tired and hungry, and so were my horses, so I put them up in the livery, had a good hot meal, and then checked into a hotel. When I woke up, it was dark, so I got up off the bed, walked to the window, looked down on the street, and saw several horses at the hitching rails on both sides of the street. I checked out of the hotel and then walked the street, looking for the brown horse and the big yellow. I walked through the town and back without finding either, so I decided to go to the livery, saddle my horse, and load up the packhorse. When I finished, I decided to get a beer, so I left my horses in the livery and went into the saloon and get a beer. I took a small table, ordered a beer, and was thinking about what I was going to do next when they walked in the place."

Morgan looked at Wade. "I about fell off my chair. They didn't see me, or if they did, they probably never remembered who I was, so I watched as they walked up to the bar and ordered beers. I started to get up when they saw a couple of men they must have known sitting with a couple of whores, walked to their table, and sat down. I sat drinking my beer and watched as they talked and laughed with the others at the table, having a good time." He paused in thought for a moment. "All of a sudden, I found myself standing, and as I walked toward them, the one with blonde hair looked up just as I drew my pistol and shot his friend in the back of the head, splattering his face all over the table. The place went silent as the one with blond hair knocked over his chair as he stood going for his gun. He never cleared leather. I shot him in the chest, knocking him back over his overturned chair. I can still see the surprised look in his eyes."

He looked at Wade. "I often wonder if he even knew who I was. The other two stood and, thinking they were going for their guns, and I shot 'em both." Morgan looked regretful. "Turns out, they were unarmed." He paused a moment. "I walked around the table and looked down at the one with blonde hair. He was still alive, coughing up blood and gasping for air as he looked up at me." Morgan paused. "I don't know if he recognized me, but I said, 'This was for my wife, Ana.' Then I cocked my gun and put another bullet in his right cheek." Morgan sat for a moment, staring at the corked bottle of whiskey he was holding. "The place was quiet as death as I turned and walked out the door and headed for the livery. I climbed up on the Appaloosa and was riding out with my packhorse when the sheriff and his deputy rode up with guns drawn, yelling for me to climb down. I knew I had just killed two innocent, unarmed men and would hang for that." He paused. "I was sorry for what happened, but I wasn't about to go to jail for killing the bastards who beat and raped my Ana. I was full of hate that night, and I didn't care if I lived or died, so I drew and killed them both."

Wade felt bad for Morgan thinking of what evil things the Bradly brothers had done.

Hunter looked bewildered. "I don't think they expected me to draw. Neither fired their pistols." He paused and looked at

Wade. "I rode out and headed west but turned north at the first river to cover my tracks." Quiet filled the room while Morgan stood and put the chair back against the wall, reached down, and picked up the bottle and cups. "That was a little over a year and a half ago." He looked down at Wade. "It won't be me who judges you for what you've done."

"Think you'll ever see your son again?"

Morgan thought about that for a moment, looking sad. "Probably not, but I know he has a good home, and that's a comfort." Then he said goodnight and walked out of the room, leaving Wade to consider all he had told him.

Jed opened his eyes, glancing around the dim jailhouse, thinking he should open the blinds and let some light inside. Feeling the early morning chill as he pushed the covers back, he thought of a fire in the potbellied stove and tossed his legs over the bed. Touching the cold wooden floor with his feet, Jed stood wearing only his faded red underwear. Wrapping himself in his arms, he rubbed his shoulders briskly while looking into the next cell at a lump of covers that was Morgan. Canon dressed, put his shoes on, built a fire in the potbellied stove, filled the coffee pot with water then poured in a handful of coffee grounds. When he finished with that, he peered in on the sheriff and quietly called the young coyote to take her outside.

Seeing she was ignoring him, he quietly called her again in a little louder voice.

She looked at him for a moment deciding if she wanted to get up, then she slowly stood and stretched, then jumped off the bed.

Jed wished she would hurry.

Pup stopped to scratch her neck and ear, yawn as she stretched again, and then slowly walked past Jed out of the room, obviously in no hurry.

Jed closed the door, walked her down the hall toward the back door, noticing that Morgan had not moved, and when he opened the back door, a scene of white snow and brisk cold air greeted him. Pausing in the doorway to take in the scene of white, quiet snow, he thought that winter had finally arrived and already wished it was spring. Stepping out into the soft snow, Jed turned and saw that Pup was hesitant. Realizing she had never seen snow before, he picked her up and carried her to a clear spot next to the door of the outhouse, set her down, then opened the door and went inside.

Pup was curious about the white snow and sniffed at it cautiously. The flakes of snow falling that disappeared into the white snow got the better of her, and she followed one flake right into the snow with her nose. Surprised at the cold, wet stuff, she jerked her head back, looked at it, and then jumped back into a fighting stance letting out a soft growl. Watching another flake falling, she growled then jumped on it as it landed.

"What's going on out there?" asked Jed.

The coyote pup stopped her assault on the snow, looked at the closed door of the outhouse, squatted, and did her business.

Jed stepped out of the outhouse, buttoning his trousers as he looked down at the yellow spot and tiny footprints in the snow, but Pup was nowhere to be seen. Fearing she had run off, he called for her as he followed her trail to the rear of the outhouse, finding her busy chewing a twig sticking out of the snow." Leave that alone," he scolded. "Let's get back inside; it's too darn cold to play right now."

She jumped up and bounded playfully in the snow on the way to the door of the jailhouse, bringing a smile to Jed's face. Once inside, she shook off the wet snow and then bolted for the bedroom. By the time Jed got to the doorway, she had laid on the bed next to Wade, licking her wet paws. Seeing she hadn't disturbed Wade, he built a fire in the small potbellied stove that sat in the corner of the bedroom then checked on the coffee. It hadn't started boiling yet, so he opened the door on the side of the potbellied stove, added more wood to the fire, and then walked to the front door. Parting the blind just enough to see, he peered out at the white street that carried no signs of horse or wagon tracks. The covered boardwalk was clean of snow except for what had drifted along the edges.

Seeing smoke rise from the chimney of Laurie's Café across the street made him think of breakfast when the bedroom door opened.

Wade leaned against the door jamb, looking at Jed. "I've got to go."

"Can't you use the pot?" asked Jed as he let go of the blind.

Wade shook his head. "I want to go outside."

Noticing Wade was barefooted, Jed said, "You need your boots. It snowed last night."

Wade looked down at his bare feet and then at Pup a few feet away, staring up at him. He turned and slowly walked back into his room for his boots.

Jed followed and helped him with his boots, helped him outside, and then back to the bedroom, where Jed helped him back into his bed. Fearing he would get a chill, Jed made sure he was covered and then checked the stove and added a little more wood. Pup jumped up on the bed and curled up next to Wade, who had already drifted back to sleep. Jed closed the door, and when he checked on the coffee, it was boiling, so he moved the big gray pot to the edge of the stove and reached for an empty cup.

Morgan walked out of the cell, looking sleepy. "How's Emmett?"

Jed turned. "I helped him to the outhouse and then put him back to bed." He gestured outside. "Snowed last night."

Looking surprised, Morgan walked to the window of the front door, pulled the blinds back, and looked outside. "Isn't it a little early for snow?"

Jed was in the process of pouring two cups of coffee. "I've seen it snow in September lots of times and as late as June." Jed shrugged while handing Morgan his cup. "Don't think it'll stay long, though."

Hunter turned from the window and took the cup, thinking about the land he bought. "Will you be all right by yourself for a few hours?"

Jed looked curious. "S'pose so. I'll keep the shotgun loaded and handy and the door locked."

Morgan set his cup down on the edge of the desk and shrugged into his sheepskin coat. "Make sure you don't shoot Doc."

A grin filled Jed's face.

"I'll go get our breakfast," said Hunter, "and if you feed Emmett, I'll be on my way."

It was close to noon when Morgan pulled his horse up in a small clearing near the Thornton's log ranch house, set in a white scene of October snow. White, lazy smoke drifted from the chimneys that quickly disappeared into the gray sky and thought of a cup of hot coffee. The Appaloosa blew a soft neigh of white breath in the chilly air and shook his head, rattling the reins and bridle. He nudged the horse into a walk through the snow chasing their white breath toward the covered porch and front door.

Jessup Thornton opened the door. "Thought that was you," he said, looking concerned. "Come in out of the cold." Then he stepped away from the doorway, yelling over his shoulder, "Ma, come see who's here!"

Hunter tied his Appaloosa to the porch post, stepped up onto the porch stomping the snow off of his boots. He walked across the porch stepping inside to the friendly warmth of the big room. He glanced at the fireplace filled with wood and dancing flames while Jessup took his hat, gloves, and coat and placed them on a nearby chair.

Mrs. Thornton was standing by the table that separated the small living room from the kitchen. "Good day Mr. Hunter."

Morgan smelled something cooking. "Good day, ma'am."

Recalling that he was from Texas, Louise smiled. "How do you like the snow?"

Morgan grinned. "To be honest, Mrs. Thornton, I wasn't expecting it quite so soon."

"It's September," she said. "We've had snow on the ground in early September before, but this one will be gone in a day or two." She looked from Morgan to her husband. "You two talk while I get on with my cooking."

Jessup pointed to a chair. "Have a seat."

Instead, Morgan walked to the big stone fireplace and stood close to the flames with his hands held out to warm them.

"What brings you out this way?" asked Thornton.

Morgan looked into the flames while his hands felt the warmth of the fire. "I bought the Chandler place."

Jessup looked pleased, and then his face filled with a grin as wide as any Morgan could remember seeing in quite a while. "Did you hear that, Mother? Morgan, done, bought the Chandler place."

Mrs. Thornton stepped from the kitchen and looked at Morgan. "Is that true, Mr. Hunter?"

He smiled. "Yes, ma'am."

"Well," she said, "you can tell us all about it over lunch."

Jessup headed for the front door. "You go get settled at the table, Mr. Hunter, while I put that fine horse of yours in the barn out of the cold. I'll see he has a nice blanket over him and a feed bag of oats."

As they ate the meal prepared by Louise, they talked about the land, cattle, and other things that made idle conversation interesting. After they had eaten, Morgan took a drink of coffee and thought of Wade, and decided he would continue to call him

Emmett. He told the Thornton's about meeting up with Emmett in Pickering, the coyote pup, of Emmett being beaten, and of Jed killing Harry Anderson over the coyote.

Mrs. Thornton looked regretful. "Not that I ever liked that Harry Anderson, but I'm sorry to hear he died in such a manner."

Jessup sat back with a worried look. "Sounds like a hell of a lot of trouble this Emmett has gotten himself into over a coyote." He looked at his wife and then Morgan. "Hell, everyone knew who beat up Sheriff Cole and ran him out of town." He shook his head, looking disgusted. "The council's no match for the likes of Francis Brodie and them others."

Morgan chuckled as he repeated, "Francis Brodie."

Thornton nodded with a sly smile. "He sure hates the name."

Hunter laughed softly. "Francis just doesn't seem to fit the big bastard." Then he looked at Mrs. Thornton and apologized for the language.

She smiled. "Heard that plenty from Jessup."

Jessup chuckled. "His pa sure had a sense of humor, all right." Then he looked concerned. "I sure hope this Emmett fella is going to be all right."

"He'll be fine," said Morgan. "Besides riding out to tell you I bought the Chandler place, I needed to tell you that I have to stay with Emmett until he can get on his feet."

Thornton thought about that for a quick moment. "You take care of your friend. We can always take care of business in the spring."

"Well," began Hunter, "I'd like to pay you for the hundred head now, and we can sort them out this spring."

"That suits me," said Jessup. "Come spring, we'll divvy up the new calves as well."

Hunter held out his hand. "Deal." They shook hands across the table while Morgan told him that he would deposit the money into his bank account when he got back to town. Then he gently slapped the table with both hands. "I best be heading back." Feeling happy about the whole thing, he stood looking at Louise. "Thanks for the meal, Mrs. Thornton."

She smiled. "Any time. I have a feeling we'll be seeing a lot of one another from now on."

Morgan grinned. "Looks that way."

Jessup stood. "I'll help you with your horse."

Chapter 14

September

The September landscape covered in a sea of white snow quickly turned to drab gray as evening approached. Morgan recalled Mrs. Thornton saying the early snows didn't stay long, but the sun hadn't shown itself all day. It remained hidden behind the gray clouds that covered the top of the mountain range to the west, low hills to the east, and everything in between. The crunching of snow under the Appaloosa's hooves broke the quiet morning, and not a bird sang, nor a squirrel chattered.

When he reached the hill overlooking Pickering, the sky and snow were the same mixture of light and dark grays. The night was rapidly approaching, and the dark buildings of town and their lighted windows of kerosene lamps lit the way. Instead of riding through town, Morgan rode the outskirts to Bennett's livery, where he apologized to Albert for having to roust him out of his warm house. After tending to the Appaloosa with food and water, he covered her with a horse blanket he borrowed from Albert Bennett. Then he checked the packhorse and Wade's mare, making sure both had food, water, and a blanket.

Chasing his breath as he walked along the lonely street to the sound of snow crunching underfoot and the sight of orange-colored shapes of doorways and windows that spread across the snow-covered street, he worried about Emmett. Stepping onto the boardwalk in front of the Gunsmith, he walked a little faster toward the door of the Sheriff's Office. Pausing at the door, he looked along the quiet, snow-covered street at a few horses with heads hanging, tied at the hitching rail outside the saloon. "Jed, it's Morgan."

Jed hurried across the wooden floor, pulled the blinds back, and looked out the window. Seeing it was Morgan, he opened the door.

Morgan Hunter stepped inside, feeling the warmth of the room, and immediately asked about Emmett.

Jed closed the door. "He's fine."

Morgan placed his hat on the edge of the desk, followed by his gloves, then stood by the potbellied stove to warm his hands.

Jed helped Morgan off with his sheepskin coat. "He had a good supper," said Jed. "He wanted to know where you were, so I told him you went out to the Thornton place." Canon looked worried. "I hope that's all right."

"It wasn't a secret." Morgan walked to the door of Wade's room and took a peek inside.

Wade was sitting up in bed with Pup curled up next to him, and upon seeing Hunter, he motioned him into the room.

Hunter walked in, moved the chair next to the bed, sat down, and touched Wade's forehead. "How are you feeling?"

"Feeling a little better every day."

"Doc been by?"

"Just before supper." Wade grinned. "Said I could eat something besides soup." He pointed to a plate of food sitting on the dresser.

Morgan smiled. "Doesn't look like you ate very much."

Wade pointed to the cut along his jaw. "Hurts when I chew."

Thinking it probably did, Morgan smiled, "It'll get better."

Wade pointed at the dresser. "Give me a half spoon of laudanum." After he swallowed it, he looked at Morgan. "Jed said you went out to the Thornton place."

Morgan nodded. "I rode out to tell Jessup I closed the deal on the Chandler ranch." He looked at the young coyote, and when he looked at Wade, his eyes were closed. He turned down the lantern on the dresser then put a couple of small logs in the potbellied stove to feed the fire. Then he picked up the plate of cold food, stepped out of the room, quietly closed the door, set the food down on the desk, and opened the bottom drawer.

"It's empty," said Jed.

Morgan closed the drawer, thinking he needed a drink.

"I'll go get us a bottle if you want," offered Jed.

Morgan considered the offer. "I'll go. I don't think it's a good idea for you to go into the saloon just yet."

"You're probably right," agreed Jed, who didn't want to venture out in the cold anyway.

Hunter picked up his black, wide-brimmed hat from the edge of the desk and headed for the door.

"Don't you want your coat?"

"It's a short walk." Morgan opened the door, put his hat on, stepped outside, and hurried across the snow-covered street, being careful not to slip and fall.

Stepping onto the boardwalk, stomping the snow from his boots, he stepped inside, greeted by the warmth of the saloon.

Goody was talking to another customer, and upon seeing Morgan, he pulled the towel off his left shoulder and wiped the bar down. "How's the sheriff?"

Morgan smiled with a quick nod. "He's getting better."

"Glad to hear it," said Goody. "What'll it be?"

"Whiskey."

Goody tossed the towel over his shoulder, put a glass on the bar, took a bottle from under the bar, and filled the glass.

Morgan gulped it down, made a face, and asked for another.

Dave obliged, which Morgan also gulped down.

Dave smiled. "Best take it easy, Morgan. This shit sneaks up on you." He quickly added, "How about a sandwich with the next one?"

Remembering he hadn't eaten since the Thornton's, he pushed the empty glass away. "Make it a beer with that sandwich."

Goody grinned. "I'll pour that beer and get one of the girls to fix you a sandwich."

Morgan watched Dave pour the beer, then took the mug and headed for an empty table away from the others, where he could eat in peace and think about the ranch. He tossed his hat on the edge of the table, sat down, and took a drink of beer. The minutes passed, and soon one of Dave's girls approached the table carrying a plate with a sandwich.

She looked at him with smiling blue eyes as she set the plate down.

"How much?"

She smiled with a sexy look. "For the sandwich?"

He grinned with a small chuckle. "Yeah, the sandwich."

Looking a little disappointed, she told him how much. "My name's Estelle. Want some company while you eat?"

Morgan handed her more than enough for the sandwich, pulled the plate closer, and lifted the bread to see what was underneath. Not sure what was between the slices of bread, he looked up at her, thinking she was pretty. Her light brown hair flowed over her bare shoulders, and the green blouse she wore was open too far down the front exposing more than he wanted to see. Thinking she had the kind of hips made for childbearing, he smiled. "Nothing personal, but I'd rather eat alone so I can think about something."

"I understand," she said, looking disappointed. Then she smiled and gestured toward the table where the others were sitting. "If you change your mind, I'll be over there."

He glanced at the table and then looked up at her. "Thanks for the sandwich." As he watched her walk away, he picked up the sandwich, opened it up, and smelled the meat. Believing it was okay, he took a bite finding the bread a little on the dry side. As he flushed it down with beer, his thoughts turned to Emmett across the street, lying in bed. Emmett reminded Morgan of his younger brother Bobby, and maybe that was why he liked him. As he took another bite of the sandwich, his memory went back to that warm spring afternoon when he and Bobby were sitting by the stream not far from their father's farm, fishing. Their chores done, they were doing what they enjoyed doing on those lazy warm Oklahoma afternoons.

Being brothers, they often fought or argued, and Morgan couldn't remember what their argument was about that day when Bobby got mad and headed home. Recalling his brother's words, "I never want to see you again, Morgan!" And his reply, "That'd be too soon for me! Go on, run home to Mama, you big baby!" After Bobby disappeared into the trees, yelling something Morgan couldn't quite hear, he turned back to the river, pulled his battered straw hat down over his eyes, and leaned back against a tree.

Sometime later, he sat up with a start knocking his straw hat off, and looked around for what it was that had awoken him. It was quiet, and only the sounds of the river and buzzing insects filled the otherwise quiet, warm afternoon. The sun was low in the sky and hidden behind the trees on the other side of the river, and he knew it was getting close to suppertime. Feeling a bit hungry, Morgan put on his hat, picked up his fishing pole, and started home. He had walked only a short distance when the distinct sound of several gunshots broke the stillness of the heavy late afternoon air.

Afraid to move, he saw plumes of smoke rise above the trees at the end of the field in the direction of the house. Gripped with fear, he dropped his pole and ran across the small meadow, losing his hat he never stopped to pick up. Reaching the tree line, he stopped short of the fields he and his pa had plowed weeks earlier, which now carried the green haze of the summer crop. Hiding in the trees, he watched as several mounted men sat their horses in front of the burning house. He saw Bobby run out of the house toward the barn, followed by a man who raised his pistol and shot Bobby in the back.

Stunned by what just happened, young Morgan crawled further back into the trees and watched the man climb up onto his horse and ride away with the others. As they disappeared around a bend beyond the barn, Morgan ran across the field, knelt next to his brother, and turned him over, asking if he was okay. Bobby opened his sleepy eyes and softly said, "Morgan." Then Bobby closed his eyes, and his body went limp.

Morgan's eyes welled as he looked at the hole in his brother's bloody shirt where the bullet had come out. As his eyes welled with tears, he gently shook his brother. "Bobby," he said tearfully. "Bobby, wake up." Knowing his brother was gone, Morgan stood and looked at the house with smoke billowing from the windows and doorway. Thinking of his ma and pa, he ran inside the burning house, calling out. Making his way through the smoke to the hall and then to his parent's bedroom, Morgan found his mother lying on the floor with her bloody clothes in disarray. Grabbing her wrists, he pulled her out of the burning room, along the hall, and out the front door placing her body next to that of his brother Bobby.

Leaning over her, he touched her face and cried out, "Ma, wake up!" It was then that he saw that she had been shot twice in the chest. Knowing she too was dead, he looked around for his pa, and not seeing him, he stood and called out, "Pa." Running toward the barn, he found his father inside lying next to one of the stalls, shot several times in the chest and face.

When he buried his family, Morgan Hunter was seventeen. He shoved his pa's old pistol under his belt and rode away on the plow horse, searching for the men who killed his family. He followed them out of Oklahoma, losing their trail somewhere in the Texas Panhandle. Tired and hungry when Morgan rode into a small town, an old man took pity on him and gave him work in his livery. He never forgave himself for not continuing his pursuit and often thought about the argument with his younger brother Bobby that day.

Laughter from the doorway spilled across the room, pulling him back from those sad memories. As he looked up, Brodie and the other two men who were with him the night Jed shot Harry Anderson walked up to the bar ordering beers. Morgan thought of Emmett lying in bed across the street and hoped he would take care of the asshole once he healed. If not, he was looking forward to it himself.

Estelle was sitting at a table near the piano that was minus its player. Seeing Brodie, she smiled as she slid out of her chair and approached Brodie. After giving her a quick look up and down, Brodie put his arm around her, pulled her close, and whispered something in her ear that caused her to giggle. She nestled under his arm next to the bar and took the beer out of Brodie's hand. He watched as she set it on the bar, took his hand, then led him to the stairs and up to a room on the second floor.

Morgan leaned forward, rested his elbows on the table, and looked down at what remained of his beer. He let his thoughts return to the ranch imagining herding cattle along the lake that Jessup said was full of trout, thinking that maybe he could be happy here. Sitting back in his chair, Morgan thought of the one thing that was missing, took the locket out of his shirt pocket, opened it, and gazed at the picture of his wife and son. Filled with hate for the men who had killed her, he placed the open locket on the table next to his beer recalling happier times.

A slightly overweight blonde girl approach the table and set a mug of beer down.

Not recalling that he ordered another beer, he looked up with a puzzled expression.

She smiled. "Dave thought you needed another."

Morgan glanced at Dave, tossed some money on the table, and thanked her.

She reached down and picked it up, noticing the locket and picture setting open on the table. "Pretty girl, your wife?"

Morgan handed her his empty mug. "Thanks for the beer."

Thinking he seemed a little unfriendly, she walked toward the bar.

Hunter returned to the locket, picked up his beer, and took a drink while thinking of his wife and son. In his mind's eye, he saw his son laughing while being chased by his Grandfather Ramos when they would visit before everything went wrong in his life. He often considered returning to El Pamito one day to see his son, but deep down, he knew he never would.

Dave Goody was at the table. "How we doing, Morgan? Another beer?"

He looked up then at the half mug of beer sitting in front of him. "I'm fine."

Seeing the open locket, Goody bent down and looked at the picture. "Who's the pretty woman?"

Hunter looked at it and smiled in memory. "My wife."

"Pretty. How come she ain't here in Pickering with you?"

"She's dead," said Morgan softly.

Dave Goody looked at Morgan, staring down at the locket, not knowing what to say but thinking that the beer and whiskey were taking a toll on him. "I'm sorry, Morgan. I didn't know."

Morgan looked up and smiled. "It was a long time ago, Dave."

"Think maybe you've had enough, Mr. Hunter?"

Irritated at first, Morgan looked up at Goody with a scowl but then smiled and shrugged. "Maybe you're right, but I need a bottle to take along so Jed can have his drink before going to bed."

"Won't be but a minute," said Dave, then he turned and headed for the bar and the bottles of whiskey stored under it.

Brodie and Estelle walked down the stairs to the table where the others were, and as Brodie sat down, he pulled her onto his lap. He laughed at something she whispered in his ear as he watched Dave returning to the bar. "Another round of beer barkeep."

"In a minute," said Goody as he walked behind the bar, bent down, and came up with a bottle of whiskey he took to Morgan under the watchful eye of Brodie.

As Dave walked back to the bar, Brodie looked at Morgan, who was staring at something he was holding in his hands, and yelled over his shoulder at Goody, "Where's our beer?"

"They're coming," replied an irritated Dave Goody.

"Well, get the damn lead out," laughed Brodie, then he smiled at Estelle and pulled her closer. "We're thirsty."

Morgan looked up at the big white face on the clock above the bar next to the buffalo head and imagined Jed anxiously waiting for the bottle of whiskey so he could have his coffee and whiskey before going to bed.

Todd touched Brodie's arm while pointing to Morgan. "Ain't that the guy who came into the Sheriff's Office the night that damn Jed Canon shot Harry?"

Brodie looked at Morgan, remembering him pointing that big colt pistol at them. "Let's have a little fun with the old boy." Then he told Estelle to get up.

Morgan drank the last of his beer, and as he set the mug down, he noticed Brodie and the other two walking toward his table and knew from their expressions they weren't going to buy him a beer. He picked up his hat, put it on, and sat back in his chair away from the edge of the table. As they approached the table, he looked up and smiled. "Something on your mind?"

"What's on my mind?" asked Brodie. "I'll tell you what's on my mind. It's that piece of shit across the street still breathing while Harry's pushing up daisies."

Morgan's eyes went to Jimmy, then Todd, and then he smiled as he looked up at Brodie. "I'm not the person you should be discussing that with."

Brodie frowned. "You trying to be funny?"

Morgan shook his head and looked from one to the other. "No, I'm not trying to be funny. I'm just telling it like it is. I'm not the law."

Brodie chuckled without humor. "You sure acted like it the other night, busting in with that big pistol of yours, giving orders."

Todd and Wilson chuckled as the three looked at one another.

Morgan wanted to punch the bastard in the face but knew he didn't stand a chance with all three, and besides, he figured Brodie would have his day once Emmett was up and around. "I was just trying to keep someone else from getting killed."

Brodie noticed the locket, quickly reached down, snatched it up from the table, and looked at the picture. "Lookie here, boys," he said while showing it to the others. "We have a picture of pretty Mex and some kid."

"I'd like to have that back," said Morgan in a soft voice.

Brodie frowned. "We ain't done looking just yet."

Dave Goody had been watching from the bar and yelled across the room. "I don't want any trouble tonight, Brodie."

Brodie turned, giving Dave a dirty look. "Stay out of this, Goody, and keep that damn shotgun under the bar. I'm tired of you pulling it every time we try and have a little fun."

Morgan glanced at Goody then sat back in his chair, so the grip of his Colt was away from the edge of the table.

"Sexy little señorita," said Wilson. "I could go for her myself."

Brodie chuckled as he looked at Morgan. "Ain't she a little young for you, old man?" Then he laughed.

Morgan looked from Wilson to Brodie, "If you don't mind, Mr. Brodie, I'd like my locket back now."

Brodie looked at the others as he grinned with a chuckle. "And if I do mind?"

Morgan slowly lifted his hat off with his left hand and held it just above the top of the table. They watched the hat and not his right hand, which had moved to the grip of his pistol. "Guess I'll have to take it, but first I have to ask you a question."

"Yeah, what's that?" asked Brodie.

Morgan smiled. "Why would any loving father name his son Francis?"

Dave Goody heard what Morgan had said and knew there would be trouble, so he set the bottle of whiskey on the bar and reached for the shotgun under it.

Morgan looked into Brodie's eyes for that tell a man always has just before he draws. "Your move Francis, if you have the guts." Then he dropped his hat, which the other two looked at, and drew his gun before Brodie ever cleared leather. Morgan's Colt exploded, and the force of the .45 slug hit Brodie's big gut.

Brodie managed to get off a wild shot that hit the wall behind Morgan as he fell backward, crashing over a table and chairs, dropping his gun. In an instant, Morgan turned to Todd and pulled the trigger as Todd managed to clear leather. The force of the .45 in the gut sent Todd back over a chair that Brodie had tipped over when he fell. Todd's shot went wide, shattering a small window in the back of the saloon. Morgan quickly turned to Jimmy, standing with his knees slightly bent, his hand just above his pistol as if he were about to draw. He looked at the big Navy Colt's barrel pointed at his stomach, and slowly put his hands up. "I ain't drawing."

"How about it, Son?" said Morgan angrily as he stood and kicked his chair away for the table. "Go for it, you little shit. I'd like nothing better than sending you to hell with the others."

Jimmy looked at Brodie and Todd lying dead on the saloon floor in a puddle of blood. Then he looked at Morgan. "I ain't drawing."

"You're sweating, sonny," said Morgan as he stared at him while holstering his big Colt. "Go for it, you little bastard. You just might get lucky and outdraw me."

Jimmy shook his head. "No, sir. I ain't drawing."

Goody stood behind the bar, stunned at what Morgan just did to Brodie and Todd.

Morgan stepped closer and slapped Jimmy with his left hand. "You cowardly little shit, I said go for it."

Jimmy looked into Morgan's eyes, knowing he'd kill him in an instant. "I ain't drawing."

Morgan slapped him again and then yelled, "Draw, damn you!"

"That's enough!" yelled Dave Goody.

Morgan turned, seeing Goody and his double-barreled shotgun pointing at him over the bar.

Dave motioned toward the door and said in a calm voice, "Pick up your bottle Morgan and go. You've made your point."

Morgan looked at Brodie and Todd lying on the floor, blood oozing from their wounds, and then at Goody. "They had to push it."

"I know," said Goody. "They been asking for that for a long time. Guess they messed with the wrong man."

"I just wanted what was mine," said Hunter. "I didn't want this tonight."

Goody nodded his understanding. "I know, now go on get out of here."

Morgan looked at Jimmy Wilson. "There's a man across the street who wanted this pleasure once he was up and around."

He smiled. "He'll mend soon, and then he'll come looking for you, you little piece of shit." He reached down and took Jimmy's gun from its holster, unloaded it, and tossed it across the room while dropping the cartridges on the floor. "That' so you won't find that piece of bravery and shoot me in the back." Then he walked to where Brodie was lying, knelt and took the locket out of his hand, then stood and put it into his shirt pocket.

"I believe you have what's yours, Mr. Hunter," said Dave.

Morgan looked at him. "I do."

Goody nodded toward the door. "Time to leave, Mr. Hunter."

Morgan walked to the bar, picked up the whiskey bottle, turned, and looked at Jimmy Wilson. "I'm sure you'll be hearing from the sheriff soon. I know for a fact that he's looking forward to it. Be interesting to see how brave you are now that your friends aren't around." Morgan glanced at Goody, still holding the shotgun across his chest, nodded, and then headed for the door.

Jed was full of questions about the gunshots when Morgan walked into the jailhouse, then followed him to the desk and watched as he set the bottle down.

Not wanting to talk to Jed about what happened, he took off his hat. "There's your whiskey for your coffee Jed."

Jed forgot about the gunshots and grinned as he picked up the bottle, pulled the cork off, poured some whiskey into his cup, and then topped it off with coffee.

Morgan sat down in the swivel chair with a troubled look.

Jed turned to him. "Everything alright, Morgan?"

He looked at Jed and only nodded. He didn't want to kill Brodie and Todd Young. He had hoped he'd left all of that behind him.

Jed could tell he was bothered by something. "That was the last of the coffee, but I'll make a fresh pot if you want."

Morgan shook his head no as he stood. "I'm gonna check on Emmett and then turn in."

Wade was sitting up in bed, resting against his pillow, when Morgan opened the door.

Morgan was surprised at finding him not sleeping. "You're awake?"

"Have been for a while," said Wade. Then looking curious, he said, "Heard some shooting earlier."

Morgan closed the door, walked to the chair under the window, moved it next to the bed, and sat down. Already knowing the answer, he asked, "Thinking about Sarah and your son?"

Wade looked at him and could see he was troubled about something. "Everything all right?"

"I had to kill Brodie and Todd Young tonight."

Feeling a little jealous, Wade looked at him. "So that's what all the shooting was about. Mind telling me what happened?"

"I was sitting in the saloon, they were drunk, and one thing led to another." He shrugged. "Brodie went for his gun."

Wade looked disappointed. "I get the shit kicked out of me, Jed shoots Harry, and you kill Brodie and Todd Young." He paused. "Doesn't seem fair somehow."

Morgan smiled just a little. "I know you wanted them for yourself, Emmett, but I had no choice. I'm sorry."

He looked at Morgan. "Doesn't make no never mind, I guess, as long as they're dead. But I was looking forward to having my own conversation with them bastards."

Morgan grinned. "All's not lost. I left you, Jimmy Wilson."

Wade looked at Morgan. "I guess I should thank you."

Morgan looked regretful. "I didn't go into the saloon looking for trouble. I went over to get a bottle so Jed could have his coffee and whiskey before going to bed. It just happened."

Wade looked doubtful. "I learned a long time ago that nothing just happens."

Morgan sighed. "Maybe so." He looked at Wade. "Perhaps it was providence. All I can tell is that they were drunk and came to my table spoiling for a fight. Brodie picked up my locket, and when I asked for it back, he refused. Words were said, he drew, I killed him and that Todd Young fella drew, and I had to shoot him."

"Guess it couldn't be helped," said a disappointed Wade.

Morgan stood, put the chair back under the window, and glanced out into the moonlight on the snow-covered ground.

Wade pointed to the laudanum. "Pour me a half spoonful so I can get back to sleep."

Morgan did as asked, replaced the bottle and spoon to the dresser, and while Wade closed his eyes, Morgan reached down and petted the young coyote pup on his way to the door.

Chapter 15

A storm made its way through southeastern Montana that night, blanketing the town of Pickering and the surrounding countryside with two feet of snow and windblown drifts of over six feet. The temperature remained below freezing, dropping into the teens at night with the gray clouds threatening more snow each day, but none fell. For the next week, no one got into or out of Pickering, which became a maze of shoveled paths from one side of the street to the other.

Doc Reid managed to visit Wade and was satisfied that he was well on his way to recovery. "I don't want you outside in this cold weather." He was packing his instruments into his black bag. "All you need now is to come down with pneumonia."

Morgan had stepped into the room and grinned. "Does that go for the outhouse, Doc?"

Reid turned to Morgan and then to Wade. "So long as you bundle up. Pneumonia would do what the ones who did this to you couldn't." Doc picked up his bag and headed for the door.

"I'll see you out, Doc," said Morgan.

Reid paused at the bedroom door and turned to Wade. "Mind what I say."

"I will, Doc," promised Wade.

Morgan walked Doc Reid to the door and watched as he shrugged into his heavy coat. "I'll see he does what you say, Doc."

Reid glanced out the window of the door, looking concerned. "Make sure the sheriff stays inside except to use the outhouse." He looked at Morgan and lowered his voice. "He's feeling better, and that's good, but it can also be deceiving. I don't want him gallivanting around town in this cold weather."

"I'll see to it, Doc."

"I'm holding you to that, Mr. Hunter," said Reid with a stubborn look. Then he stepped closer as he put on his gloves. "I heard what happened in the saloon the other night. Can't say the town's going to miss them all that much. But some of his friends might."

Morgan appreciated that. "I've known men like Brodie all my life Doc; he wasn't the kind that had friends close enough to get killed trying to avenge him."

Reid put on his hat. "I hope you're right," Then he opened the door letting in a blast of cold air, and stepped outside.

Winter

October gave way to November, which brought sunshine and warm days, melting the snow and leaving a muddy mess to deal with. Wagons regularly had to be pulled out of the mud, and it seemed that everyone in Pickering was in a foul mood. Wade was up walking around, even if he was a little slow, but at least he was healing and feeling stronger with each passing day. Most of the bruises on his face had cleared up, with the exception of swelling around the left eye that remained a dark red.

The days passed quickly, the mud dried up, and Wade walked around town performing his tasks. The coyote pup was almost full-grown, standing two feet at the shoulder, weighing a little over seventy pounds. Her coat was gray and silver, her chest more silver than black, and her long pointed nose a mixture of white and brown, the same as her large ears. Wade was proud of her, and together they turned more than one head as they walked along the boardwalks together. Morgan was spending most of his time at his ranch west of Pickering, branding the cattle with the letters MH that he bought from Jessup, and was learning the ins and outs of ranching from his good neighbor. He was a quick learner and enjoyed the hard work and long days, but there were times he was too tired to eat and just went to bed.

November turned colder as the arctic chill made its way into Montana from the north, but luckily it hadn't snowed heavily since the big storm, so there was plenty of prairie grass for cattle grazing. It was early afternoon when Morgan rode to the edge of the frozen lake, pulled up, and watched as a pack of wolves chased after a large bull elk on the other side of the lake beyond the bare cottonwoods. He watched until they disappeared over the hill in the distance, and he feared the elk wouldn't last much longer. Turning the Appaloosa away from the lake, Morgan followed the tracks of several cows that had headed northwest toward the Powder River. Approaching the river, he pulled up when he saw several men rounding up what he believed to be his cattle. He opened his sheepskin coat so he could get to his Colt Pistol then nudged his horse into a trot. Seeing it was Harold Croucher, he yelled, "Good day!"

"Good day, yourself, Mr. Hunter," greeted Harold with a friendly face.

Morgan pulled up, feeling a little nervous about the killing of Brodie and Todd Young. "Cold as hell," he said, trying to be friendly.

"Hell's a might warmer," corrected Harold Croucher with humor.

Morgan glanced at the cattle seeing they had the MH brand. "I see you corralled my cattle?"

Croucher looked at the cattle. "Afraid we have Mr. Hunter. We thought they were some of our strays at first."

Hunter grinned. "Appreciate it, Mr. Croucher."

He looked at Morgan. "Call me, Harold. We heard you bought the Chandler place." He smiled. "No need telling you that pissed my pa off."

Morgan grinned. "Didn't buy it to piss your pa off, Harold. Bought it so's I'd have my own place."

"I know that, Morgan, and I guess pa does, too. If Old Man Chandler had wanted to sell to my father, then I guess we'd own it." He smiled. "The fault's not of your making, Morgan. Bad feelings between Kyle Chandler and my pa started before I was born." He paused a moment. "Someone had to buy it. May as well be you." He paused. "I just hope we can be good neighbors."

Morgan glanced at the other three riders wondering if any were friends of Brody and Todd Young. "I'd like that."

Croucher turned and introduced his foreman. "Morgan, this is our foreman, Ted Giles."

Morgan and Ted Giles nodded to one another.

Croucher continued. "That one there with the long beard and hair is Ben Parker. The other is Cody Hayes."

Ted Giles was close to forty, broad-shouldered, and big-boned. His face was cleanshaven, and he had piercing blue eyes.

Ben Parker was a tall, lean man in his mid-thirties and resembled a mountain man more than a drover. His breath left tiny icicles on his beard.

Cody Hayes was much younger, not yet twenty. A full handlebar mustache covered in ice occupied his upper lip, and dark brown hair flowed from under an old, brown Stetson hat. His face was smooth, not yet wrinkled from days working outside in the cold and heat.

Morgan felt uneasy because of killing Brodie and Young and wanted to distance himself from the others. "Well," he said. "I best get these back to where they wandered from."

Cody Hayes glared at Morgan. "You really fast enough to outdraw Brodie and Todd?"

"Shut up, Cody," said Harold Croucher angrily. "We ain't looking for trouble."

Morgan looked at Cody. "Ask Jimmy Wilson."

Ted Giles chuckled. "You must've scared the shit out of Jimmy. He packed up and left that very night."

Morgan wasn't all that surprised but knew that Emmett would be disappointed. "I'm sure the Sheriff will be sorry to hear that. I think he was looking forward to having a nice little talk with Wilson."

Cody glared at Morgan. "Well, if it were me, I wouldn't have run."

Morgan's hand was next to the handle of his Colt. "I'm sure you wouldn't, Son." He smiled. "And that would have been your last mistake."

Harold turned to Hayes. "I told you to shut the hell up, Cody. You heard pa; there's to be no trouble."

Looking like a scolded child, Hayes settled back in his saddle.

Morgan looked at Harold Croucher. "Just to set things straight, I didn't set out that night to shoot either one. They came to my table spoiling for a fight." He looked at Cody with cold eyes. "And both got a little more than what they were looking for."

"I'm sure that's true, Mr. Hunter," said Harold. "Pa said it was just a matter of time before someone killed them, or they got themselves hung." He looked at his foreman, Ted Giles. "Give Mr. Hunter a hand with his cattle."

"Yes, sir."

Morgan quickly protested. "There ain't but a few Harold, but I appreciate the gesture."

"As you wish, Morgan." Harold looked at Giles while turning his big brown gelding northward. "Let's get back, Ted. It's cold out here."

Morgan ignored Cody's glare and turned his horse feeling sure the young fool would try and prove himself before long. He took the coiled rope off his saddle horn, patted it against the Appaloosa, and herded his cows back to the rest of his herd.

December

Christmas Eve brought a light covering of snow to eastern Montana. Morgan had dinner with the Thornton's and then went home to a cold, lonely house where he built a fire, turned out the lanterns, and sat back in a leather chair with a glass of whiskey. Hunter took the locket from his pocket and held it while sitting in the dim light, watching the flames devour the logs in the fireplace and thought of his and Ana's first Christmas. Morgan lifted his whiskey glass to his mouth, took a sip, and turned his thoughts to happier times and the Christmas' in Oklahoma when he was a small boy. He and Bobby would get an apple and some homemade candy they tried to make last as long as possible. They always ate the apple first and then nibbled on the candy, a little each night before bed.

Missing his brother, he thought of Wade as he drank the last of the whiskey, looked at the empty glass, and set it down on the table next to his chair. He felt tired and lonely, and as he stared into the fire, his eyes welled as he thought of Ana and their son. Wiping his tears, he stood and walked down the hall to the bedroom, filled with the soft light from the same fire he enjoyed in the living room. After tossing a couple of logs on the fire, he got undressed, climbed between the cold sheets, and covered up. He lay there for several minutes watching the flames dance above the wood they consumed and thought of how he and Ana would make love and then lie in bed talking. Hypnotized by the flames of the fire, his eyes grew heavy; he snuggled down into the bed, closed his eyes, and slept.

Jed Canon managed a bath on Christmas Day, got his clothes washed, and even got a shave and a haircut. Wade hardly recognized him when he returned from Noonan's Barber Shop. Not wanting to be outdone, Wade followed with a bath, shave, and haircut, then donned clean clothes as well. He treated Jed to a nice dinner at Laurie's Café, and afterward, they returned to the jailhouse, had a drink, and played checkers while reminiscing well into the night about Christmas' when they were boys.

Now, in the stillness of his room, Wade lay in the darkness staring up at the ceiling, thinking of Sarah and their son, Emmett. Pup was too big to sleep on the bed and had a bed of her own under the window next to Wade so he could reach down and pet her. With her eyes closed, she lay curled up into a ball, her bushy tail across her long pointed nose, with ears back. As Wade stared at the light coming from the crack around the door of the potbellied stove, he thought of Christmas Eve with Sarah in front of their fireplace in Santa Fe. Recalling how the wind howled that night, pushing the snow into drifts that blocked the door. While Sarah fixed breakfast Christmas Day, he had to climb out a window and clear the snow from the door. The memories of her and Emmett brought tears to his eyes that quickly turned to anger and hatred for the Hoskins family and drovers. He missed his wife and son and knowing he would never see them again saddened him greatly.

Each week the stage from Miles City brought a few wanted posters, and he would quickly go through them, looking for the name Wade Garrison, wanted for murder. In his mind, the cold-blooded murder of George Hoskins and the others were justified to save his own family. But he knew that even if a jury of his peers sided with him on that, they would find him guilty of killing Hoskins' housekeeper. He felt remorse for that killing and not that it would change things; he wished he had known her name.

Chapter 16

January

January was an unusually warm month, with temperatures in the mid to upper fifties during the day but dropping into the low thirties at night. Wade sat in front of the Sheriff's Office Saturday afternoon, enjoying the peace and quiet in the warm sun, drinking a cup of coffee with his feet propped against the porch post. The coyote was lying next to the chair, enjoying the warm sun sleeping, perhaps dreaming of roaming free as her kind was meant to do. Morgan was at his ranch, and Jed was busy out back chopping wood.

The tiny town of Pickering was bustling with farmers and small ranchers taking advantage of the warm weather to stock up on supplies and other errands before the next snow fell. Wade sipped his coffee while watching Mayor Smith down the street, supervise the unloading of five wagons filled with supplies that had just arrived from the trading post up north at Miles City. Wade chuckled as he watched the mayor, who appeared to be a little upset about something as he talked to one of the skinners.

Wade drank the last of the coffee and contemplated taking a walk around town, maybe to check on his mare and give her a good brushing. As he started to get up, he saw a lone rider coming up the street and settled back in his chair. He adjusted the gun he now wore in a cross-draw that Morgan had shown him while explaining the advantages of sitting in a chair or on horseback. Over the years, Wade, like most lawmen, had developed a sense about other men, and now that sense was warning him. He set the empty cup on the boardwalk and sat back with his right hand close to the butt of his pistol and watched the stranger as he rode slowly up the street, looking this way and that. The rider turned his horse and rode at a walk toward him from across the street. Wade thought the horse looked tired, as did the rider pulled up at the hitching rail right in front of Wade. His beard and long hair carried the same trail dust as his brown hat and slicker, which Wade noticed was unbuttoned and pulled behind his pistol.

The rider glanced around and then looked at Wade, noticing the badge he was wearing. "You Emmett Spears?"

"I am," replied Wade while watching the man's body language.

As the rider suddenly went for his gun Wade rolled out of the chair, tipping it onto the boardwalk, came up to one knee, with gun in hand, and fired. The rider's shot missed its mark by inches, but Wade's shot found its target deep in the rider's left chest. The force of the bullet knocked the rider backward over the rump of his horse that neighed and rose onto her rear legs, trotted a short distance, and stopped.

The sleeping coyote jumped up at the sound of gunfire, looking startled as she cowered against the wall of the jailhouse.

Still, on one knee, Wade looked at the coyote to see if she was alright, then with his gun on the man lying on his back in the street, he got up and slowly walked to the edge of the boardwalk and looked down at the stranger that struggled to get up. Wade ducked under the hitching rail and recalled other times he had been fooled by men he'd wounded who had a second pistol or a hidden knife. Still pointing his gun at the stranger, moaning as he rolled from side to side in pain, he kicked the man's pistol away with his foot. "Who the hell are you?"

The stranger tried to get up but collapsed back onto the dirt street, coughing up blood. Wade looked down at the hole in the man's bloody shirt, knowing he was dying. He bent down and looked into his brown eyes. "Who sent you?"

The man's lips moved, but no words escaped, and then he went limp.

Wade stared at the face of the stranger thinking of Harper and the Hoskins family, wondering if anyone was left to seek revenge or if anyone knew where he was, and that worried him.

Jed ran out of the jailhouse carrying the shotgun and stood next to Wade as he knelt over the man. "What the hell happened?"

Wade stood and looked down at the stranger. "He asked if I was Emmett Spears and then drew down on me."

Voices of those who quickly gathered filled the street, and boardwalk asked, "Who was he, Sheriff?" asked a voice. "What'd he want?" asked another, "Why did he draw on you?".

Wade ignored the questions and looked at Jed. "Get Doc Reid." Then he holstered his gun, walked to the overturned chair, put it upright, and then knelt next to Pup to make sure she was alright.

Thomas Moore, the bank president, and Mrs. Jordan stepped out of the bank, wondering what had happened when Mayor Smith approached and asked them. Moore said he didn't know, only that he heard gunshots and came outside.

"Guess we best find out," said the mayor.

Having seen enough, Mrs. Jordan went back inside the bank.

Wade saw Smith and Moore coming, so he opened the door to the jailhouse, told Pup to get inside, watched her disappear into the bedroom, then turned to greet them as he closed the door.

"What the hell happened?" asked the mayor.

Wade shrugged. "I'm not sure." Then he stepped off the boardwalk and tied the man's horse to the railing.

"What the hell does that mean?" asked Smith.

Wade finished tying the horse, turned, and looked at the dead man sprawled in the street. "He rode up, asked me if I was Emmett Spears, and when I said I was, he went for his gun. I dove off the chair and got off a lucky shot." He looked at the mayor. "Now you know as much as I do."

"That makes no sense, Sheriff," said Moore.

Wade sighed. "I know, but he came to Pickering to kill me." He looked around at the crowd thoughtfully. "Someone sent him." Then he walked to the body, knelt, and searched the man's clothing finding two hundred dollars in gold coin and no identification, but he did find a piece of paper with "Emmett Spears" scribbled on it. He stood, showed it to Smith, and Moore then emptied the man's saddlebags on the chair. Rummaging through what was inside, he found some useless papers bearing the name Bill Conners, and as he read the name, he handed the two hundred dollars in gold coin to the mayor. "There should be enough to cover the burial. It looks like his name was Bill Conners."

Earl Noonan, Doc Reid, and Jed Canon pushed through the crowd. Doc knelt, feeling the man's neck for a pulse, and at finding none, looked up at Noonan. "He's dead."

"I need a drink," said Wade. He turned to Jed, telling him to take the dead man's horse up to the livery, and then he pushed his way through the crowd toward the saloon while the others stared at the dead man, wondering who would have sent him to kill their sheriff. Wade stepped onto the boardwalk in front of the saloon, turned the doorknob of the door, and stepped inside, ignoring more questions as he walked to the bar.

Dave Goody was at the window looking at the crowd across the street, watching as Doc Reid led four men carrying the body around the corner to the Doc's office. Goody turned to Wade. "What happened, Sheriff?"

Wade gave him a quick version of the story. "How about a whiskey, Dave?"

Goody took one last look out the window, turned, walked behind the bar, picked up a bottle and glass then poured the glass to the brim with whiskey.

"Leave the bottle," said Wade as he picked up the glass, drank half of it, and then looked out the window, wondering who sent Bill Conners to kill him. He drank the rest of his drink and filled his glass a second time while playing the scene over in his mind. As the man's face and unfamiliar name marched through his memory, Wade took a drink, oblivious to the others at the bar talking about what happened. Trying to understand what just took place, he replayed the whole incident over and over in his mind, but and the whole thing was a mystery. He hadn't killed anyone, and he was the only one that's been hurt. It couldn't be a friend of Harry, or Brodie or Young that came gunning for him; he'd have gone after Jed and Morgan. He picked up the bottle and his glass, found a table, and sat down. Then he thought about someone from Harper knowing where he was, but then he wasn't using his real name. Baffled, he sat back in his chair, took a drink, and considered the mystery.

Purdy was at the bottom of the stairs, asking Dave what all of the ruckus was about. Dave glanced at the sheriff and hurried from around the bar to tell him what had happened. Tom walked over to Wade. "Are you all right, Sheriff?"

Wade looked up at Purdy and nodded that he was.

Tom patted him on the shoulder. "Glad to hear it, Sheriff." Tom turned away and went back upstairs to his room.

Wade poured another drink and dropped his hat in an empty chair. He hadn't noticed Mayor Smith walk in until the mayor was standing at his table.

"Mind if I sit down?" asked Mayor Smith.

Wade looked up from the glass he'd was staring into, pushed a chair away from the table with his foot, and smiled. "Care for a drink?"

The mayor shook his head no as he sat down and leaned on the table with his forearms. "You have any idea why this man rode into Pickering gunning for you?"

Wade took a sip of whiskey, set the glass down, closed his eyes, and started rubbing his forehead. "I have no idea, Mayor. I wish I did."

Smith thought he looked tired and hoped he felt okay.

Wade looked at Smith. "I haven't had time to make the kind of enemies of anyone who would hire someone to kill me."

Smith considered that. "What about Brodie and the others?"

Wade shook his head no. "I thought about that. If it was revenge for them, then Bill Conners would have been gunning for Jed and maybe Morgan. I had nothing to do with the killings."

The mayor looked thoughtful. "That's true." Then he put one hand on Wade's arm. "I'm glad you're alright. I have some things to take care of, but if you think of anyone with reason enough, be sure and let me know." Then he stood and walked toward the door leaving Wade to the mystery of Bill Conners.

As Wade watched the mayor walk across the room and out the door, he wondered what the hell the Mayor would do about it if he did find out.

Bill Conners' body was put in a pine coffin and placed in front of the barbershop for two days for the curious to see, then it was buried along with his secret. Only three people were present in the cemetery at the east edge of town near the church that was also the school; the gravedigger, Preacher George Arden, and Wade. Preacher George Arden stood next to the open grave, reading a small passage from an open Bible. Wade stood at the foot of the grave, his hat at his side, looking down at the pine box, wondering who the hell Bill Conners was and who sent him.

The preacher finished reading, closed the book, and asked God to have mercy on Bill Conners, and then he nodded at the gravedigger who began shoveling dirt into the grave. While the dirt loudly bounced off the wooden casket, Wade looked at the name carved on the wooden cross and contemplated the mystery of the man.

Preacher Arden was a thin man, not very tall, and the brown suit he wore was a little big and wrinkled. His face was round and had a pleasant look. He was clean-shaven with bushy eyebrows and green eyes. His thinning, brown hair moved slightly in the soft breeze as he smiled and put one hand on Wade's shoulder. "Death finds us all one way or another, Sheriff, but I'm glad the Good Lord saw fit to leave you with us a little longer."

Wade considered that as he looked into the round, friendly face of George Arden.

"You look troubled," said the preacher.

Wade thought about the housekeeper he killed. "It's never easy killing a man, justified or not."

Arden looked thoughtful. "Never having killed a man, I wouldn't know and can only suppose that's true."

Wade looked at the preacher and thought again about the woman he killed at the Hoskins ranch. "How does a man seek God's forgiveness?"

The question surprised the preacher, yet he managed to smile. Arden was educated as a schoolmaster but heard the calling of Christ several years ago and became a self-taught minister and a firm believer that judgment was best left up to God and not man. He took his hand away from Wade's shoulder and grasped the Bible in both hands. "You must seek what you need through Jesus Christ. Every man must seek out atonement and forgiveness for his sins, Sheriff." He paused. "No matter how small the sin is because, in God's eyes, there are no small sins."

Visions of the elderly woman he killed and placed in the garden at the Hoskins ranch ran through Wade's memory. "And how does a man seek out this atonement?"

212

The preacher looked thoughtful. "The Good Book says all things through our Lord are possible." He paused. "The Good Lord sends the Winds of Atonement to caress each of us, Sheriff." He paused. "All we have to do is recognize them when they come."

Wade thought on that. "Do these winds come like a storm?"

"They can," replied Arden thoughtfully. "Or in little gusts, some so small you don't even know they were there." He smiled. "I believe that sometimes things happen to give us a chance for atonement. That is what I mean by winds."

Wade thought on that. "How is one to know?"

George Arden chuckled. "You may not know."

"Sounds complicated."

"Nothing is easy when it comes to pleasing God, my son. If it were..." He paused again, gesturing at the landscape, "None of this would have meaning."

Wade thought about that for a moment remembering the kindness in the lady's eyes as she died in his arms. Pushing the scene from his mind, he put his hat on, shook the preacher's hand, and walked away.

Arden called out, "Sheriff!"

Wade stopped and turned.

"A man such as you take many lives." The preacher smiled. "But you also give life that others would take, and you bring justice to those who need it in this harsh land." Arden paused a moment. "Maybe your atonement lies in the good you do." He smiled. "Go with God." Then he turned and walked away.

Wade watched the preacher for a moment and thought about what he said, then he turned and walked away.

Three days later, a small storm passed through, leaving about six inches of snow, followed by clear skies and temperatures in the low thirties. Morgan hitched up his wagon, drove to town for supplies, and stopped by the Sheriff's Office.

Wade was sitting at his desk reading a book he borrowed from Doc Reid and looked up as Morgan walked in, closed the book, and smiled. "What brings you to town?"

Morgan took off his hat. "Supplies."

"Cup of hot coffee?" asked Jed.

"Believe I will," said Morgan as he walked to the desk and placed his hat on its edge, followed by his gloves. While Jed poured his coffee, Morgan took off his sheepskin coat, tossed it on the sofa, sat down in one of the chairs in front of Wade's desk, and took the cup of coffee from Jed. "I heard about the shooting."

Jed looked at Wade. "Coffee?"

Wade picked up his empty cup and handed it to Jed. "Thanks."

Morgan took a drink, thinking it could use something stronger. "Anything in that bottom drawer?"

Wade leaned in his chair, causing it to squeak, opened the bottom drawer, and pulled out a bottle of whiskey that was more than half full. He pulled the cork, filled Morgan's cup, and then offered some to Jed, who gladly held out his cup.

Morgan took a sip of the whiskey coffee. "Any idea at all who would have hired this man?"

Wade corked the bottle, put it back in the lower drawer of his desk, and told Morgan the story, saying he had never seen the man before.

Hunter looked thoughtful. "Someone from your past, maybe?"

Wade shook his head no. "I doubt it. If someone from Harper had sent him, he'd have asked for Wade Garrison, not Emmett Spears."

Morgan considered again. "Maybe." Then he looked at Jed as if he and Wade had spilled a terrible secret.

"Jed knows everything," said Wade. Then he shrugged. "Thought it'd make things simpler."

Jed looked at Morgan. "I ain't the sort to go spreading rumors, Mr. Hunter."

"Start calling me Morgan, will you, Jed? You make it sound like I'm older than you."

Jed laughed then took a drink of spiked coffee.

Morgan turned to Wade, looking serious. "But if someone in Harper knew where you were, wouldn't they also know what name you might be using, and if so, wouldn't the man they send ask for Emmett Spears?"

Wade shrugged and shook his head. "Maybe, but I think that's a far reach."

"Makes no sense," said Morgan.

Wade stared into his cup at the dark coffee. "I seriously doubt anyone in Harper sent Bill Conners."

"Well," said Morgan thoughtfully, "That leaves someone from Pickering."

Looking puzzled, Wade said, "I haven't killed anyone or even arrested anyone." He smiled without humor. "Shit, I'm the only one who's been hurt, so why would anyone in Pickering hire a gun to kill me?"

Morgan grinned then jokingly said, "You haven't been messing with any wives now, have you?"

Wade chuckled and shook his head no as the room fell silent once more.

Jed sipped his whiskey coffee, pondering the problem.

Morgan finished his coffee, set the cup on the edge of the desk, and stood. "Too big a mystery for me to try and solve right now. I best get on with picking up my supplies."

Wade stood. "How're things at the ranch?"

Morgan grinned. "Ain't lost any cattle yet." Then he turned serious. "Did run into Harold Croucher and three of his men a while back."

Wade looked interested.

"Had a young drover with him by the name of Cody something-or-other. Little on the slender side, tall with a handlebar mustache." He paused. "You might give him some thought. Looks like he's itching to prove himself."

"I'll keep that in mind."

Morgan shrugged into his heavy sheepskin coat. "You watch yourself. Whoever sent this Conners fella will probably send another."

"I've already considered that."

Morgan picked up his hat and gloves then headed for the door, talking over his shoulder. "See you, boys, later."

Wade grinned as he sat back down. "Say hello to Mrs. Jordan."

Morgan reached for the doorknob, stopped, and looked back at Wade. "What makes you think I'll see Mrs. Jordan?"

Wade's face filled with a grin while Morgan opened the door, walked outside, and closed the door, then he looked at Jed. "Let's get something to eat."

Two days later, a storm dropped a foot and a half of snow on Pickering, and that evening Wade and Jed were playing a game of checkers when Pup lifted her head from a sound sleep, looked at the door as she slowly stood and softly growled. Wade looked up from the checkerboard and watched as she slowly walked to the door, growling, then began scratching at it.

Jed turned in his chair to look at her. "Wonder what got her going?"

Curious at what had her spooked, Wade pulled his pistol, cocked it, got up from his swivel chair, and kneeled on the sofa by the big window. He lifted the blind just enough so he could see out while Jed attempted to calm Pup. The snow-covered street was deserted, and most of the kerosene lamps of Pickering had turned

216

out long ago. He looked at Pup, whining and scratching at the door, wondering what it was that had her spooked.

Jed was kneeling next to Pup, trying to get her to stop scratching at the door. "Should I let her out?"

"No," said Wade. "We don't know what's out there." Then he stood from the sofa, walked to the door with gun in hand, put his hand on her back, and softly told her to stop. He pulled back the blind of the window of the door and peered out, seeing nothing but the snow-covered street, boardwalk, and buildings across the street.

Jed was feeling a little spooked himself by the way Pup was acting, so he took the shotgun from the rack and stood in the corner next to the potbellied stove.

Wade looked back at Jed. "I'm going outside."

"Think that's a good idea?" asked Jed.

Wade pushed Pup aside with his leg, opened the door, stepped outside, and quickly closed it before Pup could get out. While Pup scratched at the door, Wade cautiously stepped to the edge of the boardwalk next to the porch post and looked up and down the deserted street. His breath turned white in the cold air, and Wade thought about his winter coat hanging on the peg inside, along with his hat.

Putting his hand on the handle of his pistol, he stepped off of the boardwalk into the street. The snow crunched under his boots, mixing with soft laughter from the saloon. A dog barking somewhere behind the buildings across the street brought back the night he was beaten and his face cut. As the dog stopped barking and the stillness returned to the street, Wade wondered if it had been the dog that spooked Pup. He took a long look around and then stepped back onto the boardwalk, where he paused to take one last look up and down the street, trying to see into the shadows. Seeing or hearing nothing alarming, Wade backed to the door, went back inside locked the door. Holstering his gun and seeing that Pup had settled down, he figured it must have been the dog barking.

Jed was still standing in the corner by the stove, holding the shotgun. "See anything?"

Wade shook his head. "No, a dog was barking somewhere in the distance." He looked up at the clock and then at Jed, who was putting the shotgun away. "It's almost midnight, Jed. Let's finish this game tomorrow."

"All right by me," said Jed, then he pointed to Pup. "Want me to take her out?"

Wade shook his head no as he walked toward the back door slapping his leg. "Come on, Pup, let's go outside."

Loud pounding on the front door woke Jed from a sound sleep. "I'm coming, I'm coming!" he yelled as he hurried across the dimly lit room toward the door in his long underwear. Parting the blind, he saw the shadowy face of Dave Goody and opened the door.

Dave stepped inside, looking upset. "Where's the sheriff?"

The door to Wade's room opened, and he stepped into the office with his hair a mess, wearing his faded red long johns and holding his pistol looking like he had just woken up.

Pup was at his side, staring up at Dave Goody.

Wade glanced at the clock seeing it was only five in the morning. "What the hell's got you riled up, Dave?"

An astonished Dave Goody blurted, "Estelle's been murdered."

Wade suddenly looked wide awake as his eyes went from Goody to Jed and back to Goody. "Murdered!"

Jed looked surprised. "Estelle's dead?"

Dave looked irritated at Wade. "She's dead, I tell you."

Wade turned toward his room. "I'll get dressed."

Jed lit a lantern, pulled his suspenders up over his shoulders, and, figuring he wasn't going to get any more sleep started building a fire in the stove.

A few minutes later, Wade walked out of his room and put his gun belt on.

"Want me to come along?" asked Jed.

Wade shook his head no as he bent over to tie his holster down. "Stay here with Pup. I'll need some hot coffee when I come back." Then he shrugged into his heavy wool coat, picked up his hat, and followed Goody out the door.

The sun hadn't come up yet, but the sky in the east was turning lighter, and the clouds that hung above the horizon were a mixture of gray, purple, and dark pink. The cold air found its way past the opening of Wade's coat, which he quickly buttoned as he and Dave chased their white breath across the street to the sound of crunching snow underfoot.

At the edge of the boardwalk, Dave Goody gestured toward the alleyway between the two buildings. "She's out back."

Wade looked puzzled. "Out back?"

"She's in the shitter."

Curious about that, Wade followed Goody down the narrow alleyway to the rear of the building. As they approached the outhouse in the faint light of dawn, Wade saw Estelle's shoes, legs, and bottom of her dress sticking out of the open doorway. Wade opened the door as wide as it would go, and although it was dim inside, he could see it was Estelle sitting back against the wall, fully clothed. Stepping closer, Wade put one hand on the edge of the doorway and leaned inside, greeted by the foul smell of human waste. He covered his nose with his hand, and although the light was dim inside, he could see that her eyes were open and held terror in them. "You find her like this?"

Goody nodded. "When I came out to get wood for the stove, I saw someone's feet sticking out of the door."

Wade recalled the first night he saw her when she tried to speak up for Pup. Feeling sorry for her, he looked at the white lace collar of her low-cut dress covered in dark blood from the gaping hole across her throat that almost decapitated her. There were several puncture wounds in her chest, and as he stepped back, he saw her legs were bloody, so he lifted her dress, seeing that her undergarments were torn and bloody.

Goody turned away, bent over, gagged, and emptied what little he had left in his stomach. "My God," he uttered.

Wade let go of the dress and looked into her eyes, wondering who would do such a thing? Feeling pity for her, he gently closed her eyes, moved her hair away from the side of her blood-spattered face, and then turned to Goody. "Anyone else know about this?"

Dave Goody turned his head and spit to clear his mouth of vomit. "Not that I know of."

Wade stepped back, looking at the footprints in the snow, taking particular notice of his and Dave's. "Don't move," he said as he stepped back and carefully walked around, making sure he did not step in any one of the several footprints left in the snow. He walked back toward the saloon studying the snow seeing blood here and there, and then he stopped and knelt, where the two sets of prints came together, trampling the snow. "This is where the attack came."

He stood and pointed at the snow. "These would be Estelle's footprints heading toward the outhouse. See how her dress drug along as she walked?" He pointed to another set. "These are probably the killers. It looks like whoever did this waited for her by the woodpile." He paused, staring down at them. "It wasn't any drover who did this."

Dave looked puzzled. "How do you know that?"

Wade looked up from the shoe prints. "They're city shoes, same as yours and others' in town and not boots."

Goody's face held worry. "I didn't kill her."

220

"Never believed you did," said Wade quietly without looking at him. Then he stepped toward the outhouse catching a slight scent of it, and stopped. "They struggled, and she fell there, thrashing in the snow while she bled out." He paused. "That's where he cut her throat."

"How do you know?" asked Goody.

Wade remembered how the blood spewed from the neck of the man's throat he cut that night at the Hoskins ranch. "The amount of blood, and see how it moved across the snow as it shot out of her neck while she staggered to get away."

"I wonder why she never screamed for help," said Dave.

Wade remembered Pup scratching at the door. "She may have. Maybe that's why he cut her throat." He looked at Estelle's body sitting in the outhouse and felt sorry for her. "Whoever did this must have tried to set her inside but didn't have enough strength." He paused. "Or he was disturbed by something or someone. I'll get Doc, and then we'll take her to his place."

While Wade walked across the crunching snow to get Doc Reid, Dave looked at Estelle once more, then grabbed an armload of wood and headed back into the saloon.

Doc Reid wasn't too happy about being rousted from a warm bed, but when Wade told him about Estelle, he quickly dressed and accompanied Wade to the body. Reid was leaning inside the outhouse when Goody stepped out of the rear of the saloon, closed the door, and hurried across the snow putting on his coat.

Doc stepped back. "We need a blanket to wrap her in so we can carry her to my place."

"I'll get one," offered Goody, who hurried inside and returned several minutes later with a dark wool blanket.

They had difficulty getting the stiff, frozen body out of the outhouse and laying her body on the blanket Goody had spread on the snow. They wrapped the body in the blanket, picked her up, and carried her through the small alleyway toward the street.

When they got to Doc's place, they laid Estelle's body on a table in his office, and then Doc Reid saw them to the door. He looked at Wade. "I'll examine the body and let you know what I find."

"Appears pretty obvious, doesn't it, Doc?" said Wade.

Doc's tired eyes went from Goody to Wade. "I suppose it is. I'll come by later."

After Wade and Goody left Doc's, Wade told Dave to keep this to himself for a while, and that included not saying anything to Purdy. When they reached the main street of Pickering, Dave headed for the saloon while Wade hurried to the jailhouse, ready for a hot cup of coffee.

Jed was putting more wood into the belly of the stove when Wade walked in. "Coffee?" Canon asked as he straightened.

"I could sure use a cup," said Wade as he placed his hat on the edge of the desk along with his gloves. Taking off his heavy coat, he hung it on the peg next to the closed door. When Wade turned, Jed handed him a tin cup of black coffee. It felt good against his cold hands, and the steam caressed his face as he raised the cup to his mouth.

Jed had a sad look on his face. "Is Estelle truly dead?"

Wade nodded, looking sad. "I'm afraid she is, Jed."

Canon sat down on the sofa, thinking of Estelle. "I can't believe she's gone."

Wade opened the bottom drawer of his desk, pulled out the whiskey bottle, and poured a small amount into his coffee. Hoping it would take off the chill, he offered the bottle to Jed.

Cannon shook his head no then asked what happened.

Wade set the bottle on the top of the desk and told him what he found.

Jed stared down at the floor then looked at Wade with a worried expression. "Who'd do such a thing?"

Wade stared at the far wall wearing a troubled look. "I don't know, Jed, but I'm gonna do everything I can to find out."

222

Jed stood from the sofa, picked up the bottle, and poured a small amount into his coffee, took a drink, and returned to the sofa with the cup.

Wade put the bottle away, sat back in his chair, and took a drink of coffee, imagining Estelle fighting for her life in the cold night and the horror she must have known in her final moments.

Jed looked into his cup. "Poor Estelle," he said sadly. "I always liked her." He looked at Wade with a small, affectionate smile. "She'd talk to me when none of the others would."

Wade looked at Jed feeling sorry for the old man's life as well, knowing Jed and Estelle were both lost souls, the same as him. He took a drink of coffee, looked across the room to the clock on the wall, pulled his watch from his pocket, and compared the two. Seeing it was not yet six-thirty, Wade returned his watch to his pocket and took a drink of coffee as he stood then walked to the sofa. Reaching across, he raised the blind on the window and looked into the cold, gray morning at the café across the street. "I'm gonna get cleaned up, and after we have breakfast, I'll tell the Mayor about Estelle."

The soft ring of the tiny bell above the door caused Mayor Robert Smith to look up from the ledger he was working on in time to see Sheriff Spears standing in the doorway wearing a solemn face. Robert closed the ledger and waited while the sheriff closed the door that rang the tiny bell and walked up the aisle of goods to the counter. Sensing the news wasn't good, Mayor Smith glanced at the potbellied stove surrounded by five empty chairs, some of the elders used for gossiping. Being thankful they were empty, he said, "Morning, Sheriff."

"Mayor," greeted Wade as he glanced around the empty store before looking at Smith. "Have some bad news."

Smith leaned on the counter with his hands. "What kind of bad news?"

Wanting to warm himself, Wade said, "Let's go by the stove." When they reached the stove, he gestured at the curtain hanging over the door to the backroom. "Anyone back there?"

Mayor Smith glanced at the curtained doorway and then at Wade with a concerned look. "We're alone."

Wade held his hands over the stove to warm them as he spoke in a low voice. "Estelle's been murdered."

Smith looked horrified. "Estelle at the saloon? When?"

"Sometime last night. Dave Goody found her in the outhouse behind the saloon when he went outside to get firewood early this morning." Wade went on to tell of her wounds, the disfigurement of her privates, and taking her to Doc Reid's place.

The mayor listened in horror while staring at his hands he held over the stove. "Good Lord, why so brutal?"

Wade shook his head. "Don't know, Mayor. But whoever killed her was plenty pissed off about something."

Smith looked down at the floor and asked, "Who would do such a terrible thing?"

"I don't know, but I'm gonna do my damnedest to find out."

"Does Tom know?"

Wade looked at his hands he held over the stove and shook his head. "No, I told Goody to keep quiet and let me handle that."

"He's gonna be upset," said Smith in a sad voice. "What are you gonna do next?"

"Have a talk with the rest of the whores in the saloon. Maybe someone saw or heard something, or maybe one of them will know if she was having trouble with anyone."

"Tom Purdy may not like you rousting his ladies this early."

Wade considered that briefly. "Well, he's just gonna have to deal with that."

"He's gonna be upset," said the mayor, then he looked worried. "Go easy on him."

Wade looked at the mayor curiously. "Something you need to tell me about Tom Purdy and Estelle?"

"Estelle was," said Smith, who then paused. "Well, you might say she was his favorite."

Wade thought on that. "So Tom Purdy ain't married?"

"Not to my knowledge."

Wade became more curious about the man. "How long have you known him?"

Smith thought a moment. "Close to five years. Why?"

"No reason," said Wade thoughtfully. "Just curious. Where does he live?"

"Above the saloon."

Wade sighed softly. "Guess I best go talk to him."

Chapter 17

Wade opened the saloon door, stepped inside, and paused, letting his eyes adjust from the bright snow to the dim lantern light. The saloon was empty but for Dave Goody behind the bar with his back toward Wade, facing the mirror busy with something.

Seeing Wade's reflection in the mirror, Goody turned just as Wade leaned on the bar with his elbows. Dave wiped the bar down with a towel out of habit, but instead of smiling as he usually did, he looked miserable. "I still can't get Estelle's face out of my mind."

"Terrible thing, all right," agreed Wade as he glanced around. "The other girls still sleeping?"

"Yeah. Want a beer or whiskey? I've already had two whiskeys myself."

Wade shook his head. "No, thanks, but I would like to talk to the girls."

Goody glanced up at the balcony of the second floor. "They don't usually get up before noon. The place is always dead 'til then."

Wade thought on that. "I need to talk to them before they hear about Estelle from someone else."

Dave frowned, then realizing that was a good idea, he bobbed his head a couple of times. "All at once or one at a time?"

"All at once."

Goody looked worried. "I'll have to clear it with Mr. Purdy first."

Wade shrugged. "Do what you gotta do, but I'm talking with the girls this morning."

Goody saw the determination on Wade's face and then looked upstairs with a worried expression. "I'll have to tell Mr. Purdy why."

Wade wanted to tell Tom Purdy about Estelle himself. "Tell your boss that I need to talk to him about something very important."

Dave gave a troubled sigh, said he'd be back in a minute and walked around the end of the bar toward the stairs.

Wade watched him hurry up the stairs and disappear down a hall. Moments later, he heard a slight tapping sound as Dave knocked on Tom Purdy's door. Faint voices made their way from the hall downstairs, and then it became quiet. A few moments later, Dave appeared at the top of the stairs and started down. Reaching the bottom step, he looked at Wade. "First door on the left."

Wade walked up the stairs finding the hallway, then the first door on his left, and recalling what Mayor Smith said about going easy on Tom, he gently knocked on the door.

"Come in," said a soft voice.

Wade turned the knob, opened the door, stepped inside, and took his hat off. The room was large and filled with expensive furniture and oil paintings of wealthy dressed people on city streets, flower gardens, and castles. Purdy was standing in front of the big window of sheer curtains with the heavy dark drapes pulled back, letting the gray day invade the room. He was pouring a drink, but he stopped and looked up. "Brandy?"

"No, thanks." Wade unbuttoned his coat and watched Tom take a sip of brandy.

Purdy gestured to an overstuffed chair. "Dave said you had something important you wanted to talk to me about."

Wade remained standing. "I'm sorry to have to tell you this, Mr. Purdy." he hesitated.

Tom looked up from his glass. "Yes?"

Wade fidgeted with his hat. "Don't know how else to say this, Mr. Purdy, but someone killed Estelle last night."

Tom stared at Wade in disbelief. "Estelle's dead?"

"Afraid she is, Mr. Purdy."

Purdy slowly sat on the sofa, held his drink in one hand, the other rubbing his forehead. "Estelle's dead?"

Feeling sorry for Tom, Wade told him how Dave found her early this morning, woke him up, and that after examining the body, they got Doc Reid, and that is where Estelle's body is.

"Have a seat, Sheriff, please."

Wade sat down and wondered what kind of an arrangement the two had but knew it wasn't any of his business. Most men would not take up with a whore while she was still whoring, but there wasn't a lot about Tom Purdy that made sense to Wade anyway. He was more curious than ever how such a meek, pudgy little man would end up a pimp over whores and in love with one.

Tom stared into his drink with a sad face. "Who'd do such a terrible thing?"

Wade did not answer the question where there was no answer. Then he asked one of his own. "Did you see Estelle last night?"

Purdy nodded his head a few times, looking sad. "Yes. We had dinner right here in this room before she went downstairs to work."

Wade sat forward, resting his arms on his knees, his hat in his hands. "You never saw Estelle after dinner?"

Tom Purdy took a drink of brandy then shook his head as he swallowed. "No."

Feeling he had nothing to offer, Wade stood. "If you have no objections, I'd like to speak to the other girls and see when they saw her last."

Purdy stood. "Of course. If you wait here, I'll get them ready." He set his half-empty glass on the table next to his chair and left the room.

While he waited, Wade's eyes roamed the room until the door opened, and Tom stepped inside, leaving the door open. "They'll see you now, Sheriff." He stepped back. "They're just across the hall."

Wade thanked him, and as he walked to the door, he noticed a photograph in a dark wooden frame sitting on the table next to the door of a lovely young girl of fifteen or sixteen standing next to a young boy.

"My older sister and myself."

Wade looked at Tom. "Must have been taken a long time ago."

Tom looked down at the photograph. "Yes, it was."

Wade took a last look, thanked him for his time, walked across the hall, and gently knocked on the door.

"Come in," said a female voice.

He opened the door and stepped inside, finding five girls dressed scantily in undergarments and sheer robes; none embarrassed that their breasts were showing. After the casual hellos, Wade told them about Estelle, which brought loud sobbing and questions to which he had no answers. The girls weren't much help, and they all said they had seen her the night before, but no one remembered her leaving. One thing they all did say was that none of them visited the outhouse at night. They used bedpans instead and dumped them in the morning. Wade thanked them, opened the door, walked into the hall, and paused to look at Tom Purdy's closed door, wondering how he was doing, then turned and headed for the stairs.

Dave Goody was behind the bar when Wade walked up to the bar. Goody stiffened. "How's Mr. Purdy?"

Wade thought about Tom looking sad. "All right, I guess." He paused in thought. "You know anything about your boss and Estelle?"

Dave looked uneasy as he glanced at the second-floor balcony and lowered his voice. "Tom has or had a thing for Estelle. I think he loved her."

Wade considered that and felt sorry for Tom Purdy.

Goody wiped the bar down with a towel. "Girls have anything to say?"

Wade leaned against the bar, resting on his right forearm. "Nothing that was helpful." He considered what they told him about not going outside at night and wondered why Estelle did, and wondered if she went outside to meet her killer.

Goody glanced around and then leaned on the bar, looking secretive.

Figuring he has something to say, Wade leaned closer.

Dave glanced up at the second-floor balcony and then looked at Wade. "Estelle used to sneak out once in a while after she got off work."

That answered Wade's question. "Do you know where she went?"

Goody shrugged. "Don't know. I started to follow her once but decided it wasn't any of my business."

"Wish you had," offered Wade thoughtfully.

More people attended Estelle's burial than there were at Bill Conners' the week before, though it was a select, sparse group. The sun had come out, melting most of the snow and leaving the ground muddy. Planks of wood were placed from the edge of the small cemetery to the gravesite and then around it so people wouldn't stand in the mud. While Preacher Arden read the words from the Bible he held, Wade stood with his hat in his hands, glancing at the faces of the others, wondering if her murderer was at her funeral. Mayor Smith wearing a black suit, stood next to his

230

heavyset wife, also dressed in black. Earl Noonan and his wife, both dressed in black, stood behind the Smith's with Jonathan Moore, his wife, and Mrs. Jordan. Several cowhands who had come to pay their respects were standing in the background, and Wade thought it sad that the only people crying were the five whores who worked with Estelle. Tom Purdy was at the foot of the open grave, his hands folded in front of him, looking solemn.

The preacher finished reading, then stepped back while six drovers picked up the ropes and lifted the casket while two others pulled the boards from under it. Wade watched as the pine box disappeared into the deep hole, and when the casket reached the bottom, the ropes were pulled out, rolled up, and laid on the muddy ground. Purdy bent down, picked up a handful of wet dirt, and tossed it into the grave that sent back a sad, final, lonely sound. He took a neatly folded hanky from his coat pocket and wiped his hands as he stepped back. He put his hanky away and then walked past Wade without looking up.

While the others passed by the open grave, paying their last respects to Estelle Winters' memory, which Wade thought was all for Tom's benefit, Wade put on his hat, thinking he needed to go for a ride. When he turned to walk away, he saw Jed and Pup standing a few feet away, walked over to them, and took the rope holding Pup. "I'm going for a ride."

"How long are you gonna be gone?"

"Don't know."

Jed watched Wade and Pup walk toward the livery, and then he gave a last look at Estelle's grave, where the only person left was the man shoveling dirt into it. Feeling bad about Estelle, he turned and headed for the jailhouse, thinking of a hot cup of coffee with some whiskey.

Wade had ridden about a half-mile when he pulled up at a small clearing where the snow had melted. He climbed down and let the mare feed on the grass, and while Pup got her exercise chasing prairie mice and birds that stayed the winter. Watching Pup scamper about from one mud and grass oasis to the other, Wade remembered Estelle sitting in the outhouse, eyes open, with her clothes covered in her blood. He thought of the footprints he went back to measure after they carried Estelle to Doc Reid's place. Dave Goody's feet were considerably bigger, and while he had no idea who killed her, he knew it was not Goody or a cowboy.

Hearing Pup growl, he turned, seeing she was chasing a rabbit that disappeared into a hole. Wade chuckled at the way Pup stared at the empty hole and wondered if she would survive on her own. While he watched the coyote, he sorted through the images of the men Wade knew in Pickering and could not find one he thought would do such a thing. But then again, Wade didn't really know the men of Pickering. Frustrated, he swung up onto his saddle and yelled for Pup. Then he nudged the mare into a slow trot toward the town that he could see in the distance.

He had ridden several minutes before he realized Pup was nowhere around, so he pulled up, stood tall in the stirrups, and looked around, calling out to her. Not seeing her, he became worried, turned the mare, and rode back in search of the coyote. The minutes passed, and then he saw her lying next to some rocks near a dead riverbed eating something, and as he approached, he saw that she had caught and killed a rabbit. She looked up at Wade, picked up her kill, and trotted off as if she were afraid he was going to take it away. Wade called to her as he followed, but she kept her distance, so he pulled the mare up and watched the coyote to see what she was going to do.

Pup stopped, turned with her kill hanging from her mouth, stared at him for a moment, and then lay down and continued eating.

Knowing this would take a while, he let out a frustrated sigh, climbed down, and found a nice size rock to sit on and enjoy the sun while Pup finished her meal. To pass the time, he grabbed a handful of wet snow, took a bite, and let it melt in his mouth, took another, and tossed the rest away. When smelling the blood of the rabbit, the mare put her ears back and snorted as her big dark eyes looked toward the coyote feasting on her kill. Figuring the mare was uneasy, he stood and rubbed her forehead and neck while speaking in a soft voice as he watched Pup eat.

The minutes passed, and then Pup got up and trotted toward Wade and the mare carrying what remained of her kill. Her long snout and chin were red with blood, and when she stood next to Wade, the mare became anxious and backed away. He calmed her, wondering if she would ever get used to Pup, climbed into the saddle, and pointed the mare toward Pickering. He nudged her into a trot with Pup following at a distance carrying her kill, and Wade knew she would be just fine on her own.

March

January turned into February and that into March, and Wade still had no clues about who killed Estelle. Without suspects, he knew her death would never be solved, and that festered like a cactus thorn in the thumb. To make matters worse, whenever he visited the saloon if the other girls didn't question him about it, Dave Goody or Tom Purdy would.

The weather was warm and dry, most of the mud from the last snow melting had hardened, and it felt like spring had arrived. Wade had just returned from eating lunch at the café across the street and was sitting in his swivel chair, going through some papers. Hearing a commotion outside, he turned, seeing two men jumping on their horses and gallop down the street.

A young boy burst in, yelling, "The bank's been robbed."

Jonathan Moore ran out of the bank, pointing at the two riders. "They've robbed the bank."

Not believing someone would rob a bank next door to the sheriff's office, Wade rushed back inside, grabbed his Sharps rifle

233

and bandoleer of cartridges, and ran outside just as the two men rode out of town at a fast gallop.

Wade glanced around for a horse and saw a big gray at the hitching rail in front of the saloon that looked fast. Running across the street, he untied the reins, swung up into the saddle, and rode after the two men. Minutes into the chase, he pulled up having a clear shot, stood in the saddle, aimed at the last rider, and fired. The gray, not being used to someone shooting from the saddle, reared up and bucked a couple of times. Wade settled the gray down, then rode past the body and riderless horse that had stopped.

With the Sharps and bandoleer in one hand, the reins in the other, he spurred the big gray and leaned forward with his face next to the big gray's long neck. Within minutes the gray's breathing became labored, and Wade knew it was a matter of minutes before he had to stop or the horse would collapse. Seeing a rise just off to his right, he turned the gray up the hill, and remembering what happened the last time, he pulled up, jumped down, shoved a cartridge into the breech, and knelt to one knee.

Finding his target in the crosshairs of his scope, he pulled the first trigger and then the second. The .50 caliber cartridge exploded, and the rifle kicked against his shoulder as the explosion echoed across the quiet prairie. The gray screamed at the sound rearing up on its hind legs. Wade reached for the reins but missed, and the horse trotted several yards before it stopped. Figuring the horse was not going anywhere, Wade turned back the rider, seeing a riderless horse stop, and he knew he had hit his target. Grabbing the reins of the big gray, he swung up and nudged the horse into a trot toward the riderless horse.

Pulling up a few yards from the body, he climbed down and tied the gray to a nearby bush. Still holding the Sharps and bandoleer in his left hand, he drew his Colt with his right and pulled back the hammer. The man was lying on his back, arms outstretched, hands empty, his gun still in its holster, and his hat lying a few feet away. Wade looked down at the bloody shirt and hole where the bullet from his Sharps had exited and knew he was dead, but he carefully nudged the man's thigh with the toe of his boot anyway.

With the money safely back in the bank and the two men buried, Wade's exploits became the talk of Pickering and especially his expertise with the Sharps rifle and the distance of his accuracy. And as it is always the case, both became slightly exaggerated with each telling of the story.

Chapter 18

A week passed, and Wade grew bored with town and even checkers with Jed. So, early one morning, he saddled his mare and rode out to visit Morgan. It was just short of noon when he rode up to Morgan's house, swung down, and tied the mare to the porch post while Pup curiously sniffed around. Wade knocked on the door, waited, knocked again. When no one opened the door, he walked to the edge of the porch and looked barn and corral. Seeing his black packhorse and Appaloosa in the corral, he knew he hadn't gone far. Then Wade saw him working in the pigsty and chuckled. He stepped off the porch, called Pup, and walked toward the sty.

He stopped a few feet away from the sty and watched Morgan for a moment. "The great Morgan Hunter, slopping pigs."

Morgan turned, looking a little tired and angry. "I don't recall inviting your sorry ass out here."

Wade chuckled as he walked to the fence of the sty. "Thought I'd stop by and see what you were up to."

Morgan shoved a big sow out of the way. "Filthy, stubborn things." He looked at Wade. "I'm up to my ass in hogs, that's what I'm up to?"

Wade smiled. "Looks just like what it is, I reckon."

Morgan made his way through the mud and hogs to the gate, looking annoyed. "Don't know why I let Jessup talk me into raising pigs."

Wade grinned. "It's all part of the majestic plan, Morgan."

Morgan Hunter stepped out of the sty, closed the gate, and stomped his feet to get the mud off. "Filthy bastards."

Wade looked curious. "Did you ever think to toss the slop from this side of the fence?"

"I did," he replied angrily. "I'm not stupid! But for some reason, the little one's afraid of the other two and doesn't get much to eat." He looked at Wade's grinning face. "Shut up." Then he started toward the house. "Come on, there's some coffee leftover I can heat up, and I have some apple pie, Mrs. Thornton baked." He looked back at Wade. "What brings you out here?"

"Bored." Thinking coffee and apple pie sounded good, he followed while Pup stayed behind, interested in the chickens. Hearing them getting excited, he turned and called her. "Pup! Leave the damn chickens alone."

She ignored his call and continued to run back and forth along the chicken coop scaring the chickens. Wade stopped and called her a second time and then a third with anger in his voice before she turned away from the chickens and followed him and Morgan to the house.

Reaching the porch, Morgan sat on its edge, took off his muddy boots, set them beside the door, and looked at Pup as she stood beside Wade. "I guess she's coming in?"

Wade looked at Pup and then smiled at Morgan. "She goes where I go."

"I was afraid of that." Hunter stood, opened the door, and looked at Wade. "Why don't you get yourself a real girl?"

Wade chuckled as he and Morgan stepped inside. "Not sure I'd know what to do with one."

"I believe that." Hunter gestured at the door. "Shut door. Won't be but a minute." Then he disappeared down the hall in his stocking feet. Wade waited for Pup, and after she came into the house, he closed the door and told her to lie down. He looked around the big room with its leather sofa, chairs, end tables, and a large stone fireplace. "Nice place," Wade said loud enough for Morgan to hear. Then he thought of Sarah, knowing she would like it.

Morgan walked out of the bedroom, wearing clean clothes and another pair of clean boots. "Kitchen's back here."

Wade told Pup to stay and headed for the kitchen, where he found Morgan putting some wood into the cooking stove. After he lit the wood, he set the coffee pot on top and turned to a dish covered with a towel containing half an apple pie. Taking the towel off the pie, he divided it in half, put the two pieces on a couple of plates, and handed them to Wade. "Set these on the table in the dining room."

Wade took them and headed for the dining room but stopped and looked back at Morgan. "Do we eat with our hands, or do we each get a fork?"

"Don't be a smart ass."

Wade grinned. "Just curious." He turned and walked into the dining room, set the plates down on the long table, and noticed Pup was lying underneath it. He walked around the table to the dining room window and looked out at the land of rolling hills. To the north lay the Powder River lined by cottonwood trees as far as he could see, and between the house and the river, some of Morgan's cattle peacefully grazed in the warm sun. The sound of boiling coffee spilling onto the hot stove broke the stillness, followed by Morgan's mumbled cursing. Wade grinned as he turned and looked toward the kitchen, imagining Morgan fighting with the hot handle of the coffee pot, and sat down at the long table.

Morgan walked into the room, carrying two cups of coffee and two forks. "I heard about the robbery," he said as he set a cup and fork in front of Wade and the other on the table where he sat down. "That tiny graveyard must be getting crowded."

Wade smiled. "There's plenty of room left." Then he picked up his cup and took a drink of coffee, surprised at how good it tasted.

Morgan was considering the graveyard when he suddenly jumped up, dropping his fork on the floor. "Damn it!"

Wade figured Pup must have startled Morgan, so he called her and told her to lie down next to his chair.

Morgan looked a little on the irritable side as he retrieved his fork from under the table before sitting back down. "Almost gave me a heart attack." Then he shoved a fork of pie into his mouth, followed by a drink of coffee.

Wade took a bite of pie and nodded, looking pleased. "Tell Mrs. Thornton she can send a pie into town anytime she wants."

Morgan paused, eating. "Anything new on Estelle's murder?"

Wade looked out the window toward the Powder River and shook his head in disappointment. "I don't think we'll ever know what happened."

Morgan cut a piece of crust with his fork and called Pup.

She got up, walked under the table to Morgan, looked at the hand a moment, and then smelled the crust before gently taking it.

He grinned. "I ain't never fed pie to a coyote before."

"Don't give her too much, it ain't good for her."

Morgan looked at Wade. "How the hell do you know what's good for a coyote?"

Wade looked irritated. "I don't want her getting fat."

Hunter picked up another piece of crust and gave it to her.

Wade gave him a look and shoved the fork with the last of his pie into his mouth while Morgan stood, went into the kitchen, and returned with the coffee pot.

Wade watched the coffee spew from the spout of the pot into his cup and then looked out the window at the scene of grazing cattle, rolling hills beyond the river, and a cloudless blue sky. "How are things going, Morgan?"

Hunter set the pot down on a hot plate and picked up his cup. "Not bad." Then he turned and looked over his shoulder out the window. "I've learned a lot from Jessup." Proudly, he said that neither had lost any cattle during the winter. Then he stood and picked up his cup. "Let's go outside and sit on the porch."

Wade picked up his cup, then he and Pup followed him outside where they sat in the two wooden chairs while Pup made herself comfortable at Wade's feet, her head on her paws and eyes closed. Wade looked across the yard at the barn, corral, chicken coop, and pigsty. "You've done all right for yourself, Morgan."

"Still needs a lot of work," said Hunter as he lifted his cup to his mouth.

"Always will," replied Wade in a soft voice. "And that's a good thing." The quiet moments passed filled with the sounds of horses, cows, and other ranch sounds. Then he looked at Morgan, "Best get back." He drank the last of his coffee and stood. "Someone may be trying to steal your money from the bank."

Morgan grinned as he stood and took Wade's cup while Pup, sensing a journey, got up looking anxious, staring up at Wade, her tail wagging.

Wade stepped off the porch, swung up onto the mare, and settled into his saddle.

Morgan stepped off the porch holding the two cups. "See much of Mrs. Jordan?"

Wade looked thoughtful as he shook his head. "No, I don't. Why are you asking?"

Morgan shrugged. "Just curious."

Wade leaned on the saddle horn and looked down at him. "Why don't you come to town and ask her out to dinner?" Leaving Morgan to think about that, Wade backed the mare away from the hitching rail, nudged her into a trot, and yelled over his shoulder, "See ya later, Morgan."

He watched Wade ride away with Pup beside the red sorrel mare, thinking dinner with Mrs. Jordan may not be a bad idea.

April

March quietly slipped into April, and Wade passed the warm Saturday afternoon sitting in the wooden chair on the porch of the jailhouse with his feet against the porch post. Jed opened the door, Pup stepped out, walked across the boardwalk, and relieved herself before lying down next to Wade's chair.

"Feel like a game of checkers or cards?" asked Jed.

Wade reached down and petted Pup's head and neck with his hand. "Not right now. I need to take a walk around town."

Looking disappointed, Jed said, "Maybe later?"

"Maybe," said Wade. Then he eased the chair's front legs to the boardwalk, took both feet off the post, and as he stood, three men riding up to the hitching rail of the saloon caught his eye. They glanced his way before they dismounted, tied their horses to the railing, walked across the boardwalk and into the saloon. He stared after them for a moment, getting that uneasy feeling, and then asked Jed to take Pup back inside. Pup was reluctant, but Jed managed to get her inside then watched as Wade stepped off the boardwalk and crossed the street toward the saloon.

Pausing at the hitching rail, Wade looked at the horses that had the look of a long ride and checked for a brand. Finding none, he walked up the steps to the boardwalk, opened the door, stepped into the noisy, busy saloon, and walked to the corner of the bar where he could see the entire saloon.

Goody saw him and smiled. "What'll it be, Sheriff?"

Wade glanced around the busy place. "Beer."

While Goody filled a mug with beer, Wade continued to glance around the room, looking for the three men. As his gaze wandered the room of familiar faces, he wondered if one of these good citizens of Pickering enjoying a whiskey or beer was the killer of Estelle Winters. Dave set the mug of beer on the bar about the time Wade found the three men sitting at a table with two of Goody's whores. "Them three talking to Eve and Joyce, ever see them before?"

Dave took a quick look and shook his head. "No, I ain't." He looked at Wade. "Why so interested?"

Wade thought of Bill Conners. "Just curious."

"As long as they spend money," said Dave, "and don't cause no trouble, I'm happy."

Someone down the bar yelled for a beer, and Dave hurried away.

Wade leaned against the bar looking in the big mirror at the three men who appeared more interested in Eve and Joyce than they were anything else. Deciding they were harmless, he turned and looked for an empty table. Seeing one next to the back wall, Wade picked up his beer, but instead of walking directly toward the table, he walked past the three men to have a closer look. As he approached their table, they looked up. Wade nodded, looking friendly as he walked past, noticing their boots were covered in trail dust, same as their clothes, and all three needed a shave. Figuring they were drifters, he walked to his table, tossed his hat in one chair, and sat down in another, giving him a clear view of the door and the three men. He took a drink of the beer, wiped the foam from his mouth, and glanced around, noticing the three men were watching him. Wade glanced at them for a long moment, gave a quick look around the room, then picked up his mug and took a drink of beer.

The door opened, and Morgan Hunter stepped inside.

Wade watched as he approached the bar, said something to Goody, who glanced around and then pointed toward Wade.

Morgan turned and, seeing Wade, walked across the room to Wade's table.

"What brings you to town?" asked Wade.

Morgan sat down and grinned proudly. "Took your advice."

Wade looked puzzled. "About the pigs?"

Morgan's face turned a little dark while ignoring the question. "I called on Mrs. Jordan this afternoon."

Wade smiled. "Oh, that advice. And how is Mrs. Jordan?"

"Katharine's fine." Morgan grinned like a schoolboy. "We went for a buggy ride."

Wade raised his brow. "So now it's Katharine?"

Dave was at the table with two beers Morgan had ordered and set them down.

Morgan put some money on the table and watched Goody pick it up. After he walked away, Morgan leaned on the table with his forearms and shrugged. "Seems easier than Mrs. Jordan."

Wade thought about Sarah and how much he missed her. "Mrs. Jordan seems like a right nice lady."

Morgan thought of Ana while he took a drink of beer. "She is that."

"And where did you take your lady friend for a ride?"

Hunter smiled looked a little embarrassed. "She fixed a picnic..."

"Picnic," interrupted Wade.

Morgan gave him a look. "You gonna let me finish or not?"

Wade grinned. "Sorry, go ahead." Then he drank his beer, pushed the mug away, and pulled the new one closer.

"We rode out to a nice little spot by the river where she spread a blanket." He shrugged. "We ate and talked for a couple of hours."

Wade thought of Sarah once again. "How'd you know where she lived?"

Morgan grinned. "Had to ask around, and that wasn't easy. She was a bit surprised when she opened the door."

Wade chuckled. "I bet she was."

243

Morgan gave Wade a look as he took a drink of beer. "She and her husband used to own a farm east of here, and after he died, she bought a small house up the street from Doc Reid."

"Appears you two did some talking?"

"Well, you just don't sit, eat, and look at the water pass by," said Morgan irritably.

Wade took a drink of beer, wondering what Morgan told her about his past. "What did you tell her about yourself?"

"Enough to satisfy her curiosity, I think. I kept asking questions about her and her husband."

Wade looked at the clock above the bar, seeing it was nearly five-thirty. "I'm hungry. You got time to get something to eat before you head out to your place?" Then he grinned. "That's unless you're too full from all that food, Mrs. Jordan, or should I say Katherine fixed."

"It wasn't all that much." Morgan took his watch out of his pocket. "She's not a big eater. I should be heading back soon." Then he grinned. "But I'll have a cup of coffee and keep you company."

"Good," said Wade. "Drink up."

Morgan drank his beer, and as he sat his mug down, he noticed three men walking toward them with slickers pulled back over their holsters. "You expecting company?" Then he stood, pushing the chair away from the table with the back of his legs.

Wade stood, turned, and looked at the three strangers knowing they weren't coming over to be sociable.

The one closest to him said, "This is for Elizabeth," then went for his gun.

Wade went for his and fired, first hitting the man in the belly, but he managed to get off a wild shot as he fell backward over a chair hitting Morgan's empty mug sitting on the table. At about the same moment, Morgan drew and fired at the second man, whose gun had cleared his holster, hitting him in the chest. The force of the bullet knocked him back onto a table where four men were playing poker, spilling beer, money, and cards all over the floor. In the next moment, both Wade and Morgan fired on the third man, who managed to get off a shot hitting Wade in the right thigh.

It was over in an instant, and a calm silence filled the saloon while everyone stood, or sat motionless, staring at Wade and Morgan as the smoke cleared.

Morgan hurried to each man kicking their guns away and checking their pulses. "They won't be drawing on anyone again," he said as he stood from the last man. Turing to Wade, he saw blood on Wade's right leg. "You're hit."

Wade holstered his Colt and sat down, holding his leg looking angry. "Damn it to hell."

Morgan knelt next to his chair, examining the wound. "You'll live, but we need to get you to Doc Reid's place."

Wade looked at his wound, "Damn it to hell!" Filled with anger, he looked at Morgan. "I'm sure as hell tired of getting shot."

Morgan chuckled softly, holstered his gun, and then helped him up. "Let's get you to Doc's place."

"No," said Wade stubbornly. "Take me to the jailhouse and send Jed for the doc."

Dave Goody walked up with his twelve-gauge in his hands. "What the hell was that all about?"

"Shit if I know," said Wade angrily.

Goody looked at his leg. "You all right, Sheriff?"

Wade was angry and took it out of Dave. "Does it look like I'm all right, Dave?"

Dave Goody turned to the three men lying on the floor, wishing they'd heeded his advice earlier about spending money and not causing any trouble.

Morgan and Wade started for the door when Wade stopped and looked at Goody. "Send for Noonan will you, Dave, and tell him to check for any papers that might tell me who the hell they were."

"I'll do that, Sheriff."

Jed stood on the boardwalk in front of the Sheriff's Office, wondering what happened when Morgan and Wade walked out of the saloon. Seeing that Wade was injured, Jed hurried across the street. "Let me give a hand," he said, then took Wade's other arm and put it over his shoulder.

Once inside the jail, Pup smelled the blood and was at their heels, trying to see what was wrong with Wade.

Morgan shooed her away and managed to close the door to keep her in the office while getting Wade to his bed.

"Get the doc," Morgan told Jed.

Jed opened the door to leave when Pup darted past him, jumped on the bed, and tried to sniff Wade's leg, but he pushed her away, telling her to get off.

Reluctantly she got off the bed, sat on her bed under the window, and whined as she watched Morgan help Wade off with his boots, gun belt, and pants.

Doc Reid opened the door of Wade's room, stuck his head out, and looked at Morgan and then Jed. "You can come in now."

Morgan got up from Wade's creaking chair, Jed from the leather sofa, and walked into the room looking worried. Pup was taken out of the room so Doc Reid could work on Wade, hurried past them, sniffed a sleeping Wade, and then and lay down on her bed, resting her head on her paws.

"How's he doing, Doc?" asked Morgan softly.

"It's not so bad," said Doc. "I gave him a little laudanum, so he's sleeping at the moment. No bones are broken, and no major arteries were hit. I had an easy time getting the bullet out."

He turned and picked up the bullet and handed it to Morgan. "Looks like a .44."

Morgan took the bullet, looked at it, and then gave it to Jed.

Canon examined it and then put it into his pocket.

Doc turned to the dresser and began cleaning his instruments. "He's going to be sore for a few days, and it'd be best if he stayed off that leg for the next day or so. I'll stop by and check on him tomorrow." He looked at Morgan and Jed. "I don't want him coming down with an infection."

"Don't worry, Doc," said Jed. "I'll see he stays in bed."

Reid looked at Jed. "Tomorrow, he can sit up, but he needs to keep the leg elevated."

Jed looked at Wade and shook his head in understanding.

"How long is he going to be out?' asked Morgan.

Reid looked at Wade. "He's full of laudanum and may sleep till morning." He smiled. "Maybe I should move my practice in the gun shop next door."

Morgan laughed at that. "Might be a lot easier, Doc."

Doc shook his head. "Man sure gets more than his share of trouble." He turned back to cleaning his instruments. "Maybe he ought to think about another profession."

Morgan looked at the sleeping sheriff and contemplated the same thing.

Wade opened his eyes to a dark room, sat up onto his elbows, and looked toward the light coming through the cracks of the door. "Jed!"

The door opened, and Morgan walked in, followed by Jed carrying a lantern.

"I have to go," said Wade sounding drunk.

Knowing it was the laudanum, Jed set the lantern on the dresser and reached under the bed for the pot, and then he and Morgan helped Wade stand.

247

After Wade took the pot, he realized he was bare ass naked but didn't give a damn at this point.

As Morgan helped him get back into bed, he asked, "Any more of that stuff?" Referring to the laudanum.

Morgan looked at the bottle on the dresser that had just enough left for one small dose. He picked it up and handed it to Wade. "Doc left this for you saying this is all you're gonna get."

Wade took the bottle. "Leg hurts like hell." Then he uncorked the bottle, drank what was inside, handed the empty bottle to Morgan, and closed his eyes.

The sun was up, and the room full of daylight when Wade opened his eyes and sat up the following morning, feeling the pain in his leg. He glanced at the dresser for the bottle of laudanum and, not seeing it, remembered he drank the last of it the night before. He tossed the covers back, feeling the chilly morning air on his naked body, and slowly put both legs over the side of the bed onto the cold floor. Noticing the coyote lying in her bed, watching him, he asked, "What are you looking at?"

Pup wagged her tail and whined softly, got up, and smelled the bandages on his leg.

Wade reached out and petted her neck and shoulder while he considered his clothes, then gently pushed her away and slowly stood, with the help of the bedpost and wall. In pain from the blood rushing into the leg, he moved along the wall to the dresser, slowly bent over, and opened the bottom drawer. He took out a pair of white long johns, dark blue pants from another drawer, and a folded yellow shirt.

Morgan walked in. "What the hell are you doing up?"

Wade looked at him. "Getting dressed, what the hell's it look like I'm doing?"

Morgan chuckled as he walked toward him. "Get your bare ass back to bed. The doc said you should stay in bed today."

"Screw the doc. I'm getting dressed."

Morgan took the clothes from Wade, set them down on the dresser, and then helped him back to bed. "The first thing you're gonna do is eat."

Wade looked up at him. "I ain't staying in bed, Morgan."

"You rest until we see what Doc says later today. Feel like eating?"

Wade thought on that and decided he hurt too much to argue. "I guess I could eat as long as it's not soup again."

Morgan chuckled. "Good, I'll go across the street and bring you back some breakfast." Then he said, "If Doc ain't here by the time you finish, I'll go get him. How's that sound?"

Wade looked relieved. "All right, Morgan, but I ain't staying in bed."

Morgan shook his head, thinking he was stubborn, turned, and headed for the door talking over his shoulder. "You're a stubborn bastard."

"Bring some food back for Pup!" called Wade. After Morgan left the room, Wade looked at Pup. "He'll bring you some breakfast." Then he put his hand on his hurting leg, closed his eyes, and drifted off to sleep.

Morgan sat in the chair next to Wade's bed, sipped his coffee, and watched as he ate with the same enthusiasm as Pup was eating her food. "Who's Elizabeth?"

Wade stopped chewing and looked at him with a confused look as he swallowed. "What?"

Just then, the door opened, and Doc Reid walked in carrying a pair of crutches. "You'll be needing these for a few days." He leaned the crutches against the wall at the foot of the bed. "Eating's a good sign." Then he walked to the edge of the bed and felt Wade's head. "No fever." He poked the bandage a little with his fingers. "That hurt?"

Wade flinched. "Hell, yes!"

Reid chuckled. "I need to change the bandages as soon as you finish your breakfast."

"Cup of coffee?" asked Morgan.

Reid looked interested. "Believe I will."

Morgan got up, telling Doc to have a seat while he got his coffee.

Doc glanced around the room, letting his eyes settle on Pup. "Strange seeing a coyote lying on the floor staring back at me."

Wade looked down at Pup. "I guess it does at that." Then he shoved the last of his food into his mouth, placed the fork on the empty plate, and handed it to Doc, who placed it on the dresser.

Morgan walked in with Doc's coffee.

Doc took it and thanked him after he tasted the strong, black coffee. He placed the cup on the sill of the window and asked Morgan to sit on the bottom of the bed so he could hold Wade's leg up while he took off the bandage.

Morgan did as asked and watched as Doc began unwrapping the bandage. "How's it look, Doc?"

"I was afraid he would start bleeding again," said Doc as he took off the final wrap. "There's a little seepage, is all." He looked at Wade. "Good thing you stayed in bed."

Wade and Morgan looked at one another, and then Wade asked, "So, I can get up?"

"You need to stay off this for a day or two," said Doc. "You don't have to stay in bed, but I don't want you out walking around town a lot."

"What's a lot, Doc?" asked Wade.

"You being smart?" asked Reid looking irritated.

Wade shook his head. "No, doc, I'm just curious."

Reid tossed the bandages on the floor, which caught Pup's attention, and she began sniffing at them. "Get away from there," scolded Reid as he bent down, picked them up, and placed them on the dresser next to Wade's clothes.

Jed had been at the door watching, so he called Pup and took her outside.

Reid went back to examining the wound, and then he opened his black bag, took out a bottle, some cotton, and began cleaning the skin around the stitches. "You can walk from here to the next room and the outhouse, even sit on the front porch later today, but keep the leg elevated so it won't hurt. Tomorrow we'll see how this looks."

Smiling, Wade said, "You're the boss, Doc."

"It would be good if you remembered that." Reid put the cork back into the bottle and returned it to his bag, took out a roll of gauze bandage, and began wrapping Wade's leg as he looked at Morgan. "You staying in town?"

Morgan nodded. "For part of the day, and then I have to head back to my place. I have someone to see before I leave."

Doc glanced at Morgan, recalling that he saw him and Katherine Jordan leaving in a carriage yesterday and wondered how close they were. He finished with the bandage, put the rest of the gauze into his black bag, and then looked at Wade. "Get some rest. I'll check in on you later."

Jed returned with Pup, and as she ran to Wade's bed, Jed looked at Doc Reid. "He alright?"

"I'm tired for some reason, Doc," said Wade.

"That's your body talking to you. Get some rest."

As Wade closed his eyes Doc, Jed, and Morgan left the room, leaving Pup curled up in her bed on the floor next to Wade's bed.

Two days later, Wade sat at his desk, eating lunch with his injured leg propped up on a chair when Morgan walked in. He smiled at him. "How's Katherine?"

Morgan ignored the question and said hello to Jed before he looked at Wade. "How's the leg?"

"Almost good as new," replied Wade, then shoving the last of his lunch into his mouth, he asked, "Coffee?"

"Don't mind if I do."

Jed jumped up. "I'll get you a cup."

"Sit down and finish your meal," said Morgan as he took off his gloves, hat, and coat, placing all three on the leather sofa. "I know where the cups are." He walked around the desk to the stove and poured a cup of coffee while glancing around, asking, "Where's Pup?"

Wade gestured to the bedroom. "Sleeping."

Morgan set the pot back on the stove, took a sip, thinking it was a little strong, and eased into the leather sofa. "Have you given any thought as to why those three drew down on us yesterday?"

Wade shook his head. "I have, but the reasons escape me."

Hunter stared into his coffee. "Maybe the answer lies with this, Elizabeth."

"I've thought on that," said Wade, looking puzzled. "I don't recall anyone by that name."

"Past lover?" asked Jed.

Wade shook his head. "The name means nothing to me. There's only been one woman in my life, and her name's not Elizabeth."

Morgan took a thoughtful drink of the strong coffee. "Well, since she almost got my ass killed, I'd sure as hell like to know what this is all about."

"Soon as you drink that coffee," said Wade, "we'll pay Earl Noonan a visit."

The April sun was warm, but the noon air was still crisp and chilly when Wade followed Morgan out of the office with the crutches Doc had left. Limping along the boardwalk, he thought of his son's broken leg and the man responsible. They made their way along the boardwalk to Noonan's barbershop, and when they opened the door and stepped into the empty shop. The tiny bell above the door told of their arrival and again as Morgan shut the door.

Wade called out, "Earl Noonan?"

Moments later, Earl Noonan walked out of the backroom he always referred to as the parlor, said good morning, and asked Wade how his leg was.

"Sore," replied Wade, then he gestured to Morgan. "Earl, this is Morgan Hunter."

Earl reached out and shook Morgan's hand. "We already met. You bought Kyle's place."

Before Hunter could answer, Wade asked if the three men from the saloon had any papers or identification.

Noonan shook his head no, saying each man carried two brand-new fifty-dollar gold coins in their pockets along with several other coins, but no papers that would tell who they were.

Morgan looked at Wade. "Three hundred's a good amount for revenge."

"Revenge?" repeated Noonan looking curious.

Wade was disappointed they had no papers and ignored Noonan. Then as the room fell silent, he remembered the gold coins in Bill Conners's pocket. "That fella Conners had the same amount in his pocket."

"Sometimes," began Hunter, "men carve their initials on the inside of their gun belts."

Earl gestured to the parlor door. "They're on a table back in the parlor."

Wade looked hopeful. "Let's have a look." He and Morgan followed Earl into the back room, where Wade paused on his crutches next to three coffins leaning against the wall. Each contained a body of one of them men that he and Morgan killed, thinking they looked a little cramped. Then he limped across the room, careful not to bump anything with his leg, and watched as Morgan checked the three gun belts. "This one has the initials

CT." Then Morgan picked up the second. "BM here," he said and then picked up the third. "Nothing." He shrugged. "Maybe this one couldn't write."

"Doesn't tell us much," said Wade as he looked at Noonan. "How about their saddlebags?"

Earl looked baffled. "I guess they're with the horses at the livery."

Thinking of the long walk, Wade limped toward the door. "Let's pay Bennett a visit."

Albert Bennett was busy greasing a buggy wheel when Wade and Morgan walked up to the livery. He stopped what he was doing, set the can of grease down, wiped his hands on a dirty cloth, said good morning, and then asked how the leg was.

"Sore," replied Wade while leaning on the crutches thinking they should have rested at the Sheriff's Office. "Noonan said you're holding the horses belonging to the three men that tried to gun down Morgan and me."

Bennett nodded, yes. "They're inside. We'll auction them off next week."

Wade and Morgan followed him into the livery, where he showed them the saddles and other belongings of the three men. "You go through their belongings?" asked Wade.

"Why no," said Al. "I was waiting for you."

Wade leaned the crutches against the livery wall and started through one of the saddlebags.

Morgan lit a lantern and started checking under the saddles for names. "Got a name here."

Wade stopped and looked up.

"Charlie T. No last name."

Wade waited with interest.

Morgan checked another saddle. "Nothing." Then he lifted the third saddle and held the lantern close to it. "Billy M."

Well, that's something," said Wade as he went back to looking through their saddlebags of dirty shirts, pants, spare cartridges, tobacco, and a half-bottle of whiskey.

"Check the shirt pockets," said Morgan. "You never know, one of 'em might have forgotten something."

Wade did that and found a folded piece of paper. Looking at Morgan, he unfolded the paper and started reading aloud. "Girls – Beer – Whiskey – Cards." He looked at Morgan. "Elk Horn Saloon, Miles City, Montana."

"That help?" asked Albert.

"It's a start," said Wade as he stuffed everything back into the saddlebags but the half-bottle of whiskey, which he handed to Bennett. He thanked Al for his time, grabbed his crutches then he and Morgan headed back along the street toward the jail.

"Not much to go on," said Morgan as they headed toward the boardwalk and the jail. "You ever been to Miles City?"

"Nope."

"You sure?" asked Morgan.

Wade managed the crutches onto the boardwalk. "I'd remember if I had Morgan."

When they reached the jail, Morgan said he had to get back to his ranch, said goodbye to Wade, and climbed up on his Appaloosa.

Wade watched him ride away, then went inside and spent the next few days thinking about Bill Conners and the three men in the saloon. His only explanation was that someone in Harper had figured out that Emmett Spears was Wade Garrison and wanted him dead. But who was the question? Then he realized that if someone in Harper knew his real name, it wouldn't be long until the Marshal's office in Denver did. Considering that possibility, he thought he might head west into Oregon if he had to.

Chapter 19

May

It was late May, and the afternoon sun painted everything sunset colors of deep reds and oranges that would disappear with darkness. Wade's leg had healed but would still hurt some after a long ride. He was sitting in his chair on the boardwalk, enjoying the warm May afternoon, remembering evenings such as this on the porch with Sarah while Emmett played in his room. One of Purdy's girls stepped out of the saloon and stood on the boardwalk, looking up and down the street, puffing on a thin cigar, and he thought of Estelle. Wade was no closer to solving Estelle's murder than he was the riddle of who Elizabeth was or the men sent to kill him. The only thing he was sure of was he had become suspicious of any stranger riding into Pickering.

Tom Purdy stepped out of the saloon, said something to the whore who tossed her thin cigar into the street, and went back inside. Tom stood at the edge of the boardwalk and glanced up and down the street until his eyes settle on Wade. They looked at one another for a quick moment with neither acknowledging the other, and then he stepped back inside and closed the door of the saloon. Wade stared at the closed door contemplating Tom and Estelle's relationship, finding it hard to believe that a man such as Tom Purdy owned a saloon and ran with whores. But as his father once told him, you can't judge a book by its cover.

In his mind, Wade played out the night Dave Goody found Estelle over and over, picturing the way she was stuffed into the outhouse, eyes open, her neck slashed, her chest and clothes covered in sticky blood. He thought about the shoe prints in the snow that disappeared into several other tracks and the blood in the snow where Estelle had struggled for her life. The only evidence he had was the approximate shoe size, and he couldn't go around measuring everyone's shoe.

Noticing the reds and oranges of dusk were gone, and the streets and shadows were getting darker with the coming of night. Filled with frustration over Estelle's unsolved death, he eased the front legs of his chair down to the boardwalk, took his foot off the porch post, and stood. After stretching, he picked up the chair to move it against the Sheriff's Office wall when he bumped Pup.

Startled out of a sound sleep, she jumped up, growled, and snapped at the leg of the chair.

"Easy," said Wade in a stern voice. "The chair means you no harm."

Pup looked up at Wade, stretched, and then walked into the street and squatted, leaving a small puddle on the hard soil.

The soft neigh of a horse broke the quiet evening, and both Pup and Wade turned, seeing a single rider at the far end of town. As his thumb and forefinger of his right hand found the butt of his Colt, he thought of Bill Conners and the other three men. He stepped to the edge of the boardwalk next to the porch post and watched the rider slowly make his way up the street. The horse and rider rode in and out of the light from the windows. As the rider got closer, Wade recognized him as one of the Croucher hands. Though he didn't know his name, they waved at one another, and then Wade turned, called Pup, and went inside.

Late that evening, temperatures plummeted, and a heavy, wet May snow blanketed southern Montana, leaving a half-foot of snow on the streets of Pickering and the surrounding countryside.

257

Wade filled his tin cup with coffee, stood by the old leather sofa, and looked out at the snow-covered street. Remembering other snows in Colorado in late May and early June, he hoped it would be a quiet evening, took a drink of coffee, and wondered how Morgan was doing out at his ranch.

Jed was sitting at the desk, setting up the checkers while Pup scratched at the door wanting out. "Want me to take her out?"

Wade looked at Pup. "I'll do it." Then he set his cup on the desk, got the rope, and took her outside. The snow-covered street was empty, and the shadows of lighted windows lay across the white street like islands separated by oceans of darkness. Soft piano music flowed from the saloon, and Wade pictured Chubby or the whore, Mary Lee, at the piano's keys. Pup finished coloring the snow yellow, so Wade took her inside, where she walked into an empty cell, jumped up on the cot, lay down, closed her eyes, and went to sleep.

"Checker board's set up," said Jed.

Wade put the rope away, sat down, opened the bottom drawer of his desk, and pulled out the bottle of whiskey. He took out the cork, poured a little in each of their coffees, and then corked the bottle, returning it to the drawer.

Time passed quickly, and after several games, Wade looked up at the clock seeing it was almost nine-thirty. "I've had enough, Jed. I'm going to make my rounds."

Jed dumped the checkers into a small wooden box, picked the board up, and put the game on the top shelf of the closet.

Wade shrugged into his wool winter coat, then put on his gloves and walked toward the door putting on his hat, "Be back in a while. Keep Pup inside." He opened the door and stepped onto the boardwalk, greeted by the quiet, cold night air. Light from the saloon's windows and a few other lighted windows of town left their shapes across the boardwalks and snowy street. Most windows were void of light, and he figured people were in bed by now. He adjusted the collar of his coat as he walked along the boardwalk, keeping close to the buildings for protection against the chilly breeze that made its way along the main street of Pickering. He checked the doors to the bank first, and then he continued along the boardwalk to the next door and the next until the boardwalk suddenly ended, leading to the alley where he had been beaten. He stepped off into the snow that crunched under his feet and walked across the street, glancing toward the alley regretting that Morgan had killed Brodie, and Jed, Harry Anderson. He had wanted that pleasure for himself.

Reaching the other side of the street, he stepped onto the boardwalk, checked the first door, and glanced in the window, then repeated the process until he reached the end of town where he crossed the street under a cloudless, black sky of stars and a full moon glistening off of the white snow. Stepping onto the boardwalk, he paused and looked south and Colorado. Wishing he could go home, he turned and checked the first door, then the second, and so on until he reached the saloon.

Pausing at the window, he looked past the white lettering 'Saloon,' seeing but a few familiar customers and Goody standing next to Mary Lee at the piano while Chubby was taking a break nursing a mug of beer. Dave and Mary Lee smiled at one another as they talked, and then she began playing a soft tune while Dave returned to the bar and a customer in need. Wade stepped away from the window and walked along the boardwalk to where the saloon meets the alley. Stepping into the alley, he paused to look in the direction of the outhouse, thinking of Estelle's murder. Wanting to get out of the cold, as he started walking across the street toward the jailhouse when the neigh of a horse broke the stillness. He stopped, turned, and stared down the dark alley that was a mixture of black and gray shadows on the hard, shadowy snow, wondering where the neigh came from.

Drawing his pistol, he stepped closer to the building then hurried cautiously through the narrow alleyway. Reaching the rear of the building, he poked his head around the corner and looked out across the dim moonlit-covered snow. Seeing nothing, he started to step out when a horse and rider suddenly bolted out of the dark shadows, disappearing into another alleyway further up. Wade turned and ran back along the alley to the street in time to see him ride across the street and disappear into another alley between the gunsmith shop and the land office. By the time he reached the dark alley across the street, it was empty. Wade turned and looked across the street at the alley the rider rode out of a few moments ago and got the feeling that something was wrong. Picturing Estelle laying half in and half out of the outhouse, he holstered his pistol and hurried back to the jail to get a lantern.

Jed was full of questions as Wade walked in.

"I'll explain later," Wade said as he hurried outside, leaving Jed to puzzle over the lantern. Stepping off the boardwalk, he ran down the snowy street and into the alley where he first saw the rider. With the help of the lantern, Wade found the tracks and knelt to examine them. Standing, he looked out across the open ground at the spattering of lighted windows of houses and shacks. Knowing the rider came from one of them, Wade held the lantern in front of him and followed the tracks to a dark shack with the door ajar. Thinking of the cabin in Colorado where he found Dog and the murdered family long ago, he drew his pistol, cocked it, and holding the lantern up, cautiously walked up to the door and pushed it open with the barrel of his pistol. The cold, dark night filled with the creaking sound of the door as he cautiously stepped inside. Holding the lantern in front of him with one hand, the other holding his gun, he stood in the stillness of the kitchen, moving the lantern this way and that, searching the dark corners of the small room.

Seeing a doorway leading to another room, he called out. "Hello, this is Sheriff Spears. Anyone here?" Getting no response, he stepped around the small kitchen table and chairs. Pausing at the doorway, he shoved the lantern into the other room then peered around the corner of the doorjamb. The room was crowded with inexpensive furniture, a chair, and a small table overturned on the floor. He turned with the lantern, glanced behind him into the kitchen and the open back door to make sure he was alone. Then he raised the lantern a little higher and stepped into the small living room, hearing and feeling something crunch under his foot. Looking down, he lifted his foot, seeing he had stepped on a broken glass sculpture.

It was then that he saw the leg of a woman sticking out from behind the small sofa. Stepping closer, he knelt, careful not to step in the pool of blood, and set the lantern on the floor. He holstered his pistol and gently turned her over, recognizing her as someone he had seen around town but didn't know her name. Her eyes were open, her mouth agape, and her throat cut the same as Estelle's. The left side of her face red from lying in the pool of her own blood. Just as with Estelle, there were several stab wounds in her chest and stomach. Thinking of Estelle's murder, he gently lifted the dress and looked between her legs but found no sign of disfigurement. Relieved at that, he lowered the dress and checked her arms and hands, finding both had defensive wounds. He thought she, like Estelle, had fought hard for her life.

Noticing another open door, he picked up the lantern and drew his pistol as he stood and looked inside the room, finding a neatly made bed. A piece of clothing lay over the back of a chair, and the curtain of the standing closet was pulled to one side, exposing more clothing. Nothing in either the closet or the bedroom looked in disarray. He glanced back at the body from the doorway and wondered if the dead woman and Estelle knew one another and made that the next mystery to solve. He picked up a blanket from the foot of the bed and covered the body, wondering if the two murders were connected. Wade knelt and looked at the bloody bootprints leading back into the kitchen and thought of the rider he had seen earlier. He started to get up when he noticed a second set of bloody shoe prints in the dim light and thought of those in the snow next to Estelle. Standing, he raised the lantern holding it in front of him, and followed the shoe and boot prints into the kitchen and outside into the chilly night air.

Kneeling while holding the lantern above his head, he studied the snow around the shack's door, finding the boot prints left a slight rose color in the snow next to those of a horse and the shoe prints that resembled those he found at the outhouse where Estelle was murdered. Both were leading in different directions. "Are there two of you bastards?" he asked himself in a whisper. Contemplating that, he stood in the cold, staring in the direction the horse and rider and gone, then he pulled the door of the shack closed and followed the shoeprints. They led him down another alley between two buildings to the street, where he lost them among the many tracks of wagons, horses, and people. He stood in the middle of the lonely street, glancing in both directions, trying to decide whether he should wake Doc up tonight or wait until morning. Thinking of the warm jailhouse, coffee, and getting his feet warm, he quickly decided this could wait until morning and headed for the warmth of the jailhouse.

The images of Estelle and the girl in the shack kept Wade from getting much sleep that night, so he was up before dawn, noisily stoking the stove and making coffee that woke Jed. He apologized for waking him while offering him a cup of coffee.

Jed walked out of his cell, scratching his head and looking sleepy as he took the coffee and slid into the leather sofa. Taking a drink while thinking of what Wade told him about the other girl. "Hope you catch these fella's before they kill another."

Agreeing with Jed, Wade stood and reached for his gun belt, strapped it on, and then put on his coat that hung from the back of his chair.

"Where ya going?" asked Jed.

While shrugging into his coat, Wade looked at the clock seeing it was still early. "To get Doc Reid." He picked up his black hat and, while putting it on, said, "Then I'm gonna see if I can pick up the tracks of the man I saw last night."

Thinking they may need help with the body, Jed asked, "Want me to come along?"

Wade considered the offer while looking out the window across the snow-covered street at the alley. "No, you stay with Pup." He opened the door, stepped outside to an early morning sky of gray clouds mixed with pinks and purples at the horizon. The air was cold and crisp, turning his breath white as he walked toward Doc Reid's place.

"Who's there?" asked Doc Reid from the other side of the closed door.

"Sheriff Spears."

The sound of the lock turning broke the cold stillness of the porch, and as the door opened, Reid had the look of someone being awakened from a sound sleep and unhappy about it. "What is it?"

"I need you, Doc."

Doc Reid turned and looked at the clock in the hall. "It's only five-thirty. Can't it wait?"

Wade shook his head, looking sorry. "No, it can't."

Reid opened the door and stepped back. "Come in, then. What's wrong?"

Wade stepped inside, feeling the warmth of the house, seeing Doc's mother standing in her bedroom doorway dressed in a blue robe, also wearing an unhappy look.

Wade took off his hat. "Sorry to disturb you, ma'am."

Reid closed the door and, in a soft, respectful voice, politely told her to go back to bed.

She turned in silent disappointment, stepped back into her room, and closed the door.

Reid turned to Wade. "What can be so important this time of the morning?"

Wade glanced toward the closed door of Reid's mother's bedroom, leaned his head toward him, and lowered his voice. "We have another murder."

Reid couldn't believe what he just heard. "Who?"

"I don't know her name. She lives in one of the shacks east of town."

"I'll get dressed," he said, gesturing to a chair for Wade. "I won't be a moment."

Doc Reid returned a few minutes later dressed for the chilly outdoors but quickly disappeared into his office, leaving Wade standing in the parlor. When he returned, he was carrying an old canvas stretcher. "We'll need this."

Remembering how they carried Estelle to Doc's office, Wade thought it was a good idea. As they stepped outside, the morning air was cold and crisp. The snow held the same gray mixed with pink and purple as the dawn sky as they hurried across the frozen, crunchy snow, chasing their white breath.

Reaching the small shack, they stepped inside, where Doc waited while Wade lit a couple of lanterns. Then Doc knelt next to the body while Wade placed an overturned chair upright and sat down to rest his aching right leg.

"Her name is Gracie Abbott," said Reid as he stood. "Who'd do such a thing?"

Wade rubbed his sore leg and wondered the same thing. "Can't say, Doc."

Doc Reid looked at Wade, rubbing his sore leg, thinking it was the cold air. "Well, let's get her back to my place."

When they stepped out of the shack carrying Gracie Abbott's covered body on the stretcher, the colors of the day had changed from the dark pinks and purples to lighter shades of oranges and reds. It was still early, so they managed to carry the body from the shack to his office without being seen. Inside they placed the stretcher with the covered body on one of the examining tables, and then Doc said he would go over the body after breakfast.

Wade returned to the Sheriff's Office for his Sharps Rifle, bandolier of cartridges. Not seeing Pup, he asked where she was.

Jed said she went back to bed in the bedroom.

Wishing he could, Wade grabbed a canteen, telling Jed he was going to track the man he saw last night.

"How long are you gonna be gone?"

Wade quickly considered. "Don't know, but I'll be back before sunset." Then he opened the door and stepped outside. The morning sky was a light blue with a scattering of orange and white clouds. Half of the sun that was still behind the horizon colored the hard snow a burnt orange. As he stepped off the boardwalk, he was not looking forward to waking Bennett this early to get the mare. He fussed with the front collar of his coat, pushed the fingers of his gloves tighter against his hands, and walked past the livery to Bennett's house, where he hesitated at the door before knocking.

"Who's there?" asked a sleepy Albert Bennett from behind the closed door.

"I need my mare, Al."

"And who the hell are you?"

"It's the sheriff."

Albert asked, "Kind of early, ain't it?"

"My apologies, Mr. Bennett, but I need to saddle my mare. It's important."

The door opened, and Albert stepped back, motioning Wade inside. "Come in."

"Sorry about having to wake you, Mr. Bennett."

Al scratched his messy hair and yawned as he looked at the Sharps rife. "Trouble?"

"Not yet."

265

Knowing he wasn't going to get anything more from the sheriff, he reached for a set of keys next to the door. "This key unlocks the back door." He handed the keys to Wade. "Leave them on a nail by the big doors upfront, and be sure you push them shut. There's a rock outside next to the wall you can use to set against the door so it won't open."

He took the keys, thanked Al, and headed for the back door of the livery, unlocked it then stepped inside. Greeted by the strong smell of urine and horse manure mixed with wet straw, he made his way through the dim livery and saddled the mare. When the mare was ready, he shoved his Sharps into its scabbard, tossed the bandolier over the saddle horn, then the canteen, and led the horse outside. Making sure the big doors were closed as Al asked, he swung up into the saddle, turned the mare, and rode along the street to the alleyway where the rider disappeared the night before. Once through the alley, it took him but a few minutes to find the tracks in the snow and follow them out of town.

Wade followed the tracks south, where they disappeared into the cold, icy water of the Powder River. As he sat in the saddle at the edge of the river, he considered his options for several minutes, knowing the Thornton place and Morgan's ranch were to the south. Neither had any hands working for them, so Wade looked north, thinking of the Croucher place, knowing the Big C covered a lot of land on both sides of the Powder River. He had never visited the place, so he was unsure which side of the river he would find the ranch but knew if the rider did work on the Big C, the tracks would lead him there. He also knew it was too cold to keep a horse in the river for long, so the rider had to have left the river soon after crossing.

He turned to look back at his own tracks in the bright white snow and then at the sun, which was still low in the sky and not yet warm. Concerned over snow blindness, he took off his bandana, tied it over his face just under his eyes, and then pulled his hat down a little more, leaving but a slit to see through. The flapping wings of a single bird that had been sitting on the branch of a leafless bush broke the stillness as it flew away. The mare shifted her weight, blew softly, and shook her head, rattling her bit and reins. Wade patted her neck as he looked north along the river and across to the other side, thinking the river was wide and looked shallow. Hoping it was, he nudged the mare into the shallow cold water.

Minutes later, he rode out of the river, pulled up and glanced around at the undisturbed snow, and cursed his bad luck. Keeping to plan, he rode north without finding the man's trail staying close to the riverbank, and after a mile of undisturbed snow, he pulled up in disappointment and considered his problem. Thinking he may be on the wrong side of the river, he returned to the shallow spot and crossed the river, then rode north.

It wasn't long before he found where the man he trailed had left the river heading east. "Got you, ya bastard," he said aloud as his gaze followed the tracks in the glistening, white snow toward the pine trees and hills about a half-mile due east. Nudging the mare into a gallop, he followed the tracks across the white snow into a forest of pine trees. Minutes later, he was at the edge of the trees looking at smoke drifting lazily from the chimneys of a big two-story ranch house about three hundred yards due east of him. A bunkhouse with smoke coming from three chimneys sat a couple of hundred yards behind the big house. The doors to the big barn were open, and he could see movement inside. Figuring this was the Croucher place, he turned in the saddle, took his long glass out of the saddlebag, and put it to his eye.

"Don't move," said a voice breaking the stillness.

Wade slowly raised his arms above his head.

"Pull that bandana down, and turn this way slowly so I can have a look at you."

Wade slowly did as asked, turning to see a rider hidden in the shade of the trees pointing a Winchester at him. "I'm Sheriff Emmett Spears from Pickering."

"I know who you are." The rider nudged his brown horse out of the trees.

Wade recognized Ted Giles, foreman of the Croucher ranch. "Can I put my hands down? They're getting a little tired."

Ted pulled up a few feet from Wade. "Go ahead." Then he lowered his rifle and looked at Wade with a curious face. "What the hell you doing hiding in these trees, spying on the Croucher house?"

Wade lowered his hands. "Is Ben Croucher in the house?"

"If he's who you're looking for, try riding down and knocking on the door. And just what is it you want to see Mr. Croucher about?"

Wade stuffed the long glass into his saddlebag. "I don't like explaining myself twice, Mr. Giles. If you take me to Mr. Croucher, I'll explain it to both of you."

Ted Giles shoved his rifle into the scabbard hanging from the front of his saddle and pointed toward the ranch house. "Go ahead. I'll follow."

Reaching the hitching rail next to the big covered porch, they dismounted and tied their horses. Giles watched while Wade untied his slicker from the back of his saddle and covered the mare with it. He led Wade up the steps, across the porch to the door, and knocked. While they waited, Ted stared at Wade, wondering why he was watching the house and what he wanted with Mr. Croucher.

The door opened, and a lovely lady in her fifties with brown hair and soft features dressed in a rose-colored dress with a white lace collar smiled at them.

"Hello, Mrs. Croucher," said Ted. "Could we see your husband?"

Looking puzzled, she stepped away from the door and gestured them in. "Please come in."

"Thank you, ma'am," said Ted.

268

They stomped the snow off their boots, stepped into the warm foyer, and removed their hats.

She looked at Wade. "Aren't you the sheriff of Pickering?"

Wade smiled. "Yes, ma'am. Name's Emmett Spears."

She held out her hand. "I'm Mrs. Rebecca Croucher, Mr. Spears." As Wade shook her tiny hand, she asked, "What brings the Sheriff of Pickering out on such a day?"

Wade glanced at Ted Giles and then smiled at Mrs. Croucher. "Just a little business with your husband."

She smiled. "My husband doesn't deal in small business matters, Mr. Spears."

Wade nodded. "Yes, ma'am, I suppose he doesn't."

"My husband will be with you shortly." Then she turned and disappeared through a doorway.

Minutes later, a door opened, and Ben Croucher, dressed in a brown suit, walked into the foyer looking puzzled. He glanced at Ted and then looked at Wade. "My wife said you have some business to discuss with me, Sheriff?"

Ted stepped toward Mr. Croucher. "Found this one looking at the ranch house through a spyglass."

Ben gave Wade a puzzling look. "Is there a reason for that, Sheriff?"

"Yes, sir, there is," said Wade

"Well, sir," said Croucher. "I'd like to know what that would be." Then he gestured toward a closed door. "Let's go into my study where you can explain yourself."

Wade and Ted Giles followed Ben Croucher into his study, and while Ben closed the door, Wade quickly glanced around the room of fine furniture and several paintings, one of which was of Mr. Croucher's wife above the stone fireplace filled with a warm fire. He thought of the Hoskins house the night he burned it down and the eyes of the lady in that painting, staring down at him as the painting burned.

Ben walked past the two men gesturing to a coat rack. "Take your coats off, gentlemen, and have a seat."

Wade took his coat off then sat down in one of the leather chairs in front of a big, dark mahogany desk, whose top was clean but for a small pile of papers.

Croucher walked toward a liquor cabinet, talking over his shoulder. "Can I offer you a whiskey or bourbon, Sheriff, to take the chill off?"

"Coffee would be better if it wouldn't be any trouble," replied Wade.

Ben stopped, turned, and looked at Wade. "Of course." Then he walked to the door, opened it, and called for his wife. Moments later, he was asking her to have some coffee brought to the library.

While they waited, Wade looked at the snow-covered landscape out the big window behind the desk, wondering how big the Big C was.

Mr. Croucher closed the door, turned, and asked, "How is old Jed Canon doing?"

Surprised at the concern, Wade got a puzzled look recalling how Morgan had told him that Mr. Croucher was very upset about Jed killing one of his men. "Jed's fine."

Just then, a knock came at the door, Ben walked over, opened it, and Mrs. Croucher walked in carrying a tray with three fine china cups and a silver pot of coffee. She set it down, poured a cup of coffee, and handed it to Wade. Ben told her that he could take care of the rest, thanked her, and, as she left, he poured a cup of coffee, handed it to Ted, and then poured another for himself. Ben picked up a bottle of whiskey and offered to pour some into Wade's coffee. "Take the chill off."

Wade held out his cup. "Maybe I will have a little."

Croucher poured a small amount into Wade's coffee as he smiled. "I reacted hastily over Jed, killing Harry Anderson. He and the others were always high spirited men, and I overlooked

270

certain things. When I found out the real truth about what happened between you and them, I was angry as hell."

Wade watched as Croucher poured a little whiskey into Ted's coffee cup and remembered the story about his son and the Indians. Maybe the man felt indebted to the men.

"Ain't that right, Ted?" Croucher asked.

Ted nodded. "Sure is Mr. Croucher."

Ben looked apologetically at Wade. "I've been meaning to stop by and say as much, but I don't get into town all that often these days, and when I do, it's usually on business, and then I get out just as fast as I rode in."

Wade smiled. "I understand."

Ben looked regretful. "I'm sorry about what happened between you and some of my men sheriff. If they hadn't gotten themselves shot by your friend, I'd have fired them."

Wade wondered how much of that was true. "Well, Sir, if Morgan hadn't, I would have after I healed."

Croucher stared into Wade's blue eyes, considering that, then turned toward his desk and sat down, recalling the men Brodie had beaten up or killed and smiled with doubt.

Wade recognized the skepticism in Croucher's smile. "It would be a mistake to underestimate me, Mr. Croucher."

Ben considered that as he sipped his whiskey coffee in thought. He set the cup down and studied the man sitting before him with broad shoulders and steady hands for a moment. "Yes, Mr. Spears, I believe it would be, and I'll not make that mistake." He smiled. "In either case, your friend saved us both from an unpleasant task." He smiled once more. "Do you still have that coyote?"

Wade smiled. "I do."

He stared at Wade a moment. "You're a strange man Mr. Spears, and I can't quite figure you out. You ride into town, get involved with four of my men over a little bitch coyote, become sheriff, get the shit kicked out of you, and you refuse to leave town." He picked up his coffee and stared at Wade. "Not many men would have stayed."

Wade took a drink of coffee. "I can't answer for other men, sir, but my mother always said I was stubborn."

Ben smiled, finding humor in that. "And just where is it you're from, if I may ask?"

"A little farm in South Carolina."

"And what brings you to our little town?"

Wade shrugged softly and grinned. "Pickering just happened to get in the way."

Croucher chuckled. "In the way of what?"

"The direction I was heading."

Big Ben looked at burning wood as it popped in the fireplace. "And where was that?" asked Croucher. "Or were you just drifting as so many men do these days?"

Wade thought about that as he drank the last of his coffee. "I believe you already know the answer to that."

Ben stared at Wade over the rim of his cup as he took a sip of his coffee. "You're a difficult man, Sheriff. I can understand your dear mother's dilemma." He paused, looking at Wade, wanting to know the man a little better. "You don't have the look of a sheriff."

Wade knew that Ben Croucher was trying to understand who he was, and he had to be careful. "And what does a sheriff look like?"

Ben took a drink. "More like that friend of yours from Texas."

"Morgan?"

Croucher nodded. "That'd be the one."

Wade smiled. "Morgan would make one hell of a sheriff, I'm sure."

Ben Croucher studied Wade and the scars left by Brodie and his men. "I can't tell you how sorry I am over that incident with Mr. Brodie and his friends." He paused. "Pickering is lucky to have such a man as you as sheriff."

Wade shrugged, wondering if he meant what he was saying. "I appreciate you saying so, Mr. Croucher, and as far as that other thing, it's over thanks to Jed and Morgan."

Ben stood with cup in hand, walked around the desk, taking a seat in one of the leather chairs next to Wade, and set the china cup on the small table between them. He had a troubled look. "I should have fired all of 'em a long time ago." He paused. "But there are reasons I couldn't."

"I've heard the story."

Croucher looked at him wanting to change the subject. "Now, what is all this about you spying on us from the trees?"

"I was trailing someone. One of your men, perhaps since his tracks led me here."

Ben Croucher's eyes narrowed. "Why would you be tracking one of my men?"

"I need to talk to him."

Croucher's eyes went to Ted Giles and back to Wade. "You'll not talk to one of my men unless I know what it's about."

"Fair enough." Then Wade told him about Gracie Abbot.

"That's terrible," said Ben, then he looked at Wade. "Do you think that whore, Estelle, and this Gracie girl were killed by the same man?"

"I don't know just yet, but it seems likely."

Croucher looked from Wade to his foreman Ted Giles. "Why does the name of this girl sound familiar?"

Wade looked from Ben to Ted.

Giles tossed his hands nervously. "I believe that's the little gal Logan was seeing a while back until they broke up."

"Who's Logan?" asked Wade.

Ben looked at him. "Logan Fortune. He works for me." Then he looked at Giles. "Is Logan on the place?"

Ted nodded. "He should be working in the barn."

Wade looked at Ted. "Was he in town last night?

Giles looked at Ben Croucher.

"Go on," said Ben. "Was he in town?"

Ted nodded quickly. "Yes, sir, he was."

Wade looked at Ben. "I'd like to talk to him."

Croucher looked at Ted and then Wade for a moment. "You thinking of arresting Logan over the girl's killing?"

Wade thought on that. "I'll be honest with you, Mr. Croucher. If I think he killed this girl, then I'll arrest him, but for now, I'd like to ask him a few questions."

Ben stood. "Fair enough." Then he told Ted to find Logan.

Ted Giles set his nearly empty cup on the small table and walk out of the room.

Ben walked to the coffee pot and picked it up. "Care for another coffee and a little whiskey while we're waiting for Ted and Logan?"

Wade stood with his cup and walked to the desk. "Thank you."

Several minutes passed, and when the door opened, Ted Giles walked in with another man that was a lean, strong man of forty with brown hair, dark eyes, and a clean-shaven face bearing the trophy lines of hot, dry summers in the sun and cold days. He appeared nervous as he stood facing Ben, then he looked at Wade and nodded. "Sheriff."

Wade didn't react but recognized him from around town.

Logan looked from Wade to his boss while nervously twirling his hat with his hands. "You wanted to see me, Mr. Croucher?"

Ben gestured to a chair. "Have a seat, Logan."

Fortune sat down, eyeing Wade, his badge, and pistol as he settled in the chair. He turned to Croucher and waited while his hands nervously twirled his hat.

Ben's face was heavy with concern. "Sheriff Spears wants to talk to you about that girl, you know, named Gracie."

Logan looked at Wade with a fearful expression.

Wade stood for effect, walked to the edge of the big mahogany desk, turned, and stared down at Logan. "I saw a rider leave town in a hurry last night and followed his tracks here this morning. Was that you?"

Tiny beads of sweat began to form on Logan's face. "It was me, alright," he said as he stood and turned to Croucher. "I didn't kill Gracie, Mr. Croucher. I swear I didn't." His voice was full of fear as he looked at Wade. "Gracie was dead when I got there."

"Take it easy, Mr. Fortune," said Wade as he gestured to the chair. "Sit down and tell me what happened."

Logan sat down on the edge of the leather chair, glancing from Wade, to Ted, to Croucher, and then with fear on his face, he looked at Wade.

"You want a drink, Son?" asked Ben softly.

Logan looked down at the floor, shook his head no, and then he looked up at Wade standing next to Croucher's mahogany desk. "I was in the saloon most of the night drinking and playing cards." He smiled at Ben. "I was lucky, too. Won twenty-three dollars off Cody, Billy, and three others."

Big Ben smiled warmly, feeling sorry for Logan. "That's good, Logan."

Wade remembered stopping at the saloon and looking at the clock through the window seeing it was a little after ten. He remembered some men at a table but didn't remember seeing Logan. "What time did the game break up?"

Logan looked down at his hat and thought for a moment. "Before ten."

Wade thought he could verify that with Dave Goody, and then he thought about the body in rigor and the way Doc Reid had said it took about two hours for that to take place. Logan couldn't have been the killer. "What happened then?"

"I finished my drink, and since I won a little money, I put some on the table for a couple of rounds for the others and left."

The room fell silent.

"What happened when you got to Miss Abbott's?" asked Wade.

"Well," Logan began, "the lights were out, and when I knocked, the door moved, and I thought that strange, so I stepped into the kitchen and called out to Gracie." He paused, put one hand to his wrinkled brow, and slowly shook his head, looking frightened. "It was awful."

Looking curious, Croucher asked, "What was awful, Logan?"

Wade glanced at Ben, wishing he'd let him ask the questions.

Logan shrugged. "I was supposed to meet her. She said she had something to tell me, so I lit a lamp and saw some furniture overturned."

Wade thought of stepping on the broken pieces of a statue lying on the floor.

Logan continued. "I saw her lying in that pool of blood and knew right away Gracie was dead." He paused to wipe the tears from his eyes as he looked up at Wade. "You gonna arrest me, Sheriff?"

Wade looked down at his boots and thought of the prints left by shoes. "No, but I need to ask you a few more questions."

Logan looked relieved.

"Do you have any idea what Gracie wanted to tell you?"

Fortune looked sad. "No, sir. I haven't seen too much of her lately. You see, she broke it off a couple of months back."

Wade considered that. "Why did Gracie break it off?"

Fortune shrugged. "She said there was someone else."

Wade looked interested. "She say who?"

276

Logan shook his head no. "I tried finding out, but I never saw her with anyone."

He looked up at Wade. "I thought maybe that's what she wanted to tell me."

Wade considered that a moment while thinking he could be a married man, explaining the other shoeprint. Then he thought about the same footprints near Estelle and wondered if this married man was seeing both girls. "Did Gracie know Estelle?"

Logan's face filled with anger as he raised his voice. "Estelle was a whore, and Gracie wasn't!"

Wade stiffened. "No one said she was."

Logan looked regretful for raising his voice. "She worked at the Grand Hotel cleaning rooms and went to church regularly. She weren't no whore."

Wade looked at Logan. "I meant no disrespect to Gracie. I'm just trying to figure out if the same man killed Estelle and Gracie." Wade paused. "You have something against whores, Mr. Fortune?"

He glanced at Ben Croucher and then looked at Wade. "I'd not marry one."

"But you'd poke one?" asked Wade.

"Well, sure, wouldn't anyone?"

Wade stared into Logan's eyes. "All right, Mr. Logan, I'm done."

Logan looked from Wade to Ben as he stood.

Ben told him to take the rest of the day off and then told Ted Giles to see him back to the bunkhouse.

"One more thing," said Wade looking at Logan. "Why did you try and hide your trail in the river?"

"I saw you coming out of the alley as I rode across the street. I figured you'd be following at first light." He paused. "Got scared, I guess."

"Go on now," said Ben Croucher. After Ted and Logan left, Ben stood from his chair and walked to the liquor cabinet. "Would you like a drink Mr. Spears?"

"No, thanks."

"How about another cup of hot coffee before you head out?"

Wade smiled, thinking how good the coffee was and how cold it is outside. "Another cup of coffee sounds good, Mr. Croucher."

Ben poured Wade another cup of coffee, picked up his drink, and looked up at the painting of his wife. "What sort of man does such a thing to another human being?"

Wade looked up at the painting, sipped his coffee, walked back to his chair, and sat down. "I don't rightly know, Sir."

Croucher turned from the painting and sat down in the chair next to Wade. "You ever experience anything like this before?"

Wade thought about the cabin where he found Dog and the other families while chasing the Bradley brothers. "Once."

Looking interested, Ben asked, "Where was that?"

"South of here."

Ben looked thoughtful. "I suppose a man in your position sees things the rest of us don't."

Wade took a drink of coffee. "I'm sure we do."

"Would you care for some lunch, Sheriff?"

Wade was hungry and wanted to stay, but he knew if he did, there would be more questions of where he came from, his family, and other things he had to keep secret. Wade couldn't risk slipping, so he smiled appreciatively. "I best be getting back to town, but thanks all the same."

Ben smiled, hiding his disappointment. "Perhaps another time."

Wade drank the last of his coffee. "Perhaps."

Ben looked out the window. "Winter stays a long time."

Wade looked out the same window as he stood. "Seems like it." Then he turned to Mr. Croucher. "I best be on my way."

Ben stood with an outstretched hand. "Hopefully, another time."

Wade shook his hand firmly. "I'd like that, Mr. Croucher."

That brought a big smile to Ben's face as he put one hand on the back of Wade's shoulder and showed him to the front door. Wade thanked him again for his hospitality, walked outside, took the slicker off the mare. After he rolled it up and tied it behind his saddle, he swung up onto the mare and rode away, following his own tracks back to Pickering.

The long ride back gave him time to keep going over the two killings and their similarities, and he knew that somewhere there had to be a connection between Estelle and Gracie. He also considered what Logan had told him and thought Mr. Fortune was a lucky man that night. He could have walked in on the killing and ended up dead.

The weather warmed and melted most of the snow over the next few days turning the town into a mud pit of stuck wagons and angry drivers. But the day Gracie Abbott was laid to rest, the sky filled with dark gray clouds, and the air became chilly. Wooden planks were placed ground around the grave so people wouldn't have to stand in the mud. It was a sight that Wade was becoming used to seeing.

Preacher George Arden read comforting words from the tattered Bible he always carried with him. Wade glanced around at the crowd of descent townspeople who weren't present at Estelle Winters' funeral. His eyes settled on Morgan, standing next to Mrs. Jordan, whom he discovered had known Gracie better than most. She wiped her red, welling eyes with a white hanky as she leaned against Morgan for comfort, and that brought his life with Sarah to mind, and that saddened him.

His thoughts of Sarah were interrupted by the word "Amen," and as the preacher closed his Bible, six men, including Logan Fortune, lowered the pine casket into the dark hole. Wade watched the mayor and his wife, the Noonan's, Tom Purdy, and the Moore's solemnly parade along the wooden planks to where wagons, buggies, and horses waited. After everyone left, Logan Fortune stood alone next to the grave, looking pitifully sad as a light rain began to fall, forcing people to hurry to their horses, wagons, and carriages. Wade glanced up at the dark gray sky, put on his black hat, and as the rain streamed off the wide brim, he looked once again at Logan Fortune standing in the rain at Gracie Abbott's grave.

Chapter 20

June

The weather cleared up the next day, bringing sun and warmer temperatures to Pickering for the next week. Today was just such a day, so Jed took Pup for a walk in the woods behind town so she could chase the birds and squirrels for a little exercise. Wade sat in his chair in front of the jailhouse, enjoying the warm afternoon, watching wagons and riders making their way up and down the street. The town was busy with women shoppers and children running and playing childish games, and on occasion, he had to shoo them out of the street. Having just done so, he smiled at the giggles and laughter from the children as they ran away from him, and he thought of his son Emmett.

Morgan and Katherine Jordan drove by in a buggy returning from their Saturday ride that had become a weekly outing. Morgan waved as they drove by, Wade tipped his hat to Katherine, and she nodded and smiled back. He watched them with envy thinking of Sarah as the buggy turned from the main street onto the street toward Katherine's house. Overtaken with loneliness, he turned away and stared toward the south and Colorado, wondering what his family was doing this very moment.

The sound of the stage arriving from Miles City was a welcome rescue from his thoughts of Sarah and the loneliness of his life. He watched as the stage drove past, chased by a small cloud of dust, and wondered about its occupants. The driver pulled at the reins and pushed the brake with his left foot stopping the stage in front of the Pickering Stage Depot. As the street dust caught up with the stage, the depot manager hurried out to open the stage door then step back as he greeted the travelers.

A middle-aged man climbed out, turned, and helped a young girl in her early teens step down to the boardwalk. A slightly younger man and woman having the appearance of farmers greeted both with hugs. Wade watched, thinking how happy everyone seemed to be as they smiled while everyone talked at the same time. Gathering their baggage, the four walked to a waiting wagon, put the baggage in the back, then climbed up onto a crowded seat and drove out of town.

The stage driver had stepped down, holding a large leather bag Wade knew was full of mail from the post office in Miles City and probably a new supply of wanted posters. The driver handed the bag to Harry, the depot manager, while a young teamster climbed up onto the driver's seat, released the brake, and drove the stage around back for a fresh team of horses. Lowering the chair's front legs to the boardwalk, Wade took his feet off the post, stood, then adjusted his holster that set across his left side. He started walking along the boardwalk toward the Stage Depot, hoping he didn't find a poster with his name on it in the leather bag. He smiled at the depot manager. "Morning, Harry." Then he looked at the driver whose name he didn't know. "How was the trip?"

"Bumpy," said the driver looking tired.

"Have some fresh coffee, if you have a mind," said Harry to the driver and the man riding shotgun while gesturing to a big, new gray pot sitting on top of a potbellied stove in the corner. He looked at Wade. "Help yourself, Sheriff."

"No thanks, Harry, just came down to see if you had anything for me."

Harry put the leather bag on the ticket counter, lifted a small hinged section of the counter, and stepped through, letting the counter slam down as he dragged the bag off the counter. He walked to an empty table against the far wall, set the bag down, and worked on the straps of the bag.

Wade stepped up to the counter while the stage driver and the other man busied themselves with coffee and watched Harry.

Harry opened the bag, turned it upside down, shaking the contents out onto the table. Checking inside to make sure all of it fell out onto the counter, he set the bag down and rummaged through the letters and packages. Finding a large envelope with Sheriff of Pickering written on it, he turned and handed it to Wade. "This what you looking for, Sheriff?"

Wade took the envelope, thanked him, walked out the door, and walked back to the Sheriff's Office, wondering what he'd find inside the envelope. Stepping inside the jailhouse, he took off his hat, placed it on the edge of his desk, and sat down in the old, creaking swivel chair. Wade opened the envelope then emptied the contents of six wanted posters onto the top of his desk, landing face down. He stared at them for a moment in anticipation and fear, then picked up the first one, turned it over, and looked at the name and description of a man wanted for murder in the Dakota Territory. Names of men he had never heard of who were wanted for various deeds were on the other five. As he set the last poster on his desk, he wondered why he had never seen a wanted poster with his name on it. Surely the U.S. Marshal in Denver would have sent out posters with his name on them after what happened at the Hoskins ranch.

As that night returned to him, he sat back in his chair, hearing the screams of the Hoskins' riders as they burned inside the bunkhouse and shooting those that tried to escape. The soft eyes of the woman he shot and killed raced across his memory. Standing, he pushed them away, turned, and looked at the coffee pot sitting on the stove. It had been nine months since that terrible night had passed and the shot that killed Old Man Hoskins in his hotel. Why hadn't Wanted Posters with the name "Wade Garrison" made their way to Pickering? It made no sense to him.

He felt the side of the coffee pot finding it still warm, so he poured a cup and took a drink, thinking it was strong and a little bitter as he sat back down to the sounds of the chair in the silent room. He took another sip and then set the cup down, opened the bottom drawer, and pulled out the bottle of whiskey. He poured some into his coffee, placed the bottle back in the drawer, opened the center drawer of his desk, and looked at a small pile of paper and a single pencil. He took a drink of the whiskey coffee, and after a moment of consideration, he pulled out a piece of paper along with the pencil and started writing a letter to Sarah. He told her that he loved her and missed both her and their son, but he could never return to Colorado. Because of all that had happened, he could not tell her where he was or where he was going. Then he went on to say that he was okay and hoped she and little Emmett were well. He told his wife that if she divorced him, he would understand, and perhaps that was the best thing for her to do. He signed the letter with love, folded it, stuffed it into an envelope, and addressed the envelope to Sarah Garrison c/o the Post Office in Harper, Colorado, leaving off a return address.

He stared down at the envelope and decided he would take a couple of days and ride up to Miles City, where the post office was. He considered riding over to Coulson to post it, but that was near 160 miles, and that would take too long. He had just sealed the envelope when Jed and Pup returned from the woods, both looking worn out. He shoved the letter inside his shirt as Pup ran over, put her front paws on his lap, and whined while he tried to dodge her fast, wet tongue. He laughed affectionately, petted her shoulders briskly, and then pushed her away. "You hungry, girl?"

She whined while flipping her tail in small, quick circles.

"I guess that's a yes," chuckled Jed.

"Guess so," said Wade as he stood and grabbed his hat off the edge of his desk and looked at Jed. "Let's you and I head over to the café and eat." He looked down at Pup. "Don't worry, girl; I'll bring you back something."

284

Wade was up before sunrise the next morning, shaved in cold water, and got dressed thinking of his ride to Miles City. Picking up the letter from the small dresser, he looked at his reflection in the stained and cracked mirror. Wondering how things got so far out of hand, Wade looked at the address on the envelope, pictured Sarah crying while reading it, and wondered if he was doing the right thing. Deciding he had to let her know he was alive, Wade also thought of the locket Morgan had and wished he had a picture of Sarah and Emmett, fearing that he may not recall what they looked like one day.

Ridding his mind of those fears, he turned and headed for the door calling Pup. Lazily she got out of bed, stretched, and followed him outside to do her business. Wade made coffee while Pup walked into the empty cell, jumped up onto the cot, curled up, and went back to sleep. Waiting for the coffee to boil, he put the letter in the inside pocket of his black duster and again hoped he was doing the right thing.

Jed opened his eyes and sat up, watching as Wade fussed with his duster, threw back the covers, and sat on the edge of his bed, looking tired as he yawned. Standing, he stretched and scratched the top of his head, eyeing Wade. "You going, someplace?"

Wade picked up his cup of coffee and looked at him. "I'm taking a ride up to Miles City. Might be gone a couple of days, maybe three."

Jed put on his pants and shirt, walked out of the cell carrying his shoes, curious about the trip, but didn't ask. He poured himself a cup of coffee, took a quick sip, thinking it was a little weak, and sat down. Looking out the front window at the early morning shadows of town, thinking the sun would be up soon, he looked at Wade. "What'll I tell Morgan or the mayor should they stop by and ask?"

"Tell him what I just told you."

Jed started putting on his shoes. "Suppose something happens?"

Wade considered that. "I don't see anything going wrong in two days, but if it should, go see Mayor Smith and let him handle it." Then he grinned. "I'd like to see that myself."

Jed chuckled and took a drink of his coffee. "When you leaving?"

"Soon as I pack a few things and eat breakfast." He walked to the closet next to the hall leading to the rear door, took out two cans of beans and a jar of peaches, and set them on the desk.

Jed watched as he stuffed them into the saddlebags along with the long glass he always carried and a clean shirt. "Pup's not gonna like you riding out without her."

Wade paused and looked at her, lying on the bed in the spare cell sleeping. "Be sure you keep her on a leash if you take her outside until I get back. I don't want her taking off looking for me."

Miles City, Montana

Miles City was a small town of several single-story wooden framed buildings separated by a road that led to Fort Keogh, a few miles to the west. While most of the buildings were single-story dwellings, some had false storefronts giving the appearance of a second story. Finding the post office closed, Wade rode to the livery to put the mare up for the night. With his saddlebags over his left shoulder, a bandoleer of cartridges over his right, and the Sharps cradled under his right arm, he headed for a small hotel across the street from the Elk Horn Saloon.

A heavyset lady behind the desk looked dirty and didn't smell much better than she looked. Wade signed the register, paid for the night in advance, hoping the room was cleaner than the lobby, and much to his surprise, it was. The single window overlooked the busy street giving him a clear view of the Elk Horn Saloon across the street. After tossing his saddlebags, rifle, and bandoleer on the bed, whose springs moaned in protest, he raised the window letting in the early evening fresh air.

Turning from the window, he walked to the single chair sitting by the door next to the bed, took off his hat and duster, then hung them on the line of pegs next to the door. Sitting down on the bed, he opened his saddlebags, dumped the contents on the bed, and picked up a can of beans. He turned and looked at the window, thinking of a hot meal, and shoved everything back into the saddlebags. Standing, he put on his duster and hat, then walked out of the room into the dim hallway and locked the door.

Pausing at the edge of the boardwalk, he looked up and down the street of the tiny town that had two more saloons than a town this size should have. His eyes settled on the Elk Horn Saloon across the wagon-rutted street and thought about the paper he found in the shirt of one of the men that came to kill him. Stepping off the porch, he walked across the busy street to the hitching rails crowded with horses patiently waiting to go back to a barn or corral. Stepping up onto the boardwalk greeted by piano music that flowed from the open doorway, he pushed the swinging doors open, walked inside, and bellied up to the crowded bar. Wade was eyeing the crowd of drunks and near-drunks, some wearing sidearms and some not, thinking the town was a little wild. Several soldiers from Ft. Keogh were scattered along the bar and at several tables talking to whores or one another. It looked like any other saloon on a busy night.

"What'll it be?" asked a voice.

Wade turned, looking into the face of a dwarf, the first Wade had ever encountered.

"Well?" said the midget.

"Beer," replied Wade, then he watched the little man walk with a slight wobble on bowed legs toward the mugs and beer near the center of the bar. Curious, Wade leaned over the bar seeing the little man was walking on planks that ran the length of the bar, making him appear taller.

Loud laughter suddenly drowned out the piano music, and when Wade turned, he saw a drunk crawling along the floor toward the door pausing to throw up. The midget bartender yelled at a man sitting in a chair atop a podium holding a shotgun across his lap while motioning to the drunk. The man on the podium stood, stepped down, and helped the drunk outside, giving him a kick in the rear when they reached the open doorway.

As laughter filled the room, the dwarf yelled at one of the girls to get a mop and clean up the vomit. He looked at Wade. "That'll be a dime."

Wade turned from the commotion. "A little expensive, ain't it?"

The little man looked at him with a tired expression. "Want it or not?"

Wade reached into his pocket and slapped a dime on the bar that the dwarf snapped up and tossed into an open register sitting on the back counter next to the clean beer mugs under a large elk's head. "Just a minute," said Wade.

The little man turned with a curious face. "What?"

Wade pulled out the card he found in the shirt pocket of one of the men that had tried to kill him. "This still good?"

The dwarf noticed the edge of the sheriff's badge under Wade's duster as he took the card, looked at it for a moment, smiled, and handed it back. "Just give it to me when you order your next beer."

Wade took the card, stuck it in his pocket, picked up his beer, and took a good drink. As he wiped the foam from his mouth, Wade looked around for an empty table, and seeing one next to a small dance floor, he headed across the crowded room. Smelling the fresh sawdust on the dance floor, he sat down and took another drink of beer. Thinking he was hungry, he noticed the midget step off the planks and walk to the man sitting on the podium with the shotgun. The man leaned down while the dwarf said something, and then as the dwarf walked away, the man with the shotgun got down and walked to a closed door. He knocked, and moments later, the door opened, the man disappeared into the room, and the door closed.

Curious about what the little man was up to, Wade took another drink of beer and then looked around at the people having a good time. Moments later, the man with the shotgun stepped out of the room, followed by another man in a suit. The man with the shotgun spoke to the other while nodding in Wade's direction.

The man in the suit looked at Wade for a quick moment, then started walking toward him. Wade watched the man of six feet and thin build make his way around tables between chairs and across the empty dance floor pausing now and again to visit with a patron. He looked to be around fifty with hazel eyes, thick, graying dark brown hair, and a clean-shaven face. He had a friendly smile as he approached Wade's table. "Mind if I sit?"

Curious what the man wanted, Wade pushed an empty chair out with his foot. "Not at all."

He sat down and extended a hand. "Niles Chapman." Then he gestured at the saloon. "I own the place."

Wade shook the hand, which felt smooth, unlike a cowboy's hand but strong just the same. "Emmett Spears."

Niles turned and motioned to one of the waiters working the floor and then looked at Wade. "Another beer?"

"Don't mind if I do," replied Wade wondering what he had on his mind.

Niles Chapman ordered two beers, and as the waiter walked away, he looked at Wade. "I'm led to believe that you're a man of the law."

It all made sense now that Wade realized he hadn't taken off his badge. "I'm the Sheriff down in Pickering."

Niles grinned. "Ah, yes. Nice little town."

The waiter returned with two beers, set them down, picked up Wade's empty mug, and left.

Niles picked his mug up and held it above the table. "To your health, Sheriff."

Wade picked up his mug and smiled. "I don't get that one a lot."

Niles chuckled and took a drink of beer.

Wade took a drink and set the mug on the table.

Niles set his beer on the table and looked at Wade. "I hope I'm not getting personal, but what brings you to Miles City, Sheriff Spears?"

Wade leaned forward on the table, resting on his elbows. "Never been here before, so I thought I'd see what all the talk was about."

Chapman stared into Wade's eyes, wondering if that were true. "You're not looking for anyone?"

Wade chuckled. "No, sir, I'm not."

Niles smiled, looking relieved. "I was afraid you were on the trail of someone and followed them in here." He paused. "Killings are bad for business."

Wade smiled. "I imagine they are." Then he took a drink of beer.

Niles grinned. "Staying long?"

"The night. I'm heading back in the morning."

Chapman drank the last of his warm beer. "Long ride for one night."

Wade knew he was curious about why he came to Miles City and couldn't much blame him. "Have some business to take care of."

"I see." Then he sat back in his chair. "Say hello to Tom Purdy for me."

Wade looked surprised. "You know Tom Purdy?"

"He's been in here on occasion. Him and that girl who works for him."

"Estelle?" offered Wade.

"I believe that's the one. Not a real pretty girl, but interesting if you know what I mean."

Wade didn't know because he was thinking about Bill Conners and the other three men. "He come here often?"

Niles sat back in thought. "No, not often. He was here last January with that woman and then again by himself. I believe this past April."

Wade thought the reason he was alone was that Estelle was dead.

Niles pointed to a table a few feet away. "He was sitting right there, talking to three men."

Wade glanced at the table then looked at Niles. "You know who they were?"

Chapman shook his head. "Drifters more than likely." Then he looked curious. "I thought it funny at the time."

"Why?"

Niles considered the question. "Can't say for sure. Maybe it was the way they were all leaning on the table." He chuckled. "Like they were discussing something important and secret."

Wade thought they might have been discussing the price to kill a sheriff.

He looked at Wade. "Why so curious?"

Wade sat back. "No reason. You knowing Tom just surprised me is all."

Niles looked concerned. "Is Tom in trouble?"

"No, not at all. Why do you ask?"

"You seemed interested in who he was talking to is all."

Wade smiled. "Just the law in me, I guess." He nodded at Niles. "You brought him up, not me."

"So, I did." Niles pushed his half mug of beer away. "Enjoy your stay, Sheriff. If you're hungry, I suggest the café up the street." He stood and smiled as he extended his hand. "Best food in town."

Wade shook his hand, thanked him for the beer, and then watched him walked away, stopping at this table or chatting with customers. Wade sat back in his chair, turned, and looked at the table Niles had pointed to, sipped his beer, and tried to think of a reason Tom Purdy would want him dead. He knew he was against him being sheriff, but would Purdy be mad enough to try and have him killed? Wade thought of the man saying this is for Elizabeth as the man drew down on him. Unable to wrap his mind around that, he drank the last of his beer and wondered who this Elizabeth person was and what she was to Purdy? The whole thing made no sense. Feeling tired and hungry from the long ride, he stood and walked toward the doors contemplating the mystery of Tom Purdy and Elizabeth while hoping the food at the café up the street was good.

Chapter 21

Pickering, Montana

The morning sun had been up for several hours and was warming the streets and boardwalks of Pickering when Jed walked out of the jailhouse carrying a cup of coffee. He sat down in the chair Wade usually sat in, propped his feet against the porch post, and sipped his coffee. Pup did her business in the street, then lay down next to the chair and studied the people and horses as they passed. The sun felt warm and friendly, so Jed closed his eyes, enjoying the warm, quiet morning, and hoped it would stay that way until the sheriff returned.

"The sheriff in?" a voice asked.

Jed opened his eyes and looked up at Tom Purdy, standing in the street next to the boardwalk.

"No, he ain't Mr. Purdy."

Purdy looked at Pup, who was staring up at him. "You shouldn't let a dangerous animal like her outside where decent people walk."

Canon took exception to that as he looked down at Pup, reached down, and rubbed her on the shoulder. "She's not dangerous."

Purdy stared at Pup with an unkind expression. "When will the sheriff be back?"

Jed looked across the street as he slid his hand under his hat and scratched his head. Then he frowned as he looked up at Tom.

"Tomorrow, maybe. Or the next. Ain't sure, Mr. Purdy. Something wrong?"

Purdy looked disappointed. "I was just wondering how he's coming on finding Estelle's murderer."

Canon shrugged. "Can't say."

Tom Purdy frowned. "Where'd the sheriff go anyways?"

Jed thought on that, and since Tom was on the city council, he saw no harm in telling him. "Took a ride up to Miles City."

Purdy glanced to the north. "Miles City?" He looked down at Jed. "What did he go up there for?"

Jed shrugged. "Never said. He got up early yesterday morning and said he'd be gone a day or two."

Purdy stood in the street in considering what Jed had just told him, and then he turned and walked away.

Jed watched him hurry across the street toward the saloon, thinking he sure acted strange, but then Jed always thought he was a strange little man. He took a sip of coffee, reached down and petted Pup on the shoulder, and wished the sheriff would hurry back so he wouldn't have to answer any more questions.

The streets of Pickering were dark by the time Wade took care of the mare, said goodnight to Albert, and walked out of the livery toward the Sheriff's Office. Stepping inside, he was greeted by a whining Pup that rushed to him as he knelt to one knee, trying to dodge her busy tongue. He looked at Jed sitting in the swivel chair. "Anything happen while I was gone?"

Jed got up and stepped toward the potbellied stove. "Nope. Want a cup of coffee? I just made a fresh pot."

Wade stood feeling and looking tired. "Sounds good. It's been a long ride." He walked toward the gun rack with Pup at his heels, wanting more attention. He put the Sharps and bandoleer away, then tossed his saddlebag onto the black leather sofa, put his hat on the desk. Thinking of Tom Purdy and Miles City, he took off his black duster and sat down at his desk.

"Mind telling me why you went to Miles City?" asked Jed.

Wade thought about the letter he tore up and tossed in the river on his way back as he reached down and petted Pup, now lying beside his chair. "Just needed to get out of town for a while, Jed. Did the mayor stop by?"

Jed handed him a cup of coffee. "No, but that Tom Purdy did."

Wade took the coffee. "When?"

"This morning."

Wade drank his coffee, thinking it needed a little whiskey. "What'd he want?"

Jed told him about Tom Purdy's visit asking about Estelle.

Wade pulled the bottle of whiskey out of the bottom drawer, poured a little into the coffee, and then put the bottle back. "What'd you tell him?"

"That you took a ride up to Miles City."

Wishing Jed hadn't told him, he wondered if Tom had put two and two together.

Jed sipped his coffee. "That alright that I told him you were in Miles City?"

The swivel chair creaked as Wade turned and looked out the window at the lighted windows of the saloon across the street. Thinking of Purdy sitting with those three men in Miles City, he looked at Jed. "What'd Purdy say?"

Jed shrugged. "Seemed a mite curious is all."

Thinking it was time to bring this to a head, Wade took another drink of coffee, set the cup down, grabbed his hat, and stood.

"Where you going?" asked Jed.

Wade put on his hat as he walked toward the door. "To pay Tom Purdy a visit."

Jed watched in quiet curiosity as Wade opened the door and stepped onto the boardwalk, closing the door behind him.

Wade paused at the edge of the boardwalk and stared across the street at the saloon, noticing Purdy's place above the saloon was dark. He stepped off the boardwalk, walked across the dirt street, and stepped onto the boardwalk of the saloon. Pausing at the window to look inside, Wade saw Dave Goody behind the bar, but there was no sign of Tom Purdy. He opened the door, stepped inside, greeted by cigarette smoke, laughter, and piano music, walked up to the bar, and waited for Dave.

Seeing Wade, Dave smiled. "Beer, Sheriff?"

"Tom around?"

Dave looked toward the stairs. "Should be upstairs."

Wade turned and walked up the stairs to the second floor under the watchful, curious eyes of Dave Goody. Wade walked down the narrow hall to Tom's room, paused at the door while glancing at the other closed doors, drew his pistol, cocked it, and knocked on the door. He waited, knocked again, and then turned the doorknob, and at finding the door unlocked, he pushed it open. Standing in the doorway, Wade looked around the dim room, wondering where Tom was. Seeing a lantern on a nearby table, he walked toward it.

"What are you doing?"

Startled, Wade turned, seeing it was Goody. "You could get yourself shot sneaking up on a man like that, Dave."

Goody looked at the pistol in Wade's hand. "What are you doing in Mr. Purdy's room?"

Wade turned back to the lantern. "Looking for Tom."

Goody nervously glanced around. "It looks like he ain't here, Sheriff. We shouldn't be in Mr. Purdy's room when he ain't here."

"Leave if you're nervous," said Wade as he lit a lantern.

Dave watched as Wade picked up the lantern and walked around the room as if he were looking for something, and then into Tom's bedroom. Not wanting to stand alone in the dark, he followed Wade and stood at the bedroom door watching while

Wade looked around. Dave turned and looked at the open door to the hallway fearing his boss would walk in. "We best leave, Sheriff. Being in here when Mr. Purdy is gone ain't right."

Wade ignored Goody, opened the door to a closet finding a small safe sitting on the floor in the corner with the door ajar. Kneeling, he pushed the door open with the barrel of his Colt, and finding it empty, he stood and turned to Dave. "When was the last time you saw your boss?"

Goody looked curious. "Just before lunch. Why?"

"Looks like your boss has up and left town."

Dave looked puzzled. "Why would he do that?"

Wade walked past him, carrying the lantern into the living room, knowing why.

Goody glanced around the dark bedroom, wondering what was going on, turned, and followed Wade back into the living room.

Wade stopped at a table next to the door, set the lantern down, and looked at the photograph of Tom and his older sister he had looked at the last time he was in this room.

Goody looked at Wade, and then the photograph "That's Mr. Purdy and his older sister."

Thinking Tom Purdy may be running to his older sister, he asked, "Do you happen to know where she is?"

Dave shrugged. "No, the only thing I know about his sister is that her name is Elizabeth."

Wade's head snapped toward Dave.

"Mr. Purdy has never talked about her."

Wade picked up the photograph remembering the words of the gunman, 'This is for Elizabeth.' He stared at the young face in the photograph, trying to recognize her but couldn't. He set it down, handed the lantern to Goody, and walked out of the room.

Three of Purdy's whores just stepped out of their room. "You looking for Mr. Purdy?" one asked.

Wade nodded.

"Saw him walk down the back stairs carrying a satchel and carpetbag earlier today."

Wade turned and hurried down the hallway.

Confused at what was going on, Dave blew out the lantern, closed the door, and by the time he reached the stairs, Wade was walking out the door.

Jed was lying on the black leather sofa, half asleep, when Wade walked in. Opening his eyes, he sat up with a puzzled look, watching Wade as he shrugged into his black duster. 'Where you going now?"

"After Purdy."

Jed looked confused as he glanced out the window, looking at the saloon across the street. "Wasn't he at the saloon?"

Wade pulled the Sharps from the gun rack. "He packed up, cleaned out his safe, and left town earlier today." He turned to Jed. "Tom Purdy is the person who hired those men to kill me."

Jed had a surprised look as he got up from the sofa. "Tom Purdy?"

Wade grabbed the bandoleer of cartridges. "That's right."

"How do you know?"

"I'll explain it all later, Jed."

Jed stepped closer. "I don't like saying what you should do, but oughtn't you wait til morning?"

"This won't wait until morning."

"Let your horse rest the night," suggested Jed. "She's had a long ride from Miles City."

Wade opened the door and walked outside, where he stopped on the porch and looked toward the livery. He knew Jed was right; the mare was tired, hell, so was he, and they both needed to rest. Wade considered taking another horse, but he needed the mare's steadiness for what he had to do. Giving out a soft sigh, he turned and stepped back inside, closed the door, and walked to the

298

desk where he set the rifle and bandoleer down. "You're right," he said without looking up. "He'll have to stop someplace tonight."

Jed sat down on the leather sofa. "Mind telling me what's going on?"

Wade sat down and began petting Pup while he told Jed of his conversation with a man named Niles Chapman, who told him that he saw Tom Purdy talking to one man in January and three men in April that fit the descriptions of the men who tried to gun him down.

Jed thought about that a moment. "Why on earth would Mr. Purdy want you dead?"

Wade considered that a moment. "Has something to do with his sister."

"His sister?"

Wade looked confused. "That's all I know, Jed."

Canon thought on that a moment. "Want me to go up to the livery and tell Albert to have your horse saddled first thing?"

"No, I'll go up now and talk to Al myself."

Albert Bennett opened the front door of his house and looked into Wade's tired, blue eyes. "What can I do for you, Sheriff?"

Wade looked past Albert seeing Shelly waiting at the dinner table. "Sorry to bother you, Al, but I need a favor."

Bennett recognized a troubled look on Wade's face, so he turned and told his wife he'd be right back. Then he stepped outside and closed the door. "What sort of favor?"

The light from the window shone on Wade's face. "I wouldn't ask Al, but this is important as all hell. I'll need my horse at first light."

Albert stared at him a moment, then sighed and shook his head. "All right. I'll get up early and be waiting inside the livery."

"Thanks, Al."

Albert gave Wade a look. "If this is gonna be a habit, maybe I should give you a key."

Wade chuckled. "Won't get to be a habit, Al." Then he gestured toward the door. "Sorry if I interrupted your dinner." He turned to leave but stopped. "What time did Tom Purdy leave today?"

Bennett looked thoughtful. "I'd say shortly before noon. Asked me to help saddle that big brown of his."

"Did you happen to see which way he rode?"

"Why so interested in Tom Purdy, Sheriff?"

"It's a personal matter. Did you happen to see which way he rode out?"

"South," replied Bennett wondering what this was all about.

Wade turned and started walking back to the jailhouse. "See you in the morning."

Sleep evaded Wade most of the night, and now he lay in bed, trying to find the connection between Tom Purdy, Elizabeth, and himself. He looked up at the window above his head, seeing the dark sky was getting lighter, so he got up, dressed without shaving, and headed for the door of the bedroom with Pup underfoot. He was surprised at finding Jed standing by the potbellied stove waiting for the coffee to boil.

"Thought you could use some coffee before you headed out."

Wade looked appreciative as he headed for the back door to let Pup out. Returning, he walked for his black duster and hat while Pup headed for the spare cell and the empty cot she liked.

Jed poured two cups of coffee, gave one to Wade, and sat down in one of the two chairs in front of Wade's desk. "Packed you some eats in your saddlebags and filled your canteen." He paused a moment. "You sure you can pick up his trail?"

Wade thought about the other men he had tracked over the years. "I'll have to find his tracks first, but after that, I won't have much of a problem." He paused to take a drink of coffee. "Tom

Purdy's not the type of man who'd know how to lay a false trail or hide the one he's making."

Jed took a drink of coffee, figuring that was true enough. "He sure don't seem the kind that would hire four men to kill a sheriff— or anyone else for that matter."

Wade looked out the big window with Sheriff painted in white lettering, seeing it was getting light. Anxious to leave, he finished the coffee, shrugged into his duster, put on his hat then looked at Canon. "Sorry about leaving you alone again, Jed."

Canon stood. "Just hurry back. And don't worry, none about Pup, she'll be fine."

Wade looked at her sleeping on the cot in the empty cell, where she always slept during the day, and knew Jed would take good care of her. He tossed the saddlebags over his shoulder, picked up the Sharps and his bandoleer, headed for the door, and as he put one hand on the doorknob, he paused and turned to Jed. "If Morgan should come around, tell him I'll see him when I get back."

"Should I tell him about Purdy?"

Wade quickly considered. "Yeah, but no one else."

"Be careful."

Wade nodded, opened the door, stepped out into the early morning, and closed the door.

Having opened the livery doors, Albert stood next to the mare's stall drinking a cup of coffee as Wade stepped from the shadows walking toward the livery. Bennett took a small drink of coffee and waited while wondering what was going on between the sheriff and Tom Purdy.

Wade walked into the livery and headed for the mare's stall.

"Morning, Sheriff."

Wade stepped into the stall finding the mare saddled. "Morning, Al, I appreciate you getting up early." He looked at him. "I'm beholden to you." Then he turned. "Could I bother you for a small sack of oats to take along? I may be gone a few days."

Bennett set his cup on the rail post. "Sure."

Wade backed the mare out of the stall, and when Al returned with the bag of oats, Wade looked at him. "I'm sure you're more than a little curious about what's going on between Tom Purdy and me."

Albert picked up his cup of coffee from the post of the stall and held it as he watched Wade shove his Sharps into the scabbard at the front of his saddle. "Guess you could say I was, but then I know it ain't none of my business."

Wade hung the bandoleer around the saddle horn, and then tossed the bulging saddlebags behind the saddle and tied them down, "I ain't got time to go into it right now, Al, but it looks like Tom Purdy's on the run."

Bennett looked surprised. "From what?"

Wade put one foot in the stirrup, swung up, and looked down at him. "Me."

Words escaped Albert as he stared up at the man.

Wade wrapped the thin rope of the burlap sack containing oats for the mare around the saddle horn. "That's all I can say for now."

Bennett grabbed the bridle and led the mare and Wade to the open doors, where he pointed toward the buildings on the east side of town. "Tom Purdy rode away from here behind them buildings heading south if that's any help."

"It is," said Wade, and then he nudged the mare into a trot figuring Purdy would stay off the road and headed south of town before he started looking for his tracks.

Wade followed Purdy's trail, and in the late afternoon, he came upon a used campsite near a small stream and figured this was where Purdy had spent the night. Climbing down, he let the mare drink from the stream while he knelt to one knee, took the glove off his right hand, and stuck one finger into the ashes. Finding them cold to the ground, Wade figured Purdy probably rode out at sunrise. He stood holding the reins to the mare in one hand while wiping his finger on his pants, letting his eyes track Purdy's trail along the sandy, dark soil next to the stream. Deciding to walk the mare for a spell, he followed the trail on foot through the land of sparse trees and shrubs below the rough hills of white cliffs, tall Ponderosa Pines, and White Bark Pines, thinking this was pretty country.

A half-hour passed when he noticed the strides of the horse were farther apart. Kneeling, he examined the deep impressions in the soil, thinking he was still about a half day's ride behind Tom. He turned and looked up at the mare's big dark eyes knowing Tom was pushing his horse, and told the mare, "He's running scared." Standing, he pulled the Sharps from its scabbard, took a cartridge from the bandoleer, shoved it into the breech, and put the rifle back into the scabbard. Feeling the heat from the sun, he looked up at the warm afternoon sky and took a drink from his canteen. Swinging up onto his saddle, he nudged the mare into a trot, knowing Purdy's horse would tire soon, and he would have to rest it. He also knew that each time Purdy rode his horse hard, he would have to stop more often, and it was just a matter of time before he caught up to him.

Wade followed the trail through Pinyons and Junipers across a shallow stream, then along a dry riverbed that wound between low hills of rocks and shrubs. The hours passed, and the sun was low in the western sky, soon to disappear behind the tall mountains. Pulling up, he took his long glass from the saddlebag and searched for some sign of Purdy. Seeing no sign of him, he put it away and started looking for someplace to make camp for the night. Finding a spot of White Bark Pines and Cottonwood trees at the base of a tall cliff next to a shallow stream, he climbed down and tethered the mare next to a tree. In the last of the daylight, he pulled the saddlebag from off the saddle along with his bedroll then unsaddled her. After placing the saddle in a favorable spot where he would spread out his bedroll, he fed some of the oats he brought along to the mare and then let her go to the stream.

As the mare drank, Wade's thoughts turned from Tom Purdy to Seth and the others when they trailed the four killers from Colorado into New Mexico. He smiled, remembering that Seth's concerns were always for the horses, having said several times, "You're only as good a lawman on the hunt as your horse." The mare finished drinking, so he led her back to the camp and hobbled her between two small Pinyon trees close to where he would sleep, so if she heard something she didn't like, he'd hear her.

He wanted a fire but decided against it, so he ate a can of cold beans and washed it down with water wishing he had a cup of Jed's hot, strong coffee. The sun was gone, and as darkness settled in around him, he lay down on his bedroll with his head resting on his saddle, staring up at the black, moonless sky of a thousand stars. Crickets sang while bullfrogs argued with one another from the stream, and as a solitary coyote called out, he thought of Pup and found he missed her. As he stared up into the black sky and dots of stars, his thoughts wandered to Sarah and the night they sat out under the stars after the fireworks on that Fourth of July. Then his thoughts turned to Tom Purdy and his older sister, Elizabeth, and as he searched for the answer as to what the three of them could have in common, his eyes grew heavy. Settle down under the blanket with his hand on the butt of his pistol, sleep crept into his camp.

The tip of the red sun broke over the hills to the east, shining on the low hills to the west, coloring them a soft, rose-colored orange, leaving everything dark between there and where Wade slept. Opening his eyes, he lifted his hat from his face and sat up, greeted by the chilly morning, and decided he would make a fire before starting after Purdy.

Seeing a small clump of grass nearby that he hadn't seen when he made camp, Wade moved the mare to it so she could eat while he built a small fire to take away the morning chill. He opened another can of beans, set the can next to the fire to warm then ate while watching the sun fill the lowlands. He moved his spoon around the inside of the empty can, recalling that he had but two cans left. He tossed the empty can and watched it bounce noisily off a small rock. Standing, he picked up the bag of oats and gave the mare two handfuls, let her drink from the stream, and then broke camp.

Two hours passed before he stopped to let the mare rest, and as he climbed down, he knelt to study the tracks of Purdy's horse, and it looked like the left rear leg of Tom's horse had come up lame. As he stood, he knew Tom would be traveling a little slower, which was in Wade's favor. Feeling confident he'd have him before nightfall, he took off his duster and tied it to the back of his saddle, climbed up, and nudged the mare into a trot. He followed until he found where Purdy had dismounted and began leading his horse on foot while keeping near the trees for shade. Wade climbed down and poured water into his hat for the mare. When she finished drinking, he walked her for a half-hour so she could rest, then he climbed back up into the saddle and followed Tom's trail.

Pickering, Montana

The afternoon sun was bright and warm when Morgan rode his Appaloosa up to the hitching rail in front of the jailhouse. Stepping inside, he found the office empty and Pup lying on the empty cell bed with the cell door closed. Her ears perked as she jumped off the bed, whining for attention as she walked to the bars to greet him with a wagging tail.

Morgan walked to the cell, reached through the bars, and petted her as he called out, "Anyone here?" Getting no response, he walked to the bedroom and looked inside, finding the bed made but no Emmett. He closed the door, walked down the short hall to the back door, and stepped outside. The outhouse door was partially open, and it looked as empty as the jail had inside. Morgan walked back inside, past the cell with the coyote watching him, and stepped outside onto the boardwalk. Leaving his horse tied to the hitching rail, he walked across the street to the café, and not finding them there, walked to the saloon. Stepping up to the bar, he waited for Dave Goody, who was busy at the other end of the bar talking to one of his girls.

Dave noticed Morgan at the bar waiting, walked up to him, and wiped the bar down with the towel he pulled from his shoulder. "What'll it be, Mr. Hunter?"

"Beer. Seen the sheriff?"

Dave thought of how the sheriff was acting but said nothing and turned to pour him a beer while talking over his shoulder. "Not since yesterday."

Morgan turned and looked around at the sparse crowd seeing Cody Hayes and three other Croucher drovers sitting at a table talking to one of Goody's girls.

Dave set the mug of beer on the bar and picked up the money Hunter had laid down, turned, and put it in the register.

Morgan picked up his mug and walked past Cody, who looked up, giving him a friendly nod, then went back to talking to the girl. Reaching the empty table, Morgan tossed his hat in one of the empty chairs, sat down facing the door, and leaned back, getting comfortable. He took a drink of beer, wondering where Wade and Jed were when Jed walked in.

Jed Canon headed for the bar, but he made his way through the maze of empty chairs and tables upon seeing Morgan sitting at a table. "Afternoon, Mr. Hunter."

"Jed," greeted Morgan. "When are you gonna start calling me Morgan, and where's the sheriff?"

Jed pulled a chair away from the table, sat down, leaned on the table with his forearms, and spoke in a low voice. "The sheriff thinks Tom Purdy hired those men to kill him."

Morgan started to take a drink of beer but lowered the mug and leaned forward. "How does he figure that?"

Jed's forehead wrinkled as he frowned. "He made a trip to Miles City a couple of days ago." Jed went on to tell him what Wade had told him about Purdy having a sister named Elizabeth.

Morgan considered that quickly. "That makes no sense Jed. I doubt that Wade ever met this Elizabeth."

"That's what the sheriff said," then Jed shook his head, looking puzzled and told of Purdy riding out of town after cleaning out his safe. "The sheriff wanted to go right after him, but I told him he should wait and let his horse rest. I guess that made sense because that's what he did, and he left at first light yesterday."

Morgan looked at his beer in thought. "Which way did they go?"

"South," gestured Jed. "Said he'd be back in a few days." Jed looked toward the bar as he stood. "I'm gonna get me a beer."

Morgan sat back, took a drink of beer, and pondered the problem between Wade and Tom Purdy while Jed made his way to the bar.

Jed accidentally bumped Cody Hayes as he walked past his chair and quickly apologized.

Cody Hayes grabbed Jed's arm. "You stupid old man. Watch where the hell you're walking."

Morgan thought about getting up and helping out old Jed but instead took a drink of beer, thinking Hayes was a little bit of a bully, as was Brodie and a smart ass on top of it.

Jed pulled his arm away. "I said I was sorry."

"You're sorry, all right," Hayes said hatefully. "A sorry old bastard."

307

"No need for that," replied Jed, then he turned away and walked to the bar for his beer.

Morgan could see the hurt in Jed's face, and it bothered him.

Cody had his back to Morgan, so he had to turn and look at him. Turning away, he said something that caused the others to look at Morgan.

Jed Canon paid for his beer, took a quick drink, and headed for Morgan and the table, but as he walked past Cody, he stuck his foot out and tripped Jed.

Canon tumbled to the floor, letting go of the mug that rolled across the floor, spilling his beer, bringing laughter from several people, including Cody and his friends.

That angered Morgan, but he decided to stay out of it.

Jed slowly got up, wiped off his pants and shirt, and looked at Hayes. "That was uncalled for, young fella."

Cody grinned. "I bet you're really sorry now, old man." Then he laughed.

Angry at Cody and feeling sorry for Canon, Morgan stood and walked toward their table while drawing his heavy, Navy Colt pistol.

Knowing what was coming, Goody pulled one of his shotguns from under the bar.

Hayes never saw Morgan coming and was wearing a big grin when Morgan slapped him across the side of the head with the barrel of the Colt. He struck Cody so hard that it knocked his hat off and pushed his face onto the table spilling two beers.

It took a moment for the others to realize what had just happened when one of them, who didn't look more than eighteen years old, stood and started to go for his gun.

Morgan cocked his Navy Colt pistol, reached across the table, and pointed the big barrel at his face. "Go ahead, you little asshole." Then he reached down, grabbed a dazed Cody by the collar of his shirt and pulled him back into his chair, took Cody's gun, and tucked it under his belt.

Cody had a dazed look about him as his hands went to the side of his head, feeling the blood in his hair.

Morgan looked at the young fool that started draw on him. "Put your hands on the table where I can see them." Then he looked at the others. "I mean, everyone, and keep them there unless you want to meet your maker a few years sooner."

Cody's head was clearing, and as he held the side of his bloody head, he looked around the table, trying to figure out what had just happened. Finally, he looked up at the barrel of the big Navy Colt and then at Morgan. "I'll kill you for that, you bastard."

Morgan reached down with his left hand, grabbed him by his shirt, lifted him off his chair, and then shoved him backward. "You a tough hombre Cody?" he asked, looking mean and angry. Seeing Goody had moved from behind the bar and was standing a few feet away with the shotgun, Morgan said, "Stay out of this, Dave."

"I'm just here to see no one shoots you in the back Morgan."

Hunter took Cody's pistol out of his belt, shoved it into Cody's holster then pushed him back several steps. "You said you were gonna kill me." Morgan holstered his gun and took a step back. "Now's your chance, Sonny."

The clicks of the hampers on the shotgun Dave Goody was holding seemed loud in the stillness of the saloon. "You boy's keep them hands on the table."

Cody's blood ran down his neck onto the collar of his gray shirt. He turned and looked at Dave, then at the shotgun in Dave's hands, turned seeing Morgan's right hand near the butt of his Navy Colt he wore in a cross draw. Hearing chairs shuffle, Cody looked around, seeing people behind him getting out of the line of fire. Staring into Morgan's eyes, he knew if he drew down on him, Morgan would surely kill him.

Goody broke the silence. "I think it's time to make your play Cody or time for you to head back to the Big C."

"We're on our way to Deadwood," said Cody without taking his eyes off Morgan.

Dave looked surprised. "What on earth for?"

"They say there's gold there," replied the one who had stood to draw on Morgan.

Hunter looked at the young man and chuckled. "You won't last long in Deadwood." Then he looked at Hayes. "Someone will put a bullet in your head before you're there a week."

Dave stepped back, pointed the shotgun at them, and then motioned toward the door. "Time to get on with your journey to Deadwood, boys." He looked at Cody's bloody hand, covering the gash in his head from the barrel of Morgan's gun. "I'm sure you can find someone to stitch up that head of yours between here and Deadwood." Then he took the towel he always had draped over his shoulder and tossed it to him. "You can take that with you. Now gather up what belongs to you and head for the door."

While Hayes held the towel against his head, the others gathered up their money, picked up Cody's hat, and handed it to him. He took the hat while the others walked toward the door and stared at Morgan.

"Something on your mind?" asked Morgan.

"Come on, Cody!" yelled one of the other men from the doorway. "I have your money."

Cody stared at Morgan as if he hadn't heard his friend.

Morgan smiled. "Make your move, boy, or get out of here while you can still walk."

Dave Goody, wanting to end this before Morgan killed someone, stepped closer and put the shotgun barrel against the small of Cody's back. "I'm doing you a favor, son. Your friends are waiting."

Hayes glanced at Dave and then the shotgun, looked at Morgan, then turned and walked away.

Goody followed him to the door and waited until they mounted their horses and rode out of town before closing the door.

Morgan turned to Jed. "You all right?"

He nodded that he was, but he looked a little embarrassed.

Goody headed for the bar giving Morgan a look. "I'm getting too old for this shit."

Hunter felt the same way. "Bring Jed another beer on me, Dave." He patted Jed on the back and smiled as they walked to their table. "And we could use a towel."

Southeastern Montana

Wade came upon a gully with several unshod horse tracks heading south, the same as Purdy's tracks. He pulled up, dismounted, then knelt to one knee, studying the unshod pony tracks believing there were four or five ponies. Wade was unsure whether they were following Tom, or they had passed before Tom came this way. Either way, Wade's right hand found the butt of his Colt as he stood and walked to the edge of the gully. From there, his eyes followed the pony tracks that quickly disappeared toward the low treeless hills in the distance. Wade didn't like the idea of being all alone out here in the middle of nowhere with Indians around and considered heading back to Pickering. As he studied both sets of tracks, he thought about all that happened and the many unanswered questions. He had to know why Tom Purdy wanted him dead. He put his foot in the stirrup, swung up into the saddle, and followed Purdy and the Indian pony tracks that led to a shallow, dry creek bed. It was quiet except for a slight breeze that played with the limbs of the White Bark Pines and a few birds frolicking in them. He drew his pistol, cocked it as he glanced around, then nudged the mare into a walk, following the tracks to a spot where Purdy's horse and those of the Indian ponies went in different directions.

Seeing footprints in the soft, sandy soil, he climbed down, knelt to one knee, and examined the footprints he was sure were those of Tom Purdy leading his lame horse into the dry creek bed while the pony tracks continued south. Feeling anxious, he glanced around, listening to the stillness hearing only the soft wind in the trees and an occasional bird. After studying the pony tracks for several seconds, he wondered why the Indians stayed with the creek bed instead of following Tom unless they passed this way first. If that was the case, why would Purdy follow the pony tracks? Wade considered the possibility that Tom never looked down to see the pony tracks, and if he did, he may not have known they belonged to Indians. Wade holstered his Colt, climbed back in the saddle, nudged the mare into the dry creek bed, and followed Tom Purdy through the white pine trees keeping a sharp eye on the shadows and stopping at every unfamiliar sound.

A tense hour had passed when he came upon the tracks of unshod ponies mixing with those of Purdy and wondered if it was the same group. Pulling up, he studied the trampled ground seeing Tom was still walking and leading his lame horse. Thinking Purdy may be heading for Deadwood, Wade drew his gun, nudged the mare into a walk, and cautiously followed the trail through the pines, deeper into the trees. Moments passed when a terrible scream filled the afternoon. Pulling up, Wade sat low in the saddle and glanced through the trees toward the sound, fearing it was Tom that screamed. The mare acted nervous, and that made Wade nervous, so he reached out, rubbed her neck, and softly said, "Smell something, girl?"

Another scream rushed at them through the trees, and Wade knew it was Tom Purdy. Figuring he had seen pony tracks for at least five Indians, maybe more, he again considered turning back. His need to know why Purdy wanted him dead and what it had to do with Elizabeth was too important to him. He had to know. Another chilling scream came from up ahead, and having made his decision, Wade climbed down and tied the mare loosely to the low branch of a tree as yet another haunting scream filled the air. Pulling the loaded Sharps out of its scabbard, he cocked the hammer and took the bandoleer from around the saddle horn.

Crouching down, he cautiously walked toward the screams, eyeing every tree and shadow. The screaming stopped, and quiet returned to the forest as he crept through the trees with his Sharps in one hand, his cocked Colt in the other. Hearing another scream, he stopped and wondered what they were doing to Tom, thinking if he wasn't careful, he'd be doing the screaming. Minutes passed with more screaming as he cautiously and slowly made his way through the trees until he came upon the campsite of the Indians on the other side of a small grassy clearing. He holstered his Colt, knelt next to a tree, rested the Sharps across his leg, and took the long glass he had stuffed under his belt. He pulled it apart, put it to his right eye, and looked across the clearing at five Crow Indians sitting around a campfire, sorting through what looked like Purdy's belongings. He estimated their distance to be two hundred yards, maybe a little more, but the single-shot Sharps worried him, and he wished he had a repeating rifle.

He could hear Purdy's moaning but couldn't see him because of the bushes and thick trees. Wade was considering his options when one of the Crow looked back over his shoulder, stood, walked a short distance, and knelt behind a large berry bush. Screams came from Purdy, and Wade could only imagine what the Crow was doing to him. But now he knew where they had Tom tied up.

The Indian stood with Tom's scalp in one hand, the knife in the other, and gave a loud war cry while Tom was screaming in pain. Wade wondered how much more the man could take. The Crow made a playful taunting lunge at Purdy, then sheathed his knife and walked back to the others proudly waving the scalp. Before he sat down, he gestured toward Purdy and said something the others seemed to enjoy as they continued sorting through and arguing over his belongings.

Knowing he had to do something soon before they killed Tom or him, Wade thought of the Sharps' single shot and knew he had to get close enough to use his Colt pistol. He lowered the long glass and looked toward the Indian ponies, and Purdy's saddled brown horse bunched together west of the camp and knew the horses would give him away if he went in that direction. Looking to his left, he saw thick underbrush that would give good cover, so he shoved the looking glass under his belt, picked up his Sharps and bandoleer, and started walking in a crouch.

Creeping back into the brush and woods, he drew his pistol, cocked it, and made his way around the clearing while Purdy's painful moans filled the otherwise calm air. By the time he reached a spot close to the Indian camp, Tom had stopped screaming, and Wade wondered if he were still alive, fearing he would never know why Purdy wanted him dead. Smoke from the campfire rose and disappeared into the tree limbs just ahead. He could hear the Indian's talking and figured they were arguing over who got what of Purdy's belongings.

Keeping low, he crept to a large Ponderosa Pine and a large bush of tiny red berries. Kneeling, he peered through the berry bush at the five Crow Indians that were seated some twenty or thirty yards away, apparently still discussing Tom's belongings. Hearing soft moaning off to his right, he moved a branch of the berry bush just enough to see Tom Purdy lying on the ground, barely moving. His shirt was torn open in the front, his face covered in blood from the scalping, and Wade could hear Tom praying for God or Jesus to help him. His arms and chest covered in blood, all caused by small slashing cuts meant to inflict pain and not kill. His hands and feet were bound and raised in the air by rawhide ropes tied to the low branches of the pine tree he lay under.

Wade could hear Tom's sobbing prayers for death, and even though the man had paid men to kill him, Wade felt pity for Tom Purdy. Afraid the Indians would soon discover his presence,

314

he picked up the Sharps with his left hand, held the cocked Colt in his right, and stood with his back against the truck of the big Ponderosa Pine facing away from the Crow. After he gently pulled the Sharps' first trigger, he took a deep breath and stepped from behind the tree with the butt of the Sharps against his left hip.

Seeing Wade, one of the Crow stood with a surprised look while the one that had been torturing Tom stood up behind him, looking past him at the white man. Wade pulled the second trigger feeling the Sharps kick violently against his hip as the .50 caliber cartridge exploded, sending white smoke out the barrel. The bullet ripped through the first Indian's chest and hit the second in the neck, knocking both backward. At about the same instant, he fired his pistol at another who started to get up, while the fourth jumped and rolled across the ground, unable to avoid the two quick shots from Wade's Colt. The fifth tossed a tomahawk missing Wade, then made a run for the ponies. Wade took aim and fired two quick shots, and it was over.

Wade stood in the middle of the Indian camp, looking down at the five Crow Indians he had just killed. The Indian that had taken Tom's scalp was still moving, holding onto his neck where the bullet tore into his skin. Wade calmly walked over, pulled his knife, and cut his throat. Standing, he loaded his Colt and then made sure the others were dead. Hearing Tom moaning, Wade hurried to him, knelt, and looked at what the Indians had done to him. Purdy's face and arms were covered with cuts, his ears were missing, he had been scalped, and his hands and feet were badly burned.

"Tom," said Wade in a soft voice.

Purdy opened his tired eyes and looked at Wade. His lips moved, but no sound escaped from his mouth.

Wade thought about his canteen on the mare. "I'll get you some water." Then he stood and hurried back to where he had left the mare, untied her, and brought her into the camp. He took his canteen from the saddle, knelt, and gave Purdy a small drink.

Tom swallowed a little water then looked up through tired, red, welling eyes as if he didn't know who he was.

"It's me, Tom, Sheriff Spears," said Wade softly, then he took his knife from its scabbard and carefully started on the rawhide ropes that held Purdy's legs and arms. He gently and carefully lowered them to the ground causing Tom to cry out in pain. Wade could see Tom was in a bad way and probably wasn't going to make it back to Pickering alive. He contemplated putting a bullet in his head to end the misery since he had no medical supplies with him, and even if he had, Tom's injuries were far too serious. He leaned closer and softly spoke. "Tom."

Purdy opened his eyes and stared up at him for several moments. "I know who you are." Then he stiffened while looking terrified. "The Indians…"

"They won't bother you anymore, Tom."

Tears welled in Tom's eyes as he began to cry. "Help me die." He stared into Wade's blue eyes. "You were going to kill me anyway."

Wade couldn't help but feel sorry for Purdy.

"Promise me," pleaded Tom just above a whisper. "Promise me you will kill me."

"I promise, but I need to know why you wanted me dead."

Tom suddenly stiffened in pain, and fought not to scream out as he looked at Wade, then as he relaxed, he said, "You killed my wonderful sister, Elizabeth."

Wade looked confused. "I didn't know your sister."

Tom closed his eyes and let out a low whimpering moan mixed with soft crying. "For the love of God, put me out of my misery."

Wade looked down at Purdy's badly burnt hands and feet, and then he leaned closer. "Hang on, Tom," and then he repeated, "I didn't even know your sister."

Purdy's face was filled with pain as he looked up at Wade. "I know who you are. You're Marshall Wade Garrison, and my sister Elizabeth was George Hoskins' housekeeper."

Wade stared at him in disbelief while remembering firing into the darkroom, thinking he was firing at George Hoskins.

Purdy's breathing was getting shallower. "I used to visit her, and I saw you in town weeks before you killed her."

That night flashed across Wade's memory. "It was an accident, Tom," he said softly. "I went there to kill George Hoskins and his men for what they did to my family."

"I know. I heard the story after I buried my sister in Harper. Everyone knows it was you that burned the ranch down and killed my Elizabeth." He looked up at Wade. "You'll hang for that one day."

"The house was dark, Tom. She shot at me, and I thought it was George Hoskins."

Tom looked up and smiled. "Doesn't matter now, Marshal Garrison."

"Why didn't you just tell the law where I was?"

Purdy stiffened in pain. "I wanted to see you dead in Pickering. I couldn't do it, so I tried to hire it done." Tom suddenly grabbed the collar of Wade's shirt, cried out, and stiffened in pain, and as he relaxed his grip, he smiled again. "I forgive you for her death as I forgive you for mine." He smiled. "I welcome it as I will soon be with Elizabeth, just like in that picture you were looking at."

Wade took out his pistol and thought of Purdy's feelings for Estelle. "I'll try and find out who killed Estelle."

Tom looked up at Wade. "I killed Estelle."

Wade stared at him in disbelief.

"That's right, Sheriff," he said in a whisper. "I killed Estelle and that other bitch."

Disbelief filled Wade. "Why?"

317

"Them two bitches were lovers," he said, and then he closed his eyes, whimpered, stiffened in pain, and then opened his eyes. "They were gonna run off to California."

Wade stared down at Tom's bloody face remembering Estelle's disfigured body, and suddenly what sympathy he had felt for Tom Purdy disappeared. He holstered his Colt. "You don't deserve a bullet." Then he picked up his Sharps, stood, and retrieved the bandoleer from where he left it by the tree. Taking a last look at Tom Purdy, he headed for the mare.

Tom called out, pleading for him to end his misery.

Wade shoved the Sharps into the scabbard on the saddle, tied the bandoleer around the saddle horn when the sound of flapping wings and the screeching of the vultures as they began feeding on a screaming Paul Bradley in Mexico came to him. He closed his eyes and leaned against the mare and thought about Paul Bradley, begging him not to leave him to the vultures. Then he thought of Tom's older sister, Elizabeth, dying in his arms as she smiled at him.

He turned and looked at Tom lying on the ground fighting the pain and knew that Elizabeth would want him to end her brother's suffering. For a moment, he watched Purdy thinking of Estelle and Gracie and the men Tom hired who are now dead and buried in Pickering. He dropped the reins to the mare, drew his Colt, and walked toward Tom.

Purdy opened his eyes and looked up, seeing the Colt pointed at his head, and smiled. "Tell Dave he can have the saloon and the money in the case."

Wade pulled the trigger ending Tom's suffering, and as he looked down at the disfigured body, he wondered if Estelle would think Purdy deserved what he got from the Indians. He gathered up the money the Indians were splitting and shoved it into Tom's saddlebag along with his other belongings. The left rear leg of Tom's brown horse was still swollen so that he couldn't use it to tote Tom's body back to Pickering. Wade let the ponies go keeping one for Tom's body.

After the ponies ran out of camp, he turned to the brown horse, thinking it was a long way back to Pickering. Feeling bad for the animal, he drew his pistol and aimed it at the side of the horse's head. The horse turned and looked at him with big, dark eyes, and after they stared at one another for a moment, Wade holstered his gun and patted him on the neck. "Guess we've had enough killing for one day." He grabbed the harness and looked into the horse's big eyes. "You slow me up, and I will put a bullet in that big head of yours."

He unsaddled Purdy's horse and put the saddle on the Indian pony. Then he wrapped Tom's body in a blanket, loaded it onto the pony, and tied the brown horse to the horn of the saddle. After making sure the fire was out, Wade swung up onto the mare, and as he settled into his saddle, he glanced at the bodies he was leaving for the animals and vultures, turned the mare's head north, and nudged her into a walk.

Chapter 22

Pickering, Montana

Two days later and more tired than hungry, Wade rode up the street of Pickering in the late afternoon sun with the Indian pony carrying Tom Purdy's wrapped body and the limping brown horse. Word had spread that the sheriff rode out of town after Tom Purdy, but the reason was unclear, so the curious poured out of doors or filled windows watching the slow procession. Stopping in front of Earl Noonan's barbershop, Wade climbed down and tied the mare to the hitching rail. Earl Noonan was busy shaving a customer when he looked out the window and watched Wade tie his horse to the hitching rail, then dust himself off as he stepped onto the boardwalk. Knowing the body draped over the saddle was Tom Prudy, Noonan stopped shaving the man sitting in the barber's chair and stepped toward the window for a better look. The man sat up with half of his face shaved and watched as Wade opened the door, stepped inside.

"Is that Tom?" asked Noonan.

Wade had a tired look about him as he glanced out the window at the body and then at Noonan, ignoring Earl's customer. "I could use some help getting him inside."

Earl gave Wade a dirty look. "What'd you do to Tom?"

320

Wade looked into Earl's sad eyes. "Tom was captured by some Crow south of here. Can you give me a hand with the body Earl?"

He looked from Wade to the wrapped body on the pony, set the razor down, excused himself from his customer, and followed Wade out to the horses. They carried Tom Purdy into the undertaker's part of the building, and after they laid him on one of the tables, Earl pulled the blanket away and stepped back with a horrified look. "My word," softly left his mouth. He stared at Tom's scalped head, cut up face, burnt hands, and feet. "Damn heathens." Noonan stared at the dried blood on Purdy's body, the deep cuts, lack of ears, and the bullet hole above Tom's left eyebrow. "You find him this way?"

"No," said Wade softly as he took off his hat and fussed with it in his hands. "They weren't quite through with him when I got there."

"Bastards," said Noonan, looking at his friend's bloody body.

"In case you're wondering," said Wade sounding tired. "That's my bullet hole. He begged me to kill him."

Earl looked at his friend and placed a soft hand on his shoulder. "Can't say I blame him. I've heard of such things but never saw a man tortured in this manner." He looked at Wade. "What about the Indians?"

"Dead," replied Wade softly as he turned toward the door.

Earl started to cover the body but paused as he looked at Wade. "Sheriff?"

Wade turned.

"If you don't mind me asking, what was it that caused Tom to run away, and you go after him like he was a criminal?"

Wade stared at Noonan. "It was a misunderstanding between Tom and me. It makes no difference now, and some things are better left alone."

Earl took one last look at his friend and covered the body. He followed Wade into the barbershop part of the building where his customer sat in the barber's chair, still wearing shaving cream on one side of his face, waiting. He and Earl Noonan watched Wade walk outside, untie his horse, then climbed up into the saddle.

Wade rode the mare at a walk with the two horses in tow up the street, oblivious of the people who had gathered along the boardwalk.

The mayor watched as he rode by and then hurried up the boardwalk to where Moore was standing. "He dropped a body off at Earl's. Let's go have a look."

Jed stepped to the edge of the boardwalk in front of the jail and watched Wade as he rode past, staring down at the dirt street looking tired. Jed turned and went inside to make a pot of coffee.

Albert Bennett was busy with a hammer pounding on a piece of steel when he looked up and saw Wade and the extra horses. Recognizing Purdy's limping brown horse, he shoved the steel back into the hot coals and set the hammer and nipper on the table next to the anvil. He wiped his hands with a dirty cloth, tossed it onto the table next to the nipper's, and walked toward Wade. "Where's Tom Purdy?"

Wade climbed down, looking tired, "At Noonan's place."

Al looked at Wade, guessing why he was at Noonan's, and felt regretful wondering if the Sheriff had killed him, and if so, why.

"Tom got caught by some Crow south of here," explained Wade.

Relieved that it was not Wade that killed Purdy, Bennett's expression changed to anger. "Bastards."

Wade gestured toward the horses. "Tom rode his horse too hard, and he has a back left leg that needs tending. I stopped so's he could stand in a cold river a time or two to help with the swelling." He paused in thought. "I think he'll be okay."

Bennett bent down and looked at the leg. "I'll see what I can do."

"I don't want him put down," said Wade firmly. "I don't give a shit if he's never ridden and limps for the rest of his life."

As Albert stood, he thought that was a strange thing for a man to say. "All right." Then he looked at the pony. "What about him?"

Wade started walking toward the livery. "Keep it if you want." Then he smiled. "Just don't let any Crow catch you riding him."

Al looked at the pony for a moment, then followed Wade and the horses inside the livery, where Wade led the mare into her stall.

Bennett put Purdy's brown horse in one stall, the pony in another, and began to unsaddle it. When he finished, he stepped into the mare's stall and watched as Wade wiped her down with a cloth. "I'll take care of her, Sheriff," he said. "You go on and get some rest."

"She's had a hard time of it, Al," Wade said while looking appreciative.

Albert smiled. "I'll treat her like she was my own."

Wade handed him the cloth, tossed the bandoleer over one shoulder, both pairs of saddlebags over the other, picked up his Sharps, and smiled. "Thanks, Al." Then he walked toward the big livery doors thinking of Pup, stopped, and turned. "I'll be by tomorrow to take the brown to the river so she can stand in the cold water. Maybe that will help the leg."

Jed was standing at the door, staring out the window, watching for Wade. When he saw him, he hurried across the room, filled a tin cup with fresh, hot coffee, and set it in the middle of Wade's desk.

The door opened, and when Wade walked in, the coyote jumped off the leather sofa she had claimed while Wade was gone and whined, carrying on as if he had been gone for months. Wade

323

knelt for the greeting of face licking, bushy wagging tail, whining, and rubbing her body against his.

"Appears she missed you," grinned Canon.

"About as much as I did her," said Wade as he stood. "Any coffee?"

Jed pointed to the cup on the desk. "Figured you could use a fresh cup."

Wade put set saddlebags on the edge of the desk, his Sharps in the gun rack, and then took off his hat and duster, tossing them on the sofa. The chair made its usual creaking sound as he sat down, picked up the coffee, and looked at Jed. "Anything happen while I was gone?"

Jed wanted to know what happened between him and Tom Purdy as he turned to fill his cup and told him what happened in the saloon between Morgan and Cody Hayes.

Wade was glad that Morgan didn't kill the foolish boys for picking on Jed, not wanting Morgan to get the reputation of a killer. He sat back, put his feet on the desk, and took a drink of coffee. "Morgan's not a man to mess with."

Jed chuckled. "Cody Hayes sure found that out." He sipped his coffee and wondered about Tom Purdy as he gestured at the extra saddlebag. "That Mr. Purdy's?"

The door opened, and Mayor Smith, along with Jonathan Moore, walked in, neither looking very happy.

"Gentlemen'" greeted Wade figuring what was coming next.

Moore closed the door and followed Smith to Wade's desk.

"Cup of coffee?" asked Wade.

Smith looked at Wade. "We heard you rode out after Tom Purdy, and some said you were angry." He looked from Wade to Moore and then at Wade. "Since Tom was part of the town council and our dear friend, I believe we have a right to know what was going on between you two."

"I agree," said Moore, "and Noonan feels the same."

Figuring he should leave, Jed stood, got the rope for Pup, and took her outside.

Wade watched Jed and Pup go out the back door and then looked up at them standing at the edge of his desk. He took his feet off the desk, set his cup down, and opened the bottom drawer. While Moore and Smith watched, Wade pulled the cork from the bottle of whiskey and poured a little into his coffee. While he corked the bottle and put it away, he wondered how they would feel about their dear friend if they knew he killed two women. Wade took a drink of whiskey coffee, sat back in his chair, and looked at the two men. "Sounds like you've already paid Noonan a visit and saw the body?"

"We have," said Smith looking sad.

"Then you saw what the Indians did to him?"

Smith nodded. "Terrible thing."

"Horrible," said Moore.

"Yes, it is," said Wade thinking how Purdy suffered.

All of a sudden, Smith didn't look very well. He turned and sat down in one of the two chairs in front of Wade's desk while Moore sat in the other.

Wade went on to give them a short version of killing the Indians and then killing Purdy.

Moore looked at him. "We heard about you riding out after Tom, and Al Bennett said you were angry."

Mayor Smith looked at Wade with a curious look. "Was there bad blood between the two of you that we aren't aware of?"

Wade sipped his whiskey coffee in thought, knowing he had to be careful what he said or they'd figure it all out, so he decided to tell them part of it. "What I am about to tell you, gentleman, goes no further than this room. Earl doesn't even know what I am about to tell you."

Smith and Moore looked at one another, then both agreed.

He began with the ride to Miles City, and the story he heard about Purdy talking to the three men who rode into Pickering and tried to kill him and Morgan.

Smith and Moore glanced at one another in disbelief, and then the Mayor looked at Wade. "Why would Tom Purdy want you dead?"

Wade shrugged. "That's what I wanted to know." He took a small drink of whiskey coffee and leaned forward with his arms on the desk. "When I found out Purdy had cleaned his safe out, packed a bag, and rode out of town, I became a little more than curious, so I went after him to find out why he wanted me dead."

"Yes," said the mayor. "I can see how you would." He looked at Jonathan. "Purdy's been acting strange for some time."

Moore nodded. "Yes, he has."

The Mayor looked at Wade. "But that doesn't explain why he would hire someone to kill you."

"No, it doesn't," lied Wade. "The only thing I know about Tom Purdy is that he was never in favor of me being sheriff. He was against it from the beginning."

"That's right," said the mayor thoughtfully. "But that's no reason to hire killers."

Wade shrugged and sipped his coffee. "Men kill for lesser reasons."

The room became silent, and then Smith said, "There has to be an explanation as to why Tom would hire a killer to gun you down."

"Well,' said Wade. "That's something that Tom took to his grave. And to be truthful, the fewer people around town know about that, the better for Tom Purdy's memory."

"That's true," said Mayor Smith, then he stood. "Sorry to bother you, Sheriff, I know you're tired." Then he looked at Jonathan. "I've business to tend to."

Moore stood as did Wade, they shook hands, and then Smith and Moore walked to the door. As Moore stepped outside,

Smith stopped and turned while holding the door open. "Anything new on Gracie's murder?"

"No," said Wade wondering why he never mentioned the whore, Estelle. "Nothing new."

"Well," said Smith. "Keep after it." Then he stepped out onto the boardwalk.

As the door closed, Wade picked up his cup, filled it with coffee, and returned to his chair, feeling tired, hungry, and worn out.

Jed walked in from out back with Pup, topped his cup off, sat down in one of the chairs, and looked at Wade. "I was listening at the back door, and I was wondering how you'd explain things. Guess them Crow making a mess of Mr. Purdy did you a favor."

Wade sipped his coffee and then told Jed about the Crow and killed Tom in a little more detail, leaving out the part about Tom admitting to killing Estelle and Gracie Abbott. He had thought a lot about that on his ride back to Pickering and decided they were best left as unsolved killings. He felt that the good, thoughtful citizens of Pickering would slash the two apart with gossip, and the mayor's attitude proved him right. Plus, there was Katherine Jordan to consider since she and Gracie were friends. Then he wondered if Katherine knew about Gracie and Estelle.

Wade finished his coffee, set the cup down, stood, and picked up Tom's saddlebag. As he walked to the door, he talked over his shoulder. "I'm taking this and what's in it across the street then getting something to eat. Be back in a little while." He stepped outside into the dim light of dusk, closed the door, and walked across the street to the saloon.

It was Saturday night; the place was crowded and noisy with laughter and loud voices trying to talk above the tune Tim Martin's chubby fingers pounding on the piano's keys. Goody was behind the bar drying a beer mug with his damp, white towel. When he looked up, seeing Wade walk in, and having heard about

Tom through the rumor mill, he tossed the towel over his shoulder and filled the clean mug with beer.

Goody set the beer in front of Wade. "On the house."

Wade thanked him, took a healthy drink, and wiped the foam from his mouth. "We need to talk."

Dave Goody looked around, then finding one of his girls at a nearby table, he motioned her over at the men's protests at the table. "Take care of the bar until I get back." Then looking at Wade, he nodded toward the end of the bar. "Let's go up to my room."

Wade followed Dave upstairs to his room and waited while Goody lit a lantern filling the room with soft orange light. Dave gestured to an uncomfortable looking stuffed chair, and while Wade took off his hat and sat down, Goody lit another lamp, sat down, and looked curiously at the saddlebag.

"Guess you know Purdy's dead?"

Dave nodded. "News travels fast, bad news faster."

Wade nodded thoughtfully. "A band of Crow caught him two days' ride south of here." He paused. "He was pretty far gone by the time I got to him. Before I put him out of his misery, Tom said to tell you that you can have the saloon and what's in these saddlebags."

Goody looked surprised.

"I can witness that for you when you're ready," said Wade, then he bent down, picked up the saddlebag, and slid it across the floor to Dave's feet. "There's a lot of money in there."

Goody stared at the saddlebag for a long moment and then looked up. "I don't know what to say."

Wade stood and looked down at the saddlebags. "Guess there's not a lot to say."

"Mind me asking, what the trouble was between you and Purdy?"

Wade thought for a moment. "All that doesn't matter, now Dave." Then he walked to the door, stepped into the hallway, and closed the door.

Dave slid out of his chair to his knees and started untying the straps of the saddlebags.

A small crowd filled Laurie's Café when Wade stepped inside. Laurie hurried over, said hello, and showed him to an empty table against the back wall. While they exchanged pleasantries, the other patrons got on with their meals and casual conversation, glancing at him now and again. He drank the coffee she brought and waited for his food and thought about Sarah and his son for the first time in several days. As Laurie set a plate of food on his table, he looked up, smiled, and thanked her. Ignoring the heads that turned and then quickly looked away, he finished his meal, picked up the plate Laurie had prepared for Pup, and stepped outside

Pausing at the edge of the boardwalk to put on his hat, he felt tired, thought about his bed, and walked toward the lights of the Sheriff's Office. Stepping inside, he told Jed to go over to the café and eat, and then he set the dish on the floor of the cell. Wade sat down in the creaky swivel chair as Jed walked out and opened the bottom drawer. Taking out the bottle of whiskey, he popped the cork and poured a small amount into a tin cup, replaced the cork, and leaned back in his chair to the sound of Pup's plate moving across the floor. Wade took a drink and thought about Tom Purdy and what the Indians had done to him, and then he thought of Estelle and Gracie so brutally murdered because of a forbidden relationship and jealousy.

Several minutes passed as he sat there keeping company with the regretful visions of the past year, and when the whiskey was gone, he got up and lay down on the sofa with the coyote curled up on the floor next to it. When he next opened his eyes from a sound sleep, he raised his head and looked around the room, seeing Jed sitting at the desk reading a book. He sat up. "Why didn't you wake me?"

Jed looked up from the book and closed it. "Started to, but nothing was going on, so I figured you could use the rest."

Wade looked at the clock. "Has Pup been out?"

Canon pushed the book away and shook his head. "Not for a while."

Wade stood and stretched. "It's time for my rounds. I'll take her with me." He strapped on his Colt pistol, picked up his hat, and walked toward the door calling the coyote. They stepped outside into the warm summer night, greeted by the stillness of a sleeping town. He closed the door and walked along the boardwalk, chased by the sound of his footsteps. Glancing across the street at the saloon's lighted windows, he thought that Tom Purdy made Dave Goody a wealthy man. He paused to check the bank's doors, and after peering in the window, he continued along the boardwalk, checking doors and looking in windows.

Pup stepped off the boardwalk, stopped to do her business, and after glancing around into the darkness, hurried to catch up bounding along the street in a playful run. When they reached the end of the street, Wade stopped as he always had to look south toward Colorado as his head filled with images of Sarah and Emmett. The cry of a coyote somewhere in the darkness broke the stillness causing Pup to whine and stare into the black night. Wade looked down at her and wondered if she missed her own kind. Thinking she wasn't a dog, not like Dog and Willie were, he found himself feeling sorry for her, thinking he wasn't much different than she was. Maybe that was the bond between them. He thought briefly of taking her away from town and setting her free, but in the next thought, he wondered if she would go or if he could let her go. He knelt, put his arm around her, and rubbed the underside of her neck while they stared off into the darkness, listening to the cries of distant coyotes. Wade smiled at Pup and softly asked, "I ever tell you about my friend, Emmett Spears?" Then as if she

330

understood, he told her a story about his friend when they worked on the Circle T so many years ago.

The story finished, he stood, slapped his leg with the rope he carried, and called to her. She turned, looked at Wade, and then stared out into the vastness of Montana, wondering about the cries in the night. Wade slapped his leg with the rope again. "Pup, come." She turned, ran to his side, where he reached down and rubbed her shoulder, "Good girl." As they walked, she would bump against his leg, which was common for coyotes and wolves as they walk, having their version of holding hands.

Minutes later, they paused at the saloon window, and while Pup glanced around the empty street, Wade looked inside at the small crowd. The piano was silent while Tim Martin, the player, sat at a table with two other men and a couple of whores enjoying a beer and laughing at something one of them said. Wade glanced at the other faces of the sparse crowd, then turned and continued his journey to the sound of his footsteps and the creaking boards of the empty boardwalk. At the end of the building, he stepped off the boardwalk, and as he walked across the alleyway, he glanced back toward the outhouse where they found Estelle. Reaching the other side of the alley, Wade paused, looked at the dark shadows of the livery up the street, and imagined the mare inside, and he thought about saddling her and riding back to Harper. The coyote bumped his leg and whined over something, so he reached down, rubbed, and petted her on the shoulder with the realization that he would never see Sarah and his son again. "Don't worry, girl," he said sadly. "I ain't going anywhere." Then he walked across the street to the jailhouse.

Wade lay in bed, watching the darkness of the room slowly fade away as light from the early morning crept through the open window. His mind flooded with thoughts and images of Sarah and their morning coffee, then of little Emmett. Quiet, lonely moments such as this were the ones when he missed them the most. He thought of Morgan's picture of his wife, Ana, and their son wishing he had a photo of Sarah and little Emmett. Pup moaned softly as she turned in her bed. Listening to her soft, steady breathing mixed with the quiet sounds of the morning, he was glad he bought her from Harry Anderson, recalling Morgan asking if she was worth the trouble. Not that Morgan would understand, but she was to him.

Noises from the outer office told him that Jed was tending to the fire and coffee. He was still tired from the long ride, and dreams of Tom Purdy's screaming mixing with those of Paul Bradley in Mexico had interrupted his sleep. Wade tossed the covers back and sat up, placing his warm feet on the cold floor, leaned forward, closed his eyes, and rested his face in his hands. Feeling tired and older than his age, he stood and walked to the dresser where the pitcher of cold water and washbasin awaited. Lighting a lantern that filled the room with a soft orange light, Wade poured the cold water from the pitcher into the washbasin and looked at himself in the cracked mirror. Staring at the image, Wade wondered what became of the young man he once knew. Looking down at the basin, he dipped one finger into the cold water, looked again at his image, and decided not to shave. Wanting to rid himself of the hurt he felt and the loneliness of his life, Wade decided that he would have a hot bath at the bathhouse behind the Howard Hotel. Afterward, he would put on clean clothes and then stop by Earl Noonan's for a shave, maybe even a haircut.

Dressed, he called the coyote on his way to the bedroom door and waited while Pup lazily got out of bed, stretched, and then trotted across the floor, chased by her bushy gray-and-brown tail. The heat from the fire in the potbellied stove greeted them, as did the gurgling sound and smell of boiling coffee. He smiled at Jed. "Coffee ready?"

"Think so," replied Jed as he hurried to the stove and moved the pot to one side. "Let it stand a minute so the grounds will settle."

Wade waited but a few moments, then grabbed a tin cup from the top of the chest under the gun rack and poured it full of black, hot coffee. He set the pot on the edge of the stove and sipped the hot coffee, feeling the warm steam against his face. It was strong and bitter, but it tasted good, and while Jed poured a cup for himself, Wade walked to the door with Pup at his heels and stepped outside. Greeted by the cool, dawn air, he slid into one of the two chairs sitting next to the jail door. The coyote stepped off the boardwalk into the street with her head held high, staring into the distance, looking as if she smelled or heard something. Becoming disinterested, she squatted, did her business, and then hopped onto the boardwalk and lay down next to Wade's chair. He reached down and petted her shoulder while he sipped his coffee, thinking of the hot bath he would take a little later.

Jed stepped out of the jailhouse. "Mind if I join you?"

Wade looked up, smiled, and shook his head. "Have a seat."

Jed closed the door and sat in the other chair as the quiet morning filled with the sounds of them drinking their coffee and an occasional morning cough from Jed. A sparrow landed on the street, looked at Pup, and then flew away as the first rooster somewhere behind the buildings greeted the new day. Almost immediately, others that seemed to be everywhere joined the medley. The two men drank their coffee, listening to the morning sounds and watching the sun climb above the eastern hills beyond the alleyway across the street, filling their faces with warm sunshine.

Wade closed his eyes, letting the warmth of the sun caress his face while thinking of mornings past having coffee with Sarah. He opened his eyes, took a sip of hot coffee, and thought he might ride out and see Morgan later today.

Bathed and dressed in the yellow shirt Nora Peters had given him, the red bandana Sarah had given to him tied loosely around his neck and wearing a new pair of blue pants, Wade headed for Earl Noonan's place. The tiny bell above the door jingled, announcing his arrival to an empty barbershop and then repeated its soft song as Wade closed the door and called out, "Mr. Noonan?"

The door to the undertaker's part of the building opened, and Earl stepped into the room looking like he'd had about as much sleep as Wade. His face was sad. "I was just tending to Tom."

"I'm sure that's difficult," said Wade thinking that must be hard on Earl, then gestured to the chair nearest him. "You have time to give me a shave and haircut? If not, I'll come back."

"No, no, sit, please, Sheriff. I've time."

Wade hung his hat on the hat tree next to the door, placed the package containing his dirty clothes on an empty chair, and sat down.

Earl covered him with an apron tying it around his neck, and began cutting Wade's hair.

"When's the funeral?" asked Wade.

"This afternoon at three."

"So soon?" Wade asked, thinking his ride out to visit Morgan will have to wait.

Earl ran the comb down the back of Wade's head, lifting the hair so he could cut it with the scissors. "He wouldn't last much longer in this heat. The sooner, the better." He paused in his work. "Gonna miss Tom. He was a good man."

Wade looked out the window, listening to the sound of scissors mixed with those of a passing wagon and horses, and thought of Estelle's and Gracie's bloody bodies. He couldn't find any sympathy for Purdy as he softly said, "I'm sure the town will miss him."

The July air was warm, and a soft breeze played in the leaves of the cottonwood tree. Wade and Jed stood next to watching the people of Pickering walk into the small cemetery. It seemed as if everyone in town had gathered to pay their last respects to Tom Purdy. Preacher Arden had been waiting at the head of the grave, and when the last person arrived, he opened his tattered Bible and began reading from its scriptures. His voice, low yet strong above the sobs of decent women and whores alike, and even a few men such as Earl Noonan had red eyes.

Wade leaned against the tree, his hat in his hand, as he scanned the faces of the good people of Pickering and wondered what they would say if they were to learn the truth about Tom Purdy. His eyes settled on Mrs. Jordan, holding onto Morgan's arm with one hand while the other held a crumpled white handkerchief. If the truth about Tom and the two women were to come out, she might be shunned by the other good citizens simply because she was a friend of Gracie.

The preacher stopped reading, closed his Bible, and stepped back. Dave Goody, Earl Noonan, Mayor Smith, and Jonathan Moore lowered the pine box into the black hole that would be Tom Purdy's final resting place. As the coffin was lowered into the deep black hole, Dave tossed the first shovel of dirt into the grave, sending back a lonely thunderous sound. Earl followed with a shovel full, then Smith, then Moore, and then the next until the grave was covered with fresh dirt. Mrs. Smith placed a small bouquet of wild flowers at the head of the grave where the stone headstone would be placed when it arrived from Billings. Dave Goody wanted a stone marker that would test the ages of the man who made him wealthy. Dave stood on a chair and reminded everyone of the food and free drinks in the saloon to honor their lost friend.

Jed turned to Wade and suggested they head for the saloon and get some of the free food and drinks, regardless of how they felt about Tom.

Wade would have no part of it and told Jed to go on ahead. Morgan and Wade exchanged glances, and then Morgan turned to Katharine, said something, and then walked over to Wade with an extended hand. As they shook hands, Morgan glanced back at Mrs. Jordan, looked at Wade, and lowered his voice. "Jed said that you knew Purdy had hired those men."

Wade put on his hat. "He admitted it to me before I killed him."

Morgan glanced around once again. "Have you figured out who this Elizabeth is?"

Wade nodded. "Remember me telling you about Harper and the Hoskins ranch?"

"Sure," said Morgan.

"I didn't know it until Tom told me, but Elizabeth Purdy was George Hoskins' housekeeper." Wade paused. "The lady I shot thinking it was George Hoskins was Tom's older sister."

Morgan stared at him in disbelief and then glanced at the faces of the people walking away from the cemetery. "That's unbelievable."

Wade started to say something but noticed Preacher Arden walking toward them. "Afternoon, Mr. Arden."

"Afternoon, Sheriff." He looked at Morgan while changing the Bible from his right hand to his left and extending his hand. "I'm George Arden."

Morgan shook his hand. "Morgan Hunter." He turned to Wade, saying they would talk later, said good day to the preacher, and walked toward Katharine.

Wade looked at the preacher. "What can I do for you, Mr. Arden?"

The preacher smiled softly. "There's nothing you can do for me, son, but I was hoping I could do something for you."

Wade wondered what that could be.

Arden put one hand on Wade's shoulder. "I heard what you had to do at the end to relieve Tom Purdy from his horrible

336

ordeal." He paused. "I thought I could offer my knowledge of our Lord to help lift that burden from you."

Wade stared into the preacher's eyes, thinking if he only knew what sort of man Purdy was, he'd probably toss the Bible away and dance on his grave. "There is no burden to lift, Preacher."

"You're sure?" Arden asked with a doubtful look.

"Positive," smiled Wade.

"Just the same," smiled Arden. "I'll keep you in my prayers."

Wade smiled again. "I appreciate that." Then he watched the preacher walk away, wondering if the prayers would do him any good. He turned and walked to Purdy's grave, looked down at the fresh dirt for several moments thinking of the way he died. Then he looked across the small cemetery to the graves where Estelle Winters and Gracie Abbott lay buried. He turned and walked out of the cemetery toward the jailhouse, leaving the good folk of Pickering to celebrate the life of Tom Purdy.

Chapter 23

July

Another Murder

Wade sat in the shade of the boardwalk in front of the jailhouse, watching a tiny dirt devil rush along the hot, deserted street in a soft, warm breeze. Pup was lying next to his chair, sleeping in the shade, to keep cool, and Jed was across the street at the saloon having a beer. Wade took off his hat, tossed it on the empty chair next to him, and wiped the sweat from his face and forehead with his blue shirt sleeve. Wishing it would rain, he turned his head, looking up and down the street, thinking Pickering would look like a ghost town if not for the three horses at the hitching rail in front of the saloon.

The sound of a wagon broke the heavy warm air, and when Wade looked south along the empty street, he saw a wagon and its driver racing up the street chased by a cloud of dust. Thinking the driver had better slow down before he loses control, the driver turned the team and headed for the jailhouse. As the horses and wagon approached, the driver stood pulling back on the reins yelling at Wade, "They killed 'em, Sheriff!"

Wade stood as the two horses, and the wagon slowed and then stopped a few feet from Wade and the boardwalk. Pup jumped up, trying to get closer to the jailhouse wall as dust from the wagon engulfed the boardwalk. Looking excited, the driver set the brake and repeated himself. "They killed them, Sheriff!"

Wade swatted at the dust with his hand, recognizing Dan Hurley, a dirt farmer. "Who killed who, Dan?"

Hurley turned and pointed to the back of the wagon. "Burt and Debbie Bensen, and they took little Julie."

"Who's this, Julie?" asked Wade as he put one foot in the spokes of the wagon wheel, stepped up, and looked inside, seeing what appeared to be two bodies under a tarp.

Dan had a worried look. "The Bensen's five-year-old daughter."

Thinking of the two little girls he, Frank Wells, and Seth Bowlen rescued several years ago, Wade pulled the tarp back. Burt Bensen was shot twice in the chest, and his wife Debbie once in the heart. He covered the bodies, stepped down from the wagon wheel, and looked up at Dan.

"Did you see who did this?"

Dan nodded, yes, looking regretful. "I couldn't do nothing, Sheriff. I didn't have a gun with me."

Wade thought he couldn't have done much of anything if he'd had a gun. "What happened?"

"I was going to help Burt put a roof over the back porch for shade today, and just before I got to the top of the hill overlooking his place, I heard gunshots. Pulling my team up below the top of the hill, I stood on the wagon seat so's I could see over the hill. That's when I saw three men coming out of the house, get on their horses, and ride to the corral, where they let the horses and cows out. Then I saw another walk out of the house carrying little Julie under one arm. I could hear the poor thing screaming as she kicked and fought as the man climbed on his horse." He paused to catch his breath. "The bastard was still holding little Julie as they herded the cows and horses away from the house."

"When was this?"

"A couple of hours ago, maybe less."

Wade sucked in a small breath and thoughtfully let it out slowly. "All right. Take them to Doc's place around the corner. I'll be along directly."

"Yes, sir," said Dan. "You want me to stay there?"

Wade nodded. "Yeah."

As Dan drove away, Wade picked up his hat from the chair, put it on, put the coyote inside, and headed for the saloon. As he stepped inside, he let his eyes adjust to the dim light while glancing around, looking for Jed. Seeing him at a table playing cards with a couple of old farmers, he walked over, bent down, and whispered, "I need you now."

Jed looked up at Wade, seeing a troubled face, tossed his cards down, picked up his change, and followed him outside.

Wade stopped at the edge of the boardwalk and spoke softly. "You know the Bensen family?"

Jed nodded. "They have a nice little place a few miles south of here."

Wade looked sad. "They were both murdered earlier this morning."

Jed shoved his money into his pants pocket, looking surprised. "Murdered?"

Wade glanced around. "Dan Hurley brought them in a few minutes ago. I told him to take them over to Doc's."

Jed looked worried. "And the little girl?"

"Let's get to the office." Wade stepped off the boardwalk, and as he walked across the street, he looked in the direction Dan had come. "Bastard's took her."

Jed followed, looking worried. "We gotta get her back."

Wade thought about doing just that as he paused at the boardwalk in front of the jailhouse. "I need you to go up to the livery and have Al saddle you a horse. Then I want you to ride out to Morgan's place. Tell him I need him."

Jed nodded and turned to leave

Wade grabbed his arm. "Tell Morgan he may be gone a few days."

Jed nodded his understanding and then ran along the boardwalk toward the livery.

Wade hurried along the boardwalk to Smith's store, finding Mayor Smith and his wife doing inventory. "Can we talk, Mayor?"

Recognizing a troubled look, Smith handed the pencil and pad to his wife. "Let's finish this later." Then he walked to meet Wade in the aisle.

Wade glanced past Smith to Mrs. Smith, who was watching them, so he stepped closer to the mayor, lowered his voice, and told him about the Bensen's murder earlier that morning.

Shock filled the mayor's face. "My God."

He told the mayor about Dan Hurley bringing the bodies into town and of the men taking their daughter Julie. "I'll need enough supplies for two men. We may be gone for several days."

Smith stared past Wade to the street through the open doorway, still trying to digest what Wade had told him. He looked at Wade. "Of course, we have to get that little girl back. I'll see to it myself."

"I told Dan to take the Bensen's to Doc's, and I've sent Jed to get Morgan."

"Just the two of you going?" asked the mayor.

"Two's enough."

"You sure you don't want a posse to go after these men?"

Wade shook his head. "Posse's too slow and too hard to control. When I move, I don't want to have to explain my reasons."

Smith considered that. "You're probably right. I'll have the supplies and a packhorse at the livery by the time you're ready to leave."

Wade turned to leave but stopped. "Better split the supplies up between two horses, Mayor. Two lightly packed horses are faster than one heavily loaded."

Smith nodded. "Of course."

Dan Hurley's wagon was still at Doc Reid's place when Wade got there. He hurried up the steps, knocked on the door, and waited. When the door opened, Mrs. Reid stepped back, looking troubled as she gestured to a closed-door across the room. "The doctor and that other man are waiting for you in there."

Wade thanked her as he stepped in, took off his hat as he walked to the closed door, and knocked.

A voice said, "Come in."

He opened the door and stepped inside, finding Dan Hurley sitting in a straight-back chair across the room while Doc Reid examined the body of Mrs. Bensen.

Wade looked at Dan and thought he didn't look so good.

Hurley stood and hurried out the door, saying he'd wait outside.

Wade turned to Doc Reid. "She all right, Doc?"

Reid looked at Wade over the rims of his glasses. "If you're asking whether or not she had been molested, the answer is no."

Wade felt somewhat relieved knowing she hadn't suffered in terror while being raped by four men but saddened about her death.

Doc looked at him with angry eyes. "You going after these men?"

Wade nodded. "Soon as Morgan gets here."

"I'll be ready by the time you leave."

Wade looked at him. "You're not going, Doc."

Reid looked up. "That girl may need a doctor."

"Sorry, Doc, but you're not coming."

"Who is going?"

"Just me and Morgan. I need speed, not a damn army."

Knowing he was right, Doc Reid nodded in surrender. "Just get the child back, Sheriff."

"You can count on it, Doc." Then he turned and walked out of the room, leaving Doc Reid to continue his examination. When Wade walked outside, Dan Hurley was waiting in the shade of a cottonwood tree, fussing with his battered hat he was holding in his hands. Dan was close to fifty, with troubled brown eyes, thick brown hair, and a beard. Wade stepped off the porch and walked toward Dan, who looked fearful and anxious. "You and Burt good friends?" he asked.

Looking distraught, Dan nodded they were. "Wish I'd done something."

"They were dead when you heard the shots. You couldn't have done anything except make your wife a widow and your kids fatherless."

Hurley knew that was true. "I drove my wagon down the hill to the house after they left and found the door open. I called out, and when I stepped inside the kitchen," he paused while looking at his crumpled old hat. "They were lying on the floor." He looked at the sheriff. "I checked to see if they were alive," he paused, shaking his head. "But they were both dead, so I loaded them in my wagon and came directly to town." He looked at Wade. "I didn't know what else to do, Sheriff."

Wade put one hand on Dan's shoulder, feeling sorry for him. "How do I get to the Bensen place?"

Hurley pointed with his hat. "Follow the wagon trail south till you come to a flat-top mountain with high ridges. You can't miss it. The Musk River turns, and if you look for it, you'll find the wagon trail that will lead to the top of a hill. From there, you can see the Bensen place." Dan had a sad, worried look. "I'm worried about my family sheriff. Can I go home now?"

"Go home to your family, Dan," said Wade in a soft voice. "How many cows did they take?"

Hurley looked puzzled. "Six and two horses. Does it matter?"

"It matters. They'll slow 'em up."

"Hope you catch the bastards." Hurley climbed up on his wagon, sat down, then slapped the horses with the reins, and drove away.

Wade headed for the Sheriff's Office, where he took his Sharps from the gun rack and a bandoleer of cartridges from a peg next to the rack and laid them on the desk. Then he took his Colt pistol off the rack, strapped it on, then checked to make sure it was loaded. Wade walked into his bedroom, grabbed a blanket off the bed, folded it, rolled it, and returned to the outer office. He shoved a box of medical supplies in one side of his saddlebags, tied the straps, and then put a box of .45 caliber shells for his pistol and his long glass in the other side. He started to tie the straps down, but instead, he opened the bottom drawer of his desk and pulled out the bottle of whiskey, and shoved it in the saddlebag. He tied the straps and looked at his rifle, rolled up blanket and saddlebags, wondering if he had forgotten anything. Remembering his duster, he took it off the peg next to the gun rack and laid it on top of the saddlebags. He looked at the clock on the far wall wondering how long it would take Morgan and Jed sat down, looked at Pup sleeping in the empty cell, and waited.

Wade was sitting at his desk staring at the clock, wondering when Jed and Morgan would get here when he heard horses. Looking out the window, he saw Morgan and Jed at the hitching rail. They dismounted and came through the door.

"Jed told me what happened," said Morgan.

Wade stood. "Appreciate you coming."

"Glad to help," said Morgan. "We need to get this little gal back."

Wade looked worried. "Your place gonna be all right with you gone a few days?"

344

"My two hands can handle things for a few days. I told them to see Jessup if they needed anything." He glanced around. "Who else is coming?"

"It's just the two of us."

Morgan gave a quick nod. "What's that old saying about too many hands in the pot?"

Wade started picking up his stuff. "Mayor Smith has a couple of packhorses waiting at the livery."

"Well," said Hunter. "Let's get after 'em."

Jed looked unhappy as he followed them to the door. "I'd like to tag along."

Morgan looked at Wade. "Fine with me."

Wade looked at the coyote that was at the cell door, eyeing him. "Can't leave Pup here by herself."

Jed's face lit up, looking hopeful. "Bring her along. She won't be no trouble, and she'd warn us at night if Indians were lurking about."

Wade looked at her as he considered that and then thought of her getting hurt or running away. Deciding neither would happen, he agreed. "All right, we'll all go."

Jed looked happy. "Can I take the shotgun?"

Wade gave him a look. "As long as you don't shoot Morgan or me. While I lock up here, you go to the livery and tell Bennett to give you a fresh horse. You can be the cook."

Jed grinned, grabbed his old dirty coat, the shotgun, the box of shells, and hurried out the door.

Wade looked at Morgan. "You want a fresh horse?"

Morgan looked out the window at the Appaloosa in thought. "No." Then he looked at the coyote. "You best keep up."

The Bensen Farm

It was near sundown when they rode up to the Bensen place and slowed their horses to a walk while approaching the rear of the house. Pulling up a few feet from the back porch, Pup lay down in the shade and watched the others. Wade looked at Jed, told him to stay put, and then motioned to the barn and corral, telling Morgan to check it out, then dismounted. He walked through the long afternoon shadows to the back door, stepped onto the back porch to the sound of creaking wood, and drew his pistol. Glancing back at Jed, Wade pushed the door open and cautiously stepped inside. The last of the sun's deep red-orange color eerily shone through the windows of the dim kitchen as he walked across the floor, stepping on broken dishes. A chair overturned, the coffee pot lay in a puddle of coffee on the floor, and in the dim light, he saw two large, dried pools of blood. Imagining the Bensen's lying on the floor, he walked into the living room, finding it in disarray, reminding him of the houses they found while chasing the Bradley brothers. He walked up the stairs finding the two bedrooms in the same condition as the living room downstairs with drawers pulled out and clothing scattered about. He checked the smaller room that belonged to the little girl and imagined the terror she must have known.

Morgan called out from the kitchen. "Wade."

"Be right down," responded Wade as he backed out of the girl's bedroom then hurried downstairs to the kitchen.

"I found their trail," said Morgan.

Wade walked past him and stood on the porch as the last of the sun dipped below the western hills. "We'll camp here tonight and get on it at first light."

They made camp close to the barn, and while Jed gathered firewood, Morgan and Wade tended to the horses making use of the empty stalls in the barn as well as the oats and straw the Bensen's would never use. Jed raided the henhouse for eggs, found some smoked meat in the smokehouse, and cooked a dinner of eggs and meat while proudly saving their supplies. Their dinner eaten, they sat around the campfire resting against their saddles they would later use for pillows and drank the strong, bitter coffee.

Jed took a drink and, without looking away from the flames, asked of no one in particular, "What do you think they'll do with that little girl?"

Wade gazed into the flames thinking of the two little girls living happily with Gil Robinson they saved from the Bradley brothers and the half-breed Negro Indian. "Sell her, I imagine."

Jed looked at him. "Who to?"

Morgan looked up, "Indians most likely."

Wade took a sip of coffee and nodded in agreement.

"Who'd sell an innocent child to them, heathens?" asked Jed.

Morgan shifted against his saddle. "Countries full of bad men that'd sell their own sister if the price was right."

"That's a fact," agreed Wade, and as silence fell on the camp, he recalled other bad men he had hunted and killed over the years. Drinking the last of his coffee, he set the cup next to the fire then snuggled down under his blanket. "Sun will come up early, and I aim to be gone before it does." Then he pulled his hat over his eyes and waited for sleep, feeling Pup curl up next to him for warmth.

Morgan tossed the rest of his coffee into the fire, then lay down, covered up with his blanket, and pulled his hat down over his eyes. "Better get some sleep, Jed."

The sky was turning from black and star-filled to a starless, soft pallet of blue mixed with orange, pink, and deep purple when Wade lifted his hat from his face. He sat up, disturbing an unhappy Pup, and looked at the dark figures of the house and outhouse beyond the corral fence, wondering why men did these things to nice people. The morning air was chilly, and the hard ground Wade had been sleeping on left him stiff and sore. He tossed his blanket back, covering Pup, stood, and then stretched.

Pup was still lying under the blanket and Jed, and Morgan was still asleep when he returned, so he went about the business of making a fire, and not too quietly at that. When the fire was going, he sat on his haunches and warmed his hands while Jed's snoring competed with the chirping of waking birds. Wade looked at his two companions and found himself missing Seth Bowlen, Frank Wells, and the Indian Dark Cloud. Wanting to get on with the chase, he picked up the dented coffee pot and his cup, turned toward the others, and started beating the cup against the pot. Pup jumped up from a sound sleep growling while Jed and Morgan sat up with a start, cursing. Wade chuckled as he set the cup down and headed for the water pump with the coffee pot chased by mumbled, angry words from Jed and Morgan.

Returning with the pot filled with water, Jed was sitting by the fire, staring into it as if he was still asleep, and Morgan was up stretching. Wade knelt, set the pot down next to the fire, poured a handful of coffee grounds in, replaced the lid, and set it next to the fire.

Wondering if Wade had put enough grounds in the water, Jed asked, "What time is it?"

Wade pulled his pocket watch out, held it close to the fire, and looked at the time. "It's almost five," he said as he returned the watch to his pocket and stood. "While you get breakfast, Morgan and me will feed and water the horses."

Jed got up slowly and headed for the hen house to raid the hens of their eggs, then nosed around the smokehouse, finding a slab of bacon, and went about the task of breakfast. When it was ready, he called out to Wade and Morgan while dishing up a plate for Pup.

Watching Pup eagerly lick the empty plate, Jed took a bite of breakfast. "What are we gonna do if that little girl's already been sold by the time we catch up to these fella's?"

Since this was Wade's party, Morgan waited for him to answer.

Wade paused in eating. "We see if we can trade for her."

Jed was afraid to ask what would happen if the Indians wouldn't trade, and Morgan already knew the answer.

Breakfast finished, Jed cleaned up while Wade and Morgan saddled the horses and then helped Jed pack up the two packhorses.

Wade glanced around the camp, making sure they had everything, then put one foot in the stirrup, stepped up, settled into his saddle, and waited for the others to mount up. As he watched Pup trot after something, he regretted bringing her and called out to her. "Pup!"

She stopped, looked at him, then at what had interested her, turned, and trotted back to Wade, laying down a few feet from the mare.

"They're a day or more ahead of us," said Wade.

Morgan nudged his horse next to Wade's mare. "You're probably the better tracker. Maybe you should ride on ahead while Jed and I follow with the packhorses."

Wade quickly considered that. "Might be a good idea, Morgan. They can't travel fast, herding those cows and horses." He looked toward the house. "Hang on a minute." Then he spurred the mare and rode up to the back door with Pup on his heels, jumped down, then rushed inside, leaving Pup on the porch scratching at the door. Moments later, he walked out, carrying a rag doll Pup tried to take out of his hands. Ignoring Pup, he put it into his saddlebags and swung up onto the saddle. "Julie will need something familiar." He looked at Morgan. "I'll leave a good trail."

"Be careful," said Morgan. "And if you catch them, wait for us."

Wade grinned at Morgan, called Pup, then turned the mare and nudged her into a gallop, following the tracks left by the kidnappers.

"I mean what I say!" yelled Morgan. "You wait for Jed and me!"

Wade rode at a slow trot for a couple of hours, stopped to rest the mare and the coyote, and then rode at a trot for another two hours. Coming upon an old campsite, he pulled up, dismounted, and while Pup explored, Wade knelt to one knee. Wade took off his glove to check the ashes finding them cold to the hard soil under them. Little had disturbed the ashes, so he knew the fire was from early this morning. Feeling anxious, Wade stood, looked up at the sun, thinking it would be a warm one. He took off his black duster, rolled it up, and tied it behind the saddle with his bedroll. Deciding to give the mare a rest, he followed the tracks on foot for a half-hour, stopped, loaded the Sharps, then shoved it back into its sheath. He looked back in the direction he had come hoping Morgan and Jed were not having trouble following the trail he was leaving. Calling Pup, he swung up onto the mare, settled into the saddle, and nudged her into a gallop with Pup running alongside.

The trail was easy to follow, and he wondered why anyone would steal a few cows and a couple of horses that would slow them down after killing two people and taking a young girl. But over the years, he had known a lot of dumb cattle rustlers, thieves, and killers. The smart ones were hard to catch, but these four appeared to be part of the dumb ones, and he was thankful for that.

He rode at a slow gallop for another two hours before he stopped in the shade of a tree by a narrow stream to let the mare and coyote drink and rest. While the mare drank, he knelt to one knee and touched the tracks finding them clean and firm, and he was certain he was gaining on them. Standing, he glanced back in the direction Morgan and Jed would be coming and hoped they were not too far behind. Feeling thirsty and a little hungry, he decided this would be a good time to eat and let the mare and Pup get some needed rest. Looking at his pocket watch, Wade decided on the amount of time he would rest, and then he tied the mare in the shade near some grass she could eat. Taking some jerky out of his saddlebag Jed had given him, Wade sat down on a rock in the shade.

Taking a bite of jerky, he tore off a good-sized piece and gave it to Pup, who took it and moved close to the mare that didn't seem to mind Pup's company as she once did. Finished with a second piece of jerky, he flushed it down with a drink from the canteen then looked at his pocket watch. Figuring they had rested long enough, he put the watch away, tied the canteen to his saddle horn, then swung up into the saddle. Curious about Morgan and Jed, he rode to the top of a small hill, took the long glass out of his saddlebag, and looked for them. Seeing what appeared to be their dust trail barely visible to the north, he smiled, knowing that he hadn't lost them. "Atta boy, Morgan," he said softly. "Keep coming."

He put the long glass away, called Pup, and nudged the mare into a trot across the shallow stream to continue the hunt.

Chapter 24

Southern Montana

Two hours passed, and the mare seemed tired, and Pup's tongue was hanging out, so Wade stopped at a small shallow stream. While the mare and coyote drank, he looked west at the mountains in the distance and the sun hanging above them. Thinking it would be dark in a couple of hours, Wade turned and reached into the saddlebag, took out the long glass, and searched the prairie between him and the southern horizon for some sign of the men he was tracking. After several minutes of looking, he lowered the glass, thinking tomorrow he would leave Pup with Jed and Morgan so he could ride a little harder.

He turned the mare north, stood in the stirrups, and put the glass to his eye, searching for Morgan and Jed. After a few moments of not seeing any sign of them, he eased back into the saddle, hoping he hadn't lost them. He knew the mare was tired from the long day's ride and was sure the coyote could use a good rest, so he decided to wait where he was for the others. Shoving the long glass together, he hoped they'd catch up before dark. Glancing around for a place that would offer cover, he saw a group of white bark pine trees at the base of the cliff about a hundred yards to the east that would give protection, and the trees would filter the smoke of a campfire. He nudged the mare across a small stream, dismounted, took off his saddle, and hobbled her at the base of the cliff where there was plenty of grass. He unsaddled the mare, set his saddle and saddlebags near some rocks, then went about the business of gathering wood.

With the fire going, he spread out his bedroll, then sat down with Pup at his side, leaned back against his saddle, and petted the coyote on the shoulder, hoping Morgan and Jed were not lost. As he stared into the fire, he worried about the little girl they were trying to rescue, knowing if they failed, she would have a terrible life.

The sun had set, and darkness was at hand, and still no Morgan and Jed. Wade worried that they had somehow lost his trail and may not find it again until daylight. If so, he would have to go it alone because he could not take the chance of these men getting away. It also meant that he would have to eat jerky again and wash it down with water instead of Jed's hot strong coffee. He tossed another log on the fire contemplating a jerky and water dinner, when Pup raised her head, giving a low growl deep in her throat. As she stared into the darkness, the mare blew nervously, then stood still and stared in the same direction.

Wade got up and stepped back from the fire as he pulled his Colt, cocked it, hoping it was Morgan and Jed and not Indians.

Pup stood and growled with ears up.

Hearing the sound of bushes moving, he stepped farther back from the light of the fire.

Pup whined, then bolted toward the noise.

"Pup," yelled Wade. "Stay!" Then he saw what looked like the dark figures of two men on their horses step into the dim light of the campfire.

Relieved at seeing Morgan and Jed, he grinned, holstered his pistol, and stepped from the shadows. "I was beginning to think you lost my trail."

Morgan pulled up and climbed down. "One of the ropes pulled loose, spilling some of our supplies, so we had to stop and reload it."

"My fault," said Jed as he climbed down.

"Wasn't nobody's fault," corrected Morgan.

Pup whined and danced around for Jed's attention, so he knelt and talked to her while she licked his face and rubbed against him.

Morgan turned to Wade. "Any sign of our friends?"

"No," answered Wade showing his disappointment. "I thought I'd be on them by now."

Hunter considered that. "I'm sure we're close. They can't travel all that fast with them cows."

"Maybe tomorrow," said Wade with optimism.

Jed stood from the coyote. "Sure hope you're right."

Wade pointed to where the hobbled mare stood. "You can put your stock with the mare at the foot of the cliff." Then he helped unpack the two packhorses looking forward to eating something other than beef jerky.

Wade drank the last of his coffee, set his cup next to his empty plate, and stared into the dancing flames. "Think you can handle both packhorses, Jed?"

Morgan glanced at him, wondering what he had in mind.

"Suppose I could," replied Jed with a curious look.

Wade turned to Morgan. "I thought you and I would ride ahead. We can't be but a few hours behind them." Then he looked at Jed. "Think you can handle Pup as well?"

"If she'll stay with me."

"She will if I tell her."

Agreeing on the plan, they cleaned up the tin dinner plates, put stuff away, and settled back against their saddles, passing the time talking. It was getting late, and Wade was tired, so he stood and walked across the stream into the darkness. Seeing a faint light in the distance. "Morgan," he called out. "Bring my long glass from my saddlebags."

Morgan did as asked and hurried to where Wade was standing, and as he handed it to Wade, he saw the faint light in the distance. "Campfire?"

Wade pulled the glass apart, put it to his eye, and studied the light for a few moments. "Sure is." Then he handed the glass to Morgan.

Jed was standing next to Morgan. "Think it's them?"

"Has to be," replied Wade. "Has to be," he repeated softly.

Morgan lowered the long glass from his eye and stared at the faint light. "How far, you think?"

Wade quickly considered. "Five, six miles, maybe a bit further." He paused in thought. "I should have kept going."

Jed asked if he could have a look.

Morgan handed him the long glass as he looked at Wade. "You did the right thing in waiting." Concerned about their own campfire, he said, "Hope they don't see our fire."

"I don't believe they can," said Wade. "I never saw theirs until I walked out here into the open, away from camp." Wade got quiet.

"What are you thinking?" asked Morgan.

"Thinking of another campfire years ago, some men used as a decoy."

Morgan quickly considered that. "These boys can't be that smart. After all, they killed two people, stole a little girl, and then stole six cows and a couple of horses that are slowing them down."

Wade stared through the darkness at the tiny light, thinking Morgan was right.

Wade sat on his bedroll next to Pup, put one hand n her shoulder, and looked at Jed. "Me and Morgan will head out before first light. You can either stay here or pack up and follow."

Jed thought, but for a moment. "I think I'll stay put."

Wade looked at Pup. "You may have to keep her tied up."

"I will if I have to," said Jed. "She's used to the rope."

"Best get some sleep," said Wade as he laid down using his saddle for a pillow. After he covered up with the blanket, Pup took her usual place, making herself comfortable next to him on his blanket. Without raising his head, Wade said. "Whoever wakes up first gets the others up. I want to be heading for that camp before sun up."

Greeted by the early morning chill and Jed's snoring, Wade lifted the hat from his face and looked at the dark figures of Morgan and Jed and then up through the trees to the dark, star-filled sky. Tossing the covers back, he stood wearing his duster he had slept in for warmth. Pup raised her head, looked at him, and then went back to sleep. Thinking of the campfire they saw last night, he headed across the small stream and looked south, but the horizon and everything below was pitch black. Returning to camp, he built a fire and made coffee while thinking about the little girl Julie, hoping they would have her back by the end of the day.

When the coffee began to boil, Wade decided it was time to get the others up, poured a cup of coffee, walked over to Morgan, kelt, and gently shook his shoulder. "Morgan."

Hunter raised his head and looked at Wade with tired eyes. He slowly sat up on one elbow, feeling the warmth of the fire. "What time is it?"

"A little before five." Wade set the cup of coffee in front of Morgan, returned to the fire, poured another, and shook Jed's shoulder. "Time to get up, Jed."

Canon sat up and looked around as if he didn't know where he was. He stretched and feeling the morning chill, and briskly rubbed his shoulders. "You still plan on leaving?"

Wade nodded. "Soon." Then he sat down and picked up his coffee.

Morgan took a quick sip of the hot coffee. "Have you checked to see if our friends are up?"

Wade shook his head. "I didn't see any sign of a fire. My guess is they're still sleeping."

Jed thought the coffee smelled a little weak, then took a sip.

Wade looked up at the sky, which was getting lighter by the minute, took a drink of coffee, dumped the rest, and stood. "I'll saddle our horses while you eat."

Figuring Wade was in a hurry, Morgan stood. "I ain't hungry. We can eat when this is over."

"Suits me," said Wade as he picked up his saddle and headed for the mare.

The coyote watched him with anticipation waiting for his signal to follow. Hearing Morgan's coffee hit the fire, she turned and watched him as he picked up his saddle and followed Wade to the horses.

Jed watched her and could tell she knew something was going on, so he moved next to the coyote, put his arm around her shoulder, and spoke softly. "You're gonna stay with Jed for a couple of hours, girl."

Ignoring him, she watched as Wade saddled the mare.

Finished with their saddles, Wade and Morgan led the horses away from the cliff stopping a few feet from the fire. Wade looked down at the coyote and then at Jed. "If we aren't back by late afternoon, that means we missed them, and we're are on their trail."

Jed nodded thoughtfully. "I'll pack up, and then me and Pup will follow."

"Think you can follow our tracks?" asked Wade.

Jed nodded. "Just don't ride across any rocky ground."

Wade looked around at the packhorses and supplies. "Sure, you can handle both packhorses?"

"Don't worry none about them packhorses, nor about me and Pup. You just get that little gal back. I couldn't sleep last night thinking she was with some hostile Indians."

357

Wade took off his glove, thinking it was probably his own snoring that kept him awake, knelt next to Pup, and rubbed her shoulder. "You stay with Jed, girl. You can't tag along this time."

The pup whined as if she understood, acting anxious.

He put the rope around her neck. "You gotta stay, girl." Then he handed the rope to Jed, stood, and looked at Morgan. "Ready?"

Morgan nodded, then swung up onto the Appaloosa, and as he settled into his saddle, he looked down at Jed. "You have another gun besides that shotgun?"

Jed nodded. "Brought Harry's pistol. It's in my saddlebag."

Wade put on his glove, swung up onto the mare, and as he settled into the saddle, he looked down at the coyote and spoke in a firm voice, "You stay." Then he looked at Jed. "Sure you can track us?"

Jed smiled. "Damn sure I can. If I wind up in Texas, I'll write."

Wade chuckled as he took a last look at Pup then nudged the mare into a walk across the stream.

Morgan smiled at Jed. "Don't shoot yourself."

Chapter 25

A Hard Ride

Pup pulled at the rope while he and Jed watched Wade and Morgan ride out of camp, disappearing into the trees. Then Jed tied Pup to a small tree next to his bedroll, poured another cup of coffee, and settled down on his bedroll, leaning against his saddle. Pup stared after Wade and whined pitifully. Jed felt sorry for her, but after a few minutes, she gave up and lay next to Jed, staring after Wade with sad eyes. Jed took a drink of coffee and looked around the empty camp, which was silent but for the sound of crackling, burning wood, the whisper of the small stream, and the horses blowing now and again. Taking a drink of coffee, he wished this was over, and they were back in Pickering.

Hungry and feeling sorry for Pup, he set his cup down and smiled at her. "How about old Jed fix us some breakfast?"

Wade and Morgan rode at a walk along the dim, unfamiliar terrain letting the horses pick their way in the early morning light. They rode toward one of the last stars Wade had picked out for direction when they left camp. Reaching a clearing, Wade saw a tiny light against the dark hills in the distance. "See that?"

"Barely," said Morgan. "But I see it."

Wade pulled up, took his long glass from his saddlebags, and found the tiny speck in the darkness. "Looks like they're up."

He put the long glass in the saddlebag, pulled out an old compass, and in the faint light, got the direction of the campfire.

"Got a fix?" asked Morgan.

Wade nodded. "Yep."

How far you think?" asked Hunter.

"Couple miles, maybe." Wade nudged the mare into a walk waiting for it to get light enough for them to ride at a trot or gallop. As the dawn grew lighter, they nudged their horses into a gallop while Wade guided them with the compass.

Seeing a thin line of smoke drifting skyward and figured they were close and fearing might be seen, Wade pulled up. "Smoke."

"I see it," answered Morgan.

Wade pointed to the trees some thirty yards to their left at the base of a high plateau. "Let's get in the trees before they see us."

Sitting in the shadows of the pine trees, Wade took the long glass out of his saddlebags and looked at the camp.

"See the girl?" asked Morgan.

"Looks like she's sitting down by the fire. Appears to be alright."

"We can't just go riding in there," said Morgan. "The girl could get hurt."

Wade looked at Morgan. "There's a plateau through these trees that looks like it gets pretty close to the camp,"

"Let's go have a look."

Wade nudged the mare into a trot and headed through the trees for the plateau.

They rode up the steep hill to the plateau, then rode to its edge, pulled up, dismounted, and tied their horses to a tree. Wade pulled his Sharps from the scabbard, got the long glass, the bandoleer of shells, and followed Morgan to the edge of the plateau where a cliff dropped off abruptly overlooking the campsite.

"This is perfect," said Wade as he knelt next to a tall pine tree, leaned the Sharps against it and put the long glass to his eye, and looked down on the camp that was about seventy-five yards south of them. "I see the little girl."

Morgan looked relieved. "She all right?"

"Appears to be," replied Wade. "Looks like she's eating breakfast." Then he moved the long glass around the camp, telling Morgan what he saw. "Horses are still unsaddled, so they're not ready to leave." Then he moved the glass to the right and then the left of the camp, searching for a place for Morgan to approach the camp. Seeing such a spot, he handed the long glass to Morgan while pointing to the trees to the left of the camp. "There," he said. "The big boulder just to the left of the camp."

Morgan put the long glass to his eye and followed the tree line until he came to the boulder Wade had pointed at some fifty yards to the left of the camp.

Wade looked at the camp and then at Hunter. "How long will it take you?"

Morgan lowered the glass and considered the question. "Fifteen minutes, maybe twenty, depends on the terrain." He looked back at the campsite. "You staying here?"

"Best place for a shot."

Morgan thought of another hill Wade favored against a small group of Indians. "How far you figure?"

Wade lifted his rifle and put the scope to his eye. "Close to two hundred yards."

Morgan looked at the camp. "You sure you can you hit a target from that distance?"

Wade gave Morgan a quiet look as he backed away from the tree and boulders at the edge of the cliff and stood. "Let's get to the horses." Leaving the Sharps and bandoleer against the tree, they returned to the horses, where Wade took off his black duster and tied it to the back of his saddle. "Wait till I make my first kill," said Wade. "That should surprise the others and throw them

361

into a panic." Feeling foolish, Wade smiled. "What the hell am I explaining this to you for?"

Morgan grinned as he pulled his Winchester from the sheath in the front of the saddle and made sure a shell was in the chamber. Then he took off his duster and tied it to the rear of his saddle. "When I get into position, I'll come to the edge of the clearing by that big boulder so you can see me."

"When I see you, I'll drop the closest to the girl." Wade took his watch out of his pocket. "You have twenty minutes. If you're not in position, I'm taking out the closest one to the little girl."

Morgan took out his pocket watch, noted the time, climbed up on the Appaloosa, and as he settled into the saddle, he smiled. "Don't shoot the little girl."

"You just worry about being in place twenty minutes from now."

Morgan grinned as he nudged his horse and soon disappeared over the ridge.

Wade pulled his shooting rod from the Sharps sheath, hurried back to the edge of the cliff, knelt behind a boulder, and looked at Julie with his long glass once more. Remembering he had already loaded the Sharps, he pushed the long glass together, set it down, and screwed the rod into the ground. Wade pulled four shells from the bandoleer and laid them between the fingers of his left hand. Making sure everything was as he needed it, he placed the barrel of the Sharps in the u shape holder on the rod and the scope to his eye. Searching for the little girl, he found her sitting alone just a few feet from two men who appeared to be arguing. Wondering how Morgan was doing, he looked at his pocket watch sitting on the rock next to him, then turned the scope to the boulder where Morgan was supposed to be.

Knowing that Hunter wouldn't dally and would get as close as he could to the place Wade had pointed to earlier, he looked at the time, seeing that only ten minutes had passed. Thinking it seemed longer, he put the scope to his eye and the crosshairs on the one closest to Julie, pulled the hammer of the Sharps back, and squeezed the first of the two triggers. Wishing he knew where Morgan was, he looked at the watch sitting on top of the boulder seeing that fifteen minutes had passed.

The minutes passed, and when it became apparent that the men were beginning to break camp, he looked at the watch then turned the Sharps scope to the boulder and tree line where Morgan was supposed to be. Not seeing any sign of him, he moved the scope back at the camp, where the men were saddling their horses. Fearing their time was running out, Wade found the man nearest the little girl and put the crosshairs between the man's shoulders just as the man stood drawing his gun. Without looking, he knew that Morgan had made his presence known and pulled the trigger. The .50 caliber shell exploded, and the bullet hit the man with such force it spun him around, knocking him onto the campfire.

Morgan opened up with his Winchester hitting one of the men that had just climbed onto his horse, and as the man fell, Wade fired at the third man running toward the little girl. The bullet hit him in the chest, picked him up off his feet, knocking him backward. The fourth man fired a couple of rounds of his pistol at Morgan riding out of the woods, then swung up on a horse and rode out of camp. Wade reloaded, and while Morgan kept firing as he rode after the rider, Wade saw the second man he shot was sitting up, aiming his pistol at Morgan's back as he rode after the fourth man. Wade aimed, pulled the first, then the second trigger hitting the man in the back.

Knowing the little girl would be terrified, Wade gathered his stuff and hurried back to the mare while Morgan continued after the fourth man. Wade swung up and rode down the hill toward the campsite.

The little girl was standing, her clenched hands under her chin, crying and screaming, too frightened to run. Wade pulled the mare up, jumped down, and knelt to one knee, holding out the ragdoll and spoke in a soft voice. "You're okay now, Julie." He shook the ragdoll in front of her. "I brought your friend."

With tears running down her dirty face and body shaking with fear, she stared at the familiar ragdoll looking unsure and frightened. Wade continued with the ragdoll, trying to look unthreatening as he slowly crawled toward her on one knee. She backed away, so he stopped and set the doll on the ground in front of her, and backed away. She looked down at the familiar ragdoll and then at Wade, not sure what to do at first, then she reached down, picked it up, and held it in her arms as she cried.

Wade knew she was still terrified and would be for a while with all that she'd been through, so he stood, turned to the body lying in the fire, put one foot under the man's leg, and rolled him off the flames. Grabbing a loose blanket, he smothered the man's clothes, getting a whiff of burning flesh. Hearing pistol fire, Wade looked in the direction Morgan and ridden, then hearing several rifle shots, Wade turned to Julie, hoping Morgan was alright. He smiled at Julie as he knelt to one knee. "Time to go home, Julie."

Realizing what he said, she ran into his arms and put her tiny arms around his neck, and cried, "I want my mommy!"

A single rifle shot told Wade that Morgan had just killed the last man. "I know," he whispered.

She looked into his eyes as tears ran down her dirty cheeks. "They hurt my mommy and daddy."

"Did you see them hurt your mommy and daddy?"

She nodded yes as tears rolled down her cheeks.

Wade knew that what happened would be with the girl for the rest of her life and felt sorry for her. "I'm sorry you had to see that, Julie." Then he gently hugged her and thought of his son. He felt sorry for her and would be glad when they were back with the Hurleys. She needed a woman's softness now.

Julie raised her head from his shoulder and looked at him with big, brown, tearing eyes. "I want to go home."

Wade gently pushed her head to his shoulder and turned just as Morgan rode toward him with the body of the last man draped over the saddle of a horse.

"How is she?" Morgan asked as he rode up.

Wade gave him an unsure look. "She'll be okay as soon as we get her away from this place." Then he turned her toward Morgan. "This nice man is Morgan Hunter, Julie. He's a friend of mine."

Morgan smiled and took off his hat. "Hello, Julie."

She wiped her wet cheeks and teary eyes, said "Hello," and then put her head back against Wade's shoulder.

Hunter dismounted, led the horse with the body to where the others were, slid it off the saddle, and looked at Wade. "We'll head back to Jed after we put these boys in the ground?"

"Leave 'em," said Wade

Morgan looked at the bodies. "We can't just leave 'em."

Wade continued to hold Julie. "Why not? They never took the time to bury the Bensen's."

"That don't matter none." Morgan looked at Wade. "Seems the Christian thing to do."

Wade looked past him at two men riding toward them. "We got company."

Morgan turned, seeing the two men with rifles resting against their thighs, the barrels pointing into the air as they rode toward them.

Wade smiled at Julie so she wouldn't be afraid. "I'm going to stand up now, and I want you to get behind me. Okay?"

Morgan stepped to one side, his hand resting on the grip of his Navy Colt.

Wade stood and gently pushed Julie behind him with one hand while the other rested on the butt of his Colt pistol. "Stay behind me."

The two riders pulled up a few yards away and looked at the two men, the little girl peeking out from behind Wade and then the bodies of the four men. One was an elderly man having the look of hard times, the other a young boy of fifteen or sixteen, hatless and scrubby looking. "Heard shooting," said the old man. He looked at the girl and then glanced at the bodies and worried about the boy next to him and wondered what they had ridden into. He backed his horse up a couple of steps. "What's going on here?"

Wade gestured to the badge on his shirt. "I'm the Sheriff of Pickering, Montana, and we mean you no harm." Then he gestured to Julie. "These four men kidnapped this young girl from a farm near there, and we been trailing them for two days."

"And just where are the little girl's folks?" asked the old man.

Wade glanced down at Julie and then looked at the old man and lowered his voice. "They're no longer around if you get my meaning."

Understanding what Wade meant, he relaxed and sat forward in his saddle, looking at Julie peeking from behind Wade's leg. "She all right?"

"She is now," replied Wade.

The older man glanced around at the dead kidnappers. "Hanging would have been too good for the bastards." He looked at Morgan and then Wade noticing the way they wore their guns. "My name's Herb Johnson, and this here's my grandson, Michael. We have a place not far from here," he said while gesturing toward the trees in the distance. "You're welcome to spend the night so the little one can rest a bit. My wife's a pretty fair cook, and she loves the little ones."

Wade looked grateful but shook his head no. "We have a camp a few miles from here where another man is waiting with our packhorses and supplies. We need to get Julie back as soon as we can."

Herb thought about that. "Suppose you're right about that. Too bad about her ma and pa. Someone going to look after the child?"

366

"Believe so," said Wade. "A neighbor."

Herb glanced around at the cattle. "They steal them cows too?"

"That's right," said Morgan, who wasn't about to herd the cows all the way back to Pickering if he could make a trade. "You interested in the cows, Mr. Johnson?"

Wade glanced at Morgan, wondering what he was up to.

Herb scratched the stubble on his chin in thought while he looked the stock over and then turned to Morgan. "Maybe."

Hunter looked at the man. "I'll make you a deal, Mr. Johnson. We're in a bit of a hurry to get the little girl back, and if you bury these men, you can have all the stock, horses included."

Herb gave his grandson a quick look and then looked over the animals. "Are they yours to give?"

Morgan stepped closer to the gray horse the old man was riding and lowered his voice so Julie wouldn't hear. "The cows belonged to the little girl's pa, and because time is of the essence with the little girl, we don't want to deal with herding slow cows on the way back. I'm sure you can appreciate that."

Herb looked at Julie with sympathy and softly said, "I suppose you're right." Then he glanced around at the cows and horses they were offering, thinking they looked like pretty good stock.

"He speaks the truth, Mr. Johnson," offered Wade. "You can ask the girl about these men if you want."

Herb thought but a moment, not wanting to upset the little girl. "That won't be necessary. You got yourselves a deal."

Morgan and Herb shook hands, and the old man settled back in his saddle, looking proud. "We'll get this stock home and come back later to bury these scoundrels."

Wade picked up Julie and looked at the old man. "If you don't mind, sir, we'll be on our way." Wade put Julie onto one of the men's horses, tied her to the saddle, and climbed up on the mare while Herb and Michael rounded up the rest of the stock.

367

Hunter swung up and settled in, moved his horse on the other side of Julie, so she was between them.

Wade smiled at her. "You ready?"

She nodded. "We going home?"

"Yep," said Wade, then they nudged their horses into a walk with little Julie riding between them and headed back to where Jed and Pup were waiting.

Pup jumped up, looking alert and tense as she growled deep inside her throat, pulling at the rope that held her to the tree. Jed stopped what he was doing, looked at her, and then to where she was starring. "What is it, girl?" Bending down, he picked up his pistol, untied Pup, and held the rope tightly in his left hand and the pistol in his right, thinking of Tom Purdy's fate. Pup whined and jerked at the rope pulling it out of Jed's hand, and darted across the shallow stream.

Full of worry over Wade's anger, if she should run off, Jed forgot about the Indians and chased after her, but by the time he reached the stream, she had disappeared into the trees. Jed stopped and called after her while glancing around at the trees and bushes, wondering where she could have run off to. Hearing the faint sound of a girl giggling from somewhere in the trees, he looked toward the sound just as three horses and their riders walked out of the tree line.

Recognizing Wade and Morgan and seeing the little girl on a horse between them, he smiled with relief and waited where he stood. "I see you got her."

"Julie," said Wade. "This here is Jed Canon, and he cooks the best food you've ever eaten."

Jed grinned. "That's right, I do, and I hope you're hungry?"

Julie kept staring at Pup and never answered Jed.

Jed looked at Wade and Morgan. "Come on into camp, and have a hot cup of coffee while I rustle up something to eat."

They followed Jed across the stream to camp and stepped down from their horses. Julie couldn't keep her eyes off the coyote while Wade untied the ropes holding her onto the saddle so she wouldn't fall off then lowered her to the ground.

Standing next to Wade, she took his hand, stepped behind his leg, and stared at Pup. "Is he a coyote?" she asked.

"It's a she," replied Wade. "And yes, she's a coyote."

Morgan took the reins to the horses. "I'll take care of the horses while you get her settled."

Wade found the bedroll he had rolled up that morning and spread it out close to the fire. "Sit down here, Julie, and you can pet her."

Thrilled with that, she sat down, then Wade told Pup to lie down next to her, which pleased the little girl to no end.

She hesitantly reached out, touched Pup on the shoulder. Pup turned and gently licked her arm, causing Julie to pull her arm back and giggle. She looked up at Wade. "Tickles."

Wade smiled in hopes the coyote would help Julie forget about things for just a little while. "That's her way of saying hello."

Julie turned to Pup. "I like her." Then she reached out and petted the coyote again.

Thinking of how her life was about to change, Wade told the coyote to stay, and then he stood to get a cup of coffee.

While Jed fixed the food, Julie sat on the bedroll, contented to be with Pup.

Chapter 26

Dan Hurley's Farm

Dan Hurley sat on the steps of his front porch, enjoying his pipe, letting his dinner settle, watching the day give way to evening. Inside the house, his wife was busy cleaning up the dinner dishes with the help of their two oldest daughters, while the younger children were upstairs arguing over something only they cared about. Having had enough of the fighting and arguing, he stood from the steps into the yard and looked up at the second story open windows, and yelled, "Settle down up there!"

Returning to the top step of the porch, he continued puffing his pipe while enjoying the peace and quiet his yelling brought. Hearing a horse whinny, he looked toward the sound seeing two men on horseback riding at a walk beyond the barn. Standing to get a better look, he saw three riders with packhorses and immediately thought of the Bensen's. Stepping inside, he took his rifle from above the door, looked toward the kitchen and his wife. "Rider's coming." Then he stepped back onto the porch, cocked the hammer on his rifle, and held it across his stomach, hoping they were friendly.

His wife, Ruth Hurley, was standing in the open doorway, looking at the riders as they slowly rode past the barn toward the small corral. She thought of the holster and pistol hanging on a peg next to the door in the kitchen. "Can you see who it is?"

Dan stared at the riders without comment, watching as they rode at a walk past the corral and turned toward the house. It was then that he saw a small child on a horse and recognizing the coyote by the way it ran next to the horse. Grinning, he turned his head toward the door. "It's the sheriff with little Julie."

Smiling with relief, Ruth Hurley stepped outside, followed by their seven children, who crowded around their mother watching the coyote as the riders approached the house. "You children go on back inside," she said, bringing words of complaint from each one who wanted to see the sheriff's coyote they had heard so much about. Mrs. Hurley shooed them inside, then stepped closer to her husband, taking his arm.

Dan released the hammer of his rifle, set it against the wall next to the open door, and stepped off the porch wearing a grin.

Wade and the others pulled up a few feet from the porch while Pup, as usual when around strangers, settled on a spot several yards away.

Dan looked at Julie, then Wade. "She all right?"

Wade nodded that she was. "A bit tired, I suspect."

Dan turned to his wife, who was thin and looked older than her years. "This here's my wife, Ruthie."

Wade tipped his hat. "Mrs. Hurley." He looked at the children staring out the windows, and the open front door, then gestured to Morgan and Jed, introducing them.

Looking grateful, Mrs. Hurley said, "I'm so glad you got her back." Then she stepped next to her husband, wearing a worried look. "Where are you gonna take her?"

Catching Wade by surprise, he glanced at Morgan and then stepped down, giving Julie a quick look believing her ride may not be over. Thinking of the child, he turned to the Hurley's. "Maybe we should go inside."

Dan turned toward the house. "Sure thing, Sheriff, come on in."

Wade climbed up the three steps to the porch and followed Dan and Ruth Hurley inside. After giving the Hurley's seven children in their tattered clothes, a glance he took off his hat and looked around at the meager furnishings of the household. "I was hopeful that Julie could stay with you, folks."

Dan and his wife looked at one another with guilt-ridden faces. "Got seven of our own, Sheriff," he said. "And we're barely making ends meet now." He looked at his wife and children, who had taken up every available chair and the bottom step of the stairs leading up to the second story. "I have all I can do to feed what I have." Then he pointed at his wife. "Besides, the missus has the morning sickness."

Wade looked at Mrs. Hurley, not knowing if he should congratulate her or say he was sorry. "I understand your situation Mr. Hurley, but this is a little girl we're talking about who has no parents and no place to go. She needs a place to stay, and she knows both you and your children. It seems a natural process to me."

Dan glanced at his wife, looking regretful. "I know all that, Sheriff, and I don't disagree, but we got a new mouth on the way already." He paused, looking guilty. "I'm sorry."

Ruth Hurley stepped next to her husband. "We feel bad, Sheriff, really we do, but we ain't got no choice." Then she looked hopeful. "I'm sure some nice family in Pickering will be glad to give Julie a nice home." She paused and looked out the door at Julie, who appeared to be half asleep sitting on a horse. "She's such a sweet little thing."

Wade glanced around at the family, knowing it would be a burden, and looked at Ruth Hurley. "You sure about this, Mrs. Hurley?"

She looked shameful as her eyes found the floor. "We're sorry, Sheriff, but we just can't."

"I guess you know your limits Mr. Hurley, Mrs. Hurley." Then he turned and started to walk out but stopped. "Guess you

372

folks can use the extra chickens and other things at the Bensen's place." He gave each a small understanding smile, then turned and walked outside, feeling disappointed and angry but understanding the Hurley's reasoning.

Morgan and Jed sat next to Julie while Wade climbed up onto the mare. "Looks like we'll have to find a bed in town. " Then he turned her toward Pickering.

Concerned over the little girl, Jed asked what they were going to do.

Wade glanced at Julie, wondering himself what would become of her. "She can sleep in my bed," he said. "With Pup next to her on the floor, and I'll sleep in the spare cell. First thing tomorrow morning, I'll talk to the mayor."

Morgan thought about that as he looked at Julie, then he looked at Wade. "Let's drop by Katherine's and see if she can stay with her for the night."

Wade and Jed both thought that was a good idea.

It was late in the evening when they rode up the lonely streets of Pickering and stopped in front of the jailhouse. Jed saw no reason for him to accompany them to Mrs. Jordan's, so he told Wade that he would return his horse and the packhorses to the livery and have the coffee ready. Seeing no sense in taking Pup to Mrs. Jordan's, Wade climbed down and put Pup inside, then he, Julie, and Morgan headed to Katherine's place.

Sitting at the hitching rail in front of Mrs. Jordan's, Wade kept an eye on Julie, who looked like she was about to fall asleep in her saddle while Morgan climbed down, knocked on the door, waited, and then knocked again.

The door opened, and Katherine smiled, looking relieved. "Morgan, you're back. Did you get the little girl?"

Morgan gestured at Wade and Julie. "We did. Could I talk to you inside?"

She glanced at Julie. "Poor child. Is she alright?"

"I think she's pretty tuckered out."

Katherine stepped away from the door. "Please come in."

Morgan stepped inside and told her about the Hurley's inability to take her in, and then he asked if she could stay the night with her. "It'd only be for a day or two. Wade's going to talk to the mayor first thing in the morning about finding a home for the girl."

She smiled, looking past him to the closed front door thinking of Julie in the chilly night air. "Poor child must be exhausted." Then she walked past Morgan, opened the door, stepped onto the front porch, and looked at Wade. "Sheriff, bring that poor child inside."

Relieved, Wade climbed down, untied the ropes that held her in the saddle and lifted Julie off her horse, then carried the sleepy-eyed little girl inside.

Looking worried, Katherine told him to put her on the sofa.

Wade placed Julie on the sofa and then took off his hat and looked at Mrs. Jordan. "Evening, Katherine."

"Hello, Wade." Then she knelt next to the sofa, smiled, and brushed Julie's hair to one side with her hand. "Hello, Julie, my name is Katherine. Are you tired, dear?"

Julie nodded sleepily that she was.

Katherine smiled tenderly. "I have a nice, warm bed you can sleep in tonight if you want."

Julie was almost asleep. "Can't I go home?"

Katherine smiled as she fussed with Julie's hair. "We can talk about that tomorrow. Can you walk into the bedroom, or do you want me to carry you?"

Julie reached up with both arms indicating that she wanted to be carried.

Katherine smiled and picked her up, careful not to lose the ragdoll Julie held, and carried her into the spare bedroom. Wade and Morgan sat down, and several minutes passed before the bedroom door opened, and Katherine stepped out. She carefully closed the door then sat down next to Morgan on the sofa. "She dropped right off." She looked back at the closed door. "Poor child," she said sadly. "Can't imagine what she went through." Then she looked at Wade. "Did you bring any of her clothes?"

Wade looked apologetic. "I thought it best not to stop by her place. I'll send Jed out tomorrow with a wagon to get her clothes."

Thinking that was a wise choice, she looked at Wade. "What time will you be talking to Mayor Smith?"

Wade quickly considered the question. "Soon as I can. Early more than likely."

"I would like to accompany you when you do."

Wade glanced at Morgan then smiled at her. "I'll stop by mid-morning." Then he stood. "If you'll excuse me, Katherine, I'm a mite tired myself."

Morgan stood. "Guess we best take the horses to the livery." He smiled at Katherine. "Appreciate you taking her in on such short notice."

She stood, glanced at the bedroom door, and smiled. "How could I or anyone turn her away?"

Wade thought of the Hurley's having little choice in the matter, smiled wearily, thanked her, and told Morgan he'd wait outside.

Morgan turned to Katherine with a concerned look. "You going to be all right?"

She smiled. "I'll be fine."

He gave her a quick kiss, put on his hat, and said he'd drop by in the morning.

"You're staying in town?"

He nodded, looking tired. "It's been a long day. I'm tired, and I'm sure the Appaloosa's tired as well. I'll stay in one of Wade's cells."

Katherine looked concerned. "You can sleep on my sofa if you'd like. That way, you can have breakfast with Julie in the morning."

Morgan looked appreciative but shook his head. "Thanks, but I don't think that'd look proper." Then he grinned. "A cell and I aren't strangers, Katherine. I've slept in my share."

She smiled. "Just so it's voluntary."

He chuckled, put on his hat, and walked outside where Wade was waiting on his mare, closed the door, and stepped off the porch. "Can I borrow that extra cell of yours?"

"Have to ask Pup," Wade said dryly as he turned the mare away from the porch.

Katherine locked the front door and turned down the lamps in the living room, saving one for her short journey to her bedroom. As the sounds of horses galloping away faded, she paused at Julie's door, quietly opened it, and looked inside. Seeing the child was sleeping peacefully, Katherine left the door open a crack and went into her bedroom. She changed into a nightgown, checked on Julie once again then climbed into bed. Katherine had just settled in when she heard Julie screaming and figuring a nightmare. Jumping out of bed, she rushed into Julie's room.

The child was sitting up crying and looking frightened, calling for her mother. Katherine sat down on the edge of the bed, put her arms around her, and as Julie melted into her arms sobbing, she cried for her mommy. While gently holding Julie, she rocked her back and forth for several minutes, letting her cry, believing it was something the child had to do. After several minutes the crying stopped, and Julie finally fell to sleep. Katherine watched her for a few moments feeling sorry for the girl, then carried her into her bedroom. Without waking, Julie curled up next to Katherine. Katherine spent a restless night thinking of Julie watching her mother and father die and being with those terrible men.

The night passed slowly, and now Katherine looked out the window at the sky getting lighter, and as she lay next to Julie, she thought of Mayor Robert Smith deciding this poor child's fate. She looked at Julie's soft face and knew that she was the only one left to speak for this innocent child and whispered, "No one else will have you." Knowing she would have a fight on her hands, Katherine slowly pulled back the covers, quietly got out of bed, put on her robe, and tiptoed out of the room into the kitchen. Lighting a lantern, she put firewood in the cooking stove and lit it, thinking of a hot cup of coffee for herself and breakfast for Julie. Katherine had planning to do, and her mind worked best when she was busy cooking and drinking coffee.

After the bacon was sliced, eggs beaten, and batter for pancakes ready, Katherine went back to her bedroom, sat on the edge of the bed. She watched Julie sleep for a few moments before she gently shook her shoulder. "Julie, sweetheart, it's time to get up."

Julie opened her eyes that were still full of sleep and looked around as if lost.

Katherine smiled. "Do you remember coming here last night?"

Julie looked at her for a long moment, then nodded yes.

"Would you like some breakfast?"

Julie glanced around the room as she sat up, fighting the long sleeves of one of Katherine's shirts that she wore as a nightgown. "When can I go home?"

Katherine reached out and touched Julie's arm and smiled. "Time to talk about that later, dear. Would you like some pancakes and honey?"

Julie's eyes widened with a quick nod of the head.

Katherine stood, took the girl's hand, and walked her to the kitchen, where she helped her wash for a breakfast of bacon, scrambled eggs, and pancakes.

While Julie ate with enthusiasm, Katherine sat down at the table with a cup of coffee and watched the girl. When breakfast was over, Katherine bathed Julie, dressed her in the same soiled clothes, and brushed her hair while telling her they would walk into town and see about a new dress later in the day.

Julie looked sad. "I have lots of dresses at home."

"I'm sure you do."

"When can I go home?"

Katherine didn't respond to the question as she set the brush down on the dresser and tied a red ribbon in Julie's hair. When she finished, she stood, took Julie's hand, and led her into the living room where they sat down on the sofa. Although Katherine hated to do what must be done, she knew it was necessary and looked into Julie's brown, trusting eyes. "Julie, you know you can't go home, don't you?"

Julie's eyes welled. "Yes." Then she began crying. "But I want to."

Katherine put her arm around Julie and held her tight. "There's no one there to take care of you now."

The child began to sob softly as tears flowed down her face leaving little spots on her dirty dress. She held the doll tightly in her arms and looked up at Katherine. "Can I stay here?"

Katherine smiled. "Would you like that?"

Julie nodded as she wiped her eyes and face with her hands. "Uh-huh."

They talked for a while longer as Katherine explained things as best she could to a five-year-old who had been traumatized. "We have to talk to the mayor before any decisions are made."

Julie looked worried and asked if he was a nice man.

Katherine smiled, saying that he was and that she shouldn't be afraid. "Morgan and Wade will be there."

That brought the first smile to Julie's face. "They're nice."

Katherine thought of Morgan. "Yes, they are nice."

Mayor Robert Smith showed Katherine, Julie, Wade, and Morgan into his office located in a small room in the back of his store. While the mayor dusted off the two chairs in front of his old, oak desk for Katherine and Julie, Wade and Morgan took off their hats and stood by the door.

Wade glanced around the small, dim room, taking notice of law certificates on the wall behind the mayor's dark, cherry wood desk. A few photos of dead confederate and union soldiers at what appeared to be battlefields hung on the walls.

Mayor Smith turned to the single window and raised the shade to the top, letting more light into the room. "That's better," he said, then he sat down in a slightly worn, high back, leather chair behind his desk. Getting settled, he looked at Katherine. "You're not working today, Mrs. Jordan?"

"My job is part-time, Mr. Mayor and today is one of those days that I don't work."

Smith smiled, thinking he should have known that. "I see." Then he adjusted a small stack of papers, moved them to one side, folded his hands, and smiled at Julie. "And how are you feeling today, child?"

Julie held onto her ragdoll a little tighter and never answered.

Smith looked at Katherine. "Mighty decent of you taking the child in on such short notice, Mrs. Jordan."

"It was a pleasure," said Katherine as she smiled tenderly and put her arm around Julie, who nestled her head against her. Looking concerned, she asked, "What happens now?"

The mayor sat back with a thoughtful look, even a little nervous as he glanced at Julie and then looked at Katherine. "Should this be discussed in front of the child?"

Katherine looked at Julie and then at the mayor. "Julie and I had a long talk this morning, and she is well aware of what happened to her parents." She looked from Julie to Smith. "After all, she was there when this terrible thing happened."

Smith smiled sympathetically as he looked at the child who looked up at Katherine and then at the mayor.

"I have a proposition," Katherine Jordan said suddenly.

Surprised, the mayor looked from the child to Mrs. Jordan. "What sort of proposition?"

"I can't have children, and I've always wanted a girl to teach how to cook and sew, and other things a woman needs to know." She looked at Julie, smiled, and then turned to the mayor. "I want to adopt Julie."

The mayor's mouth was agape as Morgan and Wade looked at one another with surprise while Smith stared into Katherine's unblinking brown eyes. "Giving a child to an unmarried woman..." He let the sentence fade with an uncertain look.

She smiled. "I've money of my own, Mr. Smith. My house is paid for, I go to church on Sundays, and I'm a respectable woman."

Wade suddenly thought about Gracie Abbott, hoping no one found out the truth about her and Estelle.

Smith pursed his lips in thought. "All you say is true, Mrs. Jordan." Then he sat forward, filled with concern. "I've no objections mind you, but some in the town might."

"Why?" asked Morgan.

Surprised by Morgan's intervening, the mayor looked at him. "Well," he said with a long pause, "Mrs. Jordan, you're a widow."

Katherine looked from Morgan to the mayor. "What difference does that make? There are two other widows in Pickering who have more than one child to take care of, and I must say they do it quite well."

Smith sat back with a perplexed look. "That's true, but their children were not adopted."

"Nonsense," offered Hunter sounding irritated while Wade chose to remain silent.

Katherine glanced at Morgan while holding back an approving smile.

Mayor Smith stared at Morgan for a moment, then looked at Mr. Jordan.

Katherine leaned forward in her chair. "This child has already been through more in the past few days than most people in their entire lives. Why put her through anymore? I can give her a home, an education," she paused and looked at the child, "and she wants to stay with me."

The mayor leaned forward, looking at Julie. "Is that true, child?"

Julie looked up at Katherine, hugged her ragdoll, and nodded yes. "She's nice. I like her."

Katherine smiled at that.

Wade stepped toward the desk. "Who makes the final decision, Mayor?"

Smith considered that while looking at the child, and then he looked at Wade. "Well, I suppose the town council along with the church elders."

Wade thought about that. "Will Katherine have an opportunity to address the council and the elders before they make their decision?"

"I don't see why not," replied the mayor, and then he looked at Mrs. Jordan. "We've never done anything like this before."

"I hope not," said Katherine. "And I hope never again." She glanced at Julie and then looked at the mayor. "Due to the unfortunate happening in her life Mr. Mayor, Julie has already bonded with me. Putting her with strangers now would only add to the tragedy in this child's life."

Mayor Smith looked worried as he considered that for a few minutes, and then he sat forward, folded his hands with his thumbs moving nervously around one another. "There's still the farm to consider."

Katherine shrugged. "I presume it belongs to Julie. Sell it and place the money in the bank for her future. I'll need none of it to raise her."

Robert Smith thought for a few moments fearing his wife's tongue and those of a few other women in town that may be against the idea. "Still," he said thoughtfully. "You're a single woman."

"For Pete's sake," commented Morgan dryly. "Call a town council meeting; get the elders together and let Mrs. Jordan have her say."

Irritated by Morgan's intervention, Smith looked at the child. "I suppose we could."

Katherine looked from Morgan to the mayor. "I'm sure that Jonathan will agree with me on this, Mr. Mayor, as will you once you give this some thought. I donate quite a sum each month to the church." Then she stood, held her hand across the big, old, oak desk, and shook the mayor's hand. "I thank you, Mr. Mayor, for allowing me the opportunity to speak to you about Julie. I know you're a busy man, so Julie and I will wait to hear from you."

Mayor Smith stood and watched as she took Julie's hand and walked toward the door.

Wade opened it, and as she walked past him, he thought Morgan was going to have his hands full. Then he watched as she and the child walked through the store toward the front door with the bell, where they turned and waited for him and Morgan. Thinking Sarah would like her, Wade turned to the mayor, thanked him, and stepped out of the room.

Morgan followed but paused in the open doorway, told Wade that he would be along in a moment, stepped back inside, and closed the door.

Wade was curious about what Morgan was up to as he walked across the store to Katherine and Julie. Turning back to the door, he asked, "Wonder what that's about?"

"I've no idea," replied Katherine as she stared at the door with a puzzled look.

After Morgan closed the door, he walked to the chair Katherine had been sitting in, placed his big black hat on the edge of Mayor Smith's desk, and eased into the chair. "Suppose Mrs. Jordan was still married. Would that influence the council's decision?"

Smith raised his brow and shrugged. "Of course, it would."

Morgan stared out the window at the mountains in the distance in thought before looking at the mayor. "I'm asking that you not hold that meeting for a few days, Mr. Mayor."

Robert Smith frowned, looking puzzled as he sat back in his chair. "I suppose I could delay such a meeting. May I inquire as to why?"

Morgan sucked in a deep breath then stood breathing a soft, long sigh. "I'll give you the answer to that in a day or two." Then he picked up his hat and turned to the door. "Good day, Mayor."

Wade was waiting on the boardwalk leaning against the post of the roof over the boardwalk when Morgan walked out of Smith's General Store. "Mind me asking what that was about?"

Hunter put on his hat. "Where's Katherine and Julie?"

"I believe they went home." Wade stared at him, wondering what had him by the neck. "Want to get a drink?"

"No," replied Morgan while staring along the boardwalk in thought. "I better get back to my place. I told my two men I'd be back as soon as I could." He put one hand on Wade's back. "I'll walk you to your office, and then I'll get my horse and head home."

Morgan unsaddled his horse, walked to the open door of the barn, leaned against the frame, and stared at the cottonwood trees along the banks of the small lake in the distance. His thoughts were of Katherine and Julie. Visions of his dead wife, Ana, and their only son, living in Texas with Ana's mother and father, marched

383

through his mind. A small herd of elk strolled to the edge of the small lake to drink, bringing back memories of the elk chased by the wolves last winter.

He turned from the small herd, went back inside the barn, filled a bucket with water, and set it down for the Appaloosa. Then he walked to the house where he fixed a quick lunch of fried steak that he quickly ate. Sitting in his living room sipping a glass of brandy, he thought of the way Katherine sat in the mayor's office, fighting to keep Julie. Then Ana came into his mind bringing guilt and confusion about his feelings for Katherine. He drank the last of his brandy, walked to the liquor cabinet, poured another, returned to the chair, and took a small sip. Setting the glass down on the table next to his chair, he pulled out the locket he always carried, opened it, and stared at the picture while memories of their love raced through his mind.

Closing the locket, he put it away, wishing Wade was sitting in the empty chair across from him so they could talk. Feeling the need to talk to someone, he got up, took his hat off the peg, and headed for the barn. He saddled the big brown horse he brought with him from Texas, told his ranch hands that he would be back soon, and rode toward the Thornton place.

Louise Thornton was hanging laundry on a clothesline rope that ran from the back of the house to an old oak tree a few yards from the house. Hearing a horse, she turned and seeing it was Morgan, she stepped away from the line of wet clothes, shaded her eyes with one hand to watch him, and waited.

"Hope I ain't disturbing you, Mrs. Thornton," he said, pulling up near the clothesline.

She smiled. "Always glad when something takes me away from Jessup's dirty clothes." She turned and pointed toward the barn. "He's in the barn helping one of our hands deliver a Colt."

Morgan glanced at the barn. "The truth is, Mrs. Thornton, it's you I came to talk to."

Surprised and curious, she looked up at him. "Oh?"

"Yes, ma'am."

"Well, step down," she said, wondering what business he could have with her. "I'll pour us a glass of cold water."

"Won't be necessary," replied Morgan as he climbed down.

She walked toward the house, talking over her shoulder. "Nonsense, now come on inside."

Reluctantly and filled with second thoughts, he followed her inside, took off his hat, and thought about leaving without talking to her.

"Take a chair," she said, pointing to one at the big table.

Morgan sat down as told and watched as she went about filling two glasses of water from the pump on the edge of the kitchen counter.

She handed him a glass of cold water, sat down in a chair across from him at the table, and took a long drink. "Didn't realize how thirsty I was," she said as she set the glass down. "You said you came to see me about something?"

Morgan set the glass down without taking a drink and stared into the clear water, wondering where to begin.

Louise stared at him a moment. "What bothers you, Mr. Hunter?"

The room filled with a heavy silence as he looked up with a half-smile trying to find the words to begin to tell her the story he wanted to tell her. Recalling his youth's days when he took his troubles to his mother, he took a drink of water and got comfortable in the chair. "My wife died a few years ago," he began, already having made up his mind that he was not going to tell the full story. "That's why I left Texas."

Louise Thornton felt bad for Morgan as she sat back and, like any good listener, watched as Morgan struggled with the words. "You want a drink of whiskey, Mr. Hunter?"

Morgan shook his head no. "I don't know if you've heard, but Mrs. Jordan and I have been courting for a while now."

She smiled. "Yes, I've heard. She's a very nice lady, and quite pretty, I might add."

Morgan smiled uneasily. "I won't argue that." Then he told her about the Bensen family and the little girl, Julie Bensen, how Mrs. Jordan was trying to adopt the child and what the mayor had to say.

Louise Thornton was wise in her years and stared down at the glass of water she held while listening, and when he finished, she looked at him. "You considering marriage, Mr. Hunter?"

Morgan looked at her with a surprised expression.

She smiled. "I'm a woman."

He grinned. "I'll not deny I've given marriage some thought, but the thing is, with this child and all, I..." He let the sentence die.

She smiled. "Appears you aren't quite so sure about taking that big step again."

He looked into her kind brown eyes and aging face. "It ain't that I'm afraid."

She looked puzzled. "What, then?" As if she knew the answer, she stared at him. "Is it guilt you're fearing?" She paused. "You fear that you may be betraying the love you shared with your first wife?"

He thought about that for a few moments. "Something like that, I guess."

Mrs. Thornton looked at him for a long moment. "Did your wife love you, Morgan?"

He looked at her, thinking that was a strange question.

Mrs. Thornton smiled and leaned across the table, putting her hand on his arm. "Did she love you?"

"Yes, she did, just as I loved her."

Mrs. Thornton sat back in her chair and smiled. "Then she'd want you to be happy." She looked at Morgan for a long moment. "Want to know what I think about such things as death and life, Morgan? Bury the dead and love the living." She smiled tenderly at him. "It's no sin to love again. You'll always hold on to the love you have for your wife." She leaned toward him, reached out, and touched his arm. "There's always room for more love. It's the hate we don't want to give any room to in our hearts." She sat back and drank the last of her water. "Hope I was of some help." Then she stood and looked at him with a gentle smile. "Go ask Katherine Jordan to marry you, Morgan, and give that little girl whose parents are dead a decent, happy home."

It was mid-morning the next day when a nervous Morgan Hunter, clean-shaven and dressed in a clean, light gray shirt with a blue bandana around his neck, rode up to the porch of Mrs. Katherine Jordan's house in Pickering. Pausing at the hitching rail, thinking of what he was going to say, he climbed down from the Appaloosa.

The door opened, and Katherine stepped from the house, walked to the edge of the porch, and smiled. "Good morning."

"Good morning," replied Morgan as he tied the Appaloosa to the hitching rail. "How is Julie doing?"

"She had a bad night," said Katherine. "More nightmares."

Morgan looked concerned. "They'll pass in time, I'm sure."

"I hope so," she said, looking hopeful. "What brings you to town?"

Morgan's heart beat against his chest, and his head pounded. "I'd like to talk if you have a minute."

Curious, she gestured to the two white wooden chairs sitting on the porch under the living room window.

Morgan took off his hat, stepped onto the porch, waited for her to sit down, and then sat in the other chair with his hat in his lap and looked around. "Nice day'"

Katherine glanced around. "Yes, it is."

"Not too hot yet," he said, looking up at the blue sky, at his horse, and then toward the main street, wondering what Wade and Jed were doing.

Katherine watched as he nervously played with his hat and, thinking he was acting a little strange, she smiled and asked, "Is the weather what you wanted to talk about, Morgan?"

He felt his face flush as he looked down at his hat, then sucked in a small breath, let it out, and looked into her smiling brown eyes. "I was thinking…" he paused.

"Yes?"

Feeling awkward, he stood, walked to the edge of the porch, and turned. "I," he paused, looking troubled.

"Yes?"

"How would you feel if I were to ask you to marry me?" Right away, he wished he had said it differently.

Surprise filled her face, and joy her heart at what Morgan asked. "Are you proposing marriage, Mr. Hunter?"

Morgan turned and looked past the house across the street into the prairie behind it. "I ain't much of a romantic Katherine, and I do apologize for that." He looked down at the dust covering his boots then smiled as he looked at her. "I planned on how I would say it on my way here, and it sure was different." He turned and looked at his horse. "I know you must think this is sudden," he turned to her. "But I have thought about it, probably more than I should." Morgan grinned, looking nervous as he sucked in a breath of air. "This sure ain't as easy as I figured on the way here."

Seeing he was having difficulty and loving him for it, she smiled at the torture he was putting himself through, thinking it was sweet. She had already made up her mind as she touched the arm of the white wooden chair next to her. "Please sit down, Morgan."

He turned with a flushed face looking nervous while flipping his hat in his hands, and sat down. "If you ain't inclined to marry me, I understand."

"May I ask you a question?"

"Of course," he said, looking puzzled.

"Is this what you talked to the mayor about yesterday?"

He thought about that. "No," he said. "Not exactly." He decided to be honest with her. "But I did ask him that if you were still married, would there be a problem with you adopting Julie."

"And what did the mayor say?"

"He said no, there would be no problems with you taking the child."

She looked at him for a long, thoughtful moment. "Is that the reason you're asking me now?"

"Katherine," he said softly. "I've been thinking about this for quite a spell." He looked down at the hat he held in both hands. "I started to bring it up a couple of times on our rides, but I was afraid you'd say no, and wouldn't see me anymore." He looked into her brown eyes. "I wasn't ready to stop seeing you if that had been your answer." He paused and looked at her. "Then, watching you in the mayor's office fight for little Julie..." He let the sentence drift off with a smile.

Her brown eyes welled. "I'll marry you, Morgan, if you're sure that's what you want."

Three weeks later, on the seventeenth day of August, Katherine Jordan became Mrs. Katherine Hunter in the small overcrowded church with well-wishers. Wade had the honor of being best man recalling his and Sarah's marriage in the small church in Santa Fe, New Mexico. Julie was dressed in a new white dress of satin and lace and was the flower girl, holding a colorful bouquet of wild prairie flowers. As soon as the preacher pronounced them man and wife, Morgan whisked his bride away to the ranch, and Julie spent the next couple of days with Jonathan Moore and his wife.

August faded away, followed by a warm September on the Morgan ranch. Julie's crying herself to sleep slowly faded, and she settled into a new life with Morgan and Katherine, enjoying the puppy

Wade brought her. Though she was disappointed it wasn't a coyote, she loved it just the same. Katherine decided to keep the small house in town, thinking it would be a place they could use as a getaway once in a while.

The queries of who killed Estelle and Gracie Abbott faded away except in Wade's memory as he carefully guarded the knowledge of who killed them and why. It still pained him knowing that Tom Purdy died a respected man, even a hero to some, and if it hadn't been for Katherine, he would have revealed what kind of man Tom Purdy really was.

Chapter 27

Seth Bowlen Comes to Pickering

September 1879

Seth Bowlen rode his big black horse at a slow walk up the dusty, dirt street of Pickering leading his packhorse searching the boardwalks and dusty street for the face he came to find. Seeing the wooden sign "SHERIFF" in white lettering dangling from the porch roof over the boardwalk between the bank and gunsmith, he guided his horse to the hitching rail. Climbing down and feeling the miles in his back, Seth wrapped the reins to his horse and packhorse around the hitching rail and stepped onto the boardwalk. Wondering what sort of man he would find behind the door, he put one hand on the doorknob, paused a moment, turned it, and walked inside.

Hearing the door open, Jed Canon threw his feet off the cot in the cell, stood, and walked to the bars. "Can I help you?"

Thinking it strange that a prisoner would ask if he could help, Seth walked over to the cell and looked at the old man who needed a shave. "You a prisoner?"

Jed stared at Seth's bad eye for a moment, then nodded. "Have been for two days." Then he laughed.

Seth failed to see the humor. "I'm looking for Emmett Spears."

Jed frowned. "And who might you be?"

He didn't believe the prisoner was in the position to ask questions, but he answered anyway. "A friend."

Jed's eyes narrowed, looking doubtful. "Seen a few men come here looking for the sheriff, and none of 'em were his friends, and none of 'em left town."

Seth thought about that. "Well, I am."

Canon chuckled as if he knew something Seth didn't. "You best be friends, or you'll end up in the graveyard with those that weren't."

Seth considered that wondering how many men lie in the graveyard as he looked at Jed's wrinkled, grinning face. "Can you tell me where I can find the sheriff?"

Still grinning, Jed said, "Town ain't all that big, mister. Just go out the door, and you'll find him." He looked down at Seth's holstered pistol. "If you ain't his friend, you best be faster than you look."

Wondering what sort of man Wade had become, he turned, noticing the coyote lying on the cot in the next cell staring at him. "What the hell's a coyote doing in jail?"

"Belongs to the Sheriff."

"It's a pet, like a dog?"

Jed looked at Pup. "Guess you could say that."

"Ain't natural," said Seth as he walked to the door, paused to look back at the old man and coyote, wondering what sort of town this was. Stepping outside, he closed the door, looked up and down both sides of the boardwalk and the street, seeing but a few men and several women going about their business. Wondering where to start looking, Seth saw the only saloon in town and thought he'd start there. Stepping off the boardwalk, he crossed the street, opened the door of the saloon, and stepped inside. Closing the door, he walked toward the near-empty bar while his eyes adjust to the dim light.

Dave Goody wiped the bar with a damp white towel and tried not to stare at Seth's bad eye. "Whiskey?"

"Beer," corrected Seth.

Goody shook his head. "No beer. Just whiskey."

Before Seth could answer, a familiar voice said, "Give us both a whiskey, Dave."

Seth turned and smiled.

Wade smiled as he held out his hand. "Hello, Seth."

Bowlen grinned like a small boy and, while shaking his hand, noticed the scars on his face and thought Wade looked a little thin and older, maybe even tired.

"What the hell brings you to the end of the world?" asked Wade.

"You," replied Seth as the bartender filled two glasses of whiskey, wondering who the stranger was with the bad eye.

Wade tossed some money down. "The wagon bringing our beer down from Miles City had an accident. Been out of beer for two days now." He picked up the two drinks, handed one to Seth, and then motioned to a table. "Good to see you, Seth. Let's sit a spell."

Seth followed him past several empty tables to a small table in the corner of the room by the small dance floor smelling of sawdust.

Wade took off his wide-brimmed, black hat and tossed it in a chair as he sat down. He watched as Seth tossed his hat in the other vacant chair, then pulled another chair out and plopped down. Raising his glass, he said, "Here's to you, Seth."

Noticing that Wade now wore his Colt in a cross draw, Bowlen raised his glass. "Mud in your eye."

After they took a drink of whiskey, Wade grinned. "Saw you ride up."

Seth looked at him. "Why didn't you come out and holler?"

Wade grinned. "Wanted to see how your tracking skills were." Then the smile left his face. "You come to arrest me, Seth?"

Bowlen sipped his drink and shook his head no. "I'm out of my jurisdiction."

Wade chuckled. "You're always out of your jurisdiction, but that never seemed to stop you."

Seth laughed, took another sip of whiskey, then set the glass down on the table. "No, I suppose not."

"How's Sarah and Emmett?"

The smile left Seth's face. "They're doing fine. Molly and me visit her now and again."

Wade smiled. "I'm glad that you do."

Seth took a small drink. "They're still waiting for you to come home."

He took a drink. "How's Emmett?"

"He's getting big. So's your daughter."

Wade's eyes widened with surprise as he sat forward, resting his elbows on the table.

Bowlen smiled. "Pretty little thing. Sarah named her Mary Louise. I understand that it was your mother and sister's names."

Wade looked down at his drink as images of his mother and sister standing on the train depot in South Carolina passed through his mind. "I'll be damned," he said softly. He looked across the room at Dave Goody and motioned for another drink, then waited while Dave walked from the bar to the table and poured Wade another drink.

Seth watched Wade thinking he didn't know him anymore. Wondering how he got the scars on his face, he considered them trophies of hard nights in a tough town. Seth looked up at the bartender, put his hand over the top of his glass, and shook his head no.

Dave looked into his bad eye, shrugged, and walked away.

Bowlen sat forward in his chair, putting his elbows on the table. "The ranch has been rebuilt."

Wade took a drink and smiled. "Glad to hear it."

Seth grinned as he sat back. "Janice Talbert and Tolliver Grimes got married."

Wade looked up and smiled, feeling happy for both Mrs. Talbert and Old Man Grimes. "That's good."

"Sarah has the ranch to herself," said Seth. "She needs her husband."

"I'm sure she has plenty of hands." Wade sipped his whiskey and looked at Seth. "How'd you find me?"

Seth sat back. "I was in Pritchard's saloon one night having a beer with my deputy, McIver, heard some fella telling about a lawman that had a long reach with a Sharps going by the name of Emmett Spears." He shrugged. "I just followed the stories north that led me to this place."

Wade grinned. "Guess the name wasn't very creative." He took a sip of whiskey. "Does Sarah know you came looking?"

Seth shook his head. "Didn't want to get her hopes up."

"Good," Then Wade's expression soured. "Don't take this wrong, Seth, but I wish you hadn't ridden into town." He took a drink of whiskey, set the glass down, and gazed out the dirty window painted with little white curly designs and the word Saloon. He thought about the Hoskins ranch and George Hoskins standing in the window of his hotel. "When it was all over, and Sarah and Emmett was no longer the bulls-eye of a madman," he paused and thought of Elizabeth Purdy, "I knew I had to leave or get hung."

Seth stared at him without comment, knowing he would have done the same thing if George Hoskins had tried to kill his wife, Molly.

Wade sighed as he looked at Bowlen. "The way I have things figured Seth, me staying would have brought more pain to Sarah with a trial and her watching me get hung on the main street of Harper. I don't want her and Emmett to remember me that way." He took a sip of whiskey. "They're both better off without me, and at least I'm alive while that crazy bastard and all the others are waiting for me in hell."

Seth looked down at his empty glass. "I think she'd disagree with you about being better off." Then he reached over and put his hand on Wade's arm. "Come back with me, son."

"You and I both know I can't do that, Seth. I'd be arrested, tried for murder, and hung. Just as before." He pulled his arm away. "So, nothing's changed."

Seth leaned closer, glanced around, and lowered his voice. "A bullet shattered Hoskins' backbone. There are no witnesses and no one's left who can accuse anyone of anything that happened back in Harper."

Wade glared at him, thinking of Elizabeth Purdy. "It ain't Hoskins or his damn men that I regret and think about Seth. Besides, all that don't matter none." He looked down at his drink. "There's one too many ghosts in Harper for me. I can't go back."

Bowlen sat back and thought about that for a moment. "You filled God's Coffin with a lot of men all right, Wade. I won't deny that."

Wade sighed. "They didn't give me much choice."

As Seth watched him, he could find no blame for what he had done. He'd have done the same to protect Molly just like Billy French would have his family. "No," he said sadly. "I guess they didn't."

Wade downed his drink and motioned to Dave for another.

Seth waved the bartender off.

Wade gave Seth a dirty look and motioned to Dave for another drink.

Goody filled Wade's glass, glanced from one to the other, then turned and headed for his place behind the bar.

Bowlen became angry. "When I leave this shit hole of a town, you can drink yourself shitfaced, and I don't particularly give a damn if you do. But right now, I want you to listen to what I have to say."

Wade sat back in his chair, dragging his glass across the table with his right hand. "Go ahead and have your say, Seth, if that makes you feel any better."

Bowlen started to get up and leave but decided to try and convince Wade to return to his wife and children. "You don't have to live in Harper. Take your family back to Santa Fe. Shit fire Wade, take them to California, or Oregon even." He paused. "That whole business in Harper died along with that bastard George Hoskins."

Wade gulped his drink, turned from Seth to Dave Goody, and motioned for another drink.

Frustrated with Wade, Seth sat back in his chair and waited while the bartender walked across the floor and poured Wade another drink.

"Anything else, Sheriff Spears?" asked Goody.

Wade looked up. "Leave the bottle."

Goody set the bottled down, gave Seth a quick look, then Wade, knowing they were having words over something, turned and walked back to the bar.

Seth pushed his chair back and stood, thinking Wade had changed, and it was probably best Sarah never saw him like this. He reached down and picked up his hat from the other chair. "You can't change who you are by taking a dead man's name."

Wade sipped his drink and then looked past Seth out the dirty window at the weathered buildings across the street, then into Seth's good eye. "Have a nice ride home, Seth."

"Any words for Sarah?"

Wade thought a moment and then shook his head no. "I'd prefer Sarah didn't know you found me. I'd hate to have to leave this nice little shit hole as you call it and head north into Canada."

"She'll not hear from me where you are or what you've become," said Seth. "No sense in destroying the good memories she has." Then he put on his hat, turned, and walked out of the saloon into the warm sun. He was hungry and tired but didn't want to stay in Pickering any longer than it took him to mount up and ride out. His mouth had a bad taste, and he couldn't get rid of it here, so he walked across the street to his black horse at the hitching rail. Untying the reins of both horses, he stepped up into the saddle, tugged at the packhorse, turned south, and trotted toward the end of Pickering.

Wade was at the window of the saloon as Seth rode by, lifted his glass in a quiet toast to his old friend, took a sip, and silently wished him well.

Chapter 28

Morgan Hunter walked into the saloon and glanced around, looking for Wade. Seeing him standing at the window, he walked over and looked out as a man on a black horse leading a packhorse rode down the street. "Friend of yours?"

"Once was," said Wade softly. Then he turned to Morgan. "Let's have a drink."

Sensing a troubled mood, Morgan followed him to a table where they sat down, and after glancing at Wade, Hunter motioned to Dave for a clean glass.

Wade stared down at his hands and waited for their drinks, thinking of all that Seth had said and of his new daughter he would never see.

Dave set a clean glass on the table and headed back for the bar and its one customer.

Morgan picked up the bottle, poured two drinks, set the bottle down, and raised his glass. "To old friends."

Without looking up, Wade picked up the glass and took a quick sip. Not wanting to talk about Seth, he asked, "How are Katherine and Julie adjusting to ranch life?"

"Doesn't appear to be a problem with either. Julie's a natural at feeding the chickens, gathering eggs and such, and Katherine wants to change some things in the kitchen, but I talked her into waiting until next spring." He took a drink of whiskey, wondering who the man was, then smiled. "Katherine told me to ask you out for dinner this Sunday."

Wade looked up, thinking it would be a welcome relief, and smiled. "Looking forward to it."

Morgan nodded. "Good. I'll tell her to expect you." Then he glanced at the window and then looked at Wade. "Mind me asking who that was?"

Wade looked toward the window and took a sip of his drink. "That was Seth Bowlen, Sheriff of Sisters, Colorado."

Morgan remembered the name from when Wade told him about Harper. "What the hell's he doing clear up here?"

Wade took a drink. "Came for me."

Hunter thought about the Hoskins ranch and lowered his voice. "He come to arrest you?"

"No, came to take me home to Sarah."

Morgan thought about that a moment. "How'd he find you?"

Wade looked at him with a small smile. "Heard some drunk in a bar in Sisters, Colorado, talking about a Sheriff named Emmett Spears, and decided come get me." Wade grinned. "I forgot how resourceful Seth Bowlen could be. He knew that Emmett was once my best friend." Wade looked down at his glass with a sad face. "Says I have a daughter now." He paused and looked at him with red eyes. "Shit Morgan, I didn't even know she was with child."

Morgan took a sip of whiskey and watched Wade as he stared into his glass of whiskey. Setting his glass down, he leaned forward, reached out, and touched Wade's arm. "Go home, Wade. Go home and pack them up as fast as you can and head west to California or north to Oregon. Start a new life before it's too late."

Remembering Seth saying the same thing, Wade looked up from his glass, feeling sad. "It's already too late."

"No, it ain't Wade. All you gotta do is get on that mare of yours and ride south."

Wade sat back, shaking his head. "I tell you I'd be arrested, tried, and hung." He thought of Elizabeth Purdy smiling at him as she died. "There's one killing I can't run away from."

Morgan sat back, knowing what killing Wade was referring to. "Accidents happen, and I ain't no lawman, but from what you told me, all the witnesses are dead. There ain't anyone left to point the finger at you and say you did the killing."

"That's what Seth did told me." Wade frowned as he shrugged. "Everyone in harper knows it was me, Morgan. And some of those would be on the jury."

"Knowing and proving are different animals of justice, Wade." Morgan sat back in his chair. "You know that."

Wade finished his drink, being tired of talking about Sarah, the killings, and Harper. "I'm hungry," he said as he stood. "You have time for lunch?"

Knowing a lost argument when he saw one, Morgan gulped his drink and stood. "Guess I could have a cup of coffee and maybe a slice of pie while you eat. Katherine and Julie are buying clothes, and that always takes a while."

Sunday

Wade pushed his chair back from the table, leaned back, and patted his stomach. "Dinner was exceptional, Katherine. Thanks for having me."

She smiled, thanked him, and then told Morgan and Wade to take their coffee out to the porch, and she'd bring them a piece of pie after she and Julie cleaned up the dinner dishes.

Morgan and Wade picked up their coffee and headed for the porch finding Pup and Julie's young dog lying next to the door. Both got up filled with hope trying to see inside until Wade closed the door and followed Morgan to the white, wooden chairs and sat down.

Pup and the young dog lay back down on the porch near the door in disappointment and waited.

Wade took a drink of coffee and looked out across Morgan's ranch. "You're a fortunate man, Morgan."

Hunter thought about that a moment. "I won't argue on that."

The door opened, and Julie stepped out with two plates of food and looked at Wade. "Katherine wanted me to bring this out for Pup and Kelly."

Wade looked at the coyote whose nose was almost in the plate. "You better set it down before Pup cleans her dish and Kelly's while you're still holding them."

Julie giggled as she set the plates down and watched while Pup and her dog, Kelly, ate.

Wade smiled at the child. "I'm sure if they could speak, they'd say it's the best meal they've had in a long time."

Hearing Katherine call her name, Julie turned and went inside, closing the door behind her.

Moments later, the door opened, and Katherine stepped out with two plates of apple pie, gave one to Wade and the other to Morgan, followed by forks and cloth napkins. "Julie's practicing her numbers, so if you're not in a deep discussion about something, I'd like to sit awhile."

Wade stood from the chair next to Morgan with his plate of pie and coffee. "Please, Katherine, sit down."

"Keep your chair," she said as she sat down in the third chair next to Wade.

He returned to his chair sitting between Morgan and Katherine, crossed his legs getting comfortable, and cut a piece of pie with his fork. Remembering how Sarah worked with Emmett on his schooling, he shoved the pie into his mouth, tasting the sweet syrup, firm apples, and soft crust, and smiled at her. "Pie is delicious."

"Glad you like it," she said with a smile as the porch filled with sounds of silverware on china as the men ate their pie.

Wade set his empty plate next to Morgan's on the small table between them.

Katherine stood and picked up the empty plates saying she'd better check on Julie. Seeing that Pup and Kelly's plates were empty, she bent down, picked them up, stepped inside, and closed the door behind her.

Wade stood without looking at Morgan. "Let's take a walk."

Figuring Wade had something on his mind, Morgan stood.

Stepping off the porch, they walked to the corral, where Wade leaned on the top railing and watched the Appaloosa and his mare.

Morgan turned with his back against the corral rail, looked out at his land, and waited for Wade to speak his peace.

Wade reached out and touched the mare's nose with affection as her tail swished back and forth. "I've done a lot of thinking since Seth rode out of town."

Morgan stood from the corral, turned, and looked at Wade, hoping he was going home but offering no comment.

"I'm going home, Morgan."

Hunter smiled and turned. "You're doing the right thing."

Wade looked at him. "Don't look so damn happy."

Morgan chuckled. "I am happy. I'm happy for you." Then the smile faded. "I'll miss the hell out of you, though."

"Don't go getting soft on me, Morgan."

Hunter laughed and turned to look at the house, imagining Katherine and Julie inside busy with Julie's numbers. He felt happy and wanted the same for Wade. "When you leaving?"

"Soon." Then Wade looked at him. "A couple of days, maybe, but I need a favor."

Disappointed to hear he was going to leave so soon, Morgan said, "Name it."

"I'm worried about Jed."

Morgan thought for a moment, knowing what worried him. "He can come out here. I'm sure there's things Jed can do around the place. I'd pay him a wage, and he can sleep in the bunkhouse. Do you think he'd be willing?"

"I don't know, maybe," said Wade, not sure himself. "Least ways, I hope so. I hate to think of leaving him to break in another sheriff."

Both men chuckled at that.

Morgan asked what he was going to do about Pup.

Wade looked at her as she and Kelly played. "Don't know."

"I'd take her off your hands," said Morgan, "but I doubt she'd stay."

Wade stared at her. "She'd probably try and follow me. She might stay with Jed." Not wanting to think about leaving her, he looked at Morgan. "I best be heading back."

"I'll help you with the mare, and then you can stop at the house and say goodbye to Katherine and Julie."

It was almost dark when Wade rode into the livery. After he put his horse away, he and Pup walked to the jailhouse, finding Jed at his desk drinking a cup of coffee, reading the one-sheet town newspaper.

Jed looked up and stood, asking Wade if he'd like a cup of coffee. "I just made a fresh pot," he said proudly.

"I'll get it," said Wade, then he tossed his hat on the desk as he walked by on his way to the potbellied stove.

Jed knelt and petted Pup, letting her lick his face and whine her greeting while he rubbed her shoulders affectionately.

Wade poured his coffee and watched the two thinking Jed, and the coyote belonged together. While the two fussed over one another, he sat down in his creaking chair, took a sip of coffee, and pulled the bottle of whiskey out of the bottom drawer. As he

404

poured a little whiskey into his coffee, he watched Pup and Jed play on the floor like a young boy and his dog.

Having had enough, Jed laughed as he stood and petted the coyote briskly on the shoulder and then sat down in one of the two chairs in front of the desk. "How are things out at Morgan's?"

"They're good. Little Julie seems to have settled right in." He paused a moment. "Morgan says she still has bad dreams now and again."

Jed looked thoughtful. "That little gal went through a lot, that's for damn sure."

Wade took a drink of coffee, thinking he put a little too much whiskey into it and set it on his desk. "Have you eaten supper yet?"

"No, I was just about ready to head over to Laurie's when you walked in."

"I ain't hungry, but you go on ahead. I've some thinking to do."

Jed stood, thinking Wade seemed to have a lot on his mind lately, and wondered what it was. "All right. Want me to bring back something for Pup?"

"If you want." Then he looked at her. "I don't know if she's hungry. She had a good meal at Morgan's."

"I'll bring some back just in case," said Jed, and then he walked out the front door.

Wade stared at the closed door wondering how Jed was going to take the news. Then he looked at the coyote lying on the floor, staring up at him, and wondered what he was going to do with her. He sipped his coffee, wondering if he should have set her free months ago. It was too late now; she was a domesticated animal, and wild coyotes would more than likely tear her apart. He leaned back in his creaking chair, filled with emotions of seeing Sarah, his son, and his new daughter. Every part of his body wanted to rush to Harper. Filled with that excitement, he stood, walked to the door, and stepped outside onto the boardwalk, leaving the door open for Pup. He stood in the light from the door and looked south toward Colorado for several minutes, imagining seeing Sarah and the children.

Pup walked out of the jailhouse and across the boardwalk and into the street to do her business. Wade pulled a chair away from the wall, closed the door then sat down with his feet on the porch post to enjoy the quiet evening. Soft piano music made its way from the saloon across the street, and he imagined Tim Martin's chubby fingers walking easily along the keys.

Pup leisurely returned to the boardwalk and lay next to his chair, watching the people and horses pass by.

Wade reached down and stroked her shoulder with his hand. He felt sad about leaving her with Jed remembering the first night he rode up this very street toward Bennett's Livery. Then he thought of Brodie, Harry, the others, and of Pup being tormented. Seeing Jed walking toward him carrying a plate of food, Pup watched him with anticipation. Watching her, Wade felt a little jealous of their relationship with Jed, but at the same time, he was glad, and maybe that will make leaving her easier.

Jed placed the food on the boardwalk in front of her, pulled up the other chair, and sat down next to Wade. "I like quiet evenings such as this. Brings back memories of quiet evenings with my Lisa before we decided to come west."

Wade felt sorry for Jed's loss and knew he had to see Sarah and his children before it was too late and decided he would talk to Jed in the morning after breakfast before visiting the mayor.

Wade tossed and turned most of the night, getting little sleep. His mind filled with a menagerie of thoughts of seeing Sarah and their children, mixed with the sadness of leaving Pup with Jed. Wondering if she would run away or try and follow him to Harper, he didn't know what to do. In the stillness of the dim morning light of his bedroom, he could hear her soft breathing and thought of Harry Anderson and the cigarette he was going to burn her nose. Harry was an asshole, thought Wade, and he deserved what he got. As the early morning filled the room with dim light, his thoughts turned to Estelle and Gracie and how brutally Tom Purdy had murdered them. The fact that Tom was buried as a hero in many people's eyes angered him, and he felt Tom Purdy got what he deserved. Turning his thoughts to Morgan, who turned out to be the kind of friend Emmett Spears had been, Wade knew that he would miss Morgan. As his thoughts turned to his return to Colorado, his mind filled with scenes of the burning bunkhouse, the men trying to escape the inferno he shot. He thought of Katherine Purdy, and finally of George Hoskins standing at the window with a smile on his face when he pulled the second trigger of his Sharps.

A rooster crowed, greeting the sun, then another, and another until the medley was over. Tossing the covers back, he put his feet on the cold wooden floor and looked down at Pup.

She lifted her head and looked at him with her questioning, dark eyes, and ears at attention.

Wade knew he could not leave her. "I hope you're up for a long run, girl." He smiled at her, stood, stretched, and walked to the dresser, lit a lamp, and looked back at her, wondering if she somehow knew what was going on. He moved the washbasin a little closer and picked up the pitcher of cold water, then he paused and looked into the cracked mirror at his distorted image in the pale light of the lantern. Setting the pitcher down, he stared at an older man he barely recognized with a scarred face and badly in need of a shave. Since it was his last day in Pickering, he decided he would get a bath, a shave, and a haircut at Noonan's. And when that was done, he would take Jed across the street for a good breakfast before telling him that he was leaving.

Turning from the image in the broken mirror, he got dressed to the sounds of Jed stoking the stove with firewood before he made coffee.

As Wade slid his foot into the last boot, he looked at Pup. "Time to get up." He stood, walked to the door, stopped, and looked back at Pup, seeing her scratching her ears and wished she would hurry.

Jed turned from the stove as Wade and Pup walked out of the bedroom. "Good morning."

Wade returned the greeting and headed for the back door with Pup running ahead, stopped at the door, turned, and waited.

Jed called out, "Coffee will be ready in a few minutes."

When Wade and Pup returned from outside, Jed poured two cups of coffee, handed one to Wade, picked up the other, and took a small drink.

Wade took a drink of coffee then set the tin cup on the desk. "We'll go to breakfast after I get back."

"Where ya off to?" asked Jed, hoping he wouldn't be gone long.

Wade looked out the window at the quiet street. "I'm going to have a bath, then get a shave and a haircut."

Jed was hungry and wanted to eat and saw no reason for Wade to go to all that trouble before breakfast when it wasn't even a holiday. "Pup, and I will be darn hungry by then."

Wade smiled. "I'll hurry."

Wade had the bathhouse all to himself while sitting in the hot water and leaning back against the metal tub, enjoying the quiet morning. As he watched the steam rise above the hot water, his thoughts found Raton, New Mexico, and the Chinese bathhouse. Smiling, he remembered the water fight between Seth and Frank Wells. Then he chuckled softly, remembering the Chinese woman running into the room, waving her arms and hands, yelling words no one could understand. Then sadness filled his heart as he remembered Frank's death in the saloon in Paso Del Rio when they cornered the Bradley brothers that also took the life of the Indian, Dark Cloud, outside the saloon.

The door opened, and Mrs. Ida Walker stuck her head in rescuing him for the loss of his friends, asking if the water was still hot. Wade said it was, and then she told him to yell when he wanted more hot water. After the door closed, he thought of Jed waiting and remember that Jed's favorite meal was breakfast. Wade grabbed the towel next to the tub, stood, stepped out, and dried himself. He dressed in a dark blue shirt and pants he had brought along, tied the red bandana around his neck that Sarah had given him, picked up his dirty clothes, and walked out.

Earl Noonan was sitting in the barber's chair reading yesterday's one-sheet newspaper when he looked up and smiled. "Morning, Sheriff."

Wade nodded hello as he put his dirty, folded clothes on an empty chair.

Noonan stood, dusted off the chair with an apron, and after Wade sat down, he covered him with the same white apron. "Shave? Haircut?"

Wade smiled. "Both today, Earl."

Noonan smiled. "Must be a big day."

Wade looked out the window, thinking of Sarah and his children. "Hope so, Earl."

"Looks like a nice day," said Noonan.

"Yes, it does." Then Wade put his head back and closed his eyes while Noonan gave him a close shave, followed by a haircut.

Jed was sitting on the edge of the boardwalk tossing pebbles, looking anxious, and Pup was lying next to him watching each pebble as it bounced on the hard, dirt street. Jed turned and, seeing Wade, stood up, looking like a child waiting for a parent. "We gonna eat now?"

Wade grinned and stepped into the jailhouse. While Jed and Pup watched from the open doorway, he walked into his bedroom, tossed the dirty clothes on the bed. Returning to the boardwalk, he looked at Jed. "You still hungry?"

Jed thought that was a queer question when Wade told him to wait until he was back. He shook his head once. "Yes, sir, just let me put Pup in her cell."

Not much was said over breakfast; Wade mostly watched Jed put away a big breakfast and three cups of coffee while saying he wished his coffee was as good. Seeing they were about finished, Laurie came to the table with Pup's plate as she had every day for the past year.

Wade looked up, thanked her, and then he and Jed got up and walked across the street to the jail. As they stepped inside, he handed Jed the plate, then watched him opened the cell door and set it down on the floor. "Have a seat, Jed."

Jed had a curious, worried look as he sat down and waited.

Wade sat down and looked at Jed. "How would you like to stay out at Morgan's place?"

Jed looked surprised. "You mean permanently?" Then he quickly glanced around. "Who'll take care of Pup and this place?"

Wade sat forward with his arms on the desk, causing the chair to creak. "I'm leaving Pickering, Jed."

Canon stared at Wade for several moments then asked, "For good?"

Knowing Jed knew the truth about him, Wade nodded. "I'm going home."

Jed considered that for a few moments. "I thought you couldn't go home on account of what happened."

Wade sighed. "Well, I'm going anyway." He paused and stared out the window. "I have to end this thing." He looked from the window to the old man's dark eyes. "You can't stay in this jail forever, Jed."

Canon glanced around, then watched Pup move the plate across the floor, licking it clean and thought that he'd sure miss her and softly said, "Things always have to change."

Wade thought on that. "I guess they do, Jed." He paused. "Who knows what the new sheriff will be like? I talked with Morgan, and he said he could find enough for you to do around the place for a small wage, and you can sleep in the bunkhouse. You'd have plenty to eat."

Jed turned to the window and wiped his old, welling, tired eyes.

Feeling bad about Jed and thinking he needed some time alone, Wade stood, "Think on it, Jed." Then he walked toward the door, talking over his shoulder. "I'll be back in a little while."

Jed turned from the window, wiped the tears from his eyes, and asked, "Where ya going?"

Wade opened the door, turned, and looked at Jed. "I'm going to tell the mayor I'll be leaving." Then he stepped out and closed the door.

Jed listened to Wade's footsteps fade on the boardwalk, and then he stood, looked at Pup sitting near the bars watching him. He walked to the desk, bent over, pulled the bottle out from the drawer, poured some whiskey into a cup then turned to the potbellied stove. After Jed topped the whiskey off with coffee, he sat down in Wade's chair and sipped the hot whiskey coffee as sadness filled him thinking about Wade and Pup leaving Pickering for good. He stared out the window in memory of the first time he saw the coyote pup and the night he killed Harry Anderson to protect her. Turning to watch her as she napped, he knew that he'd surely miss her.

Mayor Robert Smith looked up at the sound of the tiny bell above the door and, seeing a serious expression on Wade's face, waited to hear what the bad news was. "Afternoon, Sheriff."

"Can we have a word, Mayor?"

Smith looked curious as he called out to his wife, who stepped out of the back room. "Watch things, Martha. Me and the sheriff have some business to discuss."

Wade tipped his hat to Martha and followed the mayor to his office, located in the back of the store where they talked about Julie's future.

Smith closed the door, offered him a seat, and then leaned on his desk with his big hands looking concerned. "What's the problem, Emmett?"

Wade took off his hat and held it in his lap as he looked at the Mayor. "My name isn't Emmett Spears, Mayor. My name is Wade Garrison."

Mayor Smith looked dumbfounded as his jaw dropped. He sat down in his chair, and after finding his composure, he leaned forward with his forearms on the desk, waiting to hear more.

"I won't bore you with my past Mayor, but I will tell you that I was once a Deputy United States Marshal in Santa Fe. I have a wife and children in Colorado, where I left them over a year ago."

Still in shock from the news, Smith stared at Wade, wanting to know everything but knew he would only hear what the man wanted to tell him. "Why the charade?"

Wade thought about how to answer that. "Let's just say it was best that I left for a spell and changed my name." He shrugged, looking regretful. "I apologize for lying to you and the rest of the town council, but at the time, I had no choice."

The mayor glanced around the room, looking bewildered. "I don't know what to say or what I should call you."

"Wade, Wade Garrison," he said with a smile.

Smith looked puzzled. "But why are you telling me this now?"

"It's time I go home to my family, Mayor. But I want to tell you that as sheriff, I acted in the best interests of the town every day."

Smith smiled. "I never doubted that." Then he sighed, looking disappointed. "I don't mind saying I wish you'd stay. You've made Pickering a better and safer town, and the council appreciates all that you've done." He smiled wryly. "Quite frankly, I wasn't sure you'd stay after that beating you took."

Wade smiled softly. "Takes more than a good beating to run me out of town."

Mayor Smith grinned. "Fortunate for Pickering. When are you leaving?"

"In the morning."

"That's sort of sudden, isn't it?"

Wade thought on that a moment. "Maybe so. But I've been gone long enough, and I'd like to get home and see my family."

The mayor nodded thoughtfully. "Can't say I blame you, but I wish you'd stay on a while longer, maybe until we find another sheriff."

"The town will be all right until you get a new sheriff."

"Thanks to you, I don't think we'll have any problems."

Wade stood. "Guess this is it." He held out an open hand. "I'll say my goodbye now if you don't mind. I'm not sure how early I'll be leaving in the morning."

"You have a long ride ahead of you. What about that coyote of yours?"

"She's coming with me."

Smith smiled again, stood, and shook Wade's hand. "It's been a pleasure, Sheriff, knowing you and that coyote."

"Thank you for trusting me." Then Wade turned and walked toward the door but stopped before he opened it. "If I have any wages coming, see that Jed gets it."

"That can be arranged," said Smith with a sad smile.

Wade made a visit to the bank, closed his account, and then stopped at the livery and explained to Albert Bennett that he was leaving Pickering and asked if he could have his mare ready first thing tomorrow morning.

"Sorry to see you leave, Sheriff," Bennett said as he held out an open hand.

Wade shook it firmly. "In many ways, I hate to leave. But it's time."

"Where you headed?"

"Little town in eastern Colorado by the name of Harper."

Albert thought for a moment. "Never heard of it."

Wade grinned. "Most haven't, and that suits me just fine."

Albert told Wade that he'd have his mare ready first thing, then shook Wade's hand a second time. He watched Wade as he walked away, thinking about the first time they met and Wade's first night in his livery with the coyote pup.

Wade opened the door to the jail and walked in, finding Morgan in the creaking swivel chair, Jed on the sofa, and Pup lying on the sofa next to Jed.

The coyote jumped down to greet him with a wagging tail.

Morgan grinned. "How did the mayor take the news?"

Wade shrugged while he petted Pup. "He didn't cry, if that's what you want to know, but said he was sorry to see me leave."

Morgan stood and walked around the desk while looking at the clock. "We all are." He looked at the white-faced clock on the wall. "It's nearly three." He put his hand on Wade's shoulder. "I'll buy."

As they walked toward the door, Morgan looked back at Jed. "You coming?"

Jed grinned, got up from the sofa, grabbed his old floppy hat, put Pup in the cell, and followed them out the door.

There were just a few customers in the saloon, and the piano stood silently against the wall like a dark, dusty shadow. The three sat down at an empty table and waited for Dave Goody.

Looking like they were celebrating, Goody smiled. "What's the occasion?"

414

Morgan looked up at Dave. "The sheriff is leaving us, Dave."

Goody looked at Wade with a surprised yet puzzled look. "That true?"

Wade grinned. "True as us needing a drink."

"Well, I'm sorry to hear that, Sheriff." Dave turned and walked away and returned a short time later with a bottle and three glasses. As he set them down, he smiled. "On the house."

Wade grinned. "Have a seat Dave."

The Leaving

Wade opened his eyes to the dim light of his bedroom, greeted by a pounding headache and a dry mouth. Seeing he was wearing the same clothes he had on yesterday, he slowly sat up and put his feet on the floor. With his head resting in his hands, he looked down, seeing he was still wearing his boots. Closing his eyes, he wished the pain would go away. With head pounding, he slowly stood, walked to the pitcher of water next to the washbasin, picked it up, and took a long drink of water spilling it down the front of his shirt. Feeling something brush against his leg, he looked down, seeing Pup lapping up the water he spilled. Wade poured some water into the basin and set it on the floor, and watching her drink from the basin, he wondered if she got drunk last night. He stumbled to the door, opened it, and walked into the office, greeted by Jed's loud snoring. Leaving the door open so Pup could follow, he walked toward the back door only to have Pup run past him and wait at the door with tail wagging. Wade unlocked the door and followed the coyote outside, and while she ran around looking for the perfect spot, Wade headed for the outhouse feeling sickly.

Jed was still snoring when Wade and Pup returned from outside. Pausing at the bars to the two cells, Wade looked at Jed and then at

Morgan sleeping on the cot in the other cell. With head still pounding, he walked to the desk, slowly sat down in his creaking, swivel chair, opened the bottom drawer, and pulled out the bottle of whiskey. Taking a small drink from the bottle, feeling the warmth of it go down his throat, he hoped it would help his head. He shoved the cork back into the bottle, put it away, and after closing the drawer, he stood and stoked the potbellied stove with firewood. After the fire was going, he picked up the coffee pot, stepped out the back door, and filled it with water from the pump. Then he poured a handful of grounds into the pot and set it in the center of the stove. Turning to look out the big window at the morning growing lighter, he knew he had to leave for Colorado in a couple of hours.

Turning from the window, he looked at Jed lying on his back, mouth open, snoring, and then at Morgan laying on his back with his right leg hanging off the bed. Knowing he would remember this moment in years to come, he opened Jed's cell door and closed it with a loud bang, but neither Jed nor Morgan so much as moved; He banged the door once more, and still no movement from either. Wondering what it was going to take to get them up because he had to leave soon, he walked to the desk, picked up a tin cup, and dragged it along the bars, making a terrible noise. Again, neither so much as moved, so Wade decided to sit down at his desk to rest his head. When the coffee was ready, he poured a cup, looked at his two sleeping friends, and walked into his bedroom to shave and change clothes.

Stepping from the bedroom dressed in a yellow shirt, brown pants, and the red bandana he always wore. Carrying his bulging saddlebags and carpetbag, he set them on the floor next to his desk. He filled his empty cup with coffee and took a small drink as he looked at the clock on the wall deciding it was time for Jed and Morgan to get up. Picking up an empty cup, he walked back and forth, dragging the empty cup across the cells' bars.

416

Both stirred just a little, so he yelled, "Time to get up!" Closing his eyes and wishing he hadn't yelled, he waited for the pain to go away.

Morgan lifted his head from the pillow. "What's all the noise about?"

"Time to get up," said Wade. "I have to leave soon. Coffee's on."

Morgan sat on the edge of the cot, resting his face in his hands, feeling sick to his stomach.

Wade looked at him through the bars of the cell and smiled. "Time to get up, Morgan. Coffee's ready." Then he looked at Jed sitting on the edge of his bed, not looking any better than Morgan.

Hunter stood, stepped out of the cell, walked down the hallway toward the back door, stepped outside, leaned against the building with one hand, and threw up what little whiskey and beer he had in his stomach.

Wade sat down, drank his coffee, and waited while Morgan's stomach tried to rid itself of something that wasn't there.

Morgan wiped his mouth and stepped inside, closed the door, and walked to the sofa where he gently flopped down, leaned back, and closed his eyes.

Wade handed him a cup of black coffee. "Drinking ain't quite what it was when we were young, is it Morgan?"

"That's for damn sure." Morgan took a drink of the hot, strong coffee. Wishing he had gone home last night. Knowing Kathrine would be worried, he hoped she would understand.

Jed's cell door opened, and he stood holding onto the door, looking sleepy, and what little hair he had left was standing on end. He glanced from Wade to Morgan, turned, and walked down the hall on his way to the outhouse.

Wade smiled at the site then took a drink of coffee.

Jed returned a few minutes later to the quiet room, poured a cup of coffee, sat down in one of the chairs in front of Wade's desk, and thought about his headache.

Feeling better himself, Wade looked at Pup lying on the floor, then out the window toward Laurie's Café, and then at Morgan. "I thought I'd be gone by now."

The door opened, and Albert Bennett stepped inside and, recognizing a hangover, closed the door, and looked at Wade. "Have your mare all saddled and ready like you asked, Sheriff." He glanced at Jed and Morgan and then looked at Wade. "I got worried when you never showed, so I brought her down here." Then he paused. "You still leaving?"

"Coffee?" asked Wade.

Bennett looked at the others and shook his head. "No, thanks. It looks like you boys had a rough night of it."

Wade grinned, stood, poured a cup of coffee, and handed it to Albert. "Have one anyway."

Al took the cup and a quick drink, thinking it tasted awful. He saw Wade looking out the window at the packhorse tied up next to the mare at the hitching. "Mayor Smith came by yesterday with some supplies. Told me to put them on a packhorse and have it ready for when you left today."

Wade stared out the window in surprise at the packhorse. "I'll be."

Bennett grinned. "The mayor said the city council was paying for the horse. It's yours to keep."

Jed stood and looked outside and then at Wade. "Mighty nice of them to do that for you, Sheriff."

Morgan turned on the sofa, looked at the packhorse, and nodded his agreement. "Yes, it is." Then he looked at Wade. "Got time for one last breakfast at Laurie's?"

Wade set his cup down and looked at Albert. "Join us, Al. I won't be back this way again."

"All right," said Bennett with a big grin. "I've already eaten, but I'll join you, boys, anyways." He started to take another drink of coffee but remembered how terrible it tasted and set the cup down. "Laurie always has a cherry or apple pie on hand that goes good with coffee."

Wade looked at the nearly full cup of coffee and smiled. "Tasted like horse piss, didn't it?"

Bennett chuckled. "More like buffalo."

Wade laughed and walked around his desk, grinning as he pushed Jed and Al toward the door and motioned for Morgan to follow. "Get your lazy ass up, Morgan."

Morgan Hunter, Albert Bennett, and Jed Canon all stood on the boardwalk watching Wade as he tied his saddlebags and carpetbag behind his saddle and then waited while he went back inside for his rifle and black duster. He shoved the Sharps into the sheath located in front of his saddle, hung the bandoleer around the saddle horn, and shrugged into his long, black duster. He turned and looked around the small town of Pickering, trying to burn the scene into memory, then turned to the others with a small smile. "Guess this is it."

Morgan was first to step off the boardwalk and, after pushing Wade's hand away, hugged him, patted his back, and then gripped his shoulders. "Glad you're heading home. Good luck to you."

Wade grinned. "I have a feeling I'm going to need it."

Morgan stepped back. "You, Sarah, and the kids are always welcome for a visit."

Wade smiled, knowing that would never happen. "Someday, maybe."

"I know you can write," said Morgan. "So, let me know how things are going down there." He grinned as he leaned closer. "Send word if you need anyone to break you out of jail."

Wade smiled. "I'll do that."

419

Jed extended his hand. "Been a pleasure knowing you, Sheriff." Then he looked at Pup lying on the boardwalk, knelt, gave Pup a big hug, stood, and looked at Wade. "Take care of our little gal."

"Don't worry about Pup," said Wade. "She'll like it where we're going." Wade shook his hand. "It'd be a good thing for you to stay with Morgan."

Jed grinned as he glanced at Morgan. "We already decided on a wage."

Albert stepped up with a firm hand and wished Wade a safe trip.

Wade looked at each one feeling bad about leaving, then looked at Pup. "You ready, girl?" He put one foot in the stirrup and climbed up on the sorrel mare, glanced around Pickering one last time as he settled in the saddle. He adjusted his black duster, took the reins to the packhorse from Al, and smiled. "You boys take care, and don't let anything happen to this nice town." Then he looked at the coyote. "Come on, Pup. We have a long way to go."

The three watched as Wade turned the mare and rode at a walk along the empty street, the packhorse following and the coyote running alongside the mare.

Mayor Robert Smith stepped out of his store, watching Wade as he rode down the street, sad to see him and the coyote leave.

Wade guided the mare to the boardwalk, pulled up, and shook the mayor's hand, thanking him for the supplies and packhorse.

Then he nudged the mare and continued along the street at a walk.

Morgan watched his friend until he disappeared in the distance, feeling a sense of loss while recalling the day his brother was killed. Hearing the front door of the jail open, he turned just as Jed walked out, carrying an old dirty carpetbag containing his few belongings. "Ready?" he asked.

Chapter 29

Charlie Peters' Ranch

The sun was gone leaving that faint, dim light just before darkness settles in as Wade approached the Peters' place. Thinking things didn't look right, he pulled up several yards from the back of the house. Nora usually cooked this time of day, but there was no smoke from the tin chimney above the kitchen, yet there were lights on in the windows. Hearing what sounded like a woman scream, he quietly called Pup, guided the mare and packhorse to the far side of the barn, climbed down, and peered around the corner at the house. Seeing three saddled horses standing at the hitching rail by the front porch, he got a bad feeling.

Taking off his black duster, he draped it over his saddle and tied the mare and packhorse to the railing of the corral so they wouldn't be seen from the house. Taking Pup's rope from his saddlebag, he tied Pup up next to the mare, then took his long glass out of his saddlebag and stepped between the railings of the corral fence. Making his way through the five horses in the corral, he stopped at the corner of the barn. Looking through the long glass at the lighted windows couldn't see anything but shadows moving back and forth on Nora's heavy lace curtains. One of Charlie's horses softly neighed behind him, and as he turned toward the dark images, he remembered that Charlie always eats on time and only after he puts his stock away in the barn.

The front door opened, casting light across the porch onto the three horses. A figure stepped out of the house, closed the door, walked across the porch, and headed for the outhouse. A woman's voice he knew was Nora's cried out, followed by the sound of glass breaking. Feeling the urgency to find out what was going on inside the house, Wade hurried back to the mare, put the long glass away, and pulled out an extra .44 Colt pistol he carried in his saddlebag. Shoving it under his gun belt, he quietly made his way to the woodpile beside the outhouse where he waited.

He was close enough to the house that he recognized Nora's voice telling someone to take whatever they wanted and leave. The sound of glass breaking, followed by Nora's crying, made Wade want to get inside and help Charlie and Nora before it was too late. The door of the outhouse opened, and as the man stepped out, Wade shoved his Colt into his back. "Not a word," he warned quietly. The man slowly raised his hands while Wade reached down, pulled his pistol from its holster, and tossed it. "How many inside?"

"Two."

More glass broke inside, and Nora's screams mixed with men's voices and laughter. Wade knew he had to hurry, so he shoved his pistol harder into the man's back. "What's going on?"

"Just having a little fun is all."

"Here's my kind of fun, asshole." Then Wade struck him on the head with his gun. As the man lay dazed on the ground, Wade pulled out his big hunting knife, bent down, and cut his throat. After wiping his knife off on the man's coat, he put it away, then hurried across the yard. Stopping at the edge of the house where it met the corner of the porch and roof, he peered through the heavy lace curtains of the window. Nora and Charlie were sitting on the floor, and two men were standing over them. Neither had their guns drawn, apparently confident the Peters' was helpless.

Then the bigger of the two reached down, grabbed Nora's arm, and pulled her up against his protruding belly. "You're gonna treat me and my friends to a little fun in the bedroom."

Charlie tried to get up. "Touch her, and I'll kill ya, you bastard!"

The man grinned as he put a foot on Charlie's chest and shoved him back against the sofa. "Ah, shut up, you skinny little shit."

Nora pulled away and knelt next to her husband.

The big man reached down, grabbed her arm, and tried to pull her up, but Nora pulled away, falling against Charlie's legs. "Bitch," he said as he grabbed her leg and pulled her away from Charlie, causing her long blue dress to rise above her knees.

Charlie made it up on wobbly legs and threw a punch that landed on the big man's arm, then he fell to the floor.

The big man reached down and picked Nora up. "You either take us one at a time in the bedroom, or we do it right here, so's your man can watch."

"She's kind of old," said the other.

"She ain't that old," said the big man holding onto her arm, and then he smiled. "Ain't nothing like an experienced female, Teddy."

Teddy laughed, "If you say so, Fred."

Wade drew the spare pistol from his gun belt, figuring they would think he was their friend coming back from the outhouse. He walked across the porch with heavy feet, stood facing the door, then tapped on it with the barrel of his gun and waited.

"Come in, Ben; the fun's about to start," said a voice followed by laughter mixed with Nora's sobbing, and Charlie telling them to leave her alone.

Wade tapped on the door again.

"Damn it, Ben, come in!" yelled the same voice while another told Nora to shut up and stop crying.

424

Wade heard someone being slapped, and when the door opened, the man looked at Wade with a surprised look on his unshaven face. Wade pulled the triggers of both guns filling the doorway with white smoke. As the man fell back, crashing into a small table knocking it over, Wade stepped inside and pulled the triggers of both pistols again, hitting the big man in the chest and stomach. After he made sure both men were dead, he tossed their pistols across the floor and then looked at the Peters. "You two all right?"

Nora looked up with tears in her eyes, gave him a quick nod, and put her arms around Charlie.

Mr. Peters looked up at Wade through puffy, bloody eyes. "Sure glad you came along, Marshal." He looked at the two dead men and then at Nora. "I'm sorry, Nora, but I was helpless against them."

She put her hands on his bruised and bloody face. "You've nothing to apologize for, Charlie."

Thinking they did a pretty good job on poor Charlie, Wade asked again as he knelt beside him and looked at his face. "You sure you're alright?"

He looked at the two men lying on the floor of his house and then at Wade. "I am now, thanks to you, Marshal."

Wade holstered his Colt and set the other pistol on the table, and then he looked at Nora. "Let's get you onto the sofa," he said as he tried to help her up.

"No," she said in a soft, broken voice. "Help me get Charlie up." Then she looked at Wade with fear on her face. "There's another outside."

"I already took care of him."

Nora looked relieved. "Thank God you stopped by Mr. Garrison." She stood, and then she and Wade helped Charlie onto the sofa.

Wade turned and walked toward the door while talking over his shoulder. "I'm gonna get my horses I left out by the barn." He opened the door and turned. "I'll get rid of those two when I get back." Wade hurried across the yard to the barn and led his mare and packhorse to the hitching rail with the three horses, thinking it was a little crowded. He tied Pup to the porch post, and as she lay down on the porch, he stepped inside and stood in the open doorway. Nora was holding a pan of water on her lap, cleaning the blood off of Charlie's battered face with a damp cloth. Concerned about her, Wade asked, "You sure you're alright, Mrs. Peters?"

She paused in what she was doing. "I'll never be alright, Mr. Garrison." She looked at her husband. "I think Charlie needs a doctor."

Wade walked to the sofa, knelt, and looked at Charlie while recalling his beating in Pickering. Charlie's black eyes were swollen, cuts above his eyebrows, his lips cut, and his face badly bruised. "Looks like they worked you over pretty good."

Charlie looked at Wade through the slits of his swollen eyes and managed a small smile. "I think I'll live thanks to you, Marshal." He paused and then asked, "What brought you by this time of day?"

Not wanting to go into details said, "I was on my way back to Harper and thought I'd stop in, get a meal, and spend the night." He looked at the two bodies. "I'll drag these two outside." Then he stood and walked to the nearest one, knelt, and went through his pockets. Finding a little money and no identification that would tell him the bastard's name, not that it mattered. Getting up, he grabbed the man by the ankles and dragged him out of the house to the spot where he had killed the first man and then returned for the second.

Pup stood and watched Wade as he walked past and opened the door.

Nora looked past him out the open door, surprised at seeing Pup. "There's a coyote on our porch."

426

Wade looked at Pup and then at Nora. "She's mine, Nora, and won't hurt you none."

She stared at Wade with a bewildered expression. "Yours?"

"Long story, but yes, she's mine." Then he closed the door.

Mrs. Peters looked at Wade. "Never knew anyone who owned a coyote."

Wade glanced around at the mess of broken glass and overturned table. "As soon as I put the horses away, I'll help clean the place up." He turned to open the door but paused and smiled at Mr. Peters. "You should go into the horse business, Charlie." Then he opened the door and stepped outside.

With the horses put away and the barn closed up, he hurried back to the house, finding Nora had just finished with Charlie. Her dress was torn at the shoulder, and three buttons were missing in the back, leaving the dress slightly open. She walked past him, carrying the pan of bloody water and the blood-soaked rag. "The good Lord sent you here tonight, Mr. Garrison. No other way to explain it." Then she disappeared down the hall, returning a few minutes later wearing a clean dress and carrying one of Charlie's clean shirts. She helped her husband off with his torn, bloody shirt acting more like a worried mother would a child than a wife with a husband. She looked at Wade as he cleaned up some of the broken glass. "We haven't eaten all day, Mr. Garrison, and I'm sure you could use a good meal."

"You don't need to go to any bother, Mrs. Peters…"

"I need to keep busy," she said softly.

Understanding that, Wade smiled. "Guess I am hungry at that."

"Good," she said, then she looked at the door. "What about that coyote of yours?"

"Pup?"

"That's her name?" asked Nora with a puzzled look.

427

Wade nodded. "Yes, ma'am."

She looked at the door and then at Wade. "What on this good earth possessed you to call her that?"

Wade shrugged. "I got her as a pup, and the name just sort of stuck." He quickly thought of Seth's wife, Molly, arguing with him about giving animals a proper name. "She's a good coyote."

Nora gave Wade a long look, followed by a small, soft sigh. "Well, bring her in. Maybe the good Lord sent her as well." Then she looked at him. "I suppose she sleeps inside?"

"She has since she was a pup."

Nora turned and walked toward the stove, talking over her shoulder. "She can sleep with you. Just make sure she doesn't wander about in the darkness."

"Yes, ma'am," smiled Wade as he opened the door, untied Pup, and brought her inside, telling her to sit by the door. She did as told, and as Wade picked up the overturned table, she stared toward the kitchen, smelling food.

Charlie was watching Pup from the sofa. "Bring her over here, so's I can have a look."

Wade picked up a couple of unbroken items off the floor and set them on the small table. Then he picked up the rope and led her next to the sofa. "Tell her to sit."

Charlie told her to sit, and as she did so, his puffy lips held a small painful smile as he looked at the coyote through swollen eyes. "Well, I'll be." Then he looked toward the kitchen and Nora. "Did you see that, Nora? I told her to sit, and she sat right down."

Nora just went on with her cooking.

Charlie looked into Pup's black eyes. "Ain't never seen a live coyote up this close b'fore. Killed a few over the years." He looked at Wade. "She take to a little petting?"

"Hasn't bit anyone yet."

Charlie reached out slowly to pet her head, but she shied away.

"She doesn't like the top of her head touched all that much," cautioned Wade.

Mr. Peters gently reached out and patted her on the back and shoulder working his way around to her chest. "Look, Nora, she's licking my hand."

Nora turned from the stove, looking skeptical. "Make sure she don't take a finger in the process." She stared at Pup. "I expect she's hungry like the rest of us?"

Wade smiled. "Always is and likes most anything." He told Pup to lie down, and as she did so by the sofa, he went about picking up the pieces of broken plates and other treasures that belonged to Nora then swept the floor with an old broom that had seen better days.

"Supper's ready," Nora called out. Then she asked Wade to help Charlie to the table while she filled their plates. "Ain't too fancy this evening."

Wade helped Charlie sit down. "Looks and smells fine to me." He turned to the coyote and pointed to a spot a few feet away, telling her to lie down.

Charlie watched her with a grin. "Well, don't that beat all. I ain't never seen a dog mind that good." He looked at Nora. "Maybe I can find me a coyote pup to raise, Nora."

Mrs. Peters gave her husband one of those looks women give to their husbands when they think they're foolish. She looked at Pup, not being all that impressed, and she was not too keen on having a wild coyote sleeping in the house. But since the coyote belonged to the man who saved her and Charlie from something terrible, Nora would treat the animal as if it were royalty. Mrs. Peters sat down at the table, lowered her head, closed her eyes, folded her hands, and said a quick prayer thanking the Lord for sending Wade, and after saying "Amen," she looked at Charlie. "Want me to cut that meat up a bit?"

Charlie stubbornly shook his head no. "Still got two good hands. I'll manage."

Wade took a bite of food. "Looks like you got yourself three more horses and saddles, Charlie."

Peters looked up, trying not to smile because it hurt. "Every time you stop by, I get a few more horses." He covered his mouth so it wouldn't hurt as he laughed. "Keep that up, and I'll have to expand the place."

Wade laughed, glad to see that Charlie still had a sense of humor and was feeling better.

Nora looked from Charlie to Wade and smiled; set her fork down with a small chuckle that soon turned into laughter.

Wade looked from one to the other, knowing they would both be all right, then the laughter quickly turned into silent smiles as they went back to eating.

Nora turned and looked at Pup lying a few feet away for a long, thoughtful moment, then stood, dished up a plate of food, and set it down in front of the coyote.

Pup looked up at her with questioning dark eyes and then at Wade.

"Go on," said Nora softly. "Eat."

Pup cautiously stepped closer to the plate and began eating slowly at first, and then as if she hadn't eaten in a week.

Nora returned to the table and watched Pup for several moments before taking a bite of food.

Charlie took a bite of food and looked at Wade. "Where'd you put them, three bastards?"

Hearing Pup's plate move across the floor, he smiled and gestured outside. "They're lined up a few yards behind some bushes beyond the outhouse. I'll bury them in the morning."

Nora stood, picked up the plate, petted the coyote, and walked into the kitchen for a bowl of water.

Charlie looked at Wade through swollen eyes. "I'll give you a hand." Then he grinned. "Don't want them too close to the outhouse."

Wade thanked Nora for a fine supper, pushed his chair from the table, and took Pup outside to do her business. When she finished, they started back toward the house when the coyote stopped and stared off in the direction of the outhouse, giving a low growl. Wade reached down, put his hand on Pup's shoulder, and pushed her toward the house, and after they were inside, he closed the door and looked at Charlie. "I think the wolves are after those men," he said as he took his pistol from his holster he had set on a nearby chair earlier. "I'll shoo 'em away and move the bodies into the barn for the night."

"Leave 'em be Mr. Garrison," said Nora in a soft voice. "I'll not have you fight a pack of wolves over those bastards." Then she looked at Charlie. "You need to get to bed and get some rest."

Feeling too tired to argue, Charlie slowly stood, said goodnight to Wade, and headed for the bedroom.

Nora picked up a lantern and tried to help him with her spare hand, but he stubbornly brushed her away, saying he could manage. She turned, telling Wade his bed was turned down, and she had put a blanket on the floor for the coyote. "Turn the lamps out when you turn in."

As they disappeared down the hall to their room, Wade turned out all the lamps, save one he picked up, called Pup, and walked into his bedroom, finding it just as she said. As if knowing the blanket on the floor was hers, Pup lay down and curled up while Wade undressed down to his long underwear and climbed between the cool sheets. The pillow felt soft and friendly as he laid his head down, listening to the sounds of the Peters' getting ready for bed. Wade could hear the soft breathing of the coyote asleep on the floor mix with the sudden sound of Nora's sobbing. While listening to her, he thought of the wolves and the three bodies outside.

Wade opened his eyes and looked out the window seeing the starless morning sky was getting light, bringing a new day. Feeling something at the foot of the bed, he looked down, seeing Pup had managed to get on the bed without waking him. He moved one leg against her and pushed, but she never moved, so he pushed against her again. This time she raised her head, looked at him, moved over just a bit, and immediately went back to sleep. Wade started to tell her to get off the bed but decided to let her sleep knowing she had come a long way, and there was still a long way to go. Watching her sleep, he was glad he hadn't left her with Jed.

The stillness was interrupted by the sound of pots and pans, and Wade imagined Nora busy with breakfast in the kitchen. As he lay there staring out the window watching the sky turn lighter with morning colors of oranges and yellows, Pup got up, made the short journey to his side, and lay down next to him. Wade gently petted her as his thoughts found Preacher Arden talking about the winds of atonement that day in the cemetery. Not sure what all that meant, he watched the day out the window, thinking of Morgan and Jed and the others he had come to know in Pickering. Deciding it was time to get up, Wade tossed the covers back and got out of bed. The room was still dim, so he lit the lantern and moved it to the dresser where the washbasin and pitcher of water waited.

Shaved and dressed, he and Pup joined Nora in the kitchen.

Mrs. Peters was wrapped in a faded, white robe and was barefooted fixing breakfast. She smiled as she poured him a cup of coffee. "Sleep well?"

"Once I got to sleep. How about you and Charlie?"

She handed the coffee to him and then picked up a small piece of cooked potato and held it out for the coyote, who took it gently from her fingers. "Charlie's still sleeping. I didn't sleep well." She paused and looked at Wade, wondering about the scars

432

on his face that weren't there before. She wanted to ask but didn't think it proper. "Kept thinking about those terrible men and what would have happened had you not come along. Every sound frightened me."

The sun crested the eastern horizon, and the Peters' rooster gave its greeting.

She looked at Wade with tears in her green eyes, and as they made their way down her freckled cheeks, she wiped them with the towel she was holding. "I'm not sure I want to stay out here any longer."

Wade smiled. "All men aren't evil, Mrs. Peters."

She looked doubtful as she brushed her long, red hair away from her freckled face. "Sure seems there's enough of them."

He had no argument about that as he took a sip of hot coffee, feeling sorry for her as she returned to her cooking. As he watched her, he hoped she would be able to get over last night, but he knew in his heart she never would. Somethings just seem to hang on, and he knew that this place held a different meaning for her and Charlie Peters now. Thinking of the three men lying beyond the outhouse, he headed for the door with his coffee. "Think I'll see if the wolves are still at it."

Nora gave Pup a small piece of meat and never turned or spoke.

Wade stepped outside, walked to the far edge of the porch, stopped, and looked toward the outhouse hearing the soft, familiar growling he had heard the night before. Knowing the wolves were still at it, he took a drink of coffee, set his cup on one of the chairs, and stepped off the porch. Cautiously and quietly, he approached the side of the outhouse, peered around the corner seeing several wolves making a meal of the three men. A big gray wolf stopped eating and looked up at him with intense blue eyes, its snout covered in blood as well as its white and light brown chest. Wade turned away from the terrible sight of feeling sick at his stomach and hurried back to the porch, picked up his coffee cup, and stepped inside the house. Setting the cup down on the table, he went into the bedroom and returned with his .45 Colt pistol.

Nora looked at the gun as Wade walked by. "What's wrong?"

"Wolves are still at the three men."

Nora dropped a morsel of food for Pup and called out, "Mr. Garrison!"

He turned.

"Breakfast is almost ready." She smiled as she gestured at the table. "Come, have a seat, and I'll freshen up your coffee."

He watched as she dropped another piece of food for Pup, picked up the big gray pot of coffee, and filled his cup

"Sit down," she said. "Drink your coffee." Then she returned the pot to the stove, looked down at Pup, while she stirred the food in the frying pan, and smiled. "Don't you think you've had enough?" She looked up from what she was doing. "Go on now, Mr. Garrison. Put that gun away, sit down, and drink your coffee before it gets cold."

Setting his gun down on a nearby table, he pulled a chair from the big dining table, sat down, and took a drink of coffee, considering Mrs. Peters' hatred for the three men. As he watched her casually going about breakfast, he thought about his hatred that took him to Mexico and hoped the dreams never visited her as they had him over the years.

Charlie walked into the kitchen from the bedroom, stopped at the stove for a cup of coffee, and managed a very small smile for his wife with his cut, puffy lips. He looked down at Pup, took a piece of fried potato from the frying pan, and gave it to her.

Nora slapped his hands playfully and told him to take his coffee and go sit down.

Wade looked at Pup with her black eyes watching Nora's every move, and thought Pup would get fat living here.

Charlie attempted a smile. "Morning, Wade."

"Morning, Charlie."

Nora turned from the stove. "I'll have breakfast on the table in a minute or two."

Charlie sat down, took a drink of coffee, leaned toward Wade, and spoke softly. "We'll bury them, fellas, after breakfast."

Wade glanced at Nora, dishing up the food, leaned toward Charlie, and lowered his voice. "May not be much left. There are quite a few wolves after them. We better chase them away with gunfire, or they'll come back."

Peters glanced at his wife and whispered, "You're right about that. We'll just have to bury what's left after that."

Carrying a plate of food in each hand, Nora set one down in front of Wade, the other in front of her husband, and then she sat down next to Charlie.

"Aren't you eating, Mrs. Peters?" asked Wade, then he remembered she doesn't eat breakfast very often.

"You go on ahead." She picked up her coffee cup, took a drink, and smiled at Wade. "I bet you're in a hurry to get home."

Thinking of the three men and the wolves outside, he said he was.

Suddenly Nora's eyes welled, and she looked away as she stood then ran out of the room.

Charlie tossed his napkin on the table, excused himself, and hurried after her as fast as his injuries would allow.

Having lost his appetite, Wade pushed his plate away, picked up his cup, walked to the stove, and filled it with coffee. Taking a sip, he looked toward the hall leading to their bedroom, hearing Nora's muffled sobbing. Figuring the Peters could use some time, Wade pulled Colt from the holster setting on a chair, headed for the door with his coffee, stepped out onto the porch, and closed the door leaving Pup inside. Standing at the edge of the porch, he took a sip of coffee and wondered if Nora would ever get over last night.

Holding his cup of coffee, he stepped off the porch, cocked his gun, and walked to the outhouse. Peering around it at the wolves and what remained of the three men, he aimed and fired, kicking up dust by one of the wolves that yelped and jumped to one side. Knowing he would have to kill one so they would not come back, he took aim and pulled the trigger, hitting a big male that yelped as he fell. As the others ran off, Wade fired again and then again while taking a drink of his coffee. Figuring that ended the problem with the wolves, he turned, and headed back to the porch.

The door opened, Charlie stepped out onto the porch. "Scar them wolves away?"

"Had to shoot one. Nora, alright?"

Charlie looked sad as he sat down in one of the creaky chairs. "I apologize for Nora, Marshal, but this has been too much for her. I'm surprised she didn't break down sooner."

Wade sat down in the other chair, looking sympathetic. "No need to apologize, Charlie. Nora appears to be strong of mind, and I'm sure she'll be all right."

"Maybe we ought to get away from here," Charlie said thoughtfully. Then he stared across the land. "But where would I take her?"

Wade took a drink of coffee and made no comment or suggestions on what they should do, hoping they both get through this terrible ordeal.

"Maybe we ought to move to a town." Charlie stood. "Let's put what's left of them varmints underground."

They buried what was left of the three men, and then having more respect for the wolf, they buried it in a separate grave. Charlie wiped his forehead as he looked at the ground, thinking you would never know anyone was buried here. "Hope you don't mind me asking Wade, but you never had those scars when you were here before."

"Came by them up north."

Worried about Wade, Peters asked if he was alright.

436

Wade smiled. "Yeah, Charlie, I am." He put one hand on the man's shoulder and smiled again. "Let's put these shovels away, and then I'll saddle my horse, load up and be on my way."

Charlie helped him saddle his horse and pack what was left of his supplies onto the other horse, and when they finished, Wade led the mare out of the barn to the corner of the corral while Charlie followed with the packhorse.

The door to the house opened, and Nora stepped out, carrying a small burlap bag she handed to Wade. "It's for the coyote." Her eyes were red and puffy, but she managed a smile.

Wade thanked her and found a spot with the supplies. He turned and looked into Nora's teary eyes wishing he had the words to help her feel better and forget last night.

She stepped closer, took his broad shoulders in her small hands, looked at the scars, and hugged him. "You're a good man, Mr. Garrison."

He looked down at her, thinking of many ways he could disagree but softly said, "It's going to be all right, Mrs. Peters."

"Perhaps Charlie and me should sell this place," she said. "And head out to California. I hear the sun shines most of the year."

"Sounds good, alright," said Wade.

She stepped back, wiping the tears from her eyes, and forced a small smile. "All we can do is trust in the Lord." Then she bent over, petted Pup, and kissed the coyote on the head, to Wade's surprise. She stood, smiled once more at Wade, then turned and walked toward the house, talking over her shoulder. "God bless you and that coyote of yours, Wade Garrison."

Wade watched her for a moment hoping she would be okay. Then he took his black duster from behind his saddle and shrugged into it, then turned to Charlie, and shook his hand. Wade swung up onto his saddle and took the reins of the packhorse. As he settled in, he looked down at Charlie's battered face. "Take care of yourself and the missus." He paused a moment. "I can't explain it none, Charlie. Bad things happen to good people sometimes. I'm just glad I came by when I did."

Charlie's face held a small, worried smile. "So are we, Marshal." He looked at the house where Nora was then at Wade. "Nora believes God sent you. Why else would you come on that night at that time?"

Wade could not answer as he had questions of his own.

Charlie stepped back from the mare. "God go with you."

Wade nudged the sorrel into a walk around the corral leading the packhorse while the coyote ran ahead as if eager to get started on their new adventure. Wade turned in the saddle and gave a last wave, thinking California might be just the thing for Nora. Nudging the mare into a trot, he rode after Pup as she ran ahead into the plains of Wyoming.

Chapter 30

The Hoskins Ranch

The late afternoon September air was warm, and there wasn't a hint of breeze when Wade pulled the sorrel up and stared at two piles of rubble and burnt wood. The packhorse shook its head, rattling his bit and bridle; the mare blew through her nose, and the coyote laid down a few feet away in the shade to rest. Wade stared at the blackened pile of burnt wood, which was all that remained of the bunkhouse. The sound of creaking leather broke the stillness as he slowly climbed down from the saddle, wrapped the reins of the packhorse around his saddle horn, and stared at the pile of rubble. His mind suddenly filled with the screams, the gunfire, and the killing of that night. He glanced at the deteriorating, empty barn and collapsing fence of the corral, the only things left of the Hoskins Empire that he didn't destroy.

He turned and looked at what remained of a once a grand two-story house that was now another pile of burned and charred wood. The same as Hoskins and his men had done to the Double J. Not far from the pile was an overgrown flower garden with three weathered, wooden chairs resting in the weeds, one slightly tilted from a broken leg. Letting go of the reins of the mare, he walked the short distance to the overgrown garden and looked down at the chair he had placed the body of Elizabeth Purdy in. In his mind, he could still see the reflection of the burning house on her face as he gently put her in that chair. Feeling regret for Elizabeth Purdy, but none of the others, he walked back to the mare, swung up onto the saddle, gripped the reins to the packhorse, and called to the coyote.

The sun had not set yet, but it was near dusk when he and the coyote reached the top of the hill overlooking the white two-story house Sarah had rebuilt. With the sun low in the sky behind him, he pulled the mare up and sat in the saddle, staring down at the quiet, peaceful setting, filled with anticipation and fear. The mare whinnied as if anxious to finish the last of their long journey. Wade smiled as he stroked her neck, speaking in a soft, tired voice. "We're home, girl." A woman stepped out of the house, walked to the edge of the porch, and raised her hand to shade her eyes from the setting sun. He didn't need his long glass to tell him it was Sarah.

Staring at the rider and his packhorse bathed in the colors of the evening sun, Sarah's heart raced as she softly whispered her husband's name.

Wade stood in the saddle, hesitated for just a moment, and then waved.

With her heart pounding and tears welling in her eyes, she waved back and then rushed down the steps of the porch, almost tripping over her dress. Laughing and crying at the same time, she held her dress up with one hand as she ran across the yard toward the gates and archway, calling out his name.

Nudging the mare into a gallop down the hill, he tugged at the tired packhorse while the coyote ran alongside the mare. Riding under the archway with the initials "WS" hanging above him, Wade turned the mare across the yard toward Sarah. Before the horse came to a stop, he let go of the reins to the packhorse, jumped off the mare, and ran to her. As their bodies collided into an embrace, they kissed, and then Sarah kissed his cheeks, repeating his name.

As he held her, she put her head against his chest, wrapped her arms around him, and held him tight, afraid he would disappear. "Oh, Wade," she said softly. "I've missed you so terribly."

Holding her in his arms and smelling the freshness of her hair Wade said softly, "I've thought about you every moment of every day."

She looked up with tears in her eyes, pushed away, and wiped her eyes and cheeks. "I should punch you one."

He laughed, thinking how much he missed her.

She noticed the scars on his unshaven, thin face and worried if he was sick. She wanted to know what happened but decided she would wait, closed her eyes, and melted against him.

Hearing the blow of a horse, she opened her eyes, seeing the mare and packhorse with reins dangling, and then she saw the coyote. "Wade, there's a coyote watching us."

Wade turned and chuckled. "That's Pup."

A mixture of fear and curiosity held her as she stood in his arms. "He's yours?"

"It's a bitch, and I'm not sure if she belongs to me or me to her." He turned away from Pup, looked at Sarah, and smiled. "It's a long story."

"One I'd like to hear," admitted Sarah. "Is she friendly?"

"She is." He looked toward the house. "How are the children?"

Surprised by the question about children, she looked up at him.

He smiled. "Seth told me."

Sarah had a look of surprise. "When did you see Seth?"

"A while back up in Montana."

"Why didn't he tell me he found you?"

"That was my doing," he said with guilt. "I never thought I'd come home again. Seth was a little upset with me when he left Pickering. I need to apologize to him."

"Where's Pickering?"

"Montana, Territory. I'll tell you all about it, but right now, I want to see my son and daughter."

Smiling, she took his hand and led him toward the porch, where he tied the horses to the hitching rail. Pup followed them up the steps to the porch, where Wade turned and told her to sit and stay.

Sarah looked at the coyote. "Will she stay?"

Wade grinned proudly. "Until I tell her different."

Thinking that was remarkable, Sarah took his hand, opened the door, and led him into the house, closing the door behind them.

He paused in the foyer then stepped into the living room, glancing around at the furniture and the open doorway to the library and another open doorway to the dining room. His eyes soon found the staircase leading up to the second floor and the bedrooms.

"Well?" she asked, referring to the new house. "What do you think?"

He took off his hat. "A lot like it was before, but different somehow." He smiled at her. "I like it. You've done a good job."

Pleased by that, she took his hand and led him to the staircase, where she smiled. "Your children are up those stairs."

He handed her his hat and took off his black duster, gave that to her, and then he hurried up the steps of the stairs, two at a time. Opening the door to his son's room, he stepped inside, finding him on the floor playing with his lead iron figures of Indians and cowboys. Willie and Dog were on the bed asleep, but at seeing him, both jumped off the bed and ran to greet him, whining loudly with tails wagging as he knelt to one knee.

"Pa!" yelled Emmett as he stood, scattering his lead figures across the floor. "You're home Pa. You're really home."

Wade pushed the dogs aside to make room for his son.

442

Emmett ran into his father's arms. "Where you been, Pa? I've missed you." With tears in his eyes, Emmett looked at the two dogs. "So did Dog and Willie."

Wade hugged his son while the two dogs whined and vied for his attention, trying to push their way between Wade and his son only to push Wade and Emmett backward to the floor.

Emmett sat up laughing while pushing at Willie.

Laughing, Wade stood, helped his son to his feet, and then lifted him into his arms.

Emmett put his arms around his pa's neck, hugged him, and then looked into his eyes. "You gonna stay home now, Pa?"

Wade thought about going to prison as he turned and saw Sarah standing in the doorway, holding his hat and black duster folded over her arm. Then thinking his son felt a little light and looked a little thin, he turned to Sarah. "Seems a might undernourished."

She smiled. "Emmett's fine, just a little active. He eats like you do."

Emmett noticed the scars on his pa's unshaven face, reached out, and touched the one along his chin with the tips of his fingers. "What happed here to your face, pa?"

Feeling embarrassed, he looked at Sarah and then at his son. "I'll tell you one day." Then he said, "Hey, I hear you have a little sister to watch over."

Emmett shrugged, looking disappointed. "She doesn't say much."

Wade chuckled as he set his son down. "Give her time, son. Soon you won't be able to shut her up, and you'll wish for these silent days." Wade gestured toward the door. "Let's go have a peek." Taking Emmett's hand, they walked out of the room, closed the door on Willie, and Dog then followed Sarah to another closed door.

She opened the door, peeked in then turned to Wade. "She's sleeping."

Wade let go of Emmett's hand as he stepped into the room, quietly walked to the small crib, and looked down at his daughter.

Sarah and Emmett stood beside him.

"She looks like you," whispered Wade.

Sarah laughed softly. "I certainly hope so."

"Who do I look like?" asked Emmett.

His mother smiled affectionately. "Your father, of course." Then as Wade stared at their daughter, Sarah turned and pulled a chair up next to the crib. "Sit and visit with your daughter."

He sat down, leaned on the side of the crib with his forearms, and looked down at the sleeping child.

Thinking that Wade would like to be alone with his new daughter, Sarah took Emmett's hand and led him into the hall.

Emmett looked up at his mother. "Why'd we come out here, Ma?"

She quietly closed the door, smoothed her husband's duster affectionately with one hand as she held it, fighting tears of happiness. "Your father needs a moment with Mary Louise."

"Why?" asked Emmett. "She's sleeping, and she can't talk anyways."

Sarah chuckled softly at her son as she set Wade's hat and duster on a hall chair. "I know, but let's give him a minute anyway."

The door opened, and Wade stepped into the hall wearing a smile. "She snores." He closed the door and looked at Emmett. "I have something to show you."

"What is it, Pa?" Emmett said, looking excited.

Sarah knew what Wade was talking about, and she was afraid for her son. "Be careful, Wade. She's a wild animal."

Upon hearing that, Emmett's eyes got big. "What is it, Pa? Can I keep it?"

Wade looked at his wife. "It's going to be fine, Sarah. She's as tame as Willie and Dog." He took his son's hand and started for the stairs while Sarah followed, filled with uneasiness about the coyote.

Approaching the front door, Sarah looked worried. "Be careful, Wade."

He turned and smiled at her. "It'll be fine." He opened the door, and as they stepped onto the porch, the coyote sat up and looked at them.

Emmett stopped, let go of his Pa's hand, and backed into the house, looking frightened. "There's a coyote on the porch Pa."

Wade stepped onto the porch. "It's okay, Son, she won't hurt you." He walked to Pup, knelt, and petted her. "See, she's nice like Dog and Willie."

Emmett's eyes grew big as he smiled at the sight. "Is she yours, Pa?"

Wade nodded. "Yes, she is, son, and she's smart, too."

"What's her name?" asked a curious Emmett.

"Her name is Pup."

Looking puzzled, Emmett asked, "Why did you name her Pup?"

"Because she was a pup when I found her. Want to pet her?"

Emmett stared at Pup and nodded.

Sarah wasn't too sure about that as she put one hand on Emmett's shoulder, unsure of the coyote. "Be careful, son."

Thinking Sarah was just a little over protective, Wade took his son's hand in his and petted her on the shoulder.

With tail wagging, she smelled Emmett's hand, his arm, and then his clothes with her long snout and became excited.

"She smells Willie and Dog," said Wade.

Emmett grinned, then looked worried. "What about Dog and Willie? Will they fight with her?"

Wade couldn't answer that. "I'm not sure, but we best find out. Since Dog is the littlest, you go upstairs and bring him down first and make sure Willie doesn't get out."

Sarah protested, "Wade, please."

"It's better to get them together now." Wade turned and stepped off the porch to get Pup's rope from his saddlebags while Emmett ran upstairs to get Dog. Wade put the rope around the coyote's neck and then tied her to the porch post, told her to sit, and then knelt with his arm around her. He looked up at Sarah's worried face. "It'll be all right."

She looked unsure. "You keep saying that."

"Dog and Willie are both males," said Wade. "And Pup's a bitch."

"Great," she said. "What happens when she comes into heat?"

Wade never thought about that. "I don't know."

Wondering about that herself and not sure if that even mattered with a coyote, she waited.

The door opened, and Emmett came out carrying Dog in his arms.

Seeing the coyote, Dog fought to get down, scratching Emmett's arms. He bent down and let go of him, and Dog ran right over to the coyote and began smelling her. Pup wasn't very receptive to the attention and gave Dog a soft, low growl showing her lack of appreciation. Dog backed away, tilted his head, and whined as he walked around Pup with his tail eagerly wagging.

It took a few minutes, but they soon accepted one another, and then it was Willie's turn with much the same reaction. Watching the three get acquainted, Wade knew they were going to be alright. He took the rope off of Pup then looked at Sarah. "They're going to be fine. As I said, they're males, and Pup's a bitch."

The front door opened, and a Mexican woman, thin of build with long black hair wearing a colorful dress, looking to be around thirty, glanced curiously at Wade and then looked at Sarah. "Dinner will soon be ready, Señora."

Sarah smiled as she gestured to Wade. "Maria, this is my husband, Wade Garrison." She paused and smiled. "He's been away, as you know, but has come back to us."

Maria looked at Wade and smiled. "Buenos Noches, señor. Mrs. Garrison talks of you often. Welcome home."

Wade smiled. "Buenos Noches, Maria, and gracias."

Sarah looked at Maria affectionately. "Maria stays in one of the guest rooms upstairs." She paused. "I don't know how I would have managed without her."

Maria noticed Pup and stepped back toward the doorway. "Señora, is that a coyote with Willie and Dog?"

Sarah turned. "She belongs to my husband."

Maria's worried eyes went from the coyote to Wade and then to Sarah. "I'll set another place for dinner, Señora." Taking one last glance at Pup, she went into the house, crossing her body in prayer.

Wade took the saddlebags, rifle, and other belongings upstairs and then put the horses away for the night, giving both plenty of oats and water and a stall with fresh hay. When he finished, he washed up on the back porch, then took his place at the head of the table. It felt good to be home eating a meal with his family until his mind found the image of being arrested. Pushing that from his mind, he ate and watched his son pick through his food as if not hungry. Then he watched Sarah feeding small bites of food to their daughter, who kept staring at him.

He winked at his daughter, then looked at his son and leaned on the table with his forearms. "Something bothering you, son?"

Emmett stared into his plate a moment and then looked at his pa. "When you gonna tell us where you been all this time? We missed you."

"I will, son, but not just yet. I just got home, and I want to hear what you have been doing with your time."

Emmett frowned at his plate. "School mostly." Then he looked at his pa. "Why'd you go and leave us in the first place?"

Sarah glanced at her husband and then looked at Emmett. "Your Pa's been chasing bad men, Emmett, just as he always does."

The boy frowned. "You sure were gone a long time."

Wade looked at his son. "Couldn't be helped, boy. But right now, I think it's best if we all concentrate on the fact that I'm home."

Emmett had a puzzled look. "Did you catch them?"

Wade grinned. "What do you think?"

Emmett's face filled with a big smile. "I think, yes."

"Good," grinned Wade. "Now, finish your supper like a good boy."

While they ate, Sarah told of the rebuilding of the house, the funny things Emmett did, the birth of Mary Louise, and her mother's marriage to Tolliver Grimes.

Wade looked concerned. "I've been thinking on Mary Louise."

Sarah looked puzzled. "What about her?"

"Is your mother's feeling hurt because her name is missing from her granddaughter's name?"

Sarah smiled. "It was mother that named her."

Wade sat back in his chair. "Well, I'll be."

The kitchen door swung open, and Maria walked in, wearing a smile as she looked at Sarah. "Everything all right, Señora?"

"Everything was perfect, Maria, as usual."

She smiled proudly.

"Excellent dinner Maria," said Wade. "Gracias."

She smiled, looking grateful. "You're welcome, señor." Then she frowned. "Is the coyote to be fed with the dogs?"

Wade considered that. "Don't see why not. Is there a problem?"

448

"No, señor," she said, wearing an uncertain look. "No problem, as long as she doesn't bite me."

"Pup has been around people all her life, Maria," said Wade. "She's more a dog than a coyote."

Still not convinced, she said, "Yes, señor." Then she disappeared into the kitchen.

Wade wiped his mouth with his napkin and started to stand. "Maybe I best help the first night." He followed Maria into the kitchen, and when the coyote and dogs had been fed, he walked back into the dining room, looked at Sarah, and asked, "Is there any whiskey?"

"In the study."

"After you get the children settled, would you care to join me?"

She looked up and smiled. "I'd love to."

Wade went into the library, found the liquor cabinet, poured a small glass of brandy, smelled it before taking a small sip, and sat down on a small, light yellow, stuffed sofa that was more comfortable than it looked. As he sipped the brandy letting his eyes roam the room, he thought it was a lot like Jasper's old study before the house burned down. In the silent moments that passed whileWade waited for Sarah, he thought of the fire and how scared he was that something had happened to them. Then he remembered his relief at seeing them crowded around Billy French under the oak tree with him holding a pistol in each hand.

Taking a small sip, his mind found Jed and Morgan, and then the Peters hoping Nora would soon get over that terrible night and hoped they moved to a town or someplace safe.

As Sarah walked into the library, he stood, "Would you like a sherry?"

She politely declined, sat down on the small sofa, patted the empty place next to her, and smiled. "Sit with me."

As he sat down, she wrapped her arm around his arm and watched him take a sip of brandy while considering the night and the coyote. "Where is the coyote going to sleep?"

He took a small drink. "Never gave it any thought."

"Do you think she'll sleep in Emmett's room with Dog and Willie?"

Wade felt awkward. "I don't know. She's always slept on a blanket next to my bed." He paused. "Sometimes, on my bed."

"I was afraid you were going to say that."

He looked at her lips as they formed a small smile and then looked into her big brown eyes. "I'm sure she can sleep in Emmett's room with Dog and Willie."

Sarah smiled shyly. "Maybe I will have a small glass of sherry."

Wade gave her a quick smile, then stood from the sofa, poured her a small glass.

She took a sip then stared into the glass. "What do you think will happen now that you're back?"

He took another sip of brandy. "Is Harry Block still Sheriff of Harper?"

Looking curious, she said, "Yes, he is. Why?"

"Good. The first thing we need to do is find out if there's a warrant for my arrest."

Suddenly she was worried. "And if there is?"

Wade shrugged slightly. "I'm not sure. Harry may arrest me."

Fear gripped Sarah as she fought to keep from crying. He had just returned to her, and now she may lose him again. "Before you see Harry Block, we should go into Denver and find ourselves a good lawyer."

"Going to have to be a damn good one, I'm afraid," he said in a thoughtful voice.

Sarah bit her lip the way she did when thinking. "James Goodwyn is the attorney who handled the transfer deed from my mother to me. His office is in Denver." She looked at him. "He may have a suggestion."

Wade looked worried. "We need a good criminal lawyer."

Sarah thought about that. "We can ride into Denver first thing tomorrow and see if Mr. Goodwyn knows of one." Not wanting to talk about such things that made her sad and worrisome on his first night home, she cuddled up next to him and sipped the sherry, trying to forget the law and attorneys. She set the half glass of sherry down on the small table next to her and stood.

"Where are you going?"

"Upstairs." She smiled. "Give me half an hour."

After she walked out of the room, disappearing past the doorway of the study, he looked at the clock standing in the corner of the room, thinking thirty minutes was a long time.

It was a little after ten in the morning when Wade, wearing one of his old suits that was a little big, and Sarah wearing a long white and gray dress with matching jacket and black bonnet, arrived at the law office of James Goodwyn. He rose from his chair, giving Sarah a friendly smile, wondering who the gentleman was with her. After saying it was good to see her, he asked about her mother. Mr. Goodwyn was a heavyset man in his mid-forties with thick gray hair and a clean-shaven face, dressed in an expensive gray suit.

"James, this is my husband, Wade Garrison."

Having heard the story of Wade Garrison and the Hoskins men, he gave him a curious look as he shook his hand. "When did you return?"

"Yesterday," replied Wade.

James gestured toward two dark brown leather chairs in front of a dark mahogany desk. "Make yourselves comfortable." He returned to his high-backed leather chair on the other side of the desk and smiled, wondering why her husband wasn't in jail. "Now, how can I be of service?"

Sarah looked troubled. "My husband needs a good criminal attorney, James."

Wade shifted in his chair. "I'm sure you know more than you let on, so I won't bore you with the details, but if you could do us the service of recommending a good attorney, Sarah, and I would be grateful." Wade paused. "If there is not such a man in Denver, I'm afraid we will have to find one back east, and that may take time, which means I spend more time in jail awaiting my trial."

James sat back in his leather chair, rubbing his mouth and chin in thought, and then he leaned forward with his elbows on his dark mahogany desk. "I've heard your story several times, Mr. Garrison, and each time the number of men you killed triples." He smiled. "I'm not a judgmental man, and I believe John Stirling is as good as we have in Denver, perhaps in the entire state. His office is just up the street." He smiled as he stood. "Why don't we take a walk and see if he's in?"

A slender, dark-haired woman in her late twenties with dark brown hair and green eyes greeted them as they entered John Stirling's Law Office. She smiled at James Goodwyn. "Good morning, Mr. Goodwyn."

"Good morning, Evelyn. Is your father in?"

"Yes, he is." She stood. "I'll see if he can see you." She opened the door to another room, disappeared inside, and returned moments later. "He'll see you now."

The three walked into the room greeted by a man in his fifties, whose body resembled that of a younger man, standing behind a dark cherry desk wearing a big, friendly smile. "Good morning, James," he said with a kindly look as he walked around his desk with an open hand.

James Goodwyn shook the hand and then introduced him to Wade and Sarah.

John shook Wade's hand, kissed Sarah's hand gently, and then asked them to sit down on a small, dark, stuffed sofa offering a chair to James Goodwyn.

"I think it best," began James. "If I don't hear what the Garrisons have to say." He looked at Stirling. "Lunch later?"

"Of course."

James Goodwyn tipped his hat to Sarah, shook Wade's hand wishing him luck, and walked out of the room.

John Stirling smiled at Sarah and then Wade as he walked to a small liquor table of three bottles and several glasses. He stood six feet tall and had thick, brown-and-gray hair, brown eyes, and a clean-shaven face but for a well-trimmed, thin mustache. He turned to Sarah. "I know it's a little early, Mrs. Garrison, but could I offer you a sherry?"

"No, thank you."

"Coffee or tea, then?"

She smiled. "Nothing, thank you."

"As you wish." He turned to Wade. "Whiskey, Mr. Garrison?"

"If you don't mind." Wade thought he could use a drink.

Stirling grinned. "I don't mind. It gives me a reason to have a drink myself." He chuckled as he turned and picked up a bottle while talking. "I don't trust a man who refuses a good drink." He paused and turned to Wade. "I have found over the years that a good drink during business relaxes one." He turned back to the table, poured two drinks of expensive whiskey, walked across the room, handed one to Wade, and sat down on a matching sofa facing them. He sipped his drink while he looked at Wade. "Now, how can I help you?"

Wade frowned with a worried look. "I believe you know who I am, Mr. Stirling, and I believe that I'm about to be arrested."

Stirling sat back and crossed his legs. "Yes, Mr. Garrison, I've heard your name associated with the killings at the Hoskins ranch and the killing of George Hoskins a year ago."

"Well," began Wade. "Then you know I'll probably be arrested in the next few days and put on trial for murder."

Stirling thought for a moment, watching while Wade shifted in his chair, appearing nervous. "The first thing we need to do is find out if there is a warrant and if not, will there be."

Sarah leaned forward, looking worried. "And how do we go about that without bringing attention to my husband?"

He smiled at her. "Let me worry about that, my dear."

"Then you'll take the case?" asked Wade.

He took a drink, set the glass down on the table next to the sofa, and stared at Wade. "I always ask future clients to sit here while I make up my mind as to whether I thank them and show them out or invite them to sit in those chairs."

Wade and Sarah looked at four expensive, dark leather chairs lined up in front of the big, dark cherry desk. He gestured toward the chairs. "Let's move to the desk, so I can take notes while you talk, shall we?"

Looking relieved, Wade and Sarah smiled at one another as they moved to the leather chairs. After they sat down, Sarah reached over and took her husband's hand.

Stirling sat down behind his desk, took several clean pieces of paper from the top drawer along with a pencil, and looked at Wade. "From now on, you don't speak to anyone but me about this. Do you understand?"

Wade nodded. "Yes."

John wrote something on the paper, looked at Sarah, and then Wade. "From now on, we say alleged crimes. They still have to be proven in a court of law, and defending you against them is what I do. Now, tell me what happened."

Wade sat back, looking concerned over confessing to what happened.

Stirling sensed his apprehension. "I've taken your case, Mr. Garrison. It's not my job to judge you. That will be up to a judge and jury. Everything you tell me from now on is confidential, meaning it is between me and my client, which is you ." He smiled. "Right now, I'm your best friend, and it's up to me to get you acquitted whether you are guilty or not. That's how it works. However, to do so, I need you, to be honest with me. I want no surprises when we get into court. So, tell me all that happened."

Wade took a good drink of whiskey and told John Stirling the story from the time Billy French in Santa Fe received the telegram from Seth Bowlen.

Stirling interrupted asking who these men were, wrote something on the paper, and then asked Wade to continue.

Wade told John Stirling everything from the killings in Sisters to Jasper Talbert shot in the back, Sarah being hurt and losing the baby, and their son injuring his leg in the accident.

Stirling looked at Sarah. "You have my sympathies, Mrs. Garrison."

"Thank you."

Wade continued the story up to including the raid on the Talbert Ranch and the burning of the Talbert house. He leaned forward in his chair, looking angry. "They shot at my wife, her mother, and our son Emmett as they escaped the burning house these same men had set afire." He glanced at Sarah. "Had it not been for Billy French, they all may have burned alive in that house." Wade looked into Stirling's eyes. "I'll not let anyone harm my family."

John Stirling's face held a solemn expression as he looked at Sarah, thinking of his own family, then he looked at Wade. "Can't say I blame you, Mr. Garrison." John stood and walked to the window staring out at the people on the street, and after a minute, he turned. "I've heard enough, Mr. Garrison." He returned to his chair. "First, I want to say that I loathed George Hoskins, and I believe this country is better off without his kind. Now, I want you to do exactly as I tell you from this moment on."

Wade glanced at Sarah and then nodded. "All right."

Stirling looked from Sarah to Wade. "First of all, I want the case tried in Harper and not here in Denver. So the very first thing we do is the three of us meet in Harper tomorrow, at, say noon, and you turn yourself into the local sheriff before the marshal here in Denver hears of your return. Do you know the sheriff in Harper?"

"Yes, Sheriff Harry Block."

"What sort of man is he?"

"A good man," said Wade.

Sarah turned to Wade with a worried look. "I just got you back."

Stirling looked at her with a comforting smile. "Better he's arrested in Harper than in Denver, for a couple of reasons. The Denver jail is a long way from Harper, and if he's tried here," he paused and looked at both, "a Denver jury may not be sympathetic."

Wade and Sarah looked at one another with worried faces.

"What concerns you?" asked Stirling.

Sarah looked at him. "How can you be sure the trial will be in Harper?"

Wade asked, "Couldn't a judge have me transferred?"

John smiled. "For one, everything happened in Lincoln County, or the city of Harper, and not in the county of Denver." He smiled. "Don't concern yourself. If needed, I'll file enough motions they'll be happy to have the trial in Harper." He looked at the closed door and hollered for his secretary.

The door opened, and his secretary, Evelyn, stepped into his office, glanced at Wade and Sarah, and then looked at her father.

"Put together a retainer for six hundred fifty dollars, Evelyn. The Garrisons will sign it on their way out."

She nodded. "Yes, sir." Then she stepped out of the room.

After the door closed, he smiled. "The six hundred fifty does not include expenses while we stay in Harper. Depending on the length of the trial, I may need additional funds." He grinned. "You'll find I'm worth every penny." He settled back in his chair, looking serious. "I'll meet the two of you at this Sheriff Block's office around noon tomorrow." He smiled at Sarah. "After they arrest your husband, you, I, and my daughter will have a nice dinner and discuss our strategy."

Wade looked puzzled. "I still haven't told you what happened at the Hoskins Ranch and later."

"I've heard that story many times, Mr. Garrison, and we'll get to that another time. Right now, speed is what we need to keep you away from a Denver jail."

"Will my husband's fleeing hurt his chances?"

Stirling smiled at her. "Not necessarily, Mrs. Garrison." He started to get up but settled back into his chair and looked at Wade. "I do need to know something before you leave. Were there any witnesses left alive at the Hoskins ranch?"

Wade shook his head. "Not that I know of."

Stirling grinned wickedly. "Things are already looking up, Mr. and Mrs. Garrison." He stood and walked around the desk while Wade and Sarah stood. He kissed Sarah's hand, told her not to worry, shook Wade's hand, and told them he would see them tomorrow. Then he walked them to the door, opened it, and looked at his secretary. "Are you up to spending a few days in Harper, my dear?"

She smiled. "Yes, sir. Sounds fun."

"Good, we've some work to do in that quaint little town." He looked at Wade and Sarah. "Good day to you both."

Wade and Sarah walked along the boardwalk after leaving Mr. Stirling Office when Sarah asked, "What do you think?"

Wade kept glancing around, looking for men with badges as they walked to get their carriage. "I liked him." Then he took her by the arm and walked a little faster. "I want to leave Denver before someone arrests me."

Sarah became suspicious of everyone they passed, whether they smiled or not. Reaching the livery, Wade paid for the boarding of the buggy and horse, helped Sarah into it, climbed in beside her, and drove out of the livery. Neither spoke until Wade drove the buggy out of the city limits of Denver and were safely on the road toward Harper. She glanced behind them to see if anyone was following, and then she looked at Wade. "Do you think Mr. Stirling knows what he's doing?"

Wade frowned. "I guess we'll find out."

The Garrison Ranch

Wade spent a restless night worrying about what the day would bring for him and Sarah. Afraid he would wake her by his tossing and turning, he carefully got out of bed, picked up his clothes, went into the hall, and got dressed. He opened the door to Emmett's room, let Pup out, quietly walked down the stairs, and went outside to the front porch.

The early morning September air carried a chill, and he wished he had thought about his coat as he followed Pup down the stairs of the porch into the yard. The sky to the east was starless and slowly turning a lighter shade with the coming of dawn, while the dark western sky still held its share of night stars. He walked in the still morning thinking of the coming day while the coyote ran in front of him, happy to be out of the house.

The two hundred yards to the split rail fence passed quickly, and now he stands with one foot on the bottom rail, his hands on the top rail wishing he had a cup of hot coffee. Second guessing his decision to come back to Harper, he thought about a trial, and if the verdict were guilty, he would more than likely hang. Turning from the dark shadows of the Rocky Mountains barely visible in the distance, he thought of the mare in the barn, of saddling her and riding away.

Sarah opened her sleepy eyes to the empty pillow next to her, sat up, and glanced around the darkroom, fearing for a moment that she had dreamt of Wade's return. Wondering where her husband was, she wrapped her arms around the pillow, still heavy with his scent, and stared at the early morning outside the window. Fear of what may happen in Harper today made her heart beat faster as she realized the days and weeks ahead might end their life together.

The thought of him getting hung suddenly came to a realization, and she sat up, finding it hard to catch her breath. She looked at the closed bedroom door, tossed the covers back, and walked to the window, and knelt on the seat. Looking for Wade at the fence where he would always go when he needed to think, it took her a moment, but as it got lighter, she saw her husband at the fence. Thinking he had returned a different man in many ways, she thought of the scars on his face and head, the healed bullet holes she felt on his side, left shoulder, and right thigh while they made love. She wanted to ask about each one; she wanted to know what happened to her husband in that strange place called Pickering that had changed him.

Wiping the tears from her cheeks, she worried that maybe he would go to prison or worse for trying to keep her and Emmett safe and wondered if it had been better if he had never returned. At least when he was in this place called Pickering, he was free and alive. Getting up from the window seat, she walked back to the bed, lay down, hugged his pillow, and began to cry. Thinking he should saddle the mare, take the coyote and ride so far, no one would find him. If it weren't for the children, she would go with him.

She must have drifted off when awakened by a door closing somewhere in the house. Muffled sound of pots and pans coming from the kitchen told Maria was going about her morning chores of breakfast and coffee. Sarah sat up and wiped her eyes with the sheet listening to the muffled sounds that made their way up the kitchen's stairs. Returning her gaze to the window, she thought of the mornings, she and Wade shared coffee in their bedroom in Santa Fe. Their little house wasn't much to look at; it had only four rooms, and the furniture was old, but she was happy there. Then came the telegram from Seth Bowlen that destroyed their world, and maybe Wade in the process.

The bedroom door opened, and Wade stepped into the room with a cup of hot coffee in each hand. He smiled. "Good morning."

"Good morning," Sarah said as she quickly brushed the tears from her eyes.

Pup rushed past him and lay down on the floor next to his side of the bed while Wade managed the door with one foot.

Sarah plumped the pillows against the headboard and smiled while playing the charade of not being scared or worried.

"Coffee?" smiled Wade, then he noticed her eyes were red and knew she had been crying.

Smiling while hiding her fears, Sarah took one of the cups, sat back against the pillow and headboard. Getting comfortable, she held the cup next to her lips, feeling the soft steam on her face that somehow seemed comforting.

Wade set his cup on the nightstand, took off his boots, sat on the bed, and leaned back against the pillows with his legs, with his stocking feet stretched out in front of him.

She noticed the big toe of his left foot sticking out of a hole in his white sock and smiled to herself, thinking it needed mending. Then she thought it was such a small thing to concern herself with right now. The first rooster greeted the sun, followed by other ranch sounds, and Sarah knew she and Wade were one day closer to their destiny that started with a simple telegram. She sipped her coffee with a thoughtful look and wondered how things would be different if she and Emmett had stayed in Santa Fe instead of coming with Wade to Harper. Was this her fault, she wondered? Then an idea occurred to her. "Let's get dressed and go for a ride."

He looked puzzled. "You have someplace particular in mind this time of morning?"

"I want to ride out to that old cabin we found hidden among the rocks and boulders before Emmett Spears was killed, and you rode off to avenge him."

He remembered the cabin though it was pushed far back into the dark places of his memory, jumbled up with other things. "What on earth for?"

"Please, Wade?" she pleaded.

"What about breakfast?"

For some reason, this was more important to her. "I can stand to miss a meal." Then she got out of bed while holding her coffee. "Hurry, Wade, we have to leave early if we are to be in Harper to meet Judge Stirling."

"What about the children?"

Sarah quickly considered that. "I'll ask Maria to watch them." Then she headed for the closet, set the cup down on her dresser, and turned to him looking eager. "Put your boots on, Wade, and go saddle our horses."

Remembering how stubborn she could be, Wade took a drink of coffee, set his cup on the nightstand, and put on his boots.

Thinking he was too slow, she said, "Hurry, Wade."

Picking up his coffee cup and leaving Pup asleep on the floor next to the bed, he walked down the stairs and through the living room into the kitchen.

Maria turned, said good morning, then asked if he and Sarah were hungry.

"I guess not," he said as he set his cup down.

A puzzled Maria watched him walk out the back door, and after staring at the closed door for a moment, she shrugged her shoulders and went about fixing breakfast that no one would eat.

The ride from the ranch to the rock formation filled Sarah with excitement, hoping she could catch a happy moment from the past to hang onto during the coming ordeal. Wade, on the other hand, thought about the breakfast he was missing as they rode in silence, letting the birds do most of the talking.

"There it is," said Wade.

She looked up, and at seeing the rocks and boulders in the distance, her face filled with a smile, and her eyes lit up. "Think it's still there?"

"Think what's still there?"

"The cabin," she replied irritably, wondering where his mind was.

He thought of another rock formation the day he, Seth Bowlen, Gil Robinson, and Frank Wells, rode into Stewart's Revenge. "Probably not."

Sarah's excitement turned to disappointment, but she remained hopeful as they rode toward the big rock formation. A solitary whippoorwill sang out, and buzzing grasshoppers filled the stillness of horse's hooves against the hard, red, sandy soil. As they approached the giant rock formation that dwarfed them, Sarah looked up at the various sizes and shapes of boulders. Several were larger than wagons and some taller than a two-story house, and she wondered how they got here in the middle of the prairie.

Pulling their horses up at the base of a large boulder, Wade dismounted then helped Sarah down from her horse. Excited at finding the cabin, she took Wade's hand as they led their horses into the shady maze of narrow canyons. Walking into an opening, she stopped, shaded her eyes with one hand, and looked up at the giant boulders. "It's so quiet."

Wade paused to look up but said nothing as they continued their walk through the maze of rocks and boulders. Turning a corner, they came upon the place she had wanted to find, and as Sarah stared in disappointment at what remained of the old cabin, she fought her tears. Only one wall remained, and it was leaning against the rock wall of a cliff. The rest of the cabin of gray, weathered wood and rusty nails were strewn about as if a whirlwind had visited. The rusty potbellied stove someone once used for warmth and cooking stood in what used to be the corner of the cabin, its rusty metal chimney lying with the gray weathered wood.

Staring at the pile of rubble, Sarah thought of that day long ago when she rode out to find Wade, knowing that he and Emmett Spears were riding line for the Circle T searching for strays. While Emmett Spears said goodbye and rode toward the Circle T wearing that silly grin of his, she and Wade rode their horses at a walk while they talked about this or that. They had only ridden a short distance when a horrible summer storm suddenly appeared, filled with lightning and blowing rain that chased them across the prairie to this little cabin, where they took shelter.

A screech from a magpie broke the stillness interrupting Sarah's memory, and as she looked up into the blue sky, the bird disappeared over the boulders. She stared at the destroyed cabin in disappointment as her memory found the sound of frightened horses and thunder that shook the fragile walls of the cabin. She remembered Wade wrestling with the horses he had brought inside, crowding the tiny cabin. She took in a breath and let out a sigh. "When you were gone," she began in a soft voice, "I would sit in my room or on the front porch wondering if I'd ever see you again." She glanced back at him with a shy smile. "I often thought of this place." Her eyes suddenly welled. "It was here that I first knew I loved you with all heart." Turning away, she wiped her red, welling eyes, fearing this afternoon when they ride into Harper. Her voice quivered. "Foolish memories, I suppose."

Wade looked at the back of her head and ponytail wondering if his coming back had been the right thing to do. Perhaps she might be better off had he stayed away and let her build another life, and now he may hang for what he had to do to protect her. He reached out and touched her ponytail with his fingertips. "I knew I loved you that first day in Harper when I almost knocked your mother down as I hurried out of Mason's store."

Fighting back the tears, she sniffled and chuckled as she wiped her cheeks. "Pa sure gave you what for."

Wade grinned with a furrowed brow, recalling the dirty look on Jasper Talbert's face. "That he did." Staring at the rubble, he thought of her father's death, the burial, and the fire set by the Hoskins men that almost claimed Sarah, their son, and her mother had it not been for Billy French. The hate he had carried for those responsible still lingered deep inside with the hate for the Bradley brothers, and he knew it always would.

She turned, took his hand, stood on her toes, and kissed his cheek. "I love you, Wade."

Looking into her brown eyes, he remembered that day in the abandoned cabin. Both were soaked from the rain, and he remembered her shivering as he took her into his arms and kissed her. He let go of the reins of the mare, took her in his arms, kissed her as he had that day, and held her while fearing the future.

Sarah began to cry as she pushed away, turned, and led her horse away from the rubble that once was a cabin.

Wade picked up the mare's reins, took one last look at what remained of the cabin, and followed her through the maze of boulders.

Reaching open ground, she stopped and stood next to her horse, staring off into the distance, considering their future and their children should their father be hung for murder. She wondered how she would tell them of such a thing.

Letting go of the mare's reins, Wade stood behind Sarah with his hands on her shoulders, his face next to the side of her head. "I'm sorry about everything, Sarah."

She turned her head, looked at him over her shoulder, and smiled. "You've done nothing to be sorry for, Wade. You only tried to protect us, and I'll always love you for that." Then she turned her head and looked back at the mountains in the distance.

"It's George Hoskins. I'd like to hear an apology from." She turned and smiled at him. "Thanks for bringing me here." Then stricken with panic, she began to cry as she looked up into his blue eyes. "Let's run away, Wade. We can pack up a wagon, gather the kids, and make a run for California where you'd be safe."

Wade looked into her welling eyes and pleading face loving her for what she suggested. But he thought of Elizabeth Purdy, the one death he regretted. "I can't run away from what I am any longer, Sarah."

She looked desperate. "But why?"

"I can't explain it to you, Sarah. Hell, I can't even explain it to myself. There's an accounting that's needed, and I have to be there."

Looking disappointed, she turned, filled with apprehension and fear of Wade's death, and looked at the Rocky Mountains in the distance. Afraid she was about to cry, Sara climbed on her horse. "We best get started back."

Harper, Colorado

Sheriff Harry Block was short in stature, and age brought with it some arthritis and a little extra weight he managed without too much trouble. He had been Sheriff of Harper for many years, and his once black hair was gray and thinning. His nose was slightly crooked, and his weathered face was tan. Gray bushy eyebrows sat above bloodshot brown eyes that looked up from the newspaper he was reading when the door opened. At first, he thought his old eyes were playing a trick on him, but then he smiled as he stood from his chair and hurried around the old desk with an open hand. "I never thought I'd lay eyes on you again."

Wade grinned as they shook hands. "I wasn't so sure myself, Harry. How've you been?"

"I've been fine." Letting go of Wade's hand, he turned to Sarah, smiled, and gave her a quick hug. "Hello, darl'n."

Sarah smiled. "It's good to see you, Harry."

Block noticed the man and lady standing behind them looking important. "You together?"

Wade turned. "Harry, this is my attorney, John Stirling, and his secretary Evelyn."

John extended his hand. "My pleasure, Sheriff Block. It looks like we'll be seeing one another a lot over the next few weeks."

Curious about that, Block shook the man's hand firmly. "Mr. Stirling." Then he looked at Evelyn, gently shook her hand, and then turned and offered the ladies the only two chairs in the place while apologizing for their condition. Harry waited until the ladies sat down, and then he looked at Wade. "I was hoping you'd

466

stay gone. There is still an open warrant out for you, and I get a regular visit from one of the deputy marshals in Denver, asking if I've heard anything."

"That's precisely why we're here," said Stirling.

"Oh?" replied Harry looking curious. Then he looked at Wade. "You come to give yourself up?"

"I have," said Wade.

Harry looked at Wade. "I wish you'd stayed where ever it was you ran off to, son." Then he looked at John Stirling. "The circuit judge won't be around for another two or three weeks."

"Who is the circuit judge?" asked Stirling.

"Judge Harold Palmer, from Denver."

John Stirling smiled and looked at Wade. "I know the man well. I'll speak to him when I return to Denver and see if we can get moving on a quick trial." He looked at the sheriff. "Is there a building in Harper large enough for a trial?" He grinned. "I have a feeling it will be crowded."

Block considered that. "The Blue Sky Saloon comes to mind."

Stirling grinned. "Sounds cozy. Now, if you'll take my client into custody, I'll treat Mrs. Garrison and my daughter to an early dinner before returning to Denver to talk to Judge Palmer."

Sheriff Block looked puzzled. "You want me to arrest Wade?"

Stirling looked at Block. "You said there was a warrant for his arrest."

"Well," began the Sheriff, "yeah, but I never really considered arresting a man that was once a United States Deputy Marshal." He looked at Wade. "And a damn good one, at that."

Wade smiled at Harry.

"Well," said Stirling, "I'm sure your opinion will weigh heavily on the court, but for now, my client will be better off in your cozy little jail than in a Denver jail. Once he's taken to Denver, it will be difficult to move the trial back to Harper. I believe our chances for an acquittal are better here where people know Mr. Garrison instead of in Denver where he isn't known except by reputation."

"All right," said Harry with some reluctance, then he opened the top drawer of his desk and took out the keys to the cell doors. "This way, Wade."

Wade turned to Sarah, who looked worried. "I'll be fine, Sarah. Try and explain things to Emmett and make sure Pup doesn't run off to look for me."

She hugged him, kissed his cheek, and then watched while Sheriff Block escorted him into one of the two cells and locked the door. As Wade turned and put his hands on the bars, Sarah stepped toward them and placed her hands on his with welling eyes.

John Stirling gently took Sarah's arm. "Come, Mrs. Garrison. We've some planning to do." He looked at Wade. "When I get to Denver, I'll file a motion or two, then my daughter and I will pack some things and move into a hotel here in Harper." He walked to the jailhouse door, opened it, and waited for Sarah, who stopped at the door, turned, and looked at Wade before she walked outside.

Wade stared at the closed door and then looked through the window watching the three walk past and then disappear.

Harry Block set a small table by the cell, set a checkerboard on it, then picked up a small stool, opened the cell, and handed it to Wade.

Figuring he had nothing else to do, Wade set the stool in front of the bars and sat down with his hands through the bars thinking he should have stayed in Pickering and played checkers with Jed.

"Penny a game?" asked Harry.

Wade tossed his hat on the cot. "You'll never get rich that way, Harry."

Block chuckled, wishing Wade had never come back to Harper.

Chapter 31

Three days passed, with Wade sitting in jail awaiting trial. John Stirling and his secretary, Evelyn, had moved into rooms at the Pratt Hotel, which was once the Hoskins Hotel. Stirling visited Wade daily while planning their strategies for the upcoming trial, which was to begin in two days.

On one such day, Attorney John Stirling was sitting in an uncomfortable straight back chair outside of Wade's cell while he sat on a stool. "I sent a wire to that marshal friend of yours from Santa Fe and Seth Bowlen from Sisters a couple of days ago. They should be here any day." Then John looked at the list of character witnesses he planned to call and showed it, Wade. "Can you think of anyone else?"

Wade went over the names, which included Levi Wagner, Tolliver Grimes, and a few hands at the Grimes ranch, Sam Carney, owner of the Blue Sky Saloon, Billy French, and Seth. The last name gave him pause. He looked up and lowered his voice. "Sheriff Harry Block?"

Stirling glanced at Block bent over his desk, reading the newspaper, and whispered, "See a problem with that? Remember, he said you were a damn good Marshal."

Wade looked at Harry for a moment that was sitting at his desk reading. "No, I guess not. It just seems strange having the man who arrested me on this list."

Stirling smiled, folded the paper, and shoved it into his suit pocket. "That's the point." He stood. "I have things to take care of, and we're running out of time. Judge Palmer will be here in a day, and then we'll select the jury." He put on his hat. "We'll talk again tomorrow."

Wade watched him leave, and then he lay down on his cot, staring up at the ceiling contemplating his fate, and with nothing else to do, he drifted off to sleep.

The sound of the jailhouse door opening and closing followed by heavy footsteps woke him. Lifting his head, he saw a figure in a tan Stetson and duster was standing in the middle of the room, looking through the bars of the cell. Recognizing Seth Bowlen, Wade grinned, stood from the cot, and walked to the bars of his cell.

Seth looked away from Wade to Sheriff Block. "Hello, Harry. Mind if I talk to your prisoner?"

Harry glanced at Wade before he nodded. "Go ahead. Just don't try anything. I'd hate to have to shoot you."

Seth chuckled as he walked to the cell and took Wade's outstretched hand, sticking between the bars, and shook it firmly.

"Hello, Seth," greeted Wade.

Letting go of Wade's hand, Seth glanced at the bars. "Maybe you should have stayed in Montana."

"Maybe," agreed Wade. "Guess we'll find out in a few days. When did you ride in?"

"A couple of hours ago. Been talking to that attorney fella of yours over at the hotel that sent for me." Bowlen looked regretful. "Wish I'd never found you and talked you into coming back."

"Don't lay this on yourself, Seth. It was my choice."

Seth moved closer to the bars. "They could hang you, boy; you know that?"

Wade nodded with a worried look. "That's a fact, Seth. But I chose the road to the Hoskins place last year, no one else, and I've no regrets about that." He paused, looking sad as he thought of

471

Elizabeth Purdy. "If they do hang me, in my mind, it'll be because of Elizabeth Purdy, not any of the others." He thought of her brother Tom Purdy. "I never meant that woman any harm."

Seth looked curious. "Mind telling me how that came about?"

Wade sighed softly and gently shrugged his shoulders. "Someone shot at me from the second-story window. I thought it was Old Man Hoskins. When I got to the top of the stairs, a door opened, I saw a figure pointing a rifle at me and fired." He paused and slowly shook his head, looking sorry. "I didn't know I had shot a woman until I walked into the bedroom."

"That why you wrapped her in a blanket and set her in the garden?"

Wade nodded slowly. "I didn't want her to burn with the house."

"Damn it, Wade. I sure wish I'd never found you."

"I didn't come back because of anything you said, Seth. I was thinking on that long before you ever stepped into Goody's place."

Bowlen wanted to believe that. "This John Stirling fella, do you think he's a good attorney?"

Wade looked worried. "Hope so. Seems like it, anyway." He smiled. "How's Molly?"

Seth grinned. "Sassy like always. Says hello to you and Sarah. She wanted to come, but I told her to stay home."

"I'm sure you did the right thing," said Wade. "Though Sarah would say otherwise." He looked at Seth. "I need to apologize for the way I acted towards you up in Pickering."

Seth gestured with his waving off the apology. "No need for that son. I put you in a bad spot."

Changing the subject, Wade smiled, looking proud. "Anyway, I got to see my daughter. She's a pretty little thing."

Seth smiled. "That she is." Then he turned to Harry, who was still sitting at his desk, reading the Denver newspaper he got each week. "You have any whiskey in that bottom drawer?"

Sheriff Block opened the drawer and set a full bottle of whiskey on his desk. "With or without coffee?"

"Without." Seth looked at Wade. "I need a drink." He turned away from the cell and walked to the two chairs in front of Harry's desk, took off his Stetson, set it on the edge of the desk, and then slipped out of his tan duster. After he laid it across one chair, he sat down in the other and watched while Harry poured his drink.

Harry looked at Wade. "Sorry, Wade, but you being under arrest and all…"

"Think nothing of it, Harry," interrupted Wade. "I'll have a drink after the trial if they don't hang me." He paused. "Maybe two if they do."

Seth and Harry chuckled at Wade's sense of humor then passed the time talking of old times while drinking a quarter of the bottle of whiskey. When Seth finished his last drink, he stood, gathered his things, and thanked Harry. Feeling a little drunk, he put on his hat and walked a crooked path to Wade's cell, shrugged into his duster, and looked at Wade, lying on his cot. "I'm going to get something to eat. I'll stop by later?"

Wade smiled and thanked him for coming, then watched him walk out the door. He looked at the clock, thinking it was getting close to Sarah's visit, hoping she didn't forget to bring Pup.

The Trial of Wade Garrison

It was ten in the morning when Sheriff Harry Block and a deputy escorted a handcuffed Wade Garrison into the already crowded Blue Sky Saloon and set him down at a table next to his attorney, John Stirling. Wade settled into the chair and sat back, facing another table occupied by Judge Harold Palmer, facing him and the spectators. Several rows of chairs occupied by the curious filled the room from just behind the table where Wade and Stirling were sitting all the way back to the bar.

Wade glanced around the noisy room of unfamiliar and familiar faces, including Levi Wagner, Tolliver Grimes, and several of the Circle T cowhands. The small town of Harper had never witnessed anything like this in its history. Every step of the stairs leading to the second floor was occupied, every chair taken, and every space where someone could stand was taken. Spectators leaned over the railing of the second-floor balcony; their faces filled with excitement as they stared down at the man on trial and whispered of the things he was accused of doing.

The low, noisy rumble of inaudible voices filling the room suddenly became quiet as heads turned to the swinging doors where Sarah Garrison stood with her arm around her young son. Tolliver rose from his chair, hurried over, took her arm in his, and walked them past the table where Wade and John Stirling were sitting. As she and Wade exchanged looks, she noticed his handcuffed hands and felt her eyes begin to well. Emmett could not take his eyes off of the handcuffs that his pa tried to hide but failed to do so.

Two men sitting behind Wade stood, took off their hats, and gestured to their chairs.

Sarah smiled and thanked them for their kindness, then gently pushed Emmett toward the two empty chairs and sat down while Tolliver returned to his seat behind her.

Wade turned in his chair, smiled at Sarah, and winked at his son as if telling him everything would be alright.

Judge Palmer was a heavyset man of fifty with a thin mustache and very little of his once-black hair left to comb. He pounded the table with his gavel as he glanced around the room with a determined look. "These proceedings are now in order." He looked toward the bartender, Sam Carney. "That means the bar is closed, bartender."

Sam nodded, began picking up dirty beer mugs and wiping the bar down with an already damp cloth.

Palmer looked at Wade and then Stirling. "Will the defendant please rise while the charges are read?"

Both Wade and his attorney stood facing the Judge's table.

Judge Palmer ordered a clerk he brought with him from Denver to read the charges of twenty-two counts of murder, including that of a woman, Elizabeth Purdy. When he finished, the judge asked Wade if he understood the charges.

Wade nodded. "I do your honor."

"Then how do you plead?" asked the judge.

Wade glanced at the jury of eight men and then at the judge. "Not guilty."

The noise level suddenly raised, which irritated Judge Palmer. He pounded his gavel and looked at the crowd angrily. "If you can't keep quiet, I'll empty the place." Silence quickly filled the big room as Palmer told Wade and John Stirling to sit down. The Judge glanced around the crowded room and then looked at the jury. "You eight gentlemen have been chosen to listen to what is said under oath in these proceedings and render your verdict of either guilty or not guilty. That is to be accomplished by what evidence and witness testimony and not what you feel or imagine. Your feelings have nothing to do with this case, and it is the evidence presented that you must use to determine guilt or innocence. Now, as the judge, I will be questioning the witnesses after the defense finishes." He looked at Stirling, pounded his gavel, and said, "Call your first witnesses."

The first to be called was Seth Bowlen, who stood from a chair in the back row, made his way to the chair next to the judge's table, and stood facing the crowd and the table where Wade and Stirling were sitting. A man held a bible so that Seth could put his left hand on it, and then he told him to raise his right hand, asking if he swore to tell the whole truth and nothing but the truth, so help him, God.

"I do," said Seth.

"Have a seat," said the Judge.

John Stirling stood and walked around the table, standing next to Seth. "State your name."

"Seth Bowlen."

"And what is your occupation, Mr. Bowlen?"

"I'm Sheriff of Sisters, Colorado."

Stirling asked Seth to tell the court why he asked for help from a United States Marshal in Santa Fe instead of the United States Marshal in Denver.

Seth sat back and told of the killings in Sisters, his attempt to have the men responsible arrested by the marshal in Denver, but met nothing but resistance. When his frustration reached a boiling point, he sent a telegram to an old friend, Billy French, the US Marshal in Santa Fe. Seth looked at the judge. "Marshal French sent his deputy, Wade Garrison." Then he told of how he and Wade arrested Pete Hoskins and a Harper deputy by the name of Lee Jones in Harper for those murders and took them back to Sisters to stand trial.

Palmer leaned forward, looking interested. "Did you say, Deputy Lee Jones?"

Seth nodded. "Yes, sir."

The judge wrote that down, and then he asked, "Did these men stand trial in Sisters, Sheriff Bowlen, and if so, were they found guilty?"

Seth shook his head. "No, sir, they did not." Then he told of George Hoskins visiting his son, Pete, the same day a group of men broke Pete and the deputy out of jail.

The judge leaned forward, giving Seth a puzzled look. "Are you saying George Hoskins broke his son and this deputy out of your jail?"

"Yes, sir," said Seth. "That's what I'm saying."

476

The noise level suddenly increased, and Judge Palmer pounded his gavel on the table and shouted, "Silence!" Then he looked at Seth. "Can you prove that?"

"No, sir, but…"

Palmer interrupted as he looked at the jury. "The jury will disregard that statement since the witness can't prove the allegation." He looked at Seth. "Only stick to what you know as fact, and have proof of, Mr. Bowlen. Please, go on."

Seth nodded his understanding. "Yes, sir. Well, after the jailbreak, Pete hid out on the Hoskins Ranch." He looked at Wade, then at the judge. "We considered riding out to the ranch but were sorely outnumbered and figured we'd meet stiff resistance."

The judge wrote something on the paper in front of him. "Continue."

Before Seth could continue, Marshal Billy French pushed through the swinging doors wearing his black hat and black duster, looking like he had just ridden into town. Seth turned and stared at Billy as he quietly walked past and nodded on his way to the back of the room where he stood next to the bar, turned, and looked at Seth.

Judge Palmer also watched French as he walked past the witness chair, nodding to Seth. "Do you know this man?"

Seth turned and looked at the judge. "Yes, sir. That's United States Marshal Billy French."

Attorney John Stirling looked at Judge Palmer. "Marshal French is a witness for the defense, Your Honor. He must have just arrived from Santa Fe."

Judge Palmer looked at Billy. "Is that correct, sir?"

Billy stepped away from the bar he was leaning against and looked past the crowd. "Yes, sir, I just rode in."

Palmer looked at Seth. "Continue, Mr. Bowlen."

Seth continued by telling all that happened the weeks after that and then began to tell what he and Tolliver Grimes found at the Hoskins Ranch.

Judge Palmer stopped him. "I'll recall you at a later time for that business, Mr. Bowlen. I'd like to keep that until after we hear everything that happened up to that point." He smiled. "I like to hear things in the order as they happened. You're excused." The judge looked at Stirling. "Call your next witness."

John Stirling called Sheriff Harry Block, who, after he was sworn in, told how the town council forced him into hiring Hoskins' men as deputies, one named Booth Fox, a good friend of Pete Hoskins, and a man named Lee Jones. "They worked for George Hoskins, Your Honor." Then Block quickly pointed out that most of the council members left Harper shortly after George Hoskins was killed, avoiding the word murdered, hoping that would help Wade. "Like fleas jumping off a dog."

Laughter filled the room, causing the judge to pound the table with his gavel. As the laughter faded, he leaned in his chair toward Block. "I'm curious about that, Sheriff. Did you speak up about this or complain to the council?"

Harry scoffed. "Damn right, but it did little good. I eventually ended up quitting only to be hired back at a later date."

Judge Palmer wrote on the paper, and then he looked at Block. "Could you elaborate for us?"

Block looked at the judge.

"Tell us why," said Palmer.

Block glanced at Wade, then Seth, and then looked at the judge, thinking of Booth Fox resisting arrest and being shot by Wade. "A sudden vacancy came up."

Laughter filled the room, and Judge Palmer hit his gavel on the table, asking for silence. "Go on."

Sheriff Block glanced around at the faces of the crowd, grinned at the judge, and then continued by telling about the fight between Jasper Talbert and his deputy, Booth Fox, over a comment Deputy Fox made to Talbert's daughter, the wife of Wade Garrison.

Judge Palmer looked at Block with a curious look. "Do you know what it was that this Booth Fox said to Mrs. Garrison?

Block looked at Sarah, then Wade, and then at the Judge. "No, sir, not for sure, but whatever it was, it caused her pa, Jasper Talbert, a man in his sixties, to attack a much younger man and knock the daylights out of him."

Parker thought on that a moment. "In your opinion, Sheriff Block, was there a vendetta against the Garrison family?"

Harry frowned in thought. "I can't say for sure. I think Booth Fox had his eye on Mrs. Garrison, but she ignored him." He smiled while looking at Sarah. "Ain't too many men in Harper intelligent enough to exchange words with the likes of Sarah Garrison." He looked at the judge. "Booth Fox was at the bottom of that list."

Laughter filled the room once again, and Judge Palmer pounded his gavel, yelling silence, then asked Harry Block to continue.

Block continued his story, telling of Jasper being shot in the back an hour after the incident while driving the wagon home and that the wagon overturned. He looked at Sarah. "Mrs. Garrison was injured, as was little Emmett whose leg was broken, and both suffered concussions." He looked at Emmett. "The boy was unconscious for several days." He paused, looking at Sarah. "Mrs. Garrison was with child at the time and lost it."

Judge Palmer looked at Sarah. "You have my sympathy, Mrs. Garrison."

Sarah smiled softly and nodded her thanks.

Palmer looked at the clock behind the bar and then at his pocket watch. "I think I've heard enough for one day. It's after two, and I'm hungry." He looked at the jury. "You are not allowed to discuss this case with anyone other than yourselves. If you do, I will fine each of you heavily and toss your butts in jail for the next thirty days." He hit the table with his gavel. "Court's in recess until nine A.M. tomorrow morning." Then as he stood, he said, "Bar's open."

When Judge Palmer called the court in session the second morning, Billy French was called to the stand and sworn in. As he sat down, he looked at Wade, smiled slightly, and then watched John Stirling as he walked around the table toward him.

Stirling paused a few feet away. "State your name, please, and what your line of work is."

"Billy French, United States Marshal in Santa Fe, New Mexico."

"Thank you," said Stirling. "Now, you were in Harper prior, and during the alleged killings at the Hoskins ranch, were you not, Marshal French?"

Billy nodded. "Yes, I was."

"Would you please tell the court why you were in Harper?"

Billy told of getting a telegram from Seth's deputy that suggested Seth and Wade needed help. "So, I hopped the next train out of Santa Fe to Sisters and rode the rest of the way to Harper on my horse."

John Stirling looked at Billy. "Please tell the court what you discovered."

Billy turned slightly in his chair and looked at the judge and jury. "Sheriff Seth Bowlen and United States Deputy Wade Garrison were trying to figure out a way to get Pete Hoskins off of the ranch without starting a small war." He went on to tell how they had devised a plan to do just that, but before they could arrest him, Pete Hoskins and two of his friends made a break for Oregon. He told of the chase, of being bushwhacked, and of Seth and him getting wounded. He looked at Judge Palmer. "Me and Sheriff Bowling returned to the Double J Ranch while Wade proceeded alone after the suspects."

Judge Palmer leaned on the table. "Did the defendant catch up with the men?"

Billy nodded. "At a town called Whisper Creek."

The judge looked at John Stirling. "If you don't mind, counselor, and this has no bearing on the charges before the court, but I'd like to hear direct from Mr. Garrison what happened at Whisper Creek if he is willing to share that with us."

John Stirling stood next to Wade's chair, bent down, and whispered to him.

Wade nodded.

Stirling looked at the judge. "My client is willing to tell the court, your honor."

The Judge excused Billy telling him he was still under oath, then Wade took the stand and was sworn in. He looked at Judge Palmer and told of the gunfight in the Whisper Creek Saloon and Pete Hoskins escaping into the darkness. "Two days later, I tracked him into a canyon where Pete ambushed me. I managed to climb above Hoskins, and when a gunfight broke out between the two of us, Pete fell over the cliff." He glanced around. "I wanted to bring the man in alive, and it wasn't my bullet that killed him. Pete Hoskins tripped and fell from the cliff, and that's how he died. I brought his body back to Harper, draped over the saddle of his horse." Wade looked regretful. "I didn't want to kill another of Mr. Hoskins' sons."

The court suddenly erupted in low rumbles of surprise.

Judge Palmer rapped on his mallet, leaned forward, and looked at Wade. "Are you telling this court that you killed another son of George Hoskins?"

Wade nodded, "Yes, sir, I am."

Judge Palmer looked puzzled. "When did this killing take place?"

Wade sat back in the chair. "Dan Hoskins and I had some words over a pup I had in Sisters five or six years ago. Dan Hoskins tried to shot me in the back, but the bullet only grazed me. I turned, drew my gun, got off a shot, and killed him."

481

Palmer studied Wade for a moment. "Were there witnesses to this shooting?"

"Yes sir, several, among them was Seth Bowlen, Pete Hoskins, the younger brother, and several men in the city of Sisters."

"Was your attorney aware of this?"

Wade nodded. "Yes, sir. Mr. Stirling told me to tell the court about this incident just before I took the stand." He looked at Palmer. "Because of the incident in Sisters, it was important to me to bring Pete Hoskins in alive."

"I must say," said the judge. "I find this all very interesting, Mr. Garrison." Then he looked at Stirling. "Are any of those that were present during the gunfight in the saloon in the town of Whisper Creek on your list?"

Stirling thought a moment. "No, sir."

The judge smiled at Stirling without humor. "You may have to get some."

He looked at Wade. "Who examined the body?"

Doc Granger stood. "I did, Your Honor."

Judge Palmer looked at Granger. "Tell the court the cause of Mr. Pete Hoskins death."

Granger glanced at Wade and then looked at the judge. "The defendant told me that Pete Hoskins fell off a cliff, and I had no reason to doubt that because the injuries were consistent with such a fall."

Judge Palmer thanked Doc Granger, wrote on his paper, excused Wade, and re-called Billy French to the stand who went on to tell of the raid on the Double J by several hooded men carrying torches. The house, bunkhouse, and barn set on fire, and a young drover by the name of Billy Haroldson shot in the back. "The downstairs was on fire," said Billy. "And there was no way out. Though I was wounded in the leg, I managed to help Mrs. Garrison, her mother, young Emmett, and two dogs out of the window to the porch roof and then down the trellis of the porch."

He paused, looking angry. "That's when two bastards rode up and started shooting at Mrs. Garrison, her son, and Mrs. Talbert, Sarah's ma. I fired back, hitting one, and they rode off."

"If I may ask," said Palmer, "where was the defendant, Mr. Garrison, during this?"

Billy looked at Wade. "He and Seth were attempting to arrest this Lee Jones right here in this very saloon."

"Were they successful?" asked the judge.

"Not exactly, Judge," said Billy bringing some laughter from the crowd.

Palmer gave the crowd a dirty look and then looked at Billy. "Can you elaborate?"

"Lee made the mistake of drawing down on Wade." He glanced at Wade. "He had no choice but to kill Lee Jones." He looked around. "I believe Sam Carney saw the whole thing."

Palmer turned the paper over and wrote on the other side. "Continue."

"We found out later that Doc Granger patched up one of the Hoskins' men claiming it was an accident out at the Hoskins Ranch."

The room filled with soft voices while the judge wrote on the paper, and then he looked at Marshal French. "Do you have anything else to add?"

French shook his head no but quickly added. "Only that I believe these men who worked for George Hoskins were trying to kill Wade Garrison's family in retribution of Wade killing his two sons."

Judge Palmer looked at the jury. "You'll disregard the last statement of Marshal French. There's no proof these men worked for George Hoskins." Then he looked at French. "You're excused."

As Billy stood, the judge stood calling for a two-hour recess.

Two hours later, Judge Harold Palmer pounded his gavel on the desk calling the court to order. He impatiently waited for the crowd to quiet down, then he looked at Stirling. "Would you re-call your witness, Seth Bowlen, back to the stand?"

Stirling called Seth, who took the witness chair. "You're still under oath, Mr. Bowlen," warned the judge.

"Yes, sir."

Judge Palmer leaned on his elbows, looking at Seth. "Would you describe what you and this Tolliver Grimes found the day you rode out to the Hoskins Ranch?"

Seth described the smoldering lumber of the big house, the bunkhouse, and the bodies lying about the place.

"I understand a woman was also shot and killed," said Judge Palmer. "A housekeeper, I believe."

Seth nodded. "Yes, sir. Elizabeth Purdy was shot once in the chest. Someone wrapped her in a blanket and set her in one of the white, wooden lawn chairs in the garden. At first, I thought she was sleeping, but upon closer inspection, we saw that she was dead from the gunshot wound."

"By we, you're referring to Mr. Tolliver Grimes?"

"Yes, sir."

"Was she shot through the blanket?"

"No, sir." Seth shrugged, looking uncertain. "It appeared to me that whoever shot her didn't want to leave her inside the burning house." He paused. "Sort of like he regretted what happened to the lady."

Harold Palmer leaned forward. "That's purely speculation on your part, Sheriff." Then he turned and told the Jury to disregard that last comment and looked back at Seth. "Did you find anyone alive?"

Seth shook his head. "No, sir. Everyone was pretty much dead."

Palmer looked thoughtful. "Then, there are no witnesses?"

"No, sir. None."

484

Palmer sat back in his chair, looking thoughtful. "Thank you, Sheriff." He looked down at his notes and then at Stirling. "Your witness, counselor."

"I have no more questions of Mr. Bowlen."

"You may step down," said Judge Palmer, then he looked at Stirling. "No need in calling Tolliver Grimes to the stand unless he disputes what Mr. Bowlen has just told the court."

John Stirling looked at Tolliver, who simply shook his head and said, "There's nothing I want to dispute."

In the stillness of the room while John Stirling looked over his notes. Moments later, he looked at the judge. "I have nothing further at this time, Your Honor."

"Well," said Judge Palmer, "I guess that takes us to the charges of the killing of George Hoskins in his hotel room last year." He looked at the clock on the wall behind the bar and then at his pocket watch. "I'm going to call it a day. We'll get to the killing of George Hoskins tomorrow morning at nine." He looked at the jury. "You are still prohibited from talking about this to anyone." Then he picked up his gavel and pounded on the table. "Bar's open," which was followed by sounds of skidding chairs, shuffling feet, and loud talking.

Chapter 32

Judge Palmer sat down at the table, looked at the clock behind the Blue Sky Saloon's bar, and then at his pocket watch. Seeing it was nine AM sharp, he pounded his gavel, glanced at the faces of the spectators, looked at Sheriff Block, and asked him to stand. "Your investigation early on into the killing of George Hoskins in his hotel room lists a Levi Wagner."

Wade suddenly became worried.

Block stood. "Yes, sir. I did talk with Levi, as I did a lot of people."

The judge looked over the crowd. "Is Mr. Wagner present?"

Levi stood. "Right here, you're honor."

The judge gestured to the witness chair. "Please take a seat, Mr. Wagner, so that I can ask you a couple of questions for the state."

Levi hitched up his oversized pants and made his way to the witness chair, where he took the oath before sitting down.

Harold Palmer studied the dirty little man who owned the livery. "Please tell the court what occurred in your livery on the day George Hoskins was murdered?"

Levi looked confused. "What do you mean, Judge?"

He looked down at the paper on his desk. "I see here that you told the sheriff that you were visited by the defendant, Wade Garrison, the night before."

Levi glanced at Wade, Sheriff Block, and then looked at the judge. "Yes, sir, I was. But I didn't think that was a secret. He was badly hurt, I sewed him up, and then he spent the night in the loft of the livery."

Judge Palmer looked puzzled. "Badly hurt, you say?"

"Yes, sir."

"Please elaborate, Mr. Wagner."

Levi stared at the judge with a puzzled expression.

"How was Mr. Garrison hurt?" asked the Judge.

"He'd been shot twice. Someone up in Wyoming fixed him up, but the stitches tore out, and he was bleeding." Levi looked at Wade then turned to the Judge. "Looked to me like he was about to pass out."

"Did you say Wyoming?" asked Palmer.

"Yes, sir."

Palmer looked at Wade. "When was that?"

Wade considered the question. "Two, three days, before I rode into Levi's place, I think. I'm not sure."

Palmer looked at Levi. "Did you send for a doctor?"

Levi considered that a moment and then shook his head. "No, sir, I didn't."

"And why was that?" asked the Judge.

Wade remembered telling Levi not to send for the doctor.

Levi thought for another moment. "Well," said Levi. "I've fixed many gunshots over the years and sewn up lots of cuts in men and horses. I even sewed up my own right leg up once."

Soft laughter filled the saloon.

"It was late, and I figured I could handle it." He grinned. "And I did."

As the saloon roared with laughter Judge Palmer rapped his gavel on the top of the table and glance around at the crowd. "Any more of this, and I'll have you all escorted out."

The laughter quickly faded as Palmer turned to Levi. "When did Mr. Garrison leave your establishment?"

Levi looked at the judge in thought. "Real early the next morning, as I recall."

"Did you see which way he rode out of town?"

Levi frowned, shaking his head slowly from side to side. "No, sir. After he left, I went back inside the livery."

"Did you hear the shot that killed Mr. Hoskins?"

Levi Wagner looked puzzled. "I thought everyone did."

Laughter filled the room, and Judge Palmer rapped his gavel on the table and shouted. "Silence!" As the noise settled, he looked at Levi. "But you never saw who fired the shot. Is that correct?"

Wagner shook his head. "No, sir. I stayed inside my livery."

Judge Palmer looked at John Stirling. "Your witness."

John looked at the jury while he asked Levi, "Did the defendant ever once ask, or tell you to keep quiet or lie for him?"

Wagner shook his head. "No, sir, he never did."

Stirling smiled. "Did you ever hear him say that he was going to kill George Hoskins?"

Levi shook his head slowly. "No, sir."

Stirling returned to his chair next to Wade. "Thank you, Mr. Wagner."

Judge Palmer looked at Levi. "You're excused." Then he looked at Sheriff Block. "You found no one who witnessed the killing of George Hoskins?"

Harry stood. "No, sir."

Quiet filled the room while Judge Palmer looked down at his notes, and after several minutes he turned in his chair and looked at the jury. "It appears you have heard all the witnesses and evidence against the defendant. I am adjourning for today and sequestering you to a room upstairs for the night so you can deliberate on a verdict."

One of the men raised his hand. "What's that mean, Judge?"

"It means you'll be fed and locked in the room where you will sit down and discuss everything you have heard here until you reach a verdict of either guilty or not guilty."

The man lowered his hand, looking disappointed.

Judge Palmer pounded his gavel on the table. "Court's adjourned."

John Stirling and his daughter, Evelyn, were eating dinner in Stirling's room when a knock came at the door. He wiped his mouth with his napkin, got up, and opened the door, surprised at seeing Judge Harold Palmer.

Harold smiled. "Got a minute, John?"

Stirling stepped back. "Come in."

When the judge saw Evelyn, he quickly apologized. "I didn't mean to interrupt your dinner."

"We were about done," said Stirling.

Palmer smiled at Stirling's daughter. "Hello, Evelyn. How are you?"

She smiled. "I'm fine, Judge, thank you." Then she stood. "I'll let you gentlemen talk."

Harold watched her leave the room, and then looking troubled, sat down.

"What's on your mind?" asked Stirling as he sat down across from the judge.

Palmer stared at the floor for several moments, and then he looked at John Stirling. "I knew George Hoskins for many years, and he was a self-indulging bastard, and he was the same with both of his sons. Those two boys were trouble from the start." He looked at John. "There's not enough evidence to convict Wade Garrison of any one of these crimes. And to be honest, I have a strong feeling that your client did kill those men and George to protect his family. Hell, I can't say I wouldn't have done the same. However, there's no real evidence against him, and this whole thing should never have come to trial. Those warrants should never have been issued without proof." He sighed. "You can't try a man for what you think he did and expect a conviction."

"How did they get issued, then?" asked John.

Palmer shrugged, looking irritated. "A friendly judge, no doubt and that little shit United States Marshal. I always suspected he was on Hoskins payroll."

"Well," said Stirling thoughtfully, "I guess it's up to those eight men."

"It should never have come this far." Palmer paused and looked at Stirling. "I wonder how many of those eight men on the jury were friends of the Hoskins family."

John looked concerned. "I hope none."

Palmer smiled. "I shouldn't admit this being a judge, but so do I." Then he looked at Stirling. "Colorado's a state now, and things have changed. We can't have our law enforcement making deals and taking money from rich, powerful men. I plan on writing Washington asking for them to send someone out and investigate the actions of that piss ant Marshal and the judge that's involved." Then he stood. "He clears the son of murder but goes after another man for protecting his own family. Disgraceful. See you in court tomorrow John."

Judge Harold Palmer used his gavel to call the court to order at two PM on the second day of the jury deliberation. As the room quieted, he looked at Wade and then at the eight-man jury. "Has the jury reached a verdict?"

The foreman of the jury stood. "Yes, Judge, we have."

Judge Palmer looked at Wade. "Please stand Mr. Garrison to hear the verdict of the jury."

Wade stood with his wrists handcuffed, glanced back at a worried Sarah, and then looked at the foreman of the jury.

"How do you find the defendant?" asked Palmer.

The foreman glanced at the other jurors and then looked at the judge. "The eight of us have gone over all of the evidence,

490

your honor, just as you told us, and as far as the two men Marshal was trying to arrest, it's plain they resisted and would have killed him, so we think he had no choice in the matter."

"Very well," said the Judge. "And the charges of killing several Hoskins men and setting fire to the ranch?"

"Well, we all agree that there's no evidence to that neither, your honor. There's no one to say who was at the Hoskins Ranch that night and killed all of those men."

Palmer stared at the jury. "Very well. And the death of Elizabeth Purdy."

"The same Judge. There's no one to tell who it was that killed that poor soul."

"And of the last charge, the death of George Hoskins?"

The foreman shrugged his shoulders. "Well, we ain't heard of anyone seeing him do that neither."

Judge Palmer looked at Wade and then at the foreman. "Then you eight men find the defendant not guilty on all accounts, is that right?"

The foreman looked at the other jurors and nodded. "I guess we do."

"So be it," said Judge Palmer rapping his gavel on the desk. Then he looked at Wade and hit the table with his gavel once again. "You're a free man, Mr. Garrison."

The room erupted with cheering while Wade shook John Stirling's hand amid pats on the back from those around him. As he turned to find Sarah, someone yelled, "Gun!" Wade turned, seeing the barrel of a pistol pointed at his face, and the man holding it yell, "You Bastard!"

Tolliver Grimes grabbed the man's arm just before he pulled the trigger, and as the gun exploded in a puff of white smoke, Wade tumbled backward, shot in the left chest.

Sarah screamed Wade's name as she tried to get to him, but she and Emmett were pushed to one side. Several men, including

Tolliver Grimes, wrestled for control of the gun the man held tightly in his hand as he kept yelling, "Bastards!"

Emmett fell over a chair letting go of his mother's hand. Sarah tried to get to him, but the crowd kept pushing her toward the door. Billy appeared out of nowhere, picked him up, and escorted Sarah and the boy to where Wade lay while the mob yelled profanities wanting to hang the man who had just shot Wade.

Tolliver and Sheriff Block finally subdued the man and took his gun.

Seth, Levi, and several others pushed people away from Wade, then Seth knelt next to him and yelled, "Give him room to breathe!"

Sarah managed to push her way through the crowd and knelt beside Seth, looking at her husband.

Wade looked confused and dazed as he glanced at the faces of those standing over him. Seeing Sarah next to him, he smiled and moved his lips, but nothing came out except the tiny line of blood trickling from the side of his mouth.

Doc Granger pushed his way through the crowd, knelt beside him, and put his face close to Wade's. "Can you hear me, Wade?"

He looked at Doc Granger with a blank yet terror-filled stare. Granger looked up and yelled above the noise, "We need to get him to my office!"

"Let me through!" yelled Sam Carney as he made his way through the crowd carrying a bench.

Sarah stood, stepped back, and watched as four men lifted Wade onto the bench. Tears streamed down her face as she took Emmett's hand and followed the men carrying Wade out of the saloon. Catching up to her husband lying on the board the men carried, she took Wade's hand and kept repeating his name while he stared up at her as if in shock, then his eyes closed.

Fearing he had died, Sarah screamed his name.

Reaching Doc Granger's place, they lifted Wade off the bench and put the unconscious Wade on a table while Doc rushed everyone out except Sarah. Looking down at Emmett, Granger told her that it would be best if she took the crying boy and stepped out of the room.

Doc Granger's wife hurried into the room, asking if she could help.

Granger looked from Sarah, standing like a statue, staring at Wade to his wife, telling her to cut Wade's shirt off.

Blinking from her daze, Sarah took Emmett's hand and pulled him to the door and out of the examining room into the living room. Stopping for a moment, she glanced around, and then seeing Billy and Seth, she pulled her son by his hand across the room and told him to wait with Billy.

"How is he?" asked Seth

"I don't know." Then she hurried back into the examining room.

Doc looked at her wet face and red, welling eyes when she returned. "If you can take what I need to do, you can stay. If not, it'd be best if you waited outside."

"I'll be okay," she said with tears running down her cheeks. Filled with the fear and thought of losing her husband, she stared at Wade, feeling helpless as she watched in silence while Doc Granger worked on him.

Mrs. Granger was at her side, gently took her by the arm and sat her down in a chair across the room. "Sit here, Mrs. Garrison. Let my husband do what's needed." Then she hurried to assist her husband.

The living room and front porch of Doc Granger's place were packed with people waiting to hear about Wade. Little Emmett was sitting between Billy French and Seth Bowlen, in silence looking frightened, his cheeks wet with tears, his head resting on Seth's side. People sat in what few chairs there were, so Tolliver Grimes and John Stirling stood against the wall near the door where Doc Granger worked on Wade. Several other men, including Levi Wagner, were walking around the room, looking upset. The front door was open, and soft voices of those crowding the porch and yard made their way into the house.

It seemed forever for those who quietly waited for news of Wade Garrison, and when the door finally opened, and Doc Granger stepped into the crowded room drying his hands with a white towel, the room went quiet as death. He glanced around at the eager faces, each afraid to ask the question they all wanted to know the answer to.

Tolliver stood away from the wall. "How is he, Doc?"

Granger looked concerned. "He's alive."

Whispers of relief flowed through the room.

Granger glanced around. "The bullet missed the heart but punctured the edge of his lung."

Everyone looked worried once again.

Doc sounded positive but cautious. "We'll know for sure in the morning." He looked at Tolliver Grimes. "Sarah asked if you'd take Emmett to your place and send word to her housekeeper that she will be spending the night next to her husband."

Tolliver nodded. "Sure thing, Doc." He walked over to Emmett, reached down, and took his hand. "Come on, son. Let's go see your grandmother."

Emmett wiped his face, took Mr. Grimes' hand, and stood while looking at Doc Granger. "Is Pa gonna be alright?"

Doc looked down at the pitiful lad. "We sure hope so, son. I'm doing everything I can to see that he will be. Now you go on with your grandpa."

Tolliver and Emmett made their way through the crowd and headed to the Circle T and Emmett's grandmother.

Doc looked around at the others. "You may as well go home. Nothing you can do here." He paused. "It's in God's hands now."

Wearing the fear on their faces that Wade may die, Seth Bowlen and Billy French left Doc Granger's place and headed for the Sheriff's Office.

Harry was at his desk talking to his new deputy as they stepped inside and walked past the cell holding the man that shot Wade, sitting on the cot in his cell, staring down at the floor.

Billy walked toward Harry's desk while Seth, on the other hand, paused a moment longer, looking at the bruises on the man's face and swollen eyes. Having no pity for the man, he walked over to the cell and looked at the man. "What's your name?"

He looked up. "James Robertson."

Seth gripped the bars turning his knuckles white. "If Wade Garrison dies, you bastard, I'm gonna personally put a bullet through your head."

French was at Seth's side, gently pulling him away from the cell. "Come on, Seth, don't waste your time."

Seth gave James a mean look. "Killing this bastard would not be a waste of time, Billy."

Harry sat back in his swivel chair with a sad look. "You'll have to beat me to it, Bowlen. You boys want a drink?"

Both shook their heads no.

Seth gestured to the man he just threatened. "That son-of-a-bitch tell you why he shot Wade?"

Block leaned his head to one side, looking past them at his prisoner. "Doesn't have to." He looked up at them. "James was a friend of Pete Hoskins." Then pointing to his deputy, he introduced him. "This is my deputy, Jack Hamm. He and his wife just moved to Harper."

Seth reached out and shook his hand. "Seth Bowlen."

French shook Todd's hand. "Billy French." He patted Seth on the back and looked at Sheriff Block. "I think I will have that drink after all."

Seth turned and looked at the clock above the door. "Gonna be a long night." Then he watched Harry pour whiskey into four dented, tin cups.

They passed the next hour talking very little. Each thought about Wade in their way and feeling remorse for Sarah and the children should he die.

Seth regretted finding Wade, believing somehow he could be the cause of his friend's death. He looked down at his growling stomach and then at Billy. "I haven't eaten since this morning. You hungry?"

French nodded as he stood. "Let's find a restaurant. I'll buy." Then he looked at Block and asked if he wanted to join them.

Block glanced at the prisoner. "Can't leave him alone."

Deputy Hamm said he'd stay if the sheriff would bring him back something to eat.

Block agreed, stood, and headed for the door. "Lock up after we leave and don't let anyone in." He paused at the door with a determined look. "And I mean no one, Jack." He gestured to the gun rack on the wall behind his desk. "There's a loaded double barrel twelve gauge in the rack behind you. Keep it handy."

The three men walked across the street to the café, dodging wagons and riders, and once inside, Block asked for a table by the window so he could see the front of the jailhouse. They ordered supper, and as they ate, they spoke very little. Sheriff Block remembered the day Wade rode out of town after the four men that killed his friend, Emmett Spears.

Billy remembered days on the trail with Wade after those who broke the law and some of the impossible shots he made with that Sharps rifle.

496

Seth remembered the first day they met in Sisters and the weeks on the trail after the Bradley brothers.

Soon their plates were clean, and neither remembered eating as they pushed their empty plates away.

Seth looked out the window. "Wonder how Wade's doing."

"Hope Sarah's holding up," said Billy as he stood reaching into his pocket for money. "I need a walk."

Seth agreed and stood while reaching into his pocket for money.

"Supper's on Harper, boys," said Block. "I'll pay and wait for Hamm's supper. You two go on." He watched as they walked out of the café into the late afternoon, hoping the good men of Harper didn't get drunk and visit the jail because he didn't want to kill anyone while protecting his prisoner.

Sarah had dozed off with her head on the table where Wade was lying, and now opening her eyes, she slowly sat up and looked at Wade's sleeping face hoping he didn't die. Hearing the door open, she turned, seeing Mrs. Granger walk in and close the door. She walked to Wade, checked his forehead for a fever, and then his neck for a pulse. "No fever and a strong pulse." She smiled at Sarah. "That's good news."

Sarah looked at Wade, took his hand, and held it. "Yes, it is."

"It's been a hard day, Mrs. Garrison; maybe a little dinner would help."

Sarah looked at Wade. "Thank you, Mrs. Granger, but I'm not hungry."

"You have to eat, dear. You can come back after you eat a little. I'll stay with your husband, and if there is any change, I'll come and get you."

Reluctantly, Sarah stood, followed Mrs. Granger to the door where she paused and looked back at her husband with a worried look before stepping into the other room.

Doc Samuel Granger was at the dinner table sitting back in his chair, patiently waiting. He smiled as he stood and pulled a chair away from the table for Sarah to sit. She looked at his kindly face, and friendly brown eyes thanked him and sat down while Mrs. Granger returned to Wade's room.

Doc picked up a dish of food and handed it to Sarah. "Don't be shy, Mrs. Garrison. There's plenty."

The sound of silverware on china seemed loud as Sarah took the plate, dished a small amount onto her plate, and set the plate of food on the table. "I'm sorry. I didn't mean to be a bother."

Doc Granger smiled. "It's no bother, Mrs. Garrison." Several quiet minutes passed, and Doc Granger put his fork on the edge of his plate and gently touched Sarah's hand. "The longer your husband hangs on tonight, the better the long-term outlook. These first twenty-four hours are critical." He paused and looked at the closed door of the room where his wife and Wade were, and then he looked at her. "Wade's a fighter, Sarah. He wouldn't have come all this way to be with you and them children to die."

Trying not to look at Doc Granger, her eyes welled, and then she turned her head, put the napkin to her face, and cried into it.

He reached over and touched her hand. "The best thing for you to do right now, Mrs. Garrison, is get some food in your stomach so you'll be strong for your husband." He paused. "He's going to need your strength. And so will that boy of yours."

Sarah stopped crying, turned, and looked back toward the door of the room where her husband lay, turned to Doc and smiled, then picked up her fork and took a small bite of food.

Mrs. Granger got up from a chair as Sarah walked into the room to be near Wade. "I've fixed a cot for you, Mrs. Garrison, next to your husband." She smiled, looking sorry. "I'm afraid it may be a little uncomfortable."

Sarah looked grateful. "It will do fine, thank you, and please call me Sarah."

"If you call me Josey." Josephine Granger was forty-one, nine years younger than her husband. She was thin but not skinny with dark brown hair and eyes and a pleasant smile. She and her husband met during the Civil War, where she was a nurse in a Confederate field hospital in Tennessee, and he a doctor. They married after the war and headed for California, but when they reached Harper, Josephine gave birth to their only son, who died two days later. Unable to leave the grave of their son, they made a life in Harper.

Chapter 33

Unable to sleep, Sarah got up from the cot, moved a straight, hardback chair next to Wade, sat down, and held his hand, hoping that somehow he knew she was at his side. In the dim light of the one kerosene lantern, she looked at his face bearing the scars from Pickering, lifted his hand to her lips, and gently kissed it while praying to God to let her have him for a little while longer. Feeling tired, Sarah laid her head on the table next to Wade, closed her eyes, and dozed off without letting go of his hand. Waking a short time later, she raised her head and quickly looked to see if he was still breathing. Relieved that he was, she laid her head back down on the table, closed her eyes, and drifted off to sleep.

The crowing of a rooster woke her from a much-needed sleep, and as she sat up, she checked on Wade to see if he was still breathing. Thinking his breathing seemed stronger, she stood and walked around the small room, working the stiffness out of her exhausted body.

The door opened, and Doc Granger walked in, looking tired with both suspenders dangling along his trouser legs. "Good morning." He walked to the table and looked down at Wade. "Let's see how our patient is doing."

Sarah was beside him. "His breathing seems stronger."

He lit a couple of lanterns and then stood over Wade. "You may be right. His color looks much better." He gently pulled back the covers and examined the incision and stitches on his chest, with Sarah looking on.

Wade opened his sleepy eyes, smiled, and whispered, "Thirsty."

She looked at Wade with wide eyes bending down close to his face, and with tears filling her eyes, she smiled.

Doc Granger managed to give Wade a small sip of water, and then he put two fingers on Wade's neck. "Pulse is strong."

"Where am I?" he asked, sounding hoarse.

Sarah touched his face gently with one hand and wiped her tears with the other. "You're at Doc Granger's. A man shot you after the trial."

"I remember," said Wade sounding sleepy.

Doc looked down at Wade. "How do you feel, son?"

"Tired," he whispered.

Granger poured some laudanum in a spoon, put his hand under Wade's head, and lifted it. "Drink this."

Recognizing the taste, Wade swallowed, closed his eyes, and drifted off.

"He'll sleep a spell now, Mrs. Garrison," said Doc, then he smiled. "He's going to be alright." Putting one hand on her shoulder, he looked into her tired eyes. "Go tell your son his pa is going to be alright and get some rest? I'll stay with your husband."

Sarah sat by her husband's side, holding his hand against the side of her face watching him sleep. "You're sure he's going to be alright?"

Granger looked at Wade. "Your husband's a tough man." Then he looked at her. "With rest and nourishment, he should be good as new in a few weeks."

Josephine Granger opened the door and poked her head inside. "Sam, there's a Mr. French and a Mr. Bowlen at the front door."

Doc excused himself and followed his wife to the front door, where he invited Billy and Seth inside, offering each a chair, which they declined.

They took off their hats, and both asked, "How's he doing, Doc?"

Granger nodded several times confidently. "I think he'll make it."

Both looked relieved.

Doc looked hopeful. "He woke up a few minutes ago and asked where he was."

"Does he recall getting shot?" asked Seth.

"He did. I gave him something to make him sleep and take care of the pain. He should sleep most of the day now. The more he rests, the better."

"Is Sarah still with him?" asked Seth.

Doc nodded. "She's inside. Hasn't left his side but to eat a small amount of supper last night." He paused and looked at the door. "She needs to go see her son, but I can't convince her."

"Can we go in for a minute, Doc?" asked Billy.

Granger gave it a quick thought. "Go ahead, but be quiet. See if you can convince Mrs. Garrison to go home to her children."

Billy opened the door, and then he and Seth quietly stepped into the room, carrying their hats in their hands.

Sarah turned and smiled as they approached, then looked up and whispered, "He was awake a little while ago. Doc Granger says he'll be good as new in a few weeks."

Seth looked down at Wade as he gestured to the door. "Can we talk to you outside?"

She looked at Wade as she gently set his hand at his side and walked with them into the other room.

Billy smiled at her. "I'm glad he's going to be okay. I just wanted to check on him before I head back to Santa Fe. I'd sure like to stay longer, but I can't."

502

Sarah kissed his cheek. "Be safe, Billy. And give Matha my love." Then she turned to Seth. "Are you leaving, also?"

Seth shook his head. "No, I'll stay another day. Let me get the wagon and take you home for a change of clothes, Sarah. You need to see Emmett and little Mary. I'm sure that son of yours is worried about his pa."

She looked down at the blood on the front of her brown dress and white blouse. "Perhaps, I should." She looked at Seth. "Are you sure you wouldn't mind?"

Seth grinned. "Do I look like I'd mind?"

Billy turned to Seth and held out his hand. "I'll be leaving, Seth. Send me a wire and let me know how Wade's getting along."

Seth grabbed Billy's hand. "Count on it."

Billy French said goodbye to Sarah, and after he walked out the door, she told Seth that she would get her things and tell Doc Granger she'd be back later in the afternoon.

The next day Seth stopped by Doc's to check on Wade but found him sleeping. Disappointed he was unable to say goodbye to his friend, he kissed Sarah on the cheek, said goodbye, and rode out of town for Sisters.

In the days that followed, Sarah left Wade's side very little except to eat, and as the days passed, he got stronger. Wade looked forward to the visits by his children and often asked about the coyote. Sarah would smile and say she must like Maria's cooking because she was putting on a little weight. Wade didn't like that but figured he could work that off of her when he would be able to ride.

The day finally came when Tolliver Grimes and Doc Granger helped Wade into the back of a wagon, where he lay down on an old mattress with his head on Sarah's lap. She covered him with a blanket, and Tolliver guided the wagon out of town toward the WS Ranch. Arriving at the front porch, he backed the wagon

503

up as Emmett and Maria hurried out of the house and waited on the porch with Pup, Willie, and Dog, and as soon as the wagon stopped, the dogs jumped off of the porch with tails wagging and whining anxiously to see Wade.

After Tolliver lowered the wagon's rear gate, he and Sarah kept the coyote and dogs away while a couple of ranch hands got Wade inside and upstairs to his bed.

Sarah had to shoo the dogs out of the room several times before she managed to close the door cursing words that Wade had never heard her speak.

Tolliver patted Wade on the shoulder. "I'll stop by in a day or two."

Wade nodded, "Thanks for the ride home, Tolliver."

The old man looked at Wade. "They tried and hung James Robertson two days ago."

The vision of the barrel of the gun and Robertson's angry face filled Wade's memory, but not much else after that. "I guess that's that then." Wade watched as Tolliver kissed Sarah on the cheek, and when he opened the door, Pup bolted into the room, jumped onto the bed, and laid down next to Wade.

Sarah tried to shoo her from the bed.

Wade petted the coyote as he looked up at Sarah. "She stood by me all the while I was in Montana. Even when I almost died, she was there. She never left my side."

She looked at the coyote and then at Wade with a stern look. "Just until you heal, then she goes into Emmett's room."

As Sarah and Tolliver walked out of the room and after the door closed, he put his arm around Pup, thinking they would talk on that when he was on his feet. He turned to the window and thought of the night several years ago when he shot and killed Dan Hoskins, the oldest son of George Hoskins. Drawing in a small breath and letting out a quick sigh, he hoped the hanging of James Robertson was the end of the Hoskins nightmare.

The door opened, and Maria stuck in her head. "How are you, Señor Garrison?"

Wade smiled. "Doing okay, Maria."

You rest now, señor Garrison, and later, Maria will bring you something good to eat." She smiled, and then she looked at Pup. "Willie has been a bad dog while you were gone, Señor Garrison. That coyote of yours is going to have little coyotes soon."

The Wade Garrison Saga continues in the next book of the series 'The Last Ride.'

Other books by Richard Greene

Death of Innocence

The book Death of Innocence is a story about five families of my ancestors who lived during the Civil War. The story is based on fact, along with fiction and family lore. What happened to each of these families, for the most part, is true, but I also added in some fiction to fill in the gaps. Joseph Samuel Greene, the main character, was my great grandfather. I think you will find the story interesting as well as entertaining.

Befriended by a slave and the captain of a riverboat, a young runaway named Joseph Samuel Greene finds adventure on the river and the love of a young Mary McAlexander. The Civil War will not only test their love for one another, but the faith of the McAlexander, Chrisman, and Patterson families as each endures the war's death and destruction.

Death rides across the South in the guise of the southern home guard, taking the innocent without hesitation or regret. The sorrow they leave will last forever as each proud family endures while losing their innocence.

Wade Garrison's Promise

Wade Garrison is a simple man who, as a young man, came west chasing the stories he had read about in cheap western novels while growing up on a farm in South Carolina. He is not a violent man, and like most men of humble beginnings, he holds his name and promises in high regard.

Watching the pine coffin containing his friend Emmett Spears's lifeless body lowered into the dark grave, Wade makes a silent promise of revenge. It is a promise that will take him far from the girl he loves and the Circle T Ranch in eastern Colorado.

As young Wade Garrison trails the four men responsible for his friend's death, he will soon find himself unprepared for the death and violence he will find. He is unaware that in fulfilling his promise to avenge Emmett Spears, he will lose himself in the process.

God's Coffin

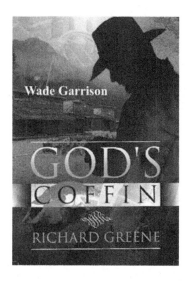

Sequel to Wade Garrison's Promise

Wade Garrison rides out of Harper, Colorado, into the New Mexico Territory in 1872, believing he is riding away from a troubled past.

Now, six years later, his old friend, Sheriff Seth Bowlen, in Sisters, Colorado, is in trouble and needs help. Sheriff Bowlen sends a wire to United States Marshal Billy French in Santa Fe, who, in turn, sends Deputy Marshal Wade Garrison to help their old friend.

Innocently, Wade decides to take his wife Sarah, and son Emmett, with him so they can visit her family in Harper, a small town northeast of Sisters. As he and his family board the train in Santa Fe, he could not have known that a terrible storm of violence was already brewing, and this fateful decision could destroy his wife and child.

Wade Garrison

The Last Ride

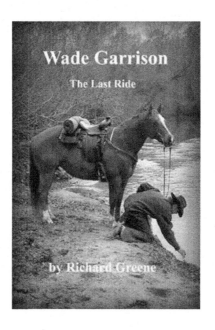

Sequel to Atonement

It has been a year since Wade was shot and nearly died after being found innocent of murder at his trial in Harper, Colorado. Keeping his promise to God and Sarah, his Colt pistol lies tucked away in the bottom drawer of a chest in his bedroom, and the Sharps rifle covered in the rawhide sheath stands in a corner behind the chest. While he misses the life of a United States

Deputy Marshal, is content being with his wife Sarah, son Emmett, and daughter Mary Louise on their ranch.

Unknown to Wade and Sarah, he is about to be thrust into a life of violence once again by events that take place in the small town of Harper, Colorado. When the people of Harper seek his help for justice, the old life pulls at him. Resisting those old ways, he fears the town, and his son will think he is a coward. How can he break his promise to not only Sarah but to God?

Feeding the Beast

1951

The Second World War has been over for six years, and the United States is now involved militarily in Korea, termed a Police Action rather than a war. On April 10, President Harry S. Truman fires General Douglas MacArthur, commander of the United States forces in Korea. This action resulted in the president's lowest approval rating of 23%, which remains the lowest of any serving president.

The Denver Police Department protecting fewer than 415,000 residents was small compared to cities such as Chicago, New York, and Los Angeles.

The use of DNA by the judicial system is far in the future. Electric-powered streetcars were the primary source of transportation and soon to be replaced by electric buses. Computers were in their infancy, and while most old newspapers and other public records are on microfilm, thousands of documents are not. Not every home could afford a television, so the radio remained the household's nightly entertainment. The closest thing to a cellular telephone was Dick Tracy's two-way wristwatch found in the comics, so the police had to rely on rotary telephones and shortwave radios. Being Mirandized was not an option criminals were given in 1951 and would not be until 1966.

The term 'Serial Killer' would not be coined until 1970 by FBI Special Agent Robert Reesler.

The last time I saw my Dad

A short story by Richard Greene

The Last Time I Saw My Dad

This short story is of my last trip to Houston, Texas, to visit my Dad and the memories it brought back of the summers I spent in Houston as a young boy.

Made in the USA
Coppell, TX
24 May 2021